ELISHA BARBER

BOOK ONE OF

The Dark Apostle

E. C. AMBROSE

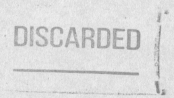

DAW BOOKS, INC.

DONALD A. WOLLHEIM, FOUNDER

375 Hudson Street, New York, NY 10014

ELIZABETH R. WOLLHEIM
SHEILA E. GILBERT
PUBLISHERS

www.dawbooks.com

Acknowledgments

This book would not have begun without the instruction of two teachers. First, Jeanne Cavelos of the Odyssey Writing Workshop, who introduced me to the joys of research. Next, Dan Brown, through his workshop at the Seacoast Writers' Group, who taught about tension.

Thanks are due, as well, to the marvelous team at DAW Books, especially my editors, Josh, who saw what this book could be, and Betsy, who helped us to get it there. I owe Barbara Campbell for the introduction, and my agent, Cameron McClure, for making it stick.

Luc Reid, founder of the Codex neo-pro online writers' group, and many of the members thereof for their support and enthusiasm. In particular, medical research advisor D. T. Friedman, without whom the surgical scenes would be much less realistic.

Others whose support came at just the right time include Cat Rambo and Sean Wallace, Ruth Nestvold, James Patrick Kelly, and the YMCA Goffstown climbers: Casey, Brendan, Daisy, Jonathan, Abby and Lauren, whose rapt attention I will never forget.

Finally, my family, who endured hair-raising drives in England, visits to torture museums, weekends at conventions, and hours of vacant stares punctuated by random plot discoveries. You know what this book means to me, and I would not be here without you.

"For the life of man is perishable and transitory,
and the wickedness of man abounds in the world—woe is me!"

—JEAN DE VENETTE

Chapter 1

❖

"**Y**ou sent her to the hospital?" Elisha whirled to face his brother, the razor still in his fist. "My God, man, what were you thinking?"

"The midwife couldn't help her, Elisha, and she's in such awful pain, for the babe won't come," Nathaniel stammered, his pale hands clenched together. He ducked in the low door of the draper's quarters, his fair hair brushing the carved oak of the lintel. "The neighbors carried her over while I came here."

"But the hospital? That place is deadly." Elisha set his razor again at his customer's chin, deftly shearing a narrow stretch of the full, and now unfashionable, beard. "What did she say?"

"Not so fast, if you don't mind. I care to keep my chin today, Barber," the draper snapped.

"Helena?" Nathaniel asked, his face a mask of anguish and confusion.

"No, you fool, the midwife!" Elisha slapped the razor through the water basin and plied it again, forcing himself to slow down. Last thing he needed was to carve the ear off the master of the drapers' guild.

Sagging, his brother balanced himself against the wall, scrubbing at his sweaty face. "The babe's turned, and wedged somehow. She thought the physicians—"

At the mention of physicians, Elisha froze. The draper glowered up at him from his best leather chair, but his brother's wife lay in the hospital, contracting God-knew-what illness added to her condition. For a moment, his conflicting duties trapped him—but Helena needed him, if it weren't already too late. The draper could abide. Flinging down his razor, Elisha roughly dried his hands on his britches. "The physicians never enter the hospital if they can advise from afar. Nobody who can afford their services goes to the hospital." He popped open the window frame nearest and flung out the dirty water.

The draper rubbed a hand across his chin and jerked it back with a cry of dismay. "You've not finished the job, Barber. I've still got half a beard!"

"Then you owe me half my fee," Elisha told him. He snatched his towel from the man's neck and spun on his heel, basin tucked under his arm. The razor he folded with a snap and gripped until his fingers hurt. "Why did you not come for me sooner?" he asked, dropping his voice to a murmur.

Instantly, Nathaniel straightened, taking advantage of his superior height. "I think you know why."

For a moment, their eyes met, and Nathaniel swallowed but gave no ground to his elder brother. Elisha had caused the breach that lay between them. He had apologized, but Nathaniel's presence here was as close as he would come to forgiveness.

They had the same intense blue gaze, though Elisha's own hair was near black and bound into a practical queue. Elisha straightened broad shoulders and flashed a furious grin. "Then let's be off while your wife yet lives."

Nathaniel stumbled out the door as Elisha bore down upon him.

"I'll be to your order about this!" The draper squawked, pushing himself up. "You'll not practice in this city again."

Rounding on the man, Elisha said, "I hope they'll consider a woman's life of more value than half a beard."

"A whore's life," the draper answered, then stepped back as Elisha held up the razor, still gripped in his fist. His mobile face registered his regret, but Elisha was in no mood to play the draper's game.

"Helena," Elisha said in a low and terrible voice, "is a whore no longer, but you'll be a bugger for the rest of your life, so I'll ask you to keep your threats to yourself."

Pale, the man's jaw dropped, his half-beard bisecting his lips.

As he turned to follow his brother, Elisha thought it a fitting image, half a beard for a man with a double life. No, the order would hear of nothing from him for a variety of reasons.

Anger was easy. It gave Elisha the distance he needed from those he must treat—and those who might die. Distance, too, from dangerous friends. Elisha would have to apologize at some point, but the draper would be a little more careful suggesting his attraction to his next barber. It would be safer for them both.

Elisha descended the narrow stairs at a run, jumping the last few to street level, emerging between the draper's shop and the neighboring woolery. Nathaniel hovered anxiously in the street, turning away toward the hospital, but only after the relief showed plain upon his face.

Elisha might have found that expression of relief touching at another time, a time when he was more certain of his skill. As it stood, he'd not dealt much with childbirth, though he'd had more experience with it

than most barbers, in the course of his work as the favored surgeon of Codpiece Alley. And even there,
many of the whores refused to accept the service of a
man, or would take advice only but no examination.
Curious, that they who spent their love at the whim of
strangers should turn prudish when it came to the touch
of an examiner's hand. Most at least knew the herbs to
take to avoid unwanted children, else they were cast
out by their keepers to give birth in the streets—or,
heaven forbid, in the hospital. Elisha's fury flared
again. His brother should have known better.

They slogged along the twisting roads of the drapers' quarter, dodging customers, wagons, and horsemen,
speaking not a word. Nathaniel stuck his shaking hands
under his arms, as if he embraced himself in his wife's
absence. He still wore his leather tinsmith's apron, the
pockets bristling with tools and bits of metal. The midwife must've fetched him up from the workshop. What
was he making that was so important he left his wife to
birth in the hands of strangers? If Helena had been Elisha's own wife—but, of course, she wasn't. Not his wife,
not his choice.

As if he could hear his brother's thoughts, Nathaniel
suddenly said, "I couldn't bear the screaming, nor the
tears. I waited at the door, I did, but I couldn't bear to
hear her like that."

The buildings loomed over them, stepping out from
the lower stories until the levels above bent together
and cut the sky into jagged shapes. In some places rods
and arches touched buildings on both sides of the
street, holding apart the tilting houses like a man inter-
vening in a tavern brawl. The graveled streets twined
between, edged by ditches to catch rain and refuse.
Straight ahead, the carriage of some fool lord had broken a wheel. Two matched horses whinnied and pulled

in opposite directions while the grooms tried to sort them out, unhitching the pair and effectively blocking the road while their master shouted from the safety of the carriage. It was just a few years ago King Hugh commissioned carriages for his family. Now every noble who could afford it had to have one, cluttering up the London streets.

With a yelp, Nathaniel stopped short, his shoulders quivering. Elisha grabbed his arm and jerked him forward again, taking to the sewage ditch that ran down the side and ducking beneath the tangled reins. "Pull yourself together, Nate, it's your family at stake," he muttered, not sure if he wanted to be heard.

The hospital at last towered before them, a story of stone at street level, topped with two more of half-timbers spanned by crumbling plaster, with birds plucking out the insulating straw for nests, or in search of insects. It was founded by the old king at the turn of the century and already decrepit. Nowadays, the current king's reputation hardly hewed to charity.

"Which ward?" Elisha asked as they entered the place. Even the refuse he scraped off his boots didn't smell so foul as the hall they faced. The scents of infection, vomit, and blood hung in the air, along with the groans, prayers, and weeping of the afflicted.

"Three?" Nathaniel suggested.

Tension gathering in his shoulders, Elisha focused a brief glare upon his brother, then pushed by him. "Sister!"

A nun passing with a bucket turned at his call. "May I . . . ? Oh." Her wide brown eyes flooded with tears.

"Is it Helena?" Nathaniel blurted, but Elisha held him back, recognizing in the woman before him an emaciated whore he had given a cure four winters back. She had sworn off the life—they all swear off it some time or another—but this oath had taken hold, and he smiled as she dropped the bucket to catch his bare forearm.

"May the Lord bless you, Elisha, and keep you in His hand."

"Sister . . ." he paused, squeezed his eyes shut, and popped them open, "Lucretia?"

She rewarded him with a nod.

"Do you remember Helena? Was she brought in here?"

"Helena? Gracious, no, I should hope not. Upstairs maybe. Follow!" Gathering up her skirts, Lucretia set a brisk pace for the stairs at the center of the ward.

Averting his eyes from the whimpering or wailing occupants of the broad beds, Elisha followed. After a moment, he thought to look back and caught hold of Nathaniel's arm once more as his brother staggered, his face gray. "Come on, Nate."

"Is it—?" He gasped for breath, recoiling from the stink. "Is it always like this?"

"It's worse in the summer," Elisha replied grimly.

Flicking him a glance, Nathaniel looked on the verge of tears himself. "I sent Helena here."

Since Nathaniel's appearance at the draper's, Elisha had felt disconcerted, allowing his brother's agitation to affect him. He'd overreacted, treating Nathaniel with less affection than he would have shown a stranger. He held Nathaniel's arm, lending him strength, as if he could communicate his apology through touch. "You've never been inside the place before. How could you know?"

"By the cross, Elisha, I could have trusted your stories."

Aye, that he could. "What reason have you to trust me, Nate?" Elisha said lightly, despite the heaviness in his heart. A ward sister met them on the landing and pointed toward the far end of the hall. A curtain there separated the wards, and the trio pushed through, pausing briefly at each bed.

Six beds lined the walls, each double width and filled with three or four women. Some of them writhed with unknown pains, moaning or cursing. At the sight of Lucretia, those who could, sat up, holding out beseeching arms.

"Sister, some water, I beg you," cried a crone with sallow flesh.

A better dressed woman in a bed of her own shouted, "Damn you, I need fresh linens!"

One piteous voice whispered, "Just a strip. I'll bind the wound myself, Sister, if you'll give me a bandage." The girl held close a ragged hand, blood streaming from an unseen wound.

Gritting his teeth, Elisha pressed his forearms over his ears, trying to block out their cries. If only he had time. "Helena!" he shouted over the din. "Helena! Where are you?"

From the fourth bed someone screamed, "Eli!" the name dissolving into a sob of pain.

They hurried over to the crowded bed, and Elisha dropped his barbering tools.

Her thick golden hair tangled on the pillow, Helena lay at the outermost. She had flung off the dirty blankets, clutching her bloody gown in a stranglehold as she shrieked. Tears tracked down her face from eyes shut tight. "Nathan! Nathan," she whimpered.

"Here, darling, I'm here." Nathaniel pushed by to grab her hand. "Oh, Love, I'm so sorry."

"Where's the midwife?" Elisha demanded, pulling the blankets down all the way to reveal Helena's perfect legs. He shut his eyes and shook himself.

"Gone," she panted, "physician."

Sister Lucretia shot him a look, her face as grim as his own.

"Sister, we'll need a cart to get the lady home," he

told her softly. He needed room to work, and peace, for his sake as well as hers.

Nevertheless, Nathaniel heard him. "You can't think of moving her, not in this condition."

Elisha stared down at his brother, the cacophony of pain beating at him from every side however he tried to ignore it. Beside Helena lay a thin woman, her eyes wide, her skin gray, her mouth stretched open in a final amazement. If Helena stayed here, he had no doubt she would soon look the same.

From the corpse's other side, a girl spoke up through blood-flecked lips. "Can you bring another blanket please? This woman's gone awfully cold."

Through clenched teeth Elisha repeated, "A cart, at once. And the midwife, if you find her."

Lucretia bobbed her head and nimbly hurried off as if she fled the pain around her. Elisha couldn't fathom how she could stand to work there, surrounded every moment by suffering.

Helena screamed again, and Nathaniel stroked the hair back from her sweaty face. "I'm here," he murmured. "And Elisha's come. We'll help you."

Kneeling down by her feet, Elisha shoved back his sleeve, but the examination was unnecessary, for one of the babe's feet could be seen. Jerking back, Elisha flung himself away from the bed. "What the hell were you thinking?" he shouted. Of all the births he'd assisted, this had to be the worst; that it was happening to his own brother's wife was unconscionable. And he knew in his heart that he was to blame. She needed a surgeon's skill and the speed of a racehorse. Skill he had, but speed he had no control over. Even if he ran for the tools he'd need and back again. Better to take her away . . .

"Please, gentlemen, I'll have to ask you to go," said an

older nun, bustling up to them as fast as her stout legs could take her. "I am the ward sister here, and you've no—"

"This is her husband," Elisha said shortly. "I'm his brother, a barber and a surgeon."

"Still and all," she huffed, "we are doing what may be done for her. The physician has been sent for."

"Do you think he'll come for her? For any of them?" He waved his arm over the beds.

"The physician is understandably busy, but he is a Christian man."

At Helena's shriek, Elisha cringed. He shoved past the nun and went back to the curtain, his hands balled into fists. The woman had no sense, or at least, no ears. Helena couldn't afford the physician's leisure. Still, he had to control himself, master his own heart before he'd be of any good to her. He started to review what he would need, to picture the tools and where to find them. Already, it was too late to turn the baby against the desperate pressure of the mother's own womb.

"Will the sister bring me a cloth?" asked a timid voice below him, and Elisha turned.

The pale girl with the gashed arm still tried to stop the blood with her hand, watching him from dark and sunken eyes.

Sinking down on the bed beside her, Elisha pulled the towel from his belt and tore it in three. "Give it here," he told her.

Blinking, she glanced away toward the distant nun, then back.

"I'm a barber," he said soothingly. "Give it here, it'll be fine."

Hesitantly, she held out her arm. The gash was long, but not too deep, cutting across the muscles of her forearm. This, at least, he knew exactly how to handle.

With the first strip of cloth, he wiped around it. Then holding her hand between his knees, he pressed together the sides of the wound and wrapped it carefully, tucking the bandage end in when he was done. From his ever-present pouch he slipped a packet of white powder and pressed it into her grasp. "Just a pinch for the pain—no more, you hear me?"

"Aye, sir."

"Get out of here," Elisha urged, drawing her up from the bed. "Go home."

With a quick glance behind her, the girl darted away, holding her injured arm close once more. He stared a moment after her, wishing Helena could be so readily healed.

A hand thrust aside the curtain, admitting Sister Lucretia followed by a plump woman with her sleeves bound back from her arms. "Elisha," she grunted. The midwife. Elisha's heart sank yet further when he recognized her: matronly, barely competent, with a demeanor soothing to pregnant women. Her combination of piety and comfort would appeal to his brother almost as much as the fact that Elisha disapproved of her.

Following close, they returned to Helena's side.

"Now, dear," the midwife said, bending down to check the infant's position. Only Elisha caught the flash of horror on her face. When she looked up again, her voice was still as calm as ever, though her hands quavered. "Now, dear, the physician recommends a cutting. We'll lift the babe from your belly and stitch't back up again, eh?"

Nodding desperately, Helena clung to her husband with both hands.

"We'll be needing water then," the midwife went on, "and a better knife than what I've brought."

With a cold certainty, Elisha laid a hand on Helena's taut belly, pressing the still form of the child she carried. Too still. He grabbed the midwife's arm and pulled her aside, turning his face from his brother. "You're going to cut her open?" he whispered urgently.

"The physician advises—"

"He knows who she is, and her circumstances?"

"Aye, Barber, he does," the midwife snapped, tugging at his grip.

Elisha swore under his breath. "So he thinks to save the babe at her expense."

The midwife dropped her gaze, her thin mouth set. "God willing, if I stitch her right up—"

Elisha didn't listen to the rest. Under the best of circumstances, cutting into the abdomen was risky—best left to the master surgeons, and even then more likely to kill than to cure.

He looked at Lucretia.

The nun nodded once. "And horses."

The first good news he'd yet been offered. Elisha grinned. "Bless you."

He lifted Nathaniel to his feet and pushed his barbering tools into his brother's hands. Then, with a nod to the imperious ward sister, he caught up Helena in both arms and drew her to his chest. "There's not a moment to spare."

"But she said—!" Nathaniel began to protest, then he whirled, seizing the midwife's hand. "Come with us."

Elisha met the midwife's eye, the fear in his brother's voice still ringing in his ears. Grudgingly he said, "She'll have need of you."

She held up her hands in a gesture of despair. "Aye, Barber, I'm coming."

"Then we have a life to save," he said, turning away to escape the hospital, and its reeking beds of corpses both living and dead.

Chapter 2

❖

They dashed from the hospital, pursued by the furious ward sister. "Only the saints may intercede for her!" she cried, tugging at Elisha's arm. "By God's grace alone, and through His physicians shall she be saved."

He snarled low in his throat, causing the nun to stumble and cross herself. He should have been there as soon as they thought she was pregnant, but his own arrogance had estranged them. He would welcome the saints if they could save her—and damn them all if they could not.

Outside waited a new wagon with tall wheels, drawn by a sturdy team of chestnut draft horses. A pair of apprentice wainwrights idled with their charge, grinning at the sight of Lucretia. Elisha had no doubt how she'd come to earn their favor in years past. Nathaniel clambered into the wagon, kneeling to draw Helena's clenched form from Elisha's arms.

With easy strength, Elisha scooped up the midwife and deposited her alongside, then started when Lucretia took a hand-hold and pulled herself in as well.

She met his gaze and murmured, "To pray for her, at the least. She may need help from more than God, but His aid is worth the asking."

"Aye, Sister." Elisha moved around to mount the

wagon beside the carter. "You'll have our gratitude to make it speedy," he told the man as the apprentices clambered up as well.

"Course." He flashed a snaggle-toothed grin. "'Twas my son's leg you saved last winter. Hya!" He snapped the reins and called out encouragement over the horses' broad backs.

Elisha pointed the way, taking them by quick turns from the main streets to byways where they could urge the team to greater speed. Behind him, he heard Helena's screams, Nathaniel's soothing tones, and the steady rise and fall of women's voices in prayer. The screams came more quickly now, and by the time they reached the tinsmithy, she let out a continuous wail of agony.

Springing down before they'd even stopped, Elisha ran to the squat house adjoining his brother's shop. Despite the hurt which lay between them, he and Nathaniel yet shared the house left them by their parents. The married Nathaniel had claimed the front rooms and—for the child they dreamed of—the loft, while Elisha, though older, had taken the low back rooms for his home and study. Now he left the others to bring Helena in while he gathered his tools.

Hooks and shelves lined the study, even concealing the little unglazed windows, for which he now cursed the lack of light. Catching up a leather satchel, Elisha tossed in a few knives as well as containers of herbs to soothe during childbirth. He knew the tool he needed, the only tool, but dreaded to carry it alone, as if doing so would be to admit failure.

He rounded the house and mounted the stoop outside, taking a deep breath before entering the open door. They'd moved the two benches and the basin stand from the center of the room to stand in the yard, with Elisha's barbering tools heaped on top. Helena screamed, a dreadful sound that tore through him. Lucretia was right, it was God they needed here.

"Feet first!" Nathaniel cried from within.

"Aye, sir, and naught I did for her would turn it," the midwife replied. Then almost timidly, "There's still time to take the physician's word."

"But Elisha—"

"Is just a barber, for all that he's got good hands."

Squaring his shoulders, Elisha ducked inside. "And whose hands would carry out the esteemed physician's advice? Yours? I find it unlikely." He leveled a cold stare at her. "Do what you can for the lady, and let me attend the child."

With a grunt, she turned away.

Gently, Lucretia tucked an arm around Nathaniel's shoulders. "Come away, sir, we're too many here. Let them do what they must. Perhaps your work would bring you some comfort now."

When they'd gone outside, Elisha knelt at the table. Helena's gown lay askew, barely covering her distended belly, which heaved and shuddered as she sobbed. The midwife held both Helena's arms, murmuring without words. Between Helena's legs protruded the tiny foot, grayish and foreign.

"How long has the child been dead?" he asked, in a quiet voice.

"Don't know what you mean," the midwife returned, adjusting her grip, her kerchiefed head lowered.

He stared at her, a strange numbness suffusing his heart. "Of course you do. You know your business, just as I know mine. This child was dead before she ever went to the hospital."

"Nothing for it but to have the baby, is there?" She dodged his glare. "Will you cut her then? That's what the physician—"

"God damn the physician!" Elisha shouted. "And God damn you," he added through clenched teeth.

Her head jerked up, her mouth working on words she could not speak.

Spilling the leather satchel onto the floor, Elisha searched among the tools for the one he needed, a slender, long handled saw with fine sharp teeth. Meant for the amputation of fingers or toes, the tool had never been put to such terrible use as what he must do. He gripped it tightly and nearly prayed himself.

"But you cannot be intending," the midwife said, her lips trembling.

"Her body won't rest until the child is out," he told her quietly. "It's already lost to me, but she is not."

From the doorway, Lucretia said, "Oh, Sweet Lord," crossing herself.

Her eyes suddenly open and wild, Helena shrieked and kicked. "You'll not! You bastard, you'll not cut my baby!" but the protests drowned in another cry, and blood stained the table beneath her. The nun crossed to her and caught her leg, shouting Bible verses to be heard above the din.

Humming in his throat, letting the sound buzz up into his skull, Elisha gripped the instrument and began his awful work, laying the child to rest in the empty leather bag as blood flowed around his arms. His namesake saint had once healed a river with salt, but Elisha knew there would be no healing this flood.

When it was done, he sat back on his heels, letting his humming die away. The delicate saw dropped from his tired hand. He applied a careful pressure to Helena's lower belly, watching intently to be sure the blood was stopping. He leaned back from her when he was satisfied. Up to the elbow, blood slicked his arms. It stained his shirt and his britches where he knelt on the floor. In his urgency, he hadn't thought to take his apron. For a long time, he stared down at his hands. Now they shook with the horror of the deed. Unsteadily, he pulled to the flap on the leather satchel and thrust it under the table, as far from himself as he could. Only then did he notice the quiet and raise his head.

Helena's legs lay at last relaxed, her belly still large, but flaccid now, draped with the ruined gown. At her side, Sister Lucretia stood, pale, lips still murmuring prayers, but with the words misplaced, the cadence trailing off, then recalling itself.

The midwife laid Helena's arms across her chest and met Elisha's helpless gaze. "So now you've done. Happy, are you, to have cost your brother his wife?"

"No," he breathed. His hands dangling, Elisha got to his feet and searched Helena's still, pale lips. "No!" he repeated. "She can't be." Unwilling to touch her, with her child's blood still on his hands, Elisha stared hard at her throat and saw no sign of pulse or breath. He stood stunned, his hands aching from the close, careful work, his skin recalling the intimacy of the mother's flesh.

"Did you cut something else down there? Did you ruin it all a'purpose, or by ignorance?" The midwife thrust herself close to him. "Putting yourself in woman's business, evading the physician's order, casting curses all about you—you've no place here, Barber. Your brother must be told." She jammed her fists onto her hips and bustled out the door.

Dazed, Elisha moved to the head of the table, near Lucretia. "What happened?" he asked. "What's gone wrong?" He wiped his hands upon his thighs, leaving long red streaks. He tried to remember through the near-trance that settled over him while he worked. He reviewed the care he had taken with each cut. He recalled being grateful when she finally lay still—merely unconscious, he thought—but there was nothing, nothing he would do differently.

"Go to your brother," Lucretia said. "Don't let it be her word he hears."

"But she's right." Leaning upon the table, Elisha felt the strain in his arms and knees. How long had he knelt there, trying to be careful, to be sure he did no harm to the mother, his brother's wife. "If he'd only got me sooner," he murmured, "maybe then, or if we'd stayed at the hospital . . ."

There was noise behind him, but he could not be distracted.

"The hospital's unclean, and full to the roof of illness, Elisha," the nun told him, reaching out to touch his arm. "I know that as well as you. 'Twas charity brought me there, not hope. If the child was already dead, what could the physician's order do but wound the mother yet again?"

What did it matter if he had done the right thing, now that it had gone so terribly wrong? Shaking his head, Elisha straightened. "What penance for the work of this day, Sister? Tell me that, if you know."

"Ask it of the Lord, Elisha," she said. "And remember that He is also merciful." She gave his arm a little squeeze. "Go to your brother. He'll be needing you, though he doubts it now."

"Aye, as would any man of sense." Edging back around the table, he kicked his scattered tools and a vial rolled beneath his foot to be crushed. Elisha did not heed them. After this, heaven forbid he ever take up his instruments to cut more than hair. "Cover her, Sister?"

"I will."

He tripped on the steps and shook himself, blinking,

in the sunlight. How dare the sun look bright upon him today? His fingers flexed and released. He had lost patients before: strangers, neighbors. It always hurt, even when he knew they could have had no better care. But this . . . . He could not imagine a loss so great, a failure so awful. Two years he hoped to reconcile with his brother, his only living kin. He would be lucky, now, if Nathaniel even came to his funeral. He had to face him and receive the curses he so well deserved. To one side, the wainwright's men stood watching, their faces slack with horror and wonder at a tragedy which touched them not. Elisha wondered why they'd not yet gone to spread the news. "Nathaniel?"

Beside the door the cleared-aside furniture, piled up and abandoned, seemed an emblem of the family he had torn apart. Something was amiss there, but it escaped his addled mind.

"Nathaniel?" He swept his gaze about the yard, settling it a moment on the apprentices who shifted uneasily.

"Workshop, I think," one of them said. "Lucy—er, Sister Lucretia took him there. We've just come back to see what help she needs."

Nodding, Elisha turned away. Knocking on the door, he heard no answer, and pushed it open with a soiled hand.

The shaft of sunlight he let in traced its path upon the dirt floor, lighting up the workbench, striking a brass gleam off a familiar item, so out of place he could not at first name it. His basin, that was it; his wide, metal basin, brimful of darkness, with his brother's blond head sunk in grief beside it.

"Nathaniel," Elisha said, coming forward from the light.

Perched on his tall stool, Nathaniel bent over the table, his arm outstretched, Elisha's razor close to his hand.

"No no no no," Elisha chanted to himself, his eyes sweeping the trail of blood, the open blade, the angle of his brother's arm.

All the breath had left him, all of his own blood, like his brother's, like his nephew's, seeping away, until he stood as a marble figure in the shaft of sunlight, struck through and dying.

And yet he alone still lived. How was it possible? How had God let it be so, that these should all lie dead while he was standing, unharmed though not unwounded? If they'd not left the hospital, if his brother had trusted him, if he'd not been such a fool two years ago—his righteous pride, his stupid conceits—ignorance indeed.

"I've killed them all," he said aloud, his fingers dripping blood into the brazen sun.

Chapter 3

❖

The constables would have to know, Elisha thought, staring at his brother's blond head, haloed by the sunlight. And the tin guildsmen must be told. If he had taken in any work, the customers must be found. Helena had a sister, somewhere in the city, married to a tradesman.

The next thought chilled him even in the sun, and caught his breath. Nathaniel had taken his own life. He would be bound for an unmarked grave, unsanctified earth despite his years of service and the tithe he made from his meager pay.

Elisha's hand reached out of its own accord, snatching up the razor at his brother's side and flinging it into the darkest corner. Quickly, he rounded the table, embracing his brother and lowering him to the floor. The loose hands fell lax and defenseless. His body was still warm in Elisha's arms. Blood dripped from the worktable to the dirt floor, soaking in, becoming part of the shadows almost as if it had never been. As if his brother had never been. It was said that inside the skull rested a seed called the Bone of Luz, and if one had the skill and knowledge, this seed could be tended, to grow into a new man. Elisha wondered where the seed·was, if he might locate it. Would the new man be another Nathaniel? He held his brother on his lap, as if they were boys again. Nathaniel's hair stroked soft against his skin, the lips parted for a trickle of blood. For the last time, he stared into his brother's face, still and pale.

"Stand up!" someone barked out from the doorway. "We've no wish to harm you."

Shaking himself, Elisha turned, starting at the sight of four armed men, their swords drawn on the instant he turned. He lowered Nathaniel at last to the unyielding ground. Elisha brought both hands slowly into the light before he rose.

"I am unarmed." He advanced a few steps from the building to be surrounded by them. Beyond, the two apprentices spoke at once, their voices high and excited, as a guard captain nodded, glaring in Elisha's direction. The captain strode across the yard, his mail coat glinting and chinking as he passed by to look into the workshop. His head jerked when he absorbed what he saw, then he spun on his heel, taking in Elisha's bloody hands and garments. "Arrest him."

Elisha bowed his head, silently crossing his arms behind him, awaiting justice.

"What have you done here, barber? Is this some revenge, or is it the house you wanted?" the captain snarled.

As Elisha wet his lips, for once at a loss, Sister Lucretia bounded down the steps from the house, upsetting the heap of benches in her haste. "Elisha!" she cried, her face lit with a grin as wide as ever he'd seen. "Elisha, where's Nathaniel?" She ran up, seizing his bloody hands in hers. "A miracle, Eli, she's alive. Helena's alive!"

For a moment, this thought crowded out all others. He let out an involuntary shout of laughter, tossing back his head. "Thank God!" His hair, flying loose from its band, shook down over his shoulders in a tumble of black waves. She lived—his work was not all in vain. For that moment, he reveled in the success of his terrible surgery, sweeping away the tragedy that followed.

"I went to cover her, as you said, and to bathe her as best I could. The water must've startled her awake, Eli." As Lucretia's words rushed out, tears sparkled in her eyes. "She breathed, and opened up her eyes. 'Sister,' she said to me, 'is my husband by?' Oh, the Lord has surely been with us today."

Elisha's joy fled as quickly as it had come, the truth of his brother's death made real with Helena's revival. As Lucretia gazed up into his face, her smile grew slim and vanished. "Eli?"

From the house, a tremulous voice called, "Nathan? Where's the baby, Nathan?"

Lucretia glanced back over her shoulder, then again to Elisha, her grip tightening.

For another endless, fleeting moment, Elisha felt himself cast back to the day of his brother's birth, his father tossing him in the air to catch him again, his tiny brother cradled against his mother's breast. Then his chin lowered to his chest, his eyes burning with tears. Shaking, tearing his hands from Lucretia's comfort, he sank to all fours, his hair hiding his face as he wept. His throat ached and he wished his heart would burst inside his shuddering chest. He curled into himself, racked with sobs, his fingers digging into the dirt of the yard. Blood and earth mingled. Dust to dust.

Nathaniel, sitting in the workshop, filing or polishing, awaiting the midwife's word. But the news she brought was the worst, not only the child but the wife as well. He had come to the door—the sound that Elisha thought he'd heard. What had Elisha said in his shock? *If he'd only got me sooner . . . ?*

Then Nathaniel, taking up the razor and basin and, retreating to the solitude of his shop, bereft of all that he loved, believing it was his own fault, setting the razor to his throat. For nothing. Helena lived! Helena lay recovering, calling out for a man who could never answer.

"If Nathaniel's the blond, then he lies within," the captain said gruffly. "With his throat cut."

"No, it can't be." Lucretia's habit rustled as she moved to the door, then quickly back. "What's happened?"

"Ask your barber, if you will, Sister."

"But he's been with me and with Helena. He saved her life today."

"Aye, is it so? 'I killed them all,' s'what he said not a few moments ago, in these young men's hearing."

A soft, warm hand lay upon Elisha's back. "He has killed no one, my lord. What has happened I cannot say, except that he acted to save the life of his sister. Perhaps the midwife can say more."

An agitated cry rang from the little house. "Nathan! I cannot rise, Love, you must come to me."

Helena's voice struck him like a blow, and he flinched. How would he ever face her? Lucretia's comforting hand lifted.

"Go to the lady, Sister, we'll clear up all else," said the captain.

"What shall be done with him?"

"He's for prison, unless we find otherwise. And for death, if the truth is plain. Pray for him if you will."

Not answering, Lucretia knelt down in a crisp movement of her woolen garments. She encircled Elisha with both arms, his forehead tucked into her slender shoulder. "You've done nothing but God's work, Eli," she whispered. "I'll see it's known."

At last, he found courage to speak. "Helena needs comfort, Sister."

"No more, nor less than you do," she replied, "and you are no less deserving."

He strangled a disbelieving laugh. If they slew him in the street, it would be more than he deserved.

"Go on, Sister." A new hand grasped his arm, drawing them apart.

They rose together, Elisha pushing back his hair, leaving a trace of blood along his cheek, Helena's or Nathaniel's, or that of their unborn child mingled on his skin, anointing him with shame. Nonetheless, Lucretia smiled gently. "May the Lord be with you, Elisha. I'll come when I may."

"Helena," he said.

"I know." Gathering up the skirts of her habit, Lucretia returned to their little house, calling out, "Lie back, Helena, I'm here with you."

Elisha stood silent while they bound his arms and led him in their midst toward the quarterhouse. What could he say to them? For his brother's sake, he'd twisted the truth already, destroying what evidence he could, implicating himself with no thought at all. If his brother's death was not to be judged suicide, then someone would be blamed—should be blamed, for the deeds that drove Nathaniel away and for the death that could be laid at Elisha's feet as surely as if he himself had drawn the blade. His brother died because of him.

Once inside the dim quarterhouse, they replaced the rope at his wrists with a chain affixed to a granite stone in the foundation. From a short distance, the captain eyed him. "Tell me all, Barber."

Nodding, Elisha wearily recounted the day from Nathaniel's finding him in the draper's house to the hospital, and their mad ride home. He told it all in what detail he could, straight until he'd left Helena's side. There, the narrative broke off, and he said no more. He was responsible to be sure, but he could not bring himself to claim the death so directly, and he would not, would never, reveal his brother's shame.

"You've left out your brother's death. How came he to be lying in the dirt, his life's blood pooled about him?"

"I can say nothing of that, my lord."

"Oh? In faith, I think you can. Unless you'll tell me you've forgotten a murder, and your own basin close by."

Elisha leaned back against the wall. Exhausted, he prayed for it to be done, for night to fall upon this day. "Then let the evidence tell all, I will not deny it."

The captain's eyes narrowed, and he chewed on his long mustache. "It seems as if that should be a confession, yet I misdoubt it."

Head cocked to one side, he regarded the captain. Elisha would not have thought the man bright enough to go even that far. He'd met him before, of course, but never for more than a few words touching on some theft or injury.

From long experience, Elisha knew that a single lie could be caught out, but in the absence of anything—lie or truth—people tended to draw the worst conclusion. "Doubt it if you will, sir, I have nothing more to say."

Still chewing on his mustache, the captain stared back then gave a slight nod. "Then I'll go interview the corpse." With a click of his heels, he turned and left. The guard brought him a basin to wash off the blood that already made his face and hands itch. Even scrubbing with both chained hands, he could not remove it all.

Sitting against the wall, his legs stretched out before him, Elisha drifted in and out of sleep, or at least, of some blessed absence of thought and remembrance.

Damp earth and blood overlaid the reek of previous in-
mates, turning his brief hunger to nausea. In the street
beyond the windowless wall, women laughed as they
shopped the market, wagons creaked to and fro, a min-
strel stopped awhile and set out his hat, grinding out
tunes on a hurdy gurdy that sounded as if several cats
were fighting inside it. A lone guard paced the hall
bounded by the iron grill, pausing to peer in at Elisha
before he passed back out to the chamber at the front
of the building. Some time later, he paced again. Some
time after that, he returned to light a torch in the hall.

Into the dim light, the captain returned, with Lucretia trailing after him, her face haunted. He fitted a key
to the lock at the grate and let them in, studying the
scene as the nun ran to Elisha's side.

"Are you well? They've not hurt you?"

Glancing over her shoulder toward the hovering captain, Elisha said, "No, of course not. I've been waiting,
that's all."

"I've found someone who'll help you, Eli." She gave
him a meager smile, her eyes worried. "Not that you'll
like it." She looked back toward the door.

With a gesture, the captain summoned in a third figure, tall and lean, wearing long, dark robes. Yards of
cloth gathered at his shoulders, draping down his arms
in elegant folds to form cuffs each wide enough to
clothe a child. A round rim at his temples gave way to a
tumble of velvet and silk—the height in fashionable
headgear. In fact, four whole families might be kept
warm in the cloth this man flaunted. The drapers must
be thriving by his custom alone.

Rising to give the smallest possible bow, his clothes
crisp with dried blood, Elisha remarked to Lucretia,
"I'm afraid you're mistaken. This man has no cause to
help me."

Ducking to enter the cell, the physician Doctor Lucius smiled, his head tilted to one side to better dangle the length of his hat. "Oh, my dear barber, do not sell yourself so short. Why, dozens of your former patients have sought us out." With an elegant hand, he indicated himself and the captain. "They plead that we must be lenient with you. I must have been approached by a hundred of whores alone." He smiled benevolently at Sister Lucretia, who tucked her hands into her sleeves and lifted her chin as he continued to address Elisha. "Holy Rood, you are covered in filth." His refined nose wrinkled his disgust.

Gritting his teeth, Elisha held his tongue.

"I have viewed the scene and investigated the evidence and the deceased, poor man. The difficulty is, you see, that the evidence tells two stories. In one, you have turned your hand against your own kin. In the other . . . well, I believe you know what the other tale might be."

"I stand accused of my brother's murder, sir, that I know."

"I've not charged you with anything," the captain said quickly.

"Why should you obfuscate a legal matter in this fashion? That is what I have asked myself." The physician waved his finger in the air. "Ah, but if your brother inflicted his own wound, he is denied his place in paradise. Ergo, you have muddied the water, so to speak, that we may not clearly determine and declare it that your brother is a suicide and damned for all eternity."

Rubbing at the chain around his wrist, Elisha evaded the man's cool gaze.

"Why would you sacrifice yourself for a God you show so little faith in? And for a man you'd not spoken to in two years, I am given to understand." He trod slowly across the brick floor to stand before Elisha. "It must be hard not to speak to a man who lives under your very roof. Especially when you are coveting his wife—"

Elisha's head jerked up. "Don't speak of things you do not understand."

"Well, the gospels of our Lord mean nothing to you, why should I expect His commandments to fare any better? Tell me, Barber, is there, in fact, anything you *do* believe in?"

Leveling his furious gaze, Elisha held up both hands, chained, blood still edging his nails, and yet steady as ever. "These," he replied.

"Ah. Hubris. I should have sought for no other antecedent to a fall such as yours." With a prim smile, the physician went on, "Then let us lay aside the issue of your brother, slain in his own workshop, by your own razor. No, let us examine the matter of the child."

The idea sickened him—the less said of it, the better. "I don't see what there is to discuss."

"Perhaps the sister should . . . ?" Doctor Lucius gestured toward the door, but Elisha shook his head.

"She was there, through it all."

"Ah. To continue, where was I? Oh, yes, ignoring the manner of your brother's death and turning to that of his child. By all accounts, you mutilated and dismembered an innocent. I was given to understand you term yourself a barber, not a butcher."

"The baby was already dead. By the time Nate came for me, it was dead. You should ask the midwife how long, and when she planned to tell the mother." The thought left him quivering with anger. Afraid of losing her fee, that woman had kept this terrible secret, even to the point of birth. A stillborn child, delivered by her, was better than one lost by other means. He'd kept his conclusions to himself as they'd raced for home, rather than add to Helena's anguish. Despair might well have tipped the balance of her own struggle.

"The midwife says the baby died during the birth," Doctor Lucius said, "when it became caught. Perhaps the delay when you took them from the hospital—"

"Then she's a liar. If she believed that, you'd never have given the order that you did."

Arching one silver eyebrow, the physician inquired, "Speaking of which, why did you not follow my advice?"

Elisha's mouth set into a hard line, every muscle in his body taut. In his lengthy schooling, the physician might have read a thousand books and studied a thousand cases and never touched a living patient, much less cut her quaking flesh. The physician had a few inches on him, but Elisha could have knocked him down like a scarecrow. "You know why."

"Because you impugn my wisdom at every turn, even to abducting a woman from the hospital I oversee. That is the only explanation I can find for you, a barber, to ignore the mandate not only of myself, but of the great physicians since the time of Hippocrates himself."

"That's a load of horse shit." He turned away, and found the captain and Lucretia exchanging a confused look.

"Maybe one of you'd better explain to me," the captain suggested, his fists planted on his hips. "Or is this part of the famous duel between doctors and barbers?"

"Legends to the contrary," Elisha began, "there's only one reason to cut open a woman to get at her child, and that's to lay them down in separate graves. Not in living memory has a woman survived such an operation." Elisha thrust his finger at the physician. "And the only reason he would advise it is that the life of one whore means nothing to him."

"Oh, come now, Barber, are you saying that even these miraculous hands of yours could not turn the operation to good effect? And without such barbarity?" The physician let out a little cackle. "One might imagine you a witch, carving up a child for the rites of the full moon. Willfully shedding its innocent blood to serve your evil ends."

Elisha lunged forward with a clanking of chains, stopping short as Lucius instinctively scrambled to escape him, white suddenly glinting in the doctor's cold eyes.

While the physician slapped his hat away from his face, and the captain looked back and forth between them, Elisha declared, "Murderer I may be, but witch I am none, and you shall find no evidence to support it."

Lucius flicked dust from his sleeves, concentrating on them while his breath still gasped a little. "If you continue to be hostile toward me, then I may rescind the offer I was to make. But perhaps your life is not worthy of my attention after all, no matter what your repugnant friends beseech of me."

"Now you're getting to the point, sir," Elisha shot back. "So tell me what you want and have done; I don't think any here believes you have my interests in mind."

"Elisha, please," Lucretia said beside him. "If you come before the peers, how shall they judge you but guilty? Please hear him out."

Folding his arms with a rattle of chain, Elisha nodded. If they judged him guilty, it would be the physician's testimony that swayed them. The chattering churl had him, and the smug little smile that played about his lips showed he knew it only too well.

Chapter 4

———————◆———————

"**I** am glad you've chosen to be reasonable, if only for a short while," the physician said. "Without further ado, my presence is requested at the front, to advise the king and his generals as to the proper treatment of battlefield injuries. There are new weapons brought to bear against us, and new procedures must be developed to cure the wounds."

A physician, concerned with the healing of wounds? Usually, they studied the urine and astrological charts of their wealthy patients and diagnosed illness without ever touching them. They didn't get involved with anything bloody. Elisha tried to be patient.

"I intend to bring several of my associates and assistants, and I am willing to include even you among that number. When I have my own university, there shall be sufficient educated doctors and surgeons. In the meantime, there are enough gross wounds of the sort you are best suited for, and where even your skill may serve. Through such service you might avoid the noose, by my grace and that of God."

"Your grace?" Elisha echoed. "You want to use me for the bloody work while you stand and blather about these new procedures with your associates. You're commanded to serve, and you're afraid to get your hands dirty."

"Why should I, when there are such as you? If you are ready to hack an infant to bits, then surely a few amputations can't turn your stomach. If you are ready to face your brother's death with no remorse, then the loss of a thousand foot soldiers won't deter you."

Elisha flicked his gaze away. "*You* turn my stomach."

"So you will turn down a position in my own retinue for what? Which story shall I tell the peers—the one which earns your death or your brother's damnation?"

He flinched. It was a devil's bargain either way. In the aftermath of his brother's death, he longed for death to escape the burden of guilt, but could not bring himself to give up life so readily.

"Which would the widow prefer to hear, do you think?"

Elisha wet his lips. "There will be rumors spread already."

"Rumors only. Rumors die with no fuel to fire them. Let each decide what he wills, and no affection lost between the widow and her friends." Gathering his courage, the physician stepped a little nearer. "Or consider that your skill may indeed be worthy, that your hands may serve a higher cause, away upon the battlefield."

At this, Elisha frowned. By God, he was a good surgeon, with the living around him as his proof. This was as close an admission as the physician might make that he knew it just as well. But Elisha had no wish to discover first-hand the wounds those new weapons could make. In silence, he studied his hands.

Dirt and blood rimmed the stubby nails and filled every line and crevice of his knuckles. They were the large, strong hands of a workman, hearkening back to his farmer forebears. Now, despite his scrubbing, Nathaniel's blood overlaid the nameless infant's. Perhaps the blame did not belong entirely to him, but also to the midwife who con-

cealed the baby's death, then revealed—prematurely—
that of the mother. These deaths were the culmination
of the trouble between himself and his brother, trouble
he had started two years ago in his arrogant, suspecting
way. If he had not been such a fool back then, he would
have been at Helena's side, not summoned in desperation when it was too late. Even if he could do nothing
for his brother's family, others needed the skills he possessed. There on the battlefield lay the penance he
asked for.

He lowered his hands and looked again to the physician. "You're going to Scotland?"

The physician made a harsh sound. "Certainly not.
Prince Thomas leads the army there, and they've got
none of the new weaponry. No, we go to the plains at
Dunbury Ford. You have heard of the battle?"

Dimly, Elisha thought. Another squabble where one
noble would be deposed and another just like him
would be given the lands while farmers and villagers
tried to put their lives back together.

Lucius sighed. "The duke has defied His Majesty.
Young Prince Alaric's called off his betrothal to the
duke's daughter, and now the duke refuses his rightful
fealty; he even claims the prince owes him an apology."
A snort. "His Majesty hopes for a quick victory."

In gentleman's terms, a quick victory meant one in
which lives were sacrificed and fortresses saved.

"His Majesty hopes the barons don't join in and recall the bastard princes from France," the captain muttered.

Lucius fixed him with a stare. "Nobody wants that,
captain. Even those who don't support our king. Are
you one of them?"

It was the same argument that brewed in alehouses
all over town, and just as meaningless there as in his

own jail cell. The succession was history, the battle of Dunbury was real. Elisha broke in: "When do we leave for this mission of mercy?"

With a smug smile, Lucius replied, "Tomorrow dawn. I trust you don't need much time to gather your things? Good. Meet us at Newgate." As he lifted the long skirts of his robe, he turned back. "You do have a horse?"

Rolling his eyes, Elisha said, "What do you think?"

With a sigh, the other said, "I shall have a wagon for my important instruments and papers. You may ride with it. Perusing them might do you some good. A little of the knowledge of the Salerno School, eh?"

Elisha reddened and looked away as the man gloated himself out the door.

"Blackmail's what that is," the captain said, frowning in the physician's wake. "I don't like it, not even for a prisoner, nor yet for an innocent man."

"No one's said I am innocent."

Shaking out his key ring, the captain gave him a stare of reproach. "Keep your own counsel then." He plucked out the proper key and fitted it into the lock at Elisha's wrist.

Rubbing the sensation back into his fingers, Elisha remarked, "I have underestimated you."

At this, the captain smiled. "Most do. I find it works to my advantage." With a brisk bow, he said, "Good luck at the front then. I don't expect you'll be back here."

"I rather guessed that myself."

"Now don't talk that way, Eli," Lucretia scolded. "Keep your wits about you, and God in your heart, and you'll not go wrong."

"In the meantime, I'll be going to war. I'd best get packing." With a nod to the captain, the two made their way into the twilight.

Looking at the sky, Lucretia muttered, "Oh, dear. I shall have missed the hour already and be late for curfew besides."

"Must be strange to go from working by night, to having a curfew."

She grinned. "You've said it, Eli, but all the same, I've a better master now than any I've ever known." Then she grew serious. "I shall be praying for you. Do keep safe, Eli."

"Of course." He gently squeezed her arms in lieu of an embrace. "See you do likewise, Sister."

Hiking up her habit, Sister Lucretia trotted off into the growing darkness. For a long time, Elisha watched her go. The Lord was lucky to have her service, as was he to be her friend. At last, he turned away, knowing full well why he dawdled. Eventually he must face the little house, awash with blood. Elisha forced himself to walk briskly. No unpleasant moment got better for waiting.

He rounded the bend of their alley and noticed the dim glow of a candle at the waxed cloth window of the upstairs loft. Surely Helena's family would be taking care of her, but there was no sign of company. Crossing the yard, Elisha opened the door and hesitated, listening, and heard nothing. Perhaps they had taken her from here to avoid the memories. As he set foot inside, however, the floorboards gave a groan, and someone gasped from above.

"Who's there? Who is it?" Helena's voice cried out.

"Only me," Elisha said. "But why are you here? Please tell me you're not alone."

"My sister's preparing a room for me."

"Good." He felt around on the shelf by the door and found flint and steel, and the lantern kept there. Nathaniel rarely bought oil, preferring a fire cheap and simple, but, even in the long months of their mutual silence, Elisha kept their oil jar full. It pleased him to fulfill another of his namesake's miracles. Nathaniel had never spoken of it, but he had to know where the extra came from.

After the lamp was lit and hung upon its chain, Helena's voice came again. "I thought I heard someone earlier, and I thought . . ."

Taking a breath, Elisha shut his eyes. "I am sorry, Helena."

"Come up," she said softly. "Let me see you."

Setting the lantern back in its place, he mounted the narrow stair on the far wall and climbed until his head emerged through the floor of the sleeping loft. On a mattress of straw Helena lay, the candle beside her and a Bible, a gift from a wealthy former admirer, resting close to hand. Of the three who'd lived here, she alone could read, a skill she'd learned before her father's ruin forced her into a different trade. Her face looked weary, with her hair bundled back in a matronly way. She fluttered a pale hand toward the book. "My only solace and company."

Folding his arms along the floor, he rested his chin upon them and watched her, even as she studied him. He hoped the light too dim to reveal the blood that stained his clothes.

"It has been a terrible day, Elisha," she breathed.

Unheeded tears seeped from his eyes to course down his cheeks. Again he prayed the darkness would hide him, and he dared not betray himself by brushing them away. His pain seemed unearned compared with hers. "A terrible day," he agreed.

"I begged him not to send for you, not after . . ."

Her words stung him, and Elisha clenched his teeth. "For that, too, I am sorry. I should have trusted you."

"And Nathan."

In a whisper, he echoed, "Him, too."

"You have not been touched by love, Elisha. You do not know its power. Or its pain. If I yet had one of them, my husband or my child, I might have felt some comfort against the loss of the other." She stared up at the peaked roof, the nails that held the roof tiles casting pointed shadows in the flickering light. "I used to wish you dead," she said, "For the wounding of my husband." Her lips curved into a ghost of her smile. "Today I have learned better. Instead, I wish you love. I wish you love to have, and love to lose, and yourself to keep on living. To know every moment that love is forever gone."

Elisha pressed his face into his arms, sobs welling up in him. He shook with the effort of silence and the pain she had struck into him with her quiet curse.

"Helena?" a woman's voice called from below. "Who's with you?" Then a round face appeared beside the stairs. "Oh. It's you." Helena's sister bore some resemblance, but as if she were the apprentice's unfinished work from which a master would carve beauty. Her lips twisted at the sight of him as if she might be ill. "Come to have another go round? Now that the husband's gone, you think Helena might yield to your wooing? And she weak from childbearing." She made a derisive sound in her throat. "We've come to get you, dearie, get you out of this dismal place." She gave Elisha a pointed stare.

Wiping his bared forearm hastily across his face, Elisha said, "I'll not be here in any event. Doctor Lucius has called me to the front."

Her mouth dropped open. "Called you? You? He's never had any use for you before."

Giving a bitter laugh, Elisha explained, "I'm the hands to do his bloody work."

"Heaven knows you're good at that," she cast back at him.

He leaned his forehead against the floor, caught on the stairs between two women who hated him, trapped as a mouse by feral cats.

"Get a move on, then," Helena's sister told him.

With an effort, he raised his head and looked across the upper floor at Helena who stared back. "The house is yours, Helena. If you rent my rooms, and the—" He couldn't bring himself to refer to his brother's workshop. "Anyhow, the money should be fair. I'll be taking some of my instruments; the rest should fetch a good price for you."

He heard her sister's husband and young son come in at the door, ready to bear her away. Elisha offered, "I can help."

For a moment, all were silent. Then came Helena's voice, stronger than before. "Two years ago, I swore never again to suffer your hands upon me."

Defeated, Elisha backed down the stairs, trying to shrink into himself so as not to brush against her sister. After a few minutes, the three had gathered up Helena and carried her back down and out the door, sparing neither word nor glare for Elisha as he stood alone in the large room.

The table dominated one end, draped over with cloth to conceal the blood which must stain it. Examining the floor, he saw the glint of his spilled instruments, and knelt down to retrieve them with unsteady hands.

"Barber?"

Elisha jerked, scattering the gathered tools once more across the floor. He turned swiftly to the door and saw the master draper there, his half-beard shaved clean by some other hand.

"Martin," Elisha gasped, trying to still the wild pulse.

Martin darted a quick glance around, then mounted the front steps, and shut the door. He bent down and collected a silver knife which lay at the turned-up toes of his shiny boots. "I came, I've been waiting—" He gave a nod toward the fireplace beyond which was Elisha's own chamber.

"About this afternoon," Elisha began. "I am sorry, I hadn't expected Nate, after so long—and to find me there—"

Laughing gently, Martin lifted another knife in his clean, beringed hand. He shook his head. "Don't apologize, Elisha. I know what's happened today. I least of all would ask any such apology from you. It is I who should apologize. I was playing at the supercilious merchant and got a little carried away. Half your fee indeed."

Still kneeling, Elisha brought one knee up before him to act as a prop for his aching head. "How long were you waiting?"

"Not long." Martin gathered a probe and a lancet, then a curved parting blade.

"Long enough to hear?"

He nodded.

Elisha blew out a breath.

Martin Draper, Master of the Draper's Guild, crouched on the floor, one by one gathering Elisha's filthy tools. Fastidiously, he avoided kneeling down and besmirching his clothes. Every so often, he wiped both tools and hands on a delicate kerchief not quite up to the task.

"Don't do that," Elisha said at last, snatching the handful of tools and reaching out for the next. "Your wife will notice blood."

Laughing again, Martin rose. "My wife is dallying with a weaver, unless I miss my mark. Handsome lad he is, too. And a good thing, since he's like to be the father of my next child."

"I've no idea how you manage."

"I am a tradesman, Elisha. I contract, I conspire, and, above all, I compromise." He remained standing, staring down at Elisha on the floor. After a time, while Elisha polished his tools on an edge of the soiled linen, Martin said, "I wish you'd just come clean; this curiosity is killing me."

Sighing, Elisha dropped the tools on the table with one hand, sitting back on his haunches. "I tried to seduce her. On the eve of their wedding."

"Oh, my." Martin's eyebrows notched upward.

"I thought she married him only to get out of the brothels, that she wanted to set up on her own at worst, or take advantage of him at best. Nathaniel was so taken with her that he wouldn't hear a word against the marriage, not from me. I told her I knew what she was up to, that I'd keep her secret, if, well, I got mine." His face flamed, and he kept it averted. "I expected her to be more than willing, and I would have my proof. I've never been so wrong about a person in my life. She called me every sort of monster, slapped me, and called my brother to throw me out. Neither one would hear an apology." He broke off, and looked up at last to Martin's sympathetic face. "It's been Hell, really, living in this house, but which of us could afford to move?"

"If you'd told me," Martin began, but Elisha cut him off.

"No, you wouldn't. You've got a position to maintain. If anyone knew—" But there was little point to finishing that sentence.

"I love you desperately," the draper said, advancing to touch Elisha's cheek.

Elisha gently withdrew from the caress. "No, you don't."

"Are you sure?"

As much at the mournful expression as at the wistful tone, Elisha smiled. "It's time you found someone to return your affections, Martin. You deserve better than a barber."

Running his fingers along his own cheek, Martin said, "A barber who doesn't even finish the job." With a shrug, he reached into a pouch at his belt and pulled out a narrow strip of cloth.

"What's that, a favor to carry into battle?"

"Consider it such, if you like. I like that idea well enough." He held it out and Elisha took the delicate fabric. "Keep it on you, Elisha, don't part with it for anything."

Frowning, Elisha looked up at his friend. "But what does it mean, Martin?"

Laying a finger across his lips, Martin smiled. "Now that would be telling. Promise me you'll keep it?"

"Is it blessed by a saint or something?" He ran the silk through his fingers, its fine fibers catching on the bits of dead skin. Threads of gold ran through in some pattern undistinguishable in the gloom.

"Charmed by a witch, perhaps. Now don't look at me like that. Just you keep it on you, and secretly."

"You do like your games," Elisha grumbled, tucking the fabric into the pouch the captain had returned.

With a final sigh, Martin slipped out of the door, back to his wealthy house, his courtly wife, and her handsome weaver.

Sometimes, Elisha would have liked to love him, would have liked to think himself worthy of such a man—or, indeed, of anyone. But he was no good at make-believe, and Martin's affection was a dangerous gift, even left unconsummated. He endured the flirtation when he tended Martin's barbering needs in the privacy of the man's chamber, but they could both be ruined if anyone knew.

Elisha rolled his neck from side to side, trying to shake the tension, and caught something out of the corner of his eye. On all fours, he crept to the table and saw beneath it the thing he had noticed: the neglected leather satchel, still seeping blood.

Chapter 5

❖

With cautious hands, Elisha drew the satchel from its hiding place, the weight of the dead child dragging it along the floor. He sat staring at the thing in front of him and thought again of the Bone of Luz, that mystical seed from which he might grow a new man. If he only knew how. The wild hope leapt within him that it might be possible, that some magic could bring it about, undo a little of the harm of this day and restore to Helena part of what she had lost, and with it, bring himself some measure of peace. Again, his heart raced. Yet how could he know if it were true? Who was there to ask without sending them both to the gallows, or worse?

He had witnessed magic once, when he was yet a boy, the last time a witch had been brought to trial. This was before even the terrible drought which had forced his family into the city to find work. His parents came in from the country to watch the execution, packing lunch for all of them, plus a few leftover vegetables from the garden gone soft and rotten, ripe for the throwing. Nathaniel, judged too young over his protests to the contrary, had been left at a neighbor's house to sulk.

The three of them rode in their pony cart, the rangy

new colt drawing them onward with the press of country folk all out in a common purpose. A tall pole had been erected outside the city wall in a patch of barren ground. The vivid purple of the royal pavilion, where the king and his two sons could recline in comfort for the festivities, brightened the gray of the city wall. Elisha had never been so close to the royal family, before or since. Nobility and townsfolk occupied the ground nearest to the site, leaving some distance for safety, so that the country farmers took up the surrounding grass, paying a few pennies to stand atop wagon seats for a better view.

Vendors wandered the makeshift rows, hawking all manner of sweets and ale from barrels slung upon their backs. Musicians roamed as well, offering songs for the ladies, while a handful of bards tossed off poems with quick wit.

Elisha begged a penny from his father to buy a little pennant of cloth painted with a hawk. So equipped, he ran about the grass, watching it flutter in the breeze. Dashing down a long slope, he stopped short.

Heedless of the direction he'd run, the boy found himself surrounded by fine carriages and ladies seated beneath stretched fabric to avoid the sun. He'd just begun to squint into the distance, searching for his parents, when the crowd around him fell silent, then let out a roar. Or so he thought until he turned around.

Elisha stood in the second rank of witnesses, not ten yards from the stake. Around him stood the king's archers, keeping a watchful eye for rioters, not caring for a wandering child. From their distant rise, Elisha's family could make out little but the pillar and its mound of wood. Close-to, he saw the woman bound there, clad in white, the pale ropes wound all about her. Her hands writhed against the bindings, and her lips moved faintly. They had shorn her hair, leaving only a rough fringe of red, revealing her terrified face.

The roar came not from the people gathered round but from a crimson flame licking the piled wood at the woman's feet.

Elisha's mouth hung open, and he shut it with a snap, his mother's scold sounding inside his head.

As the flames drew ever nearer to the woman's bare feet, the movement of her lips became fierce, until she let out a shriek that deafened him for an instant. Then the crowd roared indeed, chanting for her death. Smoke swirled around him, choking him and stinging his eyes. He rubbed them, reluctant to miss any of the spectacle. And it was then that the miracle happened.

Even as he stared, making out the woman's form within the growing flames, she seemed to sway and stretch. Then as she howled, her back bent, and the first bond broke. From both shoulders, the fabric strained, then tore. Golden and enormous, a pair of wings stretched out behind her, dwarfing her in their embrace.

Their first powerful sweep knocked Elisha down and blasted the shades around him, tearing at the ladies' hair, sending one pavilion crashing to the ground as the tethered horses bucked and ran. Nobles screamed and called out prayers. The priests scrambled back to their feet, thrusting up crosses and shouting into the wind.

Fighting that wind, Elisha rose. The sweep of her wings blew back his hair.

She glowed from head to foot, from wingtip to wingtip, the feathers glistening in the air. Even among the saints and virgins of church frescoes, he had never seen anything so beautiful. Elisha felt sure their eyes met. Her luminous eyes reflecting the flames that spat around her as she struggled to rise, then widening in agony as the first arrow struck. Blood spattered the golden wings.

Arrows tore into her feathers and slammed into flesh, piercing her legs and breast and throat.

Screaming, Elisha ran toward the fire. If he could only reach her, he could stop the bleeding, cut the ropes and set her free. Had the smoke so blinded them that they could not see she had transformed into an angel?

A priest snatched him by the shoulder, clinging despite the boy's resistance. Still, he had come close enough to be struck first by the heat, then by the tip of one powerful wing as they beat their last and vanished.

The witch's body bent into the flames, all life gone from her long before her body was consumed.

Panting, Elisha stood still, watching the flames, one hand pressed to his cheek where the angel's wing had stroked his skin.

Even now, twenty years later, that soft, delicious touch lingered in his flesh. For the first time, he wondered if he had avoided love because of that angel, because their eyes had met through a wall of flame.

His fingers traced a line across his cheek.

Too far away to see the truth, his parents thought the flames had gone out of control. When the priest returned their child, they were relieved he had not been harmed. Rumors abounded that the witch had worked some final curse upon those nearest, and Elisha was baptized again and made to attend a week of special services to rid him of whatever evil residue she had left behind. For a time, they all acted as if he had absorbed some witchcraft. His father beat him twice as hard, and four times as often, to re-instill the proper discipline, and Elisha allowed himself to be convinced that the angel had been a trick, a perversion of God's seraphim meant to ensnare the minds of the weak-willed and the

children. But as the memory of prayers and beatings receded, the angel's touch remained.

After they moved to the city, he'd found a barber in
need of an apprentice. He learned well enough how to
cut hair, pull teeth, and bleed patients on the orders of
their doctors, but he quickly surpassed his master in his
eagerness to learn the ways of surgery. If ever he had
the chance to bind an angel's wounds, Elisha would be
ready.

He laughed at himself in the darkness, fingering the
strap of the leather bag. For twenty years that memory
seemed too secret to share even with his conscious
thoughts. As an adult, he had never spoken of it to anyone, though he heard the occasional reference muttered in a tavern or whispered in the church. Certainly
he never sought out the company of witches, not that
there were any to find in these parts after that day. The
few who had been hunted down since were quietly dis-
patched with sword or arrow lest they cast another such
glamour upon an audience so vast.

Considering this, he finally stood, took up the
satchel, and gathered his tools from the table. The
Bone of Luz should be a thing of anatomy, yet he had
not seen it nor heard of any man who had. Still, even
Lucius Physician professed his belief, and he had studied at Salerno. Church law forbade dissection, except
where required for criminal investigation, but Elisha's
work had introduced him to most of the bones and organs of the body. Where might the Bone lie, then? Not
the abdomen, surely, where it might obstruct the body's
courses. Legend placed it at the top of the spine, but
wouldn't those martyrs beheaded then be denied their
resurrection? He guessed it would be found in the
skull, the sanctum of a man's intellect, and perhaps his
soul. Trepanation was not Elisha's specialty. Despite

his experience, the thought of punching a hole in someone's head, even to cure him of worse ills, worried him greatly. The Bone, if it did exist, must reside somewhere behind the eyes.

Snuffing the lamp, Elisha shut the door behind him and picked his way in the dark to the back of the house and his own chambers. There was still the packing to do—selecting the best and most needed of his tools and medicaments, the rest to be left to Helena's disposal. Before he began that, however, he located certain salts and herbs and a squat, lidded pot recently emptied of weapons ointment and suited to his needs. In the alley behind the house stood the pump and cistern. On its stone overflow rim, he set down the satchel and gently searched its contents until he found the infant's small, soft head. In the terrible operation he had performed, most surgeons would have crushed the little skull to let it pass more easily. Thankfully, he had not needed that final barbarity today. Placing it into the pot, he covered it with oils of turpentine and lavender, hoping the Bone within would not be damaged by the preservative mixture.

When that was done, Elisha washed his tools, then himself and his bloody clothes, splashing cold water by the bucket over his body. He scrubbed his hands until it felt that he would bring forth blood of his own, and finally returned to his study with his burdens, shivering in the growing chill of night. He sealed the lid of his little pot with wax and thrust it to the bottom of a small chest. He found fresh clothes, draping his wet things to dry for the morrow.

Elisha sat a long time with the sorry satchel before him. He knew what must be done, but the tools would be in his brother's workshop, and the thought of going inside, facing that terrible absence, made him feel heavy as stone. Still, he could not leave Helena to face her child's remains—or risk someone knowing what he had taken. Someday, he might return to her in triumph, restoring the baby he had cost her. Her husband was a loss for which he could not make amends.

Not far off, the church bells rang, and Elisha stirred himself to motion. He had little enough time as it was. He took up the satchel and went to the workshop. He almost knocked, but his lifted hand paused in time. No amount of knocking would rouse the dead. He pushed gently and went inside. It took a moment for his eyes to adjust—a long moment in which the shadows formed his brother's corpse. But no, the place was empty, Nathaniel's body taken away to prepare for burial, his blood merely darker shadows on the earthen floor.

Nate always started work early, and Elisha used to pause in the yard to listen to the rhythm of hammer and files. Once, he caught his brother singing while he worked and made some remark, hoping to touch him beyond the rift he had caused, but Nathaniel turned from him and sang no more.

Elisha's eyes burned with sudden tears. He forced himself to look away, forced himself to move to the neat racks of tools and find the spade for turning the coals in the hearth. On a narrow bench by the window-sill waited a row of little crosses Nate would have sold at fairs or to his other customers. Elisha took one of these, the shape pressing into his palm beneath the handle of the spade. If it should carve straight through him it would not be punishment enough.

He made his way through the narrow streets, giving a few coins to the guard at Cripplegate to let him pass. Beyond the wall, and a few more turns, Saint Bartholomew's churchyard lay before him, humped with graves. He wished he knew where his brother would lie, so he could place the child close by. Failing that, he found a place that looked too narrow for an adult's grave, not far from the church's tower. The monastic hospital rose a short way off, founded by a king's fool two centuries ago, along with the church itself. A man would have to be a fool to place his trust in either God or doctors. His brother had been failed by both.

Using the short-handled spade, awkward in his hands, Elisha peeled back the layer of grass and dug as deep as he might. He nestled the satchel into the hole, dark into darkness, and bowed his head. There should be prayers for this. On a better day, he might recall them. He wet his lips and searched for words, his hands pressed together before him. "Dear Lord," he started, and a lump rose in his throat. He stared down into the dark hole where his brother's child lay. God was too far away to hear anything Elisha might say.

To the child, he whispered, "Forgive me." His fingers knotted together and his shoulders shook, but he felt no answer. "I swear I will take care of you." He was the elder; his care was what Nathaniel should have had. He tried, hadn't he? He didn't want Helena for himself, he wanted to show Nathaniel what he thought she was, to protect him. But Elisha was wrong. He wronged his brother, he wronged his brother's wife. He became a barber to heal others, but instead he wounded them unto death.

Softly, ever so softly, as if the other graves could hear him speak, he said, "If I can, I'll see you born again. If not, if there is life in me, I'll see your spirit laid to rest."

He drew back and began to fill the little grave, pressing the grass back over it. Tomorrow he would go to war. He deserved death for the terrible day his deeds had brought, but he hoped for life. He hoped for a penance so great, a labor so severe that these dead might be appeased.

Last, he found the cross his brother made. Crosses of wood and carved stones marked the graves around him, some with words he knew to be the names of the dead, with their dates of birth and death, dates that bounded lives both long and short. April fifth, the Year of Our Lord, 1347. This child had not a year, not a month, not even a single day. If they had spoken of names for their baby in the darkness of their bed, Elisha did not know it. He pushed the end of the cross, empty of mark or word, into the grass and brushed the dirt from his hands before he crossed himself.

"I'm sorry," he whispered through his tears, his hands clutched together, begging. "I am so sorry." He squeezed his eyes shut, his throat burning, until the tears receded, and he thought he could rise without stumbling.

With the spade alone to fill his hands, Elisha walked away through the shadowed streets.

Back in his room, silence echoing overhead, Elisha set to work on his traveling chest. All around and over the dangerous jar, he packed envelopes and vials— melon seeds, slippery elm, cochineal, thistle leaves— then sat back and stared at the motley collection.

"I'm not a damned apothecary," he muttered. No doubt the physician had gotten several apothecaries already, and of more use than Elisha's mere general knowledge. And the great man himself would have a store of expensive medicines: nutmeg and cloves, powdered mummy, bezoar stone. Elisha unpacked most of the herbs and put them aside in favor of a few more instruments, a larger amputating saw, a silver crow's beak for clamping veins, a selection of probes and lances. All of his needles he added to the chest, and the rolls of suturing thread. A few ewers and bowls for bloodletting settled on top, with a smaller basin and a spare razor.

These last he hesitated over, imagining Nathaniel lying beside his best basin. That one he could not bring himself to use again, no matter its value. Let Helena sell it off.

Lastly, he dropped in his two other tunics, woolen hose with only a few holes—he meant to buy another pair once he had the money to spare—a good belt and leather apron, and draped his wet britches over the top to dry out. By candlelight, his boots didn't appear too blood-soaked, and traveling mud would conceal that soon enough. This pair had lasted a good five years so far, with only a few repairs, and he hoped to get good use out of them for some time longer. The cloak he would wear, and the thick farmer's hat his mother had made years ago.

Staring at his one small chest, Elisha wondered how many Lucius would bring, and how large. Any man who could afford the cloth of that one robe would likely have several spares besides. This triggered a thought, and Elisha brought out a long wooden box left over from childhood.

On top he found what he had recalled—his own hidden wealth, an unworn shirt procured for his brother's wedding two years back. After Elisha's foolish attempt to prove Helena's treachery, Nathaniel had threatened his life if he dared come to the church that day.

Elisha lifted out the good shirt, woven of linen with no decoration. Feeling the heavy cloth between his fingers, he sighed again at his folly. He considered himself a practical man, and yet he afforded himself the luxury of a shirt he'd never wear. As if he should save it for some special day undreamed of. Now, with today's tunic hopelessly stained, and torn besides from long use, he had need of this symbol of his betrayal. Tomorrow, he would wear it on the start of a journey far from the home that would not be his when he returned. If he returned.

Below the shirt hid his few treasures: a copper coin minted in a foreign land, a handful of embroidered tokens given him by the whores at the brothels he tended, knotted charms to ward off illness and accident, kept more for sentiment than superstition, a small tin crucifix made by his brother's hand, and, at the bottom, a rumpled cut of cloth painted like a hawk—the pennant he had begged for, which had led him to the angel of his memory. If he ever did reach Heaven, perhaps this hawk would lead him once again.

Chapter 6

❖

When the east finally began to pale toward morning, Elisha arose, dressed in the clothes he'd laid out, and combed out his hair, thick and dark. A truly practical man would have trimmed the mane of dark waves to an easier length, but it was his sole vanity, and he couldn't bring himself to cut it. He bound it back with a length of cord, slipping the comb into the pouch containing a few coppers, Martin's strip of cloth, and emergency supplies: needles, suture, a pair of small, sharp knives and the stone to whet them by, as well as a small vial of opium to dull pain. The stuff was banned, and he ought to dispose of it, but it was costly, and it let him work in peace on a relaxed patient when the wound was especially terrible. He would have liked to offer some to Helena during her ordeal, but to do so was forbidden by church law. Did not the Bible say that women must in sorrow bring forth children?

Elisha shook his head at this absurdity. Only a man who had never been there could enforce such a law. Now, knowing the midwife's deceit, he was relieved he had not used the drug, for it could have been his undoing. From behind a loose stone at the base of the wall, he removed his hoarded wealth: four silver coins, one so old it bore the worn but still proud likeness of King Edward.

He took a few minutes to stitch the coins into the hood of his cloak for safe keeping. Rolling up his blankets, he secured them with a rope fashioned into a strap to go over his shoulder. Flinging on his cloak, Elisha hefted the blankets and the chest and let himself out into a chilly dawn. He glared at the rising sun. Already, he was late, and the gate was yet a good distance off. No hammer broke the silence as he passed his brother's smithy. Steeling himself not to look back, he strode away.

He covered ground quickly enough through the city just rousing. The appointed gate stood in a richer part of town, off the end of the high street where Martin Draper kept his shop. In the peasants' quarter, tradesmen and laborers had begun their day, stoking the fires and gathering their tools. Many of these nodded to Elisha as he passed. On the merchant's row, only apprentices stirred at this hour; their duties included sweeping up and clearing refuse from the streets before their shops. Down one road, he saw a handful of shops with real glass windows, and two or three servants each, washing the glass in the leaded panes.

Dogs pursued him for much of the walk, growling and sniffing at the scent of blood which always lingered no matter how he washed. At Newgate, the guardsmen looked him over and nodded him through to the outer bailey with its portcullis not yet raised. The gate tower also served as a prison, its deep shadow reminding him of the alternative to the physician's offer: a short trial and a sharp death.

A half-dozen wagons formed the physician's train, all laden with trunks as the carters tugged each rope in turn to be sure of their hold. The heavy horses and oxen stood patiently in their traces, ears occasionally perking to a sound of interest. Fifty soldiers at least milled about, a few with tall riding mounts whose breath showed as mist in the dawn. The physician himself, in an ostentatious crimson hat, directed the arrangement of his personal wagon, lording it over the carters who cast about black looks but did as he bid them. A bright white horse stamped at the rear of the wagon, fitted out with barding of crimson and gold as if the caravan were bound for a festival. Lucius probably thought his service would win him the king's notice, and maybe the university that a royal commission could build.

Best make himself known, Elisha thought, approaching Lucius and bowing a few feet short of him.

"Ah, so you have not made off for the hills. Very good. Is that all your baggage?" His eyebrows arched upward to such good effect that Elisha suspected he had them plucked and trained for the expression.

"Aye, it is."

Tilting his head like hunting hawk, Lucius gestured up toward the seat of the wagon. "It may fit under there—I doubt there is a place for it among my things."

Lugging his chest, Elisha leaned to peer beneath the seat, and shoved the chest in, stuffing his blankets after it to keep it lodged there.

"Ay, Barber," the carter called from across the wagon. He grinned, showing his crooked teeth, and Elisha recognized the same man who had aided them in their flight from the hospital yesterday.

"How did you come here?" Elisha asked.

"Conscript. They've demanded a dozen of us, good with the horses, as know the road from here to Dunbury. Name's Malcolm." He stuck out a broad, grubby hand, and Elisha grasped it with a smile.

"Elisha's mine. I'm glad of a friendly face." He cocked his head toward the physician. "This is by way of a punishment for me. You've heard about the end of yesterday's operation?"

"No! Not too bad, I hope?"

"The worst." Elisha paused just a moment, fitting the proper words. "I lost the child and my brother also."

The man crossed himself. "Cor! And they made ye get up for this affair? It's mourning ye should be about, and seeing to the wife."

For a moment, his eyes stung. Elisha said, "She'll have none of me. Maybe it's for the best that I'll be gone."

Eyeing him sidelong, Malcolm crossed himself again. "Ye've not been to battle before then?"

"No."

Someone ahead blew on a trumpet, and the soldiers suddenly took up their reins. Elisha and the carter likewise climbed into the wagon, awaiting their place in the train as the huge portcullis ground slowly upward on its chains.

"Terrible sight, this war, and sound, too. These bombards, now, they'll cast a stone as big as your head straight through the ranks and halfway to the camp, leaving limbs and corpses behind." He added with a bitter chuckle, "I'd not want your job, sure enough. The screaming and the dying, day and night, and always with that pounding of the cannons. First time I went out, I swore the earth would rip herself apart for all the noise."

"The physician has some new treatments he plans to test out on the victims."

"If ye can scrape one up while he's still alive." Eyes to the horses, Malcolm called out, "Hya!" and the wagon pitched into motion.

Three days distant, the castle at Dunbury Ford lay under a partial siege, the king's army unable to surround it completely. Heart of the rich holdings of a duke once favored by the king, the castle occupied a hilltop alongside a deep river. Elisha did not follow the doings at court. He had enough to do to keep brothel politics straight from one day to the next, and nothing the king or his barons did was likely to touch on them. Even the mayor who ruled London preferred his manor house and let his bailiffs handle the lesser citizens. Elisha gathered from the soldiers' talk as they rode that King Hugh accused this duke of plots against the crown for his failure to deliver a shipment of new weapons from Milan. As Lucius had implied, the duke had been set to cement his loyalty with a marriage between his daughter and the king's younger son, Prince Alaric, but the whole thing had gone sour somehow.

Hugh had not been popular from the moment his father, then-King Edward, declared Hugh legitimate during a great feud with his unruly presumptive heir, Edward the Younger. Given the rushed marriage of Hugh's high-born mother to a Welsh lord, and the birth of Hugh following so soon after, many of the lords were unsurprised to find that Hugh's father had been the king himself. Apparently, King Edward hoped rewarding the loyal Hugh with legitimacy would bring his heir in line. Then both royal Edwards died within months of each other—one from sickness, the other on the front in Scotland—leaving the barons to choose between an unpleasant but powerful bastard, or the little children of King Edward's French second wife. After the declaration of Hugh's legitimacy, the queen had taken the boys home to France in a fit of anger, expecting King Edward to apologize and beg for her return, only to hear of her husband's death some time later. Given their youth, accepting the French heirs would amount to handing over the throne to the French king. The bastard Hugh had enough power from his Welsh backers to stick his own claim and prevent the French boys from returning—and now he had his own sons, the princes Thomas and Alaric. Since that difficult succession, chances were, as the captain suggested, that this new battle was merely the latest in forty years of skirmishes mounted by the restive barons.

From what Elisha's father had said of his own days at war, Elisha suspected the causes drifted high above the battlefield where peasants died until the nobles agreed to be friends once again. The high born were supposed to be better folk, more blessed, more beautiful, more wise, but they all looked the same on the inside. A king would bleed just as red as a serf.

That first afternoon, they passed through the village of Elisha's boyhood, half-empty now, long abandoned houses collapsing on themselves. Drought had driven them off, and few remained to make a living on the land he once had known. He remembered the days of growling stomachs and brittle crops before they set out for London, but the family's hardship had been his opportunity to act upon the wild dream of learning the healing arts. As they drove through, he noticed a few farmers with weathered, familiar faces. It was he who had become the stranger.

Within two days, they left behind the lands Elisha knew, setting a good pace for the king's encampment. Hills grew taller here and thickly forested. Then a heavy rain caught them up, slowing the journey and forcing Elisha down from the wagon to help heave it from the mud, and later to lift the thing up so its axle could be repaired. Lucius would not have his precious things unloaded, of course, so it required a dozen of the strongest to strain and grunt, glaring at him on his tall horse.

   The physician's assistants did not deign to speak to
Elisha, so he spent his evenings at the carters' fire,
laughing at their bawdy songs, sharing his most gruesome stories when they were in their cups. They especially enjoyed hearing anything about the whores, and
he did his best to satisfy, until some detail or memory
would bring Helena to mind and Nathaniel with her.
Then Elisha would fall silent and turn away.

   As the fifth day dawned, Elisha rolled from his blankets to a sound like distant thunder. He listened, but it
came no nearer. The carters grew almost solemn that
day as they approached the terrible noise. Yet by evening, when they entered the last town along the road, it
was the silences Elisha noticed, looking up in curiosity
when the sound had gone. The wagons creaked into
town, approaching the little church they'd known by its
tower. A few lanterns shone in the houses, but ahead a
great conflagration flared up, and almost everyone
leapt down from wagons and horses to see what the
trouble was. Elisha found himself at the lead, his long
strides equal to those of the taller physician.

   From the streets around, townsfolk rushed up as the
visitors reached the square. A mob of men surrounded
the fire with water buckets, while another group huddled to one side.

   Leading his retinue, Lucius approached the huddled
gathering, calling out, "I am a king's physician. What's
the trouble here?"

   "Witchcraft, my lord!" one of them hollered. The little band separated, revealing one man clutched in their
midst by many hands. The slight figure trembled,
bruises showing on his face. With his fair hair and
frightened eyes, he reminded Elisha chillingly of his
brother. "He's lit up the chapel with spellfire."

   The soldiers stopped short at this, muttering, but

Lucius shook his head gravely. "Nonsense. I am a learned man, and I assure you that such tricks as witches have are not equal to creating real flame. That requires spark and fuel—"

A scream tore through the night, and they whirled. A woman spun and shrieked in the churchyard, flames leaping up from her hair.

"Witchcraft!" someone shouted, and those around her cried out, stumbling back from the magic fire.

Her arms beat about her head, and she tore at her skirts. In her panic, she ran toward the center, as if pursuing the soldiers. They scattered, crossing themselves.

A few men from the fire brigade dashed forward with buckets, and Elisha swore and ran. "Stop! No water, you'll sear her to death!" He fumbled at his cloak, dodging the fleeing soldiers.

At last he ripped the garment free, throwing himself into the path of the stricken woman and pouncing on her, flinging the cloak around her.

She fought him, wailing, as he bore them both to the ground and smothered the flames.

For a moment, she whimpered in his embrace as he patted her head and shoulders muffled by cloth. "You're fine," he whispered. "Fine. Everything's all right."

Finally, he sat up, breathing hard, and unwrapped the cloak from her face.

Smoke-stained, her eyebrows singed, the woman gingerly touched her face and hair. Some of her hair was scorched, her chemise falling away from one shoulder in burnt remnants.

Elisha smiled in a way he hoped was reassuring. "Just a spark," he told her, and she offered a timid smile in return.

"Is the lady injured?" Lucius said, coming up alongside. "I'd best examine her."

Immediately, she turned from Elisha, pulling up her tattered garment. "You're the physician, sir?"

"Indeed, I am. Of the Salerno School."

Slipping off his cloak, Elisha rose, shaking out the cloth. No harm done—then a cry rose up around them.

"The witch! He's gone!" Townsfolk ran to the shout, then scattered out among the streets. "Quickly, before he enflames another!"

Elisha found himself surrounded and caught up in the rush down hill toward the river. This action the soldiers could support and they, too, joined the cry. At the river's edge, Elisha stopped, clinging to a tree. In the mad dash, his cloak had been torn from his grasp and left behind. "Damn it all," he grumbled.

After a moment, his eyes adjusted, making out the dim shape of a bridge, and the absurd sight of townsfolk and soldiers pursuing some poor man caught unawares with a sprig of mistletoe or some other supposed sign that he'd cast fire on their chapel. A pile of stones sat nearby, and Elisha made his way over, feeling for rough edges and someplace to catch his breath.

Instead, his hand encountered an arm, and someone cried out and burst up from his hiding place among the rocks.

"Bloody Hell!" Elisha shouted, as frightened as the other man. Several of the crowd turned in their direction.

The witch stumbled toward the river, and Elisha sprang after him as a soldier behind called out, "Have you got him?"

Catching the man with one hand, Elisha hauled back the other and knocked him senseless into the shallows, jumping lightly down after.

"Here, what's going on?" a soldier called, as a few townsfolk gathered, one raising a torch overhead.

Quickly, Elisha scooped the man's shoulders against his chest, looking up to them, his heart racing. "This man's fallen. I'll see to him. You'd best keep searching."

"Aye," the soldier called down, and they hurried off in search of their prey.

Bent over his captive, Elisha took a few quick breaths. His hand at the man's throat found a rapid pulse, and the man started under his touch, trying to push him away.

"Hush," Elisha urged. "Don't move, I'm not out to hurt you."

Shaking, a muffled voice replied, "You hit me, didn't you?"

"I had to—I couldn't take time to explain, could I? Now they think you're unconscious."

"I am," the witch answered, ceasing his struggle, but sitting stiffly, not trusting.

Elisha slipped his arm around the man's shoulder and helped him from the water up to the rocks. "Steady, steady," he whispered. Elisha guided him into a nook and settled beside him.

The witch shook all over, drawing his knees up and ducking his head. Quietly, Elisha replaced his arm about the other man's shoulders.

"They'll kill you," said the witch. His voice was light and soft, younger than Elisha had guessed.

"I won't tell," he replied. "Will you?"

A muffled snort answered him, a sort of nervous laugh, stifled for safety. "Who are you?"

"Elisha Barber. And you are?"

"Does it matter? I'm accused of magic."

Dropping his voice even lower, Elisha asked, "Are you a witch?"

The other jerked. "Of course not!"

"Pity. I could use a bit of magic."

Laughing, the witch rose. "I think they've gone."

"At least let me see to your injuries." Elisha tried to get a look at him, but trees obscured the feeble light of the pale moon.

"Just a beating. I've had worse. It's what I earned for trysting in a chapel." Clothing rustled as he moved, and he added, "I think your blow was the worst, actually."

"It was the best I could do in the moment."

A warm hand sought his own in the darkness and gripped it tight—a soft hand, with the slightest calluses. Not a workman's hand, nor that of any townsman he'd ever known. Elisha frowned. The young, clear voice said, "I thank you, Barber, for the blow that saved my life."

With the other's aid, Elisha pulled himself to his feet. "Take care with it, then. I've no wish to hit you again. But how did you come to this?"

"Look to yourself, Barber," the stranger said, "if you plan to save any more witches. Mobs take no more kindly to the accomplice than to the accused." Swiftly, he vanished into the night, leaving Elisha with neither cloak nor answer.

Chapter 7

❖

Elisha rose and went in search of his lost cloak, cursing the darkness when he found not a sign of it—nor of the silver coins he'd so carefully stitched into the hood. "Bloody Hell," he muttered, making a second sweep down the road he had taken. Doubtless one of the townsfolk had collected it as a prize and would only feel the more blessed when he found the coins. The spring days were warm enough, but evenings grew chilly, and he felt it especially now that he was damp from his splash in pursuit of the witch. The cloak was a sore loss. When the wagons rumbled by a little later, Elisha dusted himself off and followed along, catching up with Malcolm and pulling himself up.

"Did ye see the witch, then?" the carter asked, with an eager grin.

"Only for a moment. I think the shrine just caught a spark from something—a candle most like. The poor man's probably giving prayers of thanks right now that he got away."

Malcolm snorted. "Ye know nothing of the world, eh? These witches, they'll set fire to ye soon as look at ye. Revenge for theirs, if ye catch the meaning. And I had a cousin as turned black when he looked at one the wrong ways at market."

Elisha left off rubbing his arms to keep warm. "Black?"

"Aye, black's your hair. Took a bath in mother's milk to clean him up."

"Sounds expensive."

"Dunno, I wasn't there, was I? But that's the least mischief I've heard from a witch."

Hugging his arms close, Elisha laughed.

"Ye don't believe me," Malcolm grunted. "Suit yerself, ye'll see some doings around these parts, mark my words. I hear this duke's been accused himself."

"Well, I'll be looking forward to that," Elisha said, then noticed the carter's lowered gaze. "Just curious, that's all."

"Don't be too eager, Barber. These witches, they take blood in their rites and summon up devils to torment those as displease them. Oh, aye, that village we passed's had more trouble than a bit, let me tell you." He straightened and flicked the reins to encourage a quicker pace. "Course, we may be in for a burning, we stay long enough." He grinned at this and nodded. "Not been to one in years."

This caught Elisha's attention, and he asked, "Were you there, outside the city? Maybe twenty years ago?"

"That I was. You'd have been little more than a lad, eh? I's lucky to be a groom then, with one o' the great houses. We had a spot not five rows from the stake."

"What did you see?" Elisha leaned forward, propping his chin on one hand to see what he could of Malcolm's face.

With a flash of that suspicious look, the carter said, "She cast a glamour at the end, she did. The devil himself come into her and raised his fiery wings. Cor, that were something to see. Yet the priests held him back, so the archers got off their shots. Might'a been an awful day for all of us if they hadna taken her down." He crossed himself, staring into the distance as if he, too, could still see the scene before them. "It's the sacrifice, ye see. They're strongest at the very moment of death, when they've given themselves over to darkness."

"Like saints," Elisha murmured, but into his hand, and the carter did not hear him.

They reached the encampment shortly before dawn, led onward by the night watch. The bombards were silent all night, but Elisha saw movement on the battlements of the distant castle and doubted they would have peace for long. The vast camp stretched along the riverside, a motley assortment of common canvas tents and the brightly decorated bell tents and pavilions of the knights and nobles. Spread out all around were the cookfires and bedrolls of the common foot soldiers and camp followers.

At the heart of this stood an old monastery, its towers crooked and collapsing, rents in the walls overgrown with trees and vines. The long nave of the church lay exposed to weather through gaps in the roof and empty windows. The wagons came around the front of this structure toward the old cells where the command post was established; the lower hall, once the refectory, still had a roof by virtue of the intact second floor. From the cries and the stink, Elisha knew they'd reached his destination.

He jumped down, staring up at the granite façade before him. To the right stood the ruined church. A huge rosette window filled its peak, the stained glass mostly gone, leaving only a few petals of brilliant color that gleamed in the new sun and cast emerald and gold upon the refectory wall, adjoining the church at a corner. The smaller spire alongside it was missing its top, and a flight of doves burst free, circling it in a swooping frenzy that much resembled ecstasy.

"Take any room remaining—not far from here, naturally," the physician said. "I'm off for the generals. I'll expect to see you at the infirmary soon."

"Aye, my lord," Elisha returned, still gazing at the tower.

Making a harsh sound of irritation, the physician strode away, barking out his orders to the carters as they began untying the ropes.

After a moment, Elisha pulled out his own bedroll and small chest, carrying them toward a peaked door just visible at the base of the tower. It hung off-kilter on a single hinge, and vines draped one side. A few footprints showed the place had been explored, but Elisha hoped no other had the same idea. Entering the darkness of a windowless chamber, Elisha let his eyes adjust, then found the narrow stair upward and followed it, his boots loud on the stone steps.

As he'd expected, the second floor had a small chamber once used for storage, but long empty now save a few leaves blown in. The stairs continued up through a sagging wooden floor, but this would serve well enough for him. Under the stairs, he set down the chest and flopped his bedroll on top. He longed to spread out his blankets and get a decent rest before facing what was to come, but that would have to wait for another nightfall. Crossing the floor, he leaned to look out one of the two broken windows and found a view of the camp below. The other window afforded a sight of the castle on its hill, with sunlight just touching its highest towers. Ranks of fortifications surrounded it like trimmings on a lady's skirt, while the remains of a town spread out below. The river curved around it, a silver gleam overarched by the fortifications on that side. A few blackened areas could be seen on the castle walls, and a few bites of rubble where the king's siege

engines had struck. The scorched corpses of those engines lay scattered about, testifying to the use of burning oil by the defenders. When the wind shifted, the air
smelled of smoke and a strange metallic tang such as
Elisha had never tasted before.

Hills rose up again behind the castle, thickly grown
with spruce and oak. The plain separating the monastery from the castle was torn and dark already, crows
and vultures circling the pits where unseen bodies lay.
Standing there, Elisha realized he had never had such a
view before, unobstructed by the buildings of town. He
was used to the sight of grubby houses, gated stone
manors, and tall shops whose top floors he would never
know. The castle back in London rose abruptly to one
side, a gray obstruction, featureless and massive, its
white tower enclosed in moated walls, cut off from the
people it ruled. From a distance, perhaps, it inspired
wonder in those who approached it and fear in the
hearts of its enemies, but Elisha's work kept him to the
north, and he rarely passed that way. But this place—he
hated to imagine it destroyed, the castle brought low,
the river black with soot and blood, the trees cut down
for battering rams and ladders.

Even as he thought it, trumpets sounded below, and
the soldiers roused themselves, forming up in ranks to
greet another day of battle. Elisha turned away. His
own duty lay not on the battlefield but behind it. He
found his apron and strung it about his neck to catch
the worst of the blood.

Taking up a leather bundle of his instruments, Elisha
descended to the lower floor and out, across the grass to
the building used for a hospital. A wide aperture gaped
where double doors had once been, giving access to a
long, columned room with a few steps down to enter.
Near the entrance, a series of beds had been cobbled

together from scavenged wood or perhaps taken from
houses destroyed in the village. Each man occupying
one of these had a personal attendant, be it squire or
whore, carrying water or fresh bandages. Three men in
bloodied clothes circulated—the surgeons.

Beyond them, a makeshift curtain separated the
back half of the room. From there came the piteous
cries he'd heard earlier, and Elisha bowed his head a
moment, the long and tiring journey suddenly weighing
on him full-force. Few attendants crossed the boundary
laid by that curtain and with little in their hands to aid
those who suffered beyond it. He knew without guidance that this was the hall for the commoners, the foot
soldiers who went out first, who died first, who might
lie moaning for hours before a crew collected them
from that bloody field. His people.

Steeling himself, Elisha walked down the few steps
and inside between the beds. One of the surgeons
seemed to be directing the others, so he sought the
man's attention, joining him at the bed of an older
knight, his head wrapped in linen.

"Sir," Elisha said, with a slight bow. "I'm Elisha Barber, brought by the physician Lucius."

"What?" the man glanced up from a parchment he
had been studying. A crude sketch of the human body
filled the page, crabbed about with symbols and letters,
matched to various limbs and organs. A cord attached
the parchment to a rope belt with a half-dozen books
and a few more scrolls already dangling from it. "Who
are you?" The question furrowed his well-worn brow,
gray locks straggling from under a soft, round cap. He
looked up at Elisha from liquid brown eyes, his face
lined with a weariness beyond the flesh.

"Elisha Barber."

"Good. Been without since the last one took a ball

to the chest. Bloody sight." He looked Elisha up and down, and nodded. "Mordecai ben Ibrahim. My hospital, hear that?"

"Aye, sir."

"Where's the physician?"

Elisha shrugged. "Likely, he'll be down when he gets his things settled."

Mordecai glanced toward the heavens and sighed, a long, weary exhalation. "Man should let well enough alone. Water's in the court,"—he indicated direction with a toss of his head—"supplies in the vestry. Short on supplies as it is. Don't take what's not your due."

"Aye, sir," Elisha repeated.

Bobbing his head, Mordecai resumed his examination of the chart in his hands. "Get on then, been long enough without."

Dismissed, Elisha threaded his way back to the aisle and went to the curtain, drawing it aside to enter his new domain. A series of windows lit the inside wall, with a few narrow slots to the outside. Immediately, desperate voices assailed him from all around. Aside from the usual odor of infection, the place smelled different from the city hospital—fewer diseases and more straight-forward injuries, he guessed. And maybe fewer corpses left about. A tearing sound drew his attention to the corner where a pair of ragged women looked up from their work. "What's your business?" the older one called out.

"Barber," Elisha called back, flinching at the wash of relief which flooded their faces. They dropped the fabric they were ripping for bandages and hurried over. Their skirts were tucked up into their belts revealing sturdy legs and unshod feet.

"Lisbet," said the younger, with an awkward imitation of a curtsey.

The older offered a gapped grin. "And I'm Maeve. Praise the Lord, we've been waiting a long time for you."

"I'm Elisha. When did the last barber die?"

"Two weeks now, I mark it. The surgeons come back when they can, but there's officers and knights for them. And I hear there's a physician, eh?"

"Aye, there is. Lucius by name. I'm sure he'll be along before the day's out."

"A physician? Back here?"

Elisha nodded. "He's got some methods to try for the wounds of these new weapons."

Lisbet and Maeve stared at each other, and Lisbet shrugged. "Help is surely needed," she said. "But what's to be done aside from cautery or cutting?"

Spreading his hands, Elisha said, "I've no experience on the battlefield, so I'll count on you two. What are we facing?"

Maeve opened her arms to encompass the men all around them. "As you see, Barber. A dozen more a day, and at least half that dying at night, so we keep a steady pace."

The room held about fifty men, many unconscious while others gave only incoherent moans. They lay on the floor or on heaps of moldering straw, a few with pitchers by their heads. Flies buzzed in the air around the worst of them, those with stumps of arms or legs, those with their middles swathed in old bandages. Pale hands waved to him, one with no fingers left and a reeking putrefaction oozing down the naked arm. Sheets obscured a few faces toward the far end of the room, where one man kept up a constant stream of curses as his body twitched. Two doors opened out of that wall, one to a set of stairs going up to the second floor, the other into sunlight. Through that door, he could make out a bunch of irregular shapes. He squinted to bring them into focus: discarded feet and arms, and corpses not yet buried. Staggered, Elisha stared a long time at the ceiling. This, then, was the penance that would lay his brother to rest. He was used to handling one patient at a time, perhaps two or three if there'd been a fight or an accident.

In a low voice, Lisbet explained, "We're sure a man's to live, we give him a pitcher. Not 'nough of those to go round, see? We think he's to die, we move him toward the back. Easier to clear them out that way, to the yard." She glanced over her shoulder in that direction. "Should bring us more gravediggers, they should."

Maeve picked up the explanation. "Try to keep the cannon shots over here, in case they need the surgeons. And the minor wounds against that wall, as they don't require dressing so often. Major wounds to the inside—closer to the water—or toward the back. The master surgeon's been kind enough to pull the arrows these last few days."

"There's just the two of you?"

"Plus one at night. We try to bring in some from the whores' camp, but they get work enough to keep busy, unless they've got a favorite been injured." She shrugged one shoulder. "We stay where there's a roof against the rain. Sharing a room upstairs."

Nodding, Lisbet smiled, and he suddenly connected them as mother and daughter in the way they tilted their heads, and the dimples at their cheeks.

"I've been conscripted," he told them, "but how did you come to be here?"

Again, they shared a look, then Lisbet spoke up. "My brother's one of the king's gunners."

"Better to stay with him and know for sure than sit at home dreading to hear," Maeve put in. "Least here we've got a roof, two meals, and charitable labor."

Once more, Elisha looked around him. "Where am I needed most?"

Maeve took his arm and led him to the wall by the curtain. "New ones, not seen the surgeons yet. Stitching here, I think." She pointed to an unconscious man. "Cutting there. And this lot were hit by the bombardelles."

Bombardelles he'd never heard of, but stitching, that he could handle. It was a place to begin, to wade into the shallows of this war before he found himself up to his neck. He knelt at the man's bedside and peeled back the layers that bandaged his scalp. No sign yet of putrefaction. Good. He drew together the edges of the wound and clipped them with a silver crow's bill while he set the first stitch at the middle and tied it off. The next stitches he set to either side, drawing the lips of the wound gradually closer before stitching the gaps between. As he dealt with the bloody gash, the two women quietly returned to ripping bandages. After a time, as he drew his needle through the flesh, pinching the edges together with his off-hand, he heard the low murmur of their voices.

"Handsome, what?" the younger one said.

"Aye, he's that, but not for you. Even such as you can do better than a barber." Maeve sighed. "Doubt he'll last long here, in any case."

Finishing his first task, and paying the women no heed, he moved on to the others, checking the fellow who'd lost his fingers and another with an arrow through his thigh. When he had dealt with the pressing cases, he turned to the amputation. The man was barely conscious, his eyes roving the ceiling, his lips moving as if he were addressing the flies around him. Even beneath the wrapping, his leg looked wrong, misshapen, and Elisha braced himself before he cut away the cloth.

He palpated the limb as gently as he might, finding shards of bone that shifted beneath his hands and made the patient cry out. Both lower bones lay shattered at the ankle—too many breaks to set, and the foot skewed to one side. Elisha winced. The crushed foot already smelled foul and showed a sickly edge of green and black. At least it hadn't reached to the knee. Elisha tugged free a bandage and drew up the man's muscle and skin as much as possible before he tied it tightly around the leg just below the knee. After the amputation, the muscle and skin would relax to cover the stump of bone. He would have just a handbreadth above the break, but if the man recovered, he should do well with a wooden leg.

"Fetch us some water, would you?" he called out, and the women sighed, taking up their buckets and trudging for the far door.

To the soldier, he said, "Try to lie still. I need to cut your leg, but you'll be about with a wooden one sooner than you think. I'll be as careful and quick as I can."

The soldier moaned, but his face revealed no sign that he had heard.

Elisha unrolled his instruments, an assortment of long and short knives, some curved, along with various crows- and hawksbills to clamp off the veins and arteries. He picked one of the larger curved knives and set the blade against the flesh. As he made the first cut, the patient screamed, and Elisha began to hum, low in his throat. The flesh parted, and Elisha shifted his work to the back, supporting the leg on his own, using a smaller blade to snick between the bones and cut the oozing muscle. Too many barbers, his own master included, sometimes neglected that step.

As he reached each large vein and artery, he used a hawksbill to grip the cut end, stitching them efficiently shut. Common practice had barbers cauterize the stump either with a hot iron or caustic oils, but Elisha's journeyman years had introduced him to the brothel trade—a steady employment for any healer—where a Moorish whore who had worked in a hospital in her native land taught him the alternate technique of binding the vessels. Elisha took to it quickly, allowing him to abandon the torture of burning his patients. As if the loss of a limb were not enough.

At last faced with bone as bare and clean as he could make it, Elisha reached for the saw. His mind cast back to his brother's house, his brother's wife sobbing on the table before him as he took up a tiny, delicate saw, and he hesitated, his eyes suddenly hot with tears. He had no time for grief, not now, nor could his patient spare him this sudden reluctance. Elisha firmly took up the saw. He was needed here, and if the ghosts that haunted his memory pressed all the closer now, at least they would know they had not been forgotten.

Setting the saw carefully, Elisha made a slow draw to start the blade. The limb vibrated slightly with each push as he put his strength behind it. He let his humming drown out the sickening creak of blade into bone, silently thanking the saints that the man had lapsed into darkness.

The women settled their buckets beside him, sloshing onto the bloody floor, then went out for more, their feet tracking blood as they moved away.

Chapter 8

❖

When Elisha rose stiffly from his task, he rolled his shoulders and glanced out the windows. Across the grassy courtyard, about at the level of his chest, he saw the legs of the two women near a raised cistern. A channel ran from it out beneath a low arch in the direction of the river. They lugged two buckets each with the sort of resigned tread that told him they had done so many times before. No wonder they lost so many men, if his nurses must spend most of their time simply hauling water. He frowned. Edging between the wounded soldiers, Elisha crossed to the windowed wall, where he could study the stone and the layout of the yard. There must be a better way. He stuck his head out the window.

"Lisbet!" he called. She jerked at her name and turned. "Leave that. Find me a hammer and chisel, and a pick, if you can." As she set down the buckets with obvious relief, he added, "And a barrel or a cauldron or something." Shrugging at her mother, she turned to obey.

At his feet, one of the men said, "It's not so bad as that, is it? You're not to crack open my head with some bloody chisel?"

Glancing down, Elisha saw the man's grin and smiled

in return. "I might, if you can't keep silent." He knelt down, checking the bandages that wrapped the man's head beneath a shock of deep red hair. The wound seemed to be healing well—another day or so, the soldier could forgo the bandage altogether. It could use a change, but from what he'd seen, there were few enough bandages for the new arrivals.

Even as he thought it, the air roared with the first volley from the castle bombards, and the ground shook. Elisha steadied himself against the wall as a second impact brought screams from the unseen field. "Sweet Lord, is this what you've got all day?"

"Aye," the man answered, "we're right pleased they don't go all night. They're like dragons out there, spitting fire and boulders. Best get used to it."

"I'll try." He squatted at the man's side. "I'm Elisha, the new barber here. Can you walk?"

Lowering his voice, the young soldier leaned closer. "I can, but don't let on to the captain." He winked, and Elisha had to smile. "Ruari of Northglen," the man said, sticking out a hand for a firm shake.

"Ruari, I'll need this area cleared. It'd be a help to me if you can move some of these men, and yourself, out of the way."

"What're you planning, then?" Ruari slowly got to his feet, standing a moment to be sure they would hold, and straightened to his full height, a head taller than Elisha.

"Just an idea I have." Elisha returned to the latest arrivals as Maeve came up with her buckets. They sloshed a bit as she dropped them and rubbed her back. Patting her shoulder, Elisha told her, "Don't worry, I'm working on that as well. In the meantime, give a hand with this fellow's arm."

The fellow in question, little more than a boy, had

his arm hanging limp and awkward—dislocated at the shoulder without doubt. He sat solemn, his lower lip gripped between his teeth to keep from crying.

Kneeling, Elisha said, "There'll be a sharp pain, then you'll be all right, hear me?"

The boy nodded fiercely, his eyes flicking first one way, then another as Elisha directed Maeve to the boy's other side, to hold him firmly.

"Excellent. I'll bet you've seen some things in this battle, eh? Do you have a girl back home to tell the stories?" As he spoke softly, Elisha took a careful hold of the boy's arm.

Brightening, the boy replied, "Aye, sir, and she can milk a cow so—" He broke off at a yelp as Elisha twisted his arm back into place. Pulling away, red-faced, the boy stopped. Staring first at Elisha, then at his hand, he slowly waved his hand, then his face spread in relief. "That be a good deal better, thanks!"

A blast sounded outside, and his smile trembled into apprehension.

Studying his face, Elisha said, "Better, but not yet well. You'll need at least a day of rest to recover. Maybe you can help our Ruari with my little project."

"Aye, sir," said the boy as he scrambled to his feet, eager enough for anything that kept him from the line of fire.

Maeve met Elisha's eye and shook her head. "Ach, but you'll have us done out of soldiers, you will."

Quietly, never moving his gaze from her scowling face, he replied, "Let him live an extra day. Or don't you think his mother would approve?"

"We've all been here a bit longer than you, Barber, and some like to be here longer yet." She got up without his offered help, but she relaxed a little, the scowl settling into a rote expression rather than an offense.

Still on his knees, he turned to the next patient, but a voice called out, "Come, Barber, it's time I apprise you of my plans."

Lucius Physician stood at the door, just the other side of the curtain, a cloth scented with rosewater bound over his face. His gown today was of a modest cut, the outer sleeves turned back as if he might actually perform some labor, worn with a hat that trailed only halfway to the ground.

Elisha rose even as his two soldier-assistants collapsed, moaning together as if they could stand no longer. It was a near thing: if Lucius suspected them recovered, he'd send them back to the front. Elisha bowed to the physician, and extended his arm to usher the man inside.

Shifting his gaze about, Lucius declined. "I'd like the surgeons to consult." When Elisha had joined them, garnering the stares of the physician's three assistants and the younger surgeons as well, Lucius said, "I have formulated a sort of liquid cautery to be tried on these bombard wounds. Not the larger cannons, mind you, but the portable variety."

Cannons were the latest way for lords to devastate each other's knights, but they were monstrous things it took special wagons to haul. Now they were *portable*? Crossing his arms, Elisha tried not to show his surprise. From the look on Lucius's face, he did not succeed. "I suppose one could hardly expect a barber to be familiar with the new weapons. They are fashioned much like the larger variety, but are of a size to be carried forth, propped by a rod to steady the shot. These duke's men have a store of them which they were meant to deliver to the royal armory. They fire a ball the size of your thumb at high speed. Bombardelles."

"Ah," Elisha returned, as if this made everything clear.

With a long-suffering huff, the physician continued, "Since there are not enough skilled men to apply the irons, we needs must have a system of cautery which might be employed by such as you. Therefore, I have developed a solution of hot oil with such herbs as may draw forth the poison of the powders."

The surgeon Mordecai nodded sagely but without taking his eyes from one of his documents.

"I propose that half the men so wounded shall be treated with my solution, the others with cautery, so that we may better compare the effects of the one to the other. One of the surgeons," —he waved his fingers in the air until one of them stepped forward— "shall perform the cautery on such victims as he feels appropriate."

Those most likely to live in any event, Elisha thought.

"Then my assistants will show you how to apply my solution." The physician patted his senior assistant fondly, then swung about to Elisha. "Do you understand?"

"Aye, sir," Elisha growled.

"Benedict,"—he gestured to the senior assistant— "has recently returned from his own studies at Salerno. If you are alert, perhaps he may impart some of his knowledge." Lucius gazed vaguely into the distant reaches of the hall. "I understand there is a hearth where Benedict may assemble the ingredients?"

Over his shoulder, Elisha called, "Maeve?"

When she appeared beside him, he said, "Show these men to the kitchen, would you?"

Maeve bobbed a curtsey and said, "Follow me, my lords." She set off down the aisle, Benedict and another assistant, loaded down with a large jug and a variety of parcels, following more slowly. In profile, Benedict looked a touch pale as he passed the moaning soldiers lying on the dirty floor.

Turning back, Elisha found the physician staring at him, his arched brows drawn down now. "You are an ignorant, arrogant wretch, Barber, and I cannot guarantee your position here if you fail to show the proper deference to myself and my assistants. Need I remind you what may await your return home?"

Chastened, Elisha replied, "No, sir."

"Good." He spun on his heel and bade a hasty retreat from the stink and the noise.

When Lucius had gone, the young surgeon fetched a handful of long rods, each tipped with a slightly different shape of forged iron. Elisha had a few years and a few inches on him, but the surgeon succeeded in adopting the physician's supercilious manner as he swept by into the room full of common soldiers. Sighing, Elisha pointed out the area Maeve had indicated earlier. Surveying the victims of the bombardelles, the surgeon pointed with his bundle. "These four will do. Bring that one first." So saying, he took off down the aisle, as if he hoped to avoid the importuning cries of those he left behind.

Looking toward the men who hadn't been seen, Elisha sighed again, and bent to the man in question. "Sorry," he muttered, getting his arms around him and heaving him up, trying to avoid jostling the bloody side.

"Ach! For the love of God," the soldier moaned, gripping a handful of Elisha's shirt, and not a little hair along with it.

Wincing, Elisha carried him the length of the room, into the adjoining kitchen. Here, the two assistants had roused the fire again from banked embers and were mucking about with an enormous pot and a book which presumably held the physician's recipe. The surgeon thrust his irons into the fire and waited, arms crossed, fingers drumming on his hip.

"While those heat up, can I . . . ?" Elisha pointed back toward the waiting soldiers, but the surgeon snorted.

"The physician specifically said you were to assist me. What will he think of your trying to get out of it so quickly?"

Hands on hips, Elisha replied, "He might think I wanted to do my work."

"Now how likely does that seem to you, Benedict?" The surgeon raised his eyebrows to the physician's assistant.

Benedict's head shot up, and he rounded on the surgeon with one finger pointing like a blade. "You've no right to my name, Surgeon, and see you remember it. As for him," he poked the finger in Elisha's direction, "he's got little right to even share this room as far as I'm concerned."

Shutting his jaw with a snap, the surgeon stared at Benedict's back for a long moment, then turned to Elisha, mustering his former air as if he had not been rebuked.

Anyone would think these men were enemies, not allies. Elisha shrugged out of his shirt and draped it over a broken chair, then adjusted his apron.

"What're you doing?" the surgeon snapped.

Elisha willed himself to calm. "Getting comfortable. Unlike some, I have a lot of work to do."

"You've never done military service, have you?" asked the surgeon, his voice suddenly warming and curious.

Suspicious, Elisha lowered his gaze. "No."

"Then let me inform you. Insubordination is a crime here. That means insulting anyone above your station. Myself included." Ticking them off on his fingers, he said, "First offense: flogging. Second offense: branding. Third offense: hanging. Is it clear?"

Elisha swallowed. "Clear, sir. Forgive me." He settled to the ground beside the wounded man.

Rolling his head, the wounded soldier said, "I'd give him a mind, you'll not be the first he's reported."

With an ironic smile, Elisha said, "I thought the last barber was shot by one of these bombardelles."

"Why'd ye think he was on the field?"

Back home, physicians and master surgeons often made diagnoses and ordered treatments that were carried out by barbers. They disdained their lesser partners, but never before had the power to kill them. Losing his smile, Elisha leaned over the soldier and started to tear away the fabric around the injury. "I expect you know this'll hurt like the devil."

"Worse than the shot?"

"I don't know. You'll have to tell me." *If you live so long,* he did not add. From the look in the man's eyes, he didn't have to. The shot had cut through just below the man's ribs, tearing a wicked furrow in the flesh. Given a choice, Elisha might have packed the wound with wadding or created a tent dressing to keep out the grime. It looked no more poisoned than any other wound, aside from the threads that clung to it from his ruined tunic. Elisha plucked these with a pincer as he awaited his orders.

The lower ceiling of the kitchen gave the room a closed in feeling, with one wall dominated by an open hearth where the two assistants worked. An old table stained with blood took up the center of the room, surrounded by an assortment of chairs scavenged from here or there. Hooks held a few iron and brass pots, as well as a couple of ladles that were clearly recent additions. Heaped wood filled the far end, much of it showing the decorative carving of church pews and rood screens.

"Ready," said the surgeon. He donned a long leather glove. "Hold him still."

With the soldier's head in his lap, Elisha wrapped his arms through the soldier's, pinning them.

"Lord bless me," the man muttered, then the surgeon applied his iron, scorching the flesh with a terrible sizzle. The scent took Elisha right back to the witch's stake.

Every muscle in the soldier's body tautened and strained against Elisha's grasp. The soldier screamed until his throat went hoarse, then the surgeon returned with another iron, jabbing it to the wound, and the man fainted dead away. Shutting his eyes, Elisha relaxed his arms and took a deep breath.

"Barber! Roll him over, let me be sure I got the back."

Gently, Elisha did as he was told, cradling the soldier's head. After a parting burn, the surgeon waved them off, turning his back to plunge the iron into a bucket of water, then back into the fire.

Carefully, Elisha gathered the soldier and carried him back to the room, the dark head lolling over his arm, the legs dangling loose. Laying him back on the ground, Elisha checked the pulse at his throat to satisfy himself. Then he helped up the next man, who had taken a shot to the arm. As he passed toward the kitchen, he realized that the moaning, cursing, and praying had gone silent. Those who were able turned their heads to watch them go by, crossing themselves, prayer still evident in the furtive movements of their lips.

By the time Elisha returned for the third man, the fourth one lay still, one hand pressed to the gaping wound in his chest. Checking his pulse, looking into his wide eyes, Elisha wondered if the shot had killed him, or if the dread of the treatment had finished him off.

Chapter 9

❖

*T*hankfully, Elisha had little part in the second round of treatments. Benedict barely trusted him to restrain the soldiers and instead insisted that he carefully watch the procedure, which entailed wound-cleaning, probing for shot—which he noted the surgeon had neglected to do—and then dousing the poor patient with boiling oil. This they did in the main room rather than transport the victims to the kitchen, so all could watch them writhe in agony and hear the screams without the baffle of even a wall between. Well satisfied, Benedict rose from the last weeping soldier and nodded sharply to Elisha.

"Dress the wounds," he directed. "We'll keep a pot of the solution by the fire for the next clearing of the injured." With a smile, he wiped his hands on a cloth and discarded it on the ground, then led his lesser counterpart away.

Dismayed, Elisha bowed as they went by, then immediately dropped beside the last victim. Brushing blond hair back from the man's eyes, he murmured, "I'm sorry. I'll do what I may."

The soldier slapped his hand away, his teeth bared in a rictus of pain.

"What's your name?"

"What's that to you?"

"I'm trying to do my best for you, what little that is, and a bit of courtesy from anyone today would go a long way for me."

From the slit of his eye, the soldier studied him, blinking back the tears. "William, of Fells."

Elisha smiled. "William. I'm sorry to meet you under these circumstances. How about a drink?"

"Ale, if ye've got it," William said, trying a grin, despite the sweat trickling along his lips.

"Only the best for His Majesty's troops, I'm sure." Patting the man's shoulder, Elisha rose to find the room strangely silent. Mordecai, the head surgeon, stood in the aisle, his arms held behind him, regarding Elisha from under his bushy brows. Immediately, Elisha dropped his gaze, bowing his head. "What can I do for you, sir?"

"Came to view those my assistant cauterized." For a moment, the surgeon continued to regard him, pursing his lips. "As for you, carry on." He turned away about his own work, the books and tablets hanging from his belt, swaying as he stooped.

Fetching one of the buckets, Elisha gave each man a long drink, sending Ruari to collect the few bandages they had. He bound them up as best he could, with little help from the men themselves, starting to hum as he did so. Anything to block their pain.

"Eh, Barber?"

Elisha started at a touch on his shoulder and turned to find Ruari's cheerful face. "Which lot do you reckon screamed the louder? Surely they got the better cure."

With a weak smile, Elisha wiped his hands on his knees and drooped. "I need to get out of here," he muttered.

"Don't we all. The girls'll be through with supper soon."

Even as he said it, a pair of young women, their hair tucked up beneath caps, struggled down the aisle with an enormous stewpot carried on staves between them. A few small boys followed with towers of wooden bowls and a spoon each. They deftly scooped out servings and distributed them, returning again to collect the bowls with a melancholy efficiency so they could be used by another. Maeve came away from the men she was tending to assist with the meal. Catching on to the routine, Elisha followed after, supporting the men who could barely sit to drink their soup, and steadying the bowls of those yet weak.

By the time he and Maeve sat with their own portions, the pottage had gone cold. Still, they ate eagerly enough. The beans and barley tasted delicious, and Elisha realized he'd had nothing else since dawn. Outside the battle rumbled on, with periodic blasts from the bombards and the occasional blare of trumpets. Leaning back from his empty bowl, Elisha muffled a yawn.

Tilting her head, Maeve nodded at him. "Best get some rest now—you'll get none in a few hours when they've called the hold."

"But I've not yet seen all the men," he protested, trying to convince himself as much as the woman.

"Ach! I'll do for them for a while. Go on."

Grateful, he pushed himself up and retrieved his shirt from the kitchen, where he washed away the worst of the blood. He shrugged the shirt over his damp skin as he made his way out to the officer's infirmary. The physician and his avid assistants clustered around a stout man in a fine bed. While they spoke in low murmurs, a lovely whore poured the officer a draught of ale, cooing over him as he drank. Turning away, Elisha found the surgeon Mordecai staring at him again, and ducked his head in acknowledgement. Quickly, the man shuffled out one of his charts and turned his eyes to it as Elisha passed.

Returning to the little room he had chosen, Elisha wrapped himself in his blankets and settled against the wall. He couldn't sleep through the shaking of the building, but he might at least sit still and keep his own counsel awhile.

Even so, he woke a few hours later, when the small windows showed dusk in the sky, and no bombards split the air. Instead, an unearthly wailing drifted on the breeze. Chilled, Elisha rose and crossed to the window. In the failing light, he saw the ruin of the battlefield, littered with still forms and writhing masses he knew to be men. A few picked their way among them, searching out the wounded, and Elisha realized what Maeve had meant when she warned him of the hold.

Shaking the sleep from his limbs, he hurried back to the hospital. Already, a stream of soldiers waited outside, some carrying the fallen, others cradling injuries of their own. Apparently word had gotten out, for he'd barely left the tower when soldiers surrounded him, each begging for his attention. Behind them, the two lesser surgeons stood at the door of the hospital waving some few men inside while they shunted others off to wait along the wall until it was their turn.

"Please, my arm!" a young man cried out, grabbing hold of Elisha's sleeve.

Instantly another man pushed through the growing crowd. "Ye bastard, we were here first," he snapped, lugging a companion over his shoulder.

"Nowt but a head wound, there, I'm the one who—"

"I'll give ye a head wound," the other replied, balling his bloody hand into a fist.

While they were distracted, a boy hurried up, as fast

as he could, dragging another by the arm behind him. "Sir! It's Robbie, sir," he pleaded. Glancing down, Elisha noted the lolling head, the sunken chest, and knew he could do nothing.

"Give over, boy, let the fighting men go first." The speaker caught up both children and thrust them behind.

"Hold! Hold, all of you!" Elisha cried, throwing up his arms. The mob fell uneasily silent, shifting their eyes to those around them, as if expecting treachery. He searched the faces before him, weary, hurt, and frightened. If there had been a hundred of him, he might have reached them all. He looked to the surgeon and his assistants at the door beyond. Matthew, one of the assistants, met his gaze coolly, with the hint of a smile, then urged the man before him into the mob at Elisha's door. Shoulders sinking, Elisha rubbed his face.

"Here's how it'll be. Any of you who can stand and walk, who's not bleeding so much he can't stop it with his hand, get back. I'll see to you, but you'll have to wait." A groan of frustration rose from the crowd.

"It's not fair!" the soldier with the wounded arm shouted, echoed by several around him.

"Nothing is," Elisha shot back. "But you'll have to trust me sometime, why not start now?" He met their angry eyes without flinching, and a few clutched their wounds a little tighter, moving back out of the way. "Thank you. First, let me see anyone unconscious or not breathing. Can everyone hear me?"

Triumphantly, the man before him pulled his companion along. Elisha stepped up, checking the man's pulse. The bearer watched him, an angry grimace stuck upon his lips. Shifting his fingers on the cooling throat, Elisha wet his lips, but did not need to speak, for the bearer's teeth set hard, and he turned away, still hauling his mate. Elisha saw them go, the mob parting silently before them.

As he had suspected, most of the unconscious would never awake, and only the desperation of a battlefield friendship had brought them this far. "After these, I'll take the heavy bleeders, then chest or stomach wounds of any kind, next anyone shot with an arrow or lead, then leg wounds, then the rest of you."

"Here, barber—now!" cried a desperate voice as Elisha dismissed the last of his initial group of patients. A pair of men came his way, bearing a third between them, blood seeping around a field dressing that looked like another man's tunic. They lay their comrade down before him, and Elisha took in the gasping mouth, the pale face, the way the man's body thrashed with each breath.

"We're at the top of the siege tower, see?" said one of the bearers, himself breathing heavily, "and they start with the guns, so close—" He broke off and crossed himself.

"So he's been shot?" Elisha prompted.

The other bearer faced him then, and Elisha froze at the sight. The man's face was burned, a spray of blackened flesh around an angry red furrow, one eye swollen shut. Blood trickled down his cheek. "Went right by me, it did, where I knelt, and into Tom afore he got his shield back up."

Elisha turned his gaze back to the patient. The bearer would be scarred for life, but he would live. As for the patient—cutting away the layers of fabric, Elisha cleared the wound. He wiped the area clean with a piece of toweling, seeing the burned flesh around the hole before it welled up again with blood: a tunnel angling under his ribs, with bits of torn fabric pointing the way. "Through the back?" Elisha asked, but the bearer hesitated, and Elisha wrapped one arm around the patient's shuddering shoulders and turned him gently away. The man cried out, his heart thundering under Elisha's touch. At the back, blood gushed from a raw, open crater larger than Elisha's hand. Shards of bone and viscera specked the blood.

The man's chest went still, his head sagging against Elisha's arm. His weight settled full on Elisha, as if in giving up the ghost, he gave over all the earthly self he left behind.

Elisha bowed forward, mastered his breathing, and laid the man down. Dead. Even if this one had been the first patient of the night, no power on earth could repair such a wound. "I'm sorry," he said as he moved away. The burnt, mutilated bearer stared at him with his good eye, blood seeping down his face instead of tears. Elisha thought of his brother's blood overflowing the basin and trickling down. For a moment, the pain was like that wound, small at first glimpse, opening onto a pit of despair from which there could be no return.

Around him, men were crying, shouting, calling for him, and Elisha turned away from death and memory, and lost himself as best he could in healing the living.

For the next round, he opened his pouch, threading his needles to set to work, directing some of the healthier men to pinch their wounds shut. An hour of stitching returned some of his confidence, so that he could face the night with stronger resolve. Knowing the physician's wishes for them, he put aside any who had been shot and were likely to last the next few hours. The shot wounds they had dealt with that morning were simple ones, not too different from arrow wounds. Those he saw now made the first batch look trivial. If the shot encountered no resistance, it often passed straight through, leaving a dreadful hole at the entry and a hideous crater at the exit, like the man who had died in his arms. If it struck bone, like as not both bone and ball would break, leaving little shards that must be removed. And the shot often carried bits of cloth or powder into the wound, bringing a risk of infection. The amputations, too, must wait until the crowd had thinned, and he could undertake them with a little peace. By the time the walking wounded had dispersed, the sun had long since gone.

Stiffly, Elisha rose and replaced his needles. To the remaining men, he said, "Wait here, I'll clear the way for you." Blood slicked his fingers and screaming still echoed in his ears. As he walked to the doors, he wondered how many of these would be dead by the time he returned. There had to be a better way to manage the wounded, even among the few healers present. Passing Matthew, Elisha turned and asked, "Is it always done this way?"

With a huff, Matthew replied, "It's war, Barber, men are dying all day long, and you've the gall to complain." He snorted and strode away.

Shaking his head, Elisha resumed his pace, finding Mordecai before him.

"Such a question," the master surgeon said, without judgment.

"I wondered why we didn't go to them. Surely a few more would live, if we met them during the hold rather than let them be dragged all the way down here, that's all," Elisha snapped, the day's frustrations overwhelming him. Then, recalling Matthew's earlier words, he added, "Forgive me, sir, I shouldn't question those with more experience."

Leveling that watery gaze, Mordecai said, "I have

done. Battlefield, that is." He pursed his lips, and let out a puff of air. "Harder to tell the living from the dead." Stepping aside, he waved Elisha past him.

Unsettled, Elisha pushed aside the curtain and stepped through. Once again, the room echoed with shouts and curses from all sides. In the center of the aisle, Maeve stood with her arm around Lisbet's shoulders, watching. About a dozen men walked slowly amongst the soldiers. Every so often, they nudged one of the patients with the toe of a boot, then kicked a little harder. If the soldier didn't answer, his abuser roughly grabbed him by wrist and ankle, and toted him out the back door, dumping him into the courtyard and returning. These sorters had dull eyes, their faces devoid of expression as they rooted out the dead.

One after another, the gravediggers carried off his patients. Already, the back wall had been cleared. They kept at it until all the remaining men were cursing at them, eager to prove they lived.

One of the gravediggers, a thick man with a hunched shoulder, gave Elisha a flat stare. He nodded slowly, then, as silently as they had worked, they filed out the back door, and began the grisly night's work.

Bile rose in Elisha's throat, and he shut his eyes, waiting for his sickness to pass.

When he opened them, he saw Maeve and Lisbet helping some of the soldiers to new positions, rotating some to the few open spaces of the inner wall, others, over their feeble moans, to the area at the back. Going toward the inner wall, Elisha directed, "I'll need a bit of room here, for a basin."

Maeve shrugged. "As ye wish."

Then he snatched at her arm, looking wildly around him. "Where's William?"

Frowning, she asked, "Who?"

"William, the last man who got the physician's cure. I spoke to him this afternoon."

Again, she shrugged, pausing to wipe sweat from her creased forehead. "In the yard, I'd guess."

Releasing her, Elisha searched her face. "The yard. With the dead, you mean."

"Aye, if he's a dead man, that's where he'd be."

"But he wasn't. He was fine when I left here, he made a joke . . ." the words ran out as she sighed.

"Best to avoid the names and faces, Barber. There's no point knowing corpses."

Elisha tucked his trembling hands under his arms, and tried to pretend it was only the cold as he turned from her. In London he did not always know if his patients survived; he rarely had to face their absence, never mind seeing them hauled off by charnel men. He thought of the moment he might have chosen execution rather than come here, to this anteroom of Hell. It seemed he must not only work away his guilt, but his arrogance as well. Together, he and Maeve brought in the new arrivals, making them as comfortable as may be.

As they worked, Lucius Physician popped his head around the curtain. "Barber!"

Setting down a bucket of water, Elisha walked swiftly to the border. "How can I help you, my lord? We've yet much to do."

"No doubt, no doubt. How fare the men who received my solution today?"

Elisha scowled, "Three dead, and two of the cauteries."

"Three? How strange. This method should be much more effective." He rubbed his chin, assuming a thoughtful expression.

Most people poured boiling oil on their enemies, not on their own men, Elisha thought, but he was alert enough to hold his tongue.

Pulling himself up to aim a glare down his nose, the physician said, "Well, the fault most likely lies in your failure to apply the cure properly."

At this, Elisha nearly laughed, an inappropriate noise in a room full of tears. "Your Benedict wouldn't allow me to do it, my lord, for that very reason."

The eyebrows arched upward. "Mmm. I shall adjust the formula. Please put aside the shot victims as I shall require them to be given the cure in the morning."

Biting back a sharp reply, Elisha said, "Very good, my lord. Shall I stack them in the yard?"

Blinking, the physician said, "Wherever is appropriate," with a dismissive flicking of his fingers.

Elisha plied his needles and his saw well into the night, removing a hand here, splinting a leg there, humming all the while as if it could distract him. From beyond the curtain, he heard the shouts and moans of officers and knights, and Mordecai's even voice directing his crew. For himself, having seen Lisbet go pale at the sight of the saw, Elisha asked Maeve's assistance while her daughter hauled buckets and washed the stiffness out of bandages that might be re-used.

By the time he stitched the last cut, Elisha's arms and fingers ached. The tile floor rubbed his knees nearly raw so that he winced when he stood. Many of these men would never walk away, and certainly not with so little to complain of. Limping, he slipped through the curtain, past the snoring officers in their comfortable beds, even managing to ignore the distinctly different moans from one bed where the lovely whore opted to perform a cure of her own.

Shaking, Elisha sagged beneath the stairs in his quiet room, chafing his arms and knees. He rolled the blankets around him, and shut his eyes. Before him in the darkness, he saw a parade of faces and heard the echo of the names he had not known.

Chapter 10

❖

The next morning, Elisha dragged himself from beneath the stairs, and reached the hospital about the same time as the servers bringing porridge and bread to break the fast. Again, the surgeon's assistant Matthew cauterized the shot wounds of a group of men while Benedict oversaw the pouring of hot oil onto the rest. This time, he deigned to allow Elisha to do the work, not because he thought him capable, as his stance made clear, but because the physician willed it so. Elisha took a long time over the task, careful not to burn any more than he had to. Those duties done, Elisha made a round of the men, checking on bandages and frowning over infections. By the time all this was through, the sun had risen high, and the bombards' blasts faded to the back of his mind.

Lisbet brought him the tools he had requested, gave him her brightest smile, and left saying she must continue the search for a barrel. Exhausted, Elisha merely nodded, then swung about to face his charges. "Any here with two arms, who can wield a chisel?" He waved the tool before them.

For a time, nobody spoke, glancing one to the other as if to figure what he might be up to. Then, from the back wall, where men were placed to die, a stout man raised his hand. "Arthur Mason," he said gruffly, his look daring any to object, "I can do it."

Looking him over, Elisha realized his right leg was missing from the hip. He glanced briefly around the room, then nodded. "Right, Arthur. Ruari, give me a hand. Maeve, fetch us a chair from the kitchen."

Together, Elisha and Ruari made a seat of their arms and carried the mason over beneath the window where a space had been cleared. Curious eyes watched the process, while some of the men continued to moan. Maeve set down the chair, and they placed Arthur on top.

Tapping a stone below the window, about at the height of Arthur's shoulder, Elisha said, "I need a hole through here. I think this mortar is—"

"I know my trade," the mason snapped, glaring from beneath wiry eyebrows.

Noting the breadth of the man's shoulders and the swell of muscle in his arms, Elisha did not doubt it. "Go to. Let Lisbet know if you need some other tools."

Arthur made a show of examining the chisel, hefting the hammer, and said, "She'll do." Cautiously at first, he started tapping around the chosen block. Then, finding a section of loose mortar, he set on it with vigor.

Miraculously—unless something went wrong with one of his patients—Elisha had done all he could until the next hold. Satisfied, Elisha took up his pick. He had time for a project of his own. "I'll be in the courtyard if I'm needed. Oh—Maeve? Is it possible to get some eggs?"

"Ha!" she snorted. "Eggs? Had we chickens, then mayhap. As it is, we're boiling the townsfolks' stew-bones, and them not too pleased for it."

Shouldering his pick, Elisha crossed to the far end, taking the door into the stairwell. To the right at the

bottom of the stairs, another doorway opened onto the
broad inner courtyard. A cloister followed one side,
connecting the church with a dormitory. At the opposite corner, by the ruin of the main gate, stood a tall bell
tower with a small cluster of men at the top, watching
the progress of the distant battle. In its shadow Elisha
saw a small cottage, well-maintained. As he studied the
place, the physician emerged, stretching as if he'd only
just gotten up. Simmering, Elisha turned away, toward
the cistern at the center of the tiled court. Grass and
weeds thrust up between the stones and rimmed the
pool as well as the channel he had noticed the day before. As he suspected, this channel diverted water from
the nearby river by way of a low arch at the main gate.

Leaning the pick against the cistern wall, he stripped
off his apron and shirt and studied his course. He
dragged the point of the pick to mark a line across the
tiles from the nearest edge of the culvert to the spot beneath the window where Arthur Mason worked on the
inside.

Arthur struck his chisel with evident enjoyment,
while a few other men who were able clustered about,
muttering and peering out the windows. With a nod to
them, Elisha set about his own labor, prying up the
stones in the path he had laid out. Lounging in the
shadow of the tower, Lucius regarded him with a vague
smile, as if puzzling over the activity.

Every so often, Elisha took a break and splashed water over his face and back. Though it was only April,
the sun grew steadily hotter, and he was down to the
hard labor, hacking through the roots and dirt, carving
a path for the water to follow.

When he'd gotten into the rhythm of the work, he
started to sing one of the ballads his mother had favored.

"Oh, there was a brook, and a very bonny brook,
The rushes grow so gre-en, oh!
There was a lass, and a very bonny lass,
The like has ne'er been se-en, oh!"

With an irritated exhalation, Lucius abandoned his place and stalked away.

It was the first song that came to mind—and the last song his brother sang, at least in his hearing. He might have broken off when he remembered, but inside the hospital a few voices joined his own. He was not here for his grief but for his service, even if that service was a song. By the time they'd done a few verses, even those not familiar with the song had picked up the refrain. From the officer's infirmary, the pretty whore stuck her head through the window.

"Hey! Hey, you!"

Elisha rested on his pick and turned. "Aye, madam?"

Peevishly, she tossed her head. "Some of the lords want it quiet."

Another of the bombards shook the ground, and Elisha sighed. "Tell it to the enemy."

The whore disappeared, and a well-trimmed gray head replaced her. "What are you about, man? This is a churchyard!"

"I'm cutting through a channel to get us all some water without having to fetch it in buckets, my lord." He wiped his brow.

"Then there's no need for your caterwauling, is there?" the man barked in a voice accustomed to command.

"Oh, let be, my lord," a new voice purred, and a lady came through into the yard. She curtseyed low to the man in the window and smiled. "Surely the trouble saved will be worth a few songs?"

Blinking at the newcomer, the captain barked, "And who might you be?"

"My name's Brigit, my lord. My father holds the village yonder. I came down to see if I might offer assistance to His Majesty's doctors." Again, she smiled.

This time, the captain stuck up his chin, taking her in, and nodded once. "Carry on, then." He vanished inside.

Lady Brigit closed the distance between herself and Elisha in graceful strides almost like dancing, her figure as fair as any whore back home in London, and fairer than many of the ladies. She wore well-made garments carefully embroidered—a task for those with few cares beyond the uniformity of their stitches. The sun warmed her creamy, indoor complexion and struck sparks from her long red-blonde hair, though her head seemed lop-sided somehow. Elisha squinted, then smiled in recognition. The hair on one side of her head was chopped just past her shoulder, raggedly cut off where it had been singed by the fire of two nights before. He bowed and straightened as she came before him, then his smile fell away as his mouth dropped open. He must look an idiot, he realized, but there was nothing to be done for it.

Elisha's hand flew to his cheek, feeling again the stroke of an angel's wing. The breath had left him, and he felt suddenly light-headed though the sun might have stopped shining for all he knew. Those luminous eyes, shot with gold as if lit from within—or reflecting a fire, or meeting his own from the embrace of magnificent wings.

"It's you," he breathed.

Her hands leapt to her chest and Brigit started back with a quick intake of breath, the whites showing at her pale green eyes.

"The fire," he whispered.

After a moment, the animation returned to Brigit's face. Laughing too sharply, she smiled, pulling her hands away to smooth her fine skirt. "Of course, the fire. You must have seen me then."

Tilting his head to one side, Elisha frowned. "Aye, that I did, but I meant . . ." But what *had* he meant? That this woman was the image of a witch, burned at the stake twenty years ago? Shivering, he shook his head, feeling the brush of long hair against his bare skin. That brought another shiver, and he forced his eyes to look away. "Sorry." He caught a shaky breath and let it out slow before taking another not quite so ragged as the first.

"Yes, well, it's about that that I came."

"To see me?" he asked, a giddy hope taking the place of his astonishment.

With a negligent flip of her hair, Brigit said, "No, the physician, the man I spoke with afterward."

Elisha's hope withered. "The physician. Of course." It had been dark that night, and between that and her terror, no doubt she hadn't got a good look at him. He pointed across the court. "He's taken the cottage, though I think he's gone out."

"Thanks," she replied brightly, her expression still vague as if she had not quite recovered from whatever impact his words had brought upon her. "I'll leave a note for him, then. Thanks," she said over her shoulder as she left.

Watching the gentle sway of her hips as she went, Elisha sighed, wiping a hand across his sweaty brow. She probably thought him a workman, out in the sun at such a time, laboring on behalf of the army. She rapped sharply on the cottage door, waited, and rapped again. As if summoned, the physician emerged from the base of the tower, noticed Brigit at the door of his cottage, and came forward, his imperious bearing falling away. With a hand draped casually upon her shoulder, he guided Brigit inside his cottage, and the door shut behind them.

Elisha grumbled to himself. So she wasn't all the proper woman she seemed, if she was willing to enter the man's house alone and unaccompanied. Other men, like the assistant surgeon Matthew, looked up to Lucius for his long and distant education, but could his schooling draw on even a woman like that? Laughing at his own folly, Elisha hefted the pick again in both hands. Perhaps letters had some value after all.

Before long, he started up a new song, and the soldiers joined in. Still, he had not made much progress when he became aware of Lisbet, standing nearby, gazing at him.

Straightening, Elisha tipped his head to her, then realized it was about time for a break and crossed to the water, took a long draught, and splashed some over his head and shoulders. He shook back his hair, smoothing down the wild dark waves which had sprung loose from their bounds. Coming back from the cistern, he pulled the ribbon free so the mass of his hair fell all around him, then he gathered it all into one hand to bind it up again. To his surprise, Lisbet was still there. "Did you come to see me?"

A flush coming to her cheeks, Lisbet said, "Oh, aye. I've found a barrel, as you asked." Then she looked crestfallen as she said, "But it's got a hole in the bottom as big as my hand. It's the best I could find, though. Most others're already in use."

With the briefest glance toward the physician's cottage, Elisha said, "Show me. Maybe it can be repaired."

Bobbing a needless curtsey, Lisbet led the way into the dormitory and down a flight of stairs to a windowless basement.

"You came down here?" Elisha peered into the darkness.

With a giggle, Lisbet took up a candle from someplace. "I knew you needed it, so I looked everyplace I could go."

Casting her a look, Elisha nodded slowly. He would need to dissuade her of her interest in him more directly— if her brother the gunner didn't appear from nowhere and take care of it himself. "Thank you. I'm sure all the men will appreciate your effort."

Her shoulders slumped a bit, but she brought him resolutely onward, then held up her light with a triumphant gesture. "There it is. Will it do?"

Hunkering down, Elisha examined the barrel. Once, it had held wine but had clearly been put to many uses since. The hole gaped open just as Lisbet had told him, but he thought there must be some way to repair it. "It's excellent, just the right size. Thank you." Bending down, he took it in both arms, and followed her back to the surface. Lugging the musty thing into the hospital, he plopped it on the floor by Arthur's chair.

The mason, who had been resting from his exertions, lifted his chisel again and started pounding as if his life depended on it. Already, he'd demolished a good two inches of mortar all the way around.

Elisha slapped his shoulder. "Excellent! Keep it up—within reason, of course."

"I'll do that," Arthur replied, then, under his breath, he said, "Teach them to put me by the yard—not yet a deadman."

"I need someone to put a patch to this hole," Elisha called out. This time, there was no hesitation before two men volunteered and set to bickering over who could do it. One had a pierced chest, and wheezed out his protests, while the other shook a fist at him with half the fingers gone.

"Either one, or both. Lisbet can help you get what you need."

The girl glowed at the mention of her name, and the hand he might have set on her shoulder hovered then slipped back to his side.

"Back to work," he mumbled, retreating into the sun.

Once out the doors, he froze, his feet rooted to the spot.

Up in the courtyard, Brigit paced near the cistern, drumming her fingers on it, then turning a circle as if looking for something. When her gaze fixed on him, her face lit up, and she came forward to meet him.

Somehow, Elisha got his feet moving again, though he stumbled on the uneven stones. Too quickly, he grabbed the handle of the pick. "So you found him, then."

"I did, yes, and thank you again." She tipped her head, her pale hands gripping each other in consternation. "You must think me completely daft. The fire." She tossed her head. "It was you put your cloak over me."

"Aye, that it was." He studied the ground as if he might count the weeds remaining between where he'd left off and the culvert.

Soft fingers rested upon his forearm, and he looked up into the brilliance of her smile. "For that also, I owe you thanks. I was lucky not to be badly burned."

"You seem—that is, you look—fine." Elisha shook his head, chuckling. "That's not what I mean at all, as no doubt you are aware."

Her laughter rang like the absent bells of the broken church and lifted his heart and his eyes back to her face. "Elisha Barber, is it? I had no idea a barber could be so silver-tongued."

Giddiness welling up in him, he muttered, "Tongue-tied, more like."

From the windows behind them, a chorus of rude noises and lewd offers echoed into the court.

Elisha flushed, turning to focus an angry stare at his patients. "Enough! Be off with you, or I'll discharge the lot of you!"

"Besides," Brigit called out, "you should know I'm spoken for."

The disappointed moans of the soldiers covered for Elisha's own moment of loss, or so he hoped, before he faced her again.

Her smile now seemed wistful. "Anyhow, I should be off myself."

"Aye, lady. I'm glad you're well."

Nodding, Brigit turned away, picking her steps carefully across the court.

Watching her go, Elisha's heart made a lurch like none he'd ever felt. She was the image of the angel of his childhood—he could not simply let her leave. Before he could stop himself, he called after her, "My lady!"

Brigit stopped and turned her head to look back at him. "What is it?"

Arrested again by those gleaming eyes, Elisha wet his lips and lost his voice.

She turned full to face him. "Well?"

"I am a barber," he said, foolish again, but what could be lost? He settled the pick and leaned one elbow on top, making every effort to relax. "So let me cut your hair."

Chapter 11

❖

Across the miles between them, Brigit stared, those luminous eyes searching his face for he knew not what. Just when he thought he must collapse beneath the weight of that stare, her face cleared, and she nodded slowly. "Yes, very well. I've no hurry."

Blinking at her, Elisha hesitated a moment, then leaned his pick against the cistern and approached her, cautiously, as if she might start up and flee. Indeed, the pulse leapt at her throat as he neared her, her eyes still roving. "I have shears in my trunk, and combs. Won't be a minute." His heart threatening to explode, he passed her by and entered the little door to his steeple. Quickly, he found the things he needed, threw on his fresh tunic, and emerged again into the sunlight to find her gone.

Dazed, he drooped. Betrothed though she was—no, even if she were already wed—he must know her, he must find out how she came by those eyes and the face of an angel he watched burn. For a moment, in the sun, he thought he might have imagined her, or at least, transformed an ordinary woman on an ordinary errand into his angel. Then he heard laughter behind him and turned.

Brigit popped her head out of the church door. "Well, then, I'm waiting!"

"In there?"

"Are you always so bright?" she asked, with a twinkle in her eyes.

Elisha replied, "I always seem dimmer by daylight." He gripped the shears and cocked his head in the direction of the hospital. "Wouldn't you rather have others about?"

With a cool smile, Brigit vanished into the church, her voice trailing over her shoulder. "I'm not afraid of you. What are you afraid of?"

She was a whore; she had to be—no proper woman would speak so to a stranger. Vaguely deflated, Elisha followed, and found her seated on the mossy altar, swinging her bare feet above the flowers that carpeted the ruin. Her cast-off shoes lay to one side, along with the shawl she had held about her shoulders. The altar stood on a low rise which must once have been a platform of stone. A few stone benches stood around the walls, but the nave of the church held only flowers and fallen roofing, forming mounds for the delight of rabbits and weeds alike. At the far end, the arch of the main entrance stood empty, the hinges rusted into the air, lacking their doors. Two rows of columns marched along the sides, helping to support the high ribs of stone which soared overhead. The style of the church was new; light and lofty in comparison to the churches he knew. Back in London, they had torn down the older church to build just such a place, but of cathedral proportions. Fifty years later, only half-done, the place looked empty and forlorn. This church must only just have been built by the time it was abandoned. If things had gone badly with the fire in Brigit's village, their own church might have ended up like this.

Following his gaze, Brigit said, "The old lord deeded this land to the church, and they built their monastery

here in my grandparents' time. But the place had a reputation for healing disease. Victims came from miles
around to pray here."

When her voice died away, Elisha saw her staring up
where the roof should be.

"There was an epidemic. Two or three survived, not
enough to carry on, and the monastery was dissolved,
the church deconsecrated."

The pale arch of her throat drew him nearer, watching it quiver as she spoke and breathed, the blouse she
wore draping just barely upon her shoulders, the remaining long hair drifting down her back, caressing it
like familiar hands. Lowering her chin, she smiled out
the distant doorway. "It's beautiful here. Like a church
for the sky and the flowers."

"Beautiful," he murmured. When the gaze swiveled
around toward him, he looked away and came around
behind her, dropping the shears on the altar beside her.
He plied his comb through the softness of her hair, gently untangling the long ends.

"It doesn't bother you," she asked. "Me sitting
here?"

Everything about her drove him to distraction, so
that he must watch his hands every moment lest they
take undue advantage. "It's a good height." But perhaps she wanted him to take advantage, perhaps that
was why she'd brought him here.

Annoyed, she said, "I mean on the altar. This is—or
at least, it was—a church of the Lord."

"I was a barber to the street of brothels, my lady. Not
much offends me."

She made a curious little noise but did not press him.

When he'd combed out the fine hair, he came to
stand in front of her, avoiding her eyes, surveying the
damage of the fire. He took a bit of hair at either shoul-

der, measuring what remained against what had been. Well, he would do what he could. She was lucky to have her eyebrows. Elisha glanced down. Yes, she had her eyebrows, slightly singed, raised now so she could peer up at him without moving her head.

He retreated again, this time to the side to start trimming. "You seem quite well-recovered, my lady," he remarked.

"Why shouldn't I be?"

"Most women would have had more of a fright, catching on fire like that. I haven't seen—" He broke off, shying away from the image of the angel in flames.

"What?" she asked lightly. "You've not seen flaming hair, or witchfire?"

"Neither," he lied, and she twitched so that he had to pull away the shears before he trimmed more than he should. "Stay still. Actually, the fire seemed right ordinary to me. As for the witch—" He broke off again. He longed to question her, discover if she knew of the burned witch of two decades past, but dared not scare her off with too much talk of witches.

"What about the witch?" She prodded a bit of moss, twisting a sprig of it between her fingers.

"He seemed ordinary as well. But I have little experience."

"Ordinary? But how can a witch be ordinary? Shouldn't he have claws and a hump and horrible fangs?" Her voice had sunk low despite the energy it conveyed, and he paused a moment in his snipping.

"As I say, I have little experience." But the image of the angel flashed again before him, the bright wings sweeping out, raising a riot of sparks into the air.

"Haven't you ever seen a witch, even one? Or perhaps heard tell of them?"

Snip, snip. "Of course there are stories. The carter I

rode out with claimed his cousin was turned black by one, and one of the whores told me a witch cursed her to become pregnant."

Brigit laughed, but the sound was brittle. She started to turn her head to see him, but he placed a hand quickly on top of her head to still her. "Please, I don't want to make this worse than it is."

"Sorry." For a moment she sat silent beneath his attention, then asked, "But have you not once laid eyes on one, for yourself?"

"Apart from two nights ago?" Why was she pressing him? Tension gripped his shoulders, and, for the first time in his life, he had difficulty steadying his hands. She spoke as if she wanted information from him, just as much as he from her. Could she be spying? Following up on something the physician said about him?

"That was no witch you saw," she said, "just a man in the wrong place."

"I thought as much." Her confirmation of his conviction drained some of his tension. Snip, snip, snip. The scorched ends of her red-gold hair fell away, settling onto the toes of his boots and draping over the green grass below. His hands withdrew the shears resting briefly against his lips with a chill of metal before he lowered them. What harm could come of his admission? "Yes, I saw one. A woman, years ago. The last witch executed outside the city."

Strangely subdued, Brigit asked, "What was she like?"

"I don't know, I only saw her from a distance." He longed for a moment to see Brigit's face, but could not move, his eyes finding the form of the angel in clouds beyond the over-arching stone. "She was beautiful."

"They said she cast a glamour on the crowd, so they could not see her true nature." Brigit's voice caught, and she shivered.

"Perhaps it was so."

"Do you believe it?"

"I was a boy, and it was a long time ago." *I had to be cleansed*, he wanted to say, *I had to be beaten until I believed what they told me, and not what my eyes could swear. I saw an angel,* he wanted to say. The compulsion to speak burned within him, the longing to reveal this most secret memory, the thing never spoken to another soul. *An angel touched my face, and I could not be the same.*

His throat ached with the need to speak, but his stubborn teeth refused, and he shoved the thought away. "I'm done," he told her, his voice harsh.

Brigit jerked as if he had slapped her and sprang down from the altar, fumbling with her shoes and shawl. "Thank you."

She was going. She would leave, and he would never see her again, and he wouldn't even know why. Cursing himself, Elisha rounded the altar. "I don't have a mirror, I'm sorry," he said, forcing his voice to be gentle, trying not to reveal the nervous awareness that jittered inside.

"I'm sure it's fine. If not, my father's maidservant can fix it."

Nodding, Elisha picked up his comb, running a finger along the teeth of bone.

Still not facing him, Brigit patted her hair, the burnt parts cut away and evened out to meet the longer section. "Imagine, I didn't come down looking for a barber, but for a doctor." At this, she turned, her bright, blank expression once more in place as she held out a hand. "Thank you, barber."

He bent over the offered hand, not brushing it with his lips. Whoever she might be, it was clear that her position was far above his own—he hadn't earned the privilege of a kiss.

"And thanks for rescuing me the other night, as well. If there's ever anything . . ." she broke off and turned sharply away.

Say something, he urged himself, *do something so she doesn't walk away.* "Actually," he blurted, "There is something."

She froze, the shawl pulled taut about her shoulders.

Uninvited, he blundered on, "That night, in the hunt for the witch, I lost my cloak. The one I'd put around you. If anyone's found it, or if you hear of anything, I would appreciate having it back."

She nodded again, her new short hair sliding over her shoulders.

Before he could come up with another way to cling to the sight of her, a voice from without broke the stillness. "Barber!" someone roared. "Barber! Where've you got to?"

Clenching his teeth, Elisha turned to face the physician as he stormed through the little door.

"Ah, this is where I find you. Praying, are you? You'd better be—" Suddenly, his face froze as he spotted their audience: Brigit, looking back at him, plainly astonished. "My apologies, my lady, I did not know you were still present."

She curtseyed her acknowledgement. "The barber offered to cut my hair."

"Ah, yes, well, that's good, then." He looked from one to the other, his hands in fists at his sides.

Bowing, Elisha said, "Sorry, my lord, I'm through here, let me just put my shears away."

"Through?" thundered the physician, recalling his fury. "The surgeons tell me you've not been cauterizing the amputees. What do you mean by that? These men could die by your neglect!"

Shutting his eyes, Elisha cursed himself yet again.

He found the binding of arteries to be just as effective and much less painful. But he should've known that these doctors would expect the orthodox treatment. His own training would carry no weight compared with the words of the long-dead physicians of old. "I've bound them tight, my lord, and meant to—"

"Meant to? What have your intentions to do with the lives of His Majesty's soldiers?"

In the pause after the shout, Elisha heard a little, strangled noise. Still half-bowed, he glanced behind and caught sight of Brigit's face, stark pale, her rosy lips parted, her eyebrows creeping up her forehead. He frowned.

"You're a medical man," she bleated, bringing a hand to her mouth as if she had spoken some wrong.

"So he claims," the physician said. "After today, we shall have to see about that. He barely deserves the title, never mind the honor of working on His Majesty's men. Get on, you scoundrel, get you to the hospital, and perhaps my skill can yet save them from your malpractice."

Thus browbeaten, Elisha made for the door, but he paused to glance again behind him. Brigit had not moved, nor had the stunned expression left her face. With a slight gesture, he bowed his head to her, but she stared on, as if it were not even he she saw. He let himself out, leaving the physician behind with the lady, hoping the rest of the world still made sense.

Chapter 12

What else might be said in his absence, Elisha had no idea. He was grateful to the lady for keeping the physician off his back while he returned his barbering tools before hurrying into the hospital. The work on the water must wait for tomorrow. He found Matthew in the kitchen, his irons in the fire and a fierce glower on his face.

"It's high time you showed your face. Or are you ashamed to?" the assistant surgeon demanded.

"Are you planning to cauterize my amputees?"

"Of course I am. Some of us are not barbarians."

"No, naturally, sir. But should you have to stoop to such labor? I'm sorry for my absence—I understand the trouble it must have caused you."

Straightening, Matthew folded his arms and glared. "I don't believe you have any idea of our troubles, Barber."

Bowing quickly, Elisha said, "How could I? I'm ignorant in the proper procedures, as you know, sir."

Matthew looked flustered, not sure how to take Elisha's apparent capitulation. "Obviously, or you would know that the great physician Galen advised cautery for amputations and ligature only for injuries touching the vessels."

"But," Elisha said brightly, "I've had the opportunity to observe your technique these past two days. I think I can manage it, and you can return to your own work. You shouldn't be bothered with these men. A few of the more able-bodied soldiers can assist me."

Matthew narrowed his eyes. "And if you botch the job, there's only you to blame."

"Even so, sir." Elisha kept his head bowed, as Matthew debated with himself and finally quit the room with admirable speed.

Taking a deep breath, Elisha sighed and leaned against the door frame, arms crossed.

"Sorry, I should've paid closer mind," Maeve said, rushing up to him. "Who's to be first, then?"

"Who's the best screamer?"

"Sorry?" Her head pulled back as her brow wrinkled.

"I need a good screamer." He led her out of the kitchen to survey the men before him.

"I'm not understanding you, Elisha," she complained. "How's the sound of his scream going to be of help?"

"Here's the question for you, Maeve, have we lost any of the men I've cut since I got here?"

The frown deepened, and she plunked her hands on her hips. "Nowt that I recall."

"And how many before, when the surgeons got at them?"

Maeve's eyes sought out the doorway nearby, leading into the yard of corpses. "Most, I'd guess, most the night they come in."

He lowered his voice, leaning close to her ear. "What they do beyond the curtain, I don't care a whit. If I'm wrong, then on my head be it, but I'll appreciate your silence on this point."

"But it's always been done, cutting, then cautery."

"On my head be it," he repeated urgently. "I'd rather not cause more pain than I must." Or have to explain the treatment he'd learned from a woman, and a Moorish one at that. Ligature was reputedly a technique of witchcraft as well as of surgery.

Pursing her lips Maeve appraised him in a way so like his mother used to, as if she couldn't tell if he deserved punishment or reward.

"Please," he said. "Give me a few days. If we start losing them, I swear I'll do the cautery."

Shaking a finger in his face, she said, "Your head."

"My head, absolutely."

She frowned out at the soldiers. "Maclean's your best screamer, then."

"Bless you!" He grinned.

"Cor!" She slapped at him, then bustled off to check on the latest gunshot victims.

"Ruari? I'll need a hand. Which one's Maclean?"

A burly fellow recovering from a sword to the gut raised his head. "That's me."

Elisha realized that, on the day he'd arrived, Maclean was the one shouting curses at the ceiling.

"Do you trust me?" Elisha asked, swinging around to direct the question to the room at large.

Lowering his chisel, Arthur called, "Aye! And why not? How long's it been since we've heard any singing?"

A few men burst into laughter, then one of them piped up, "And ye bring that girl round here, we'll trust ye right enough!"

"If only I could," he sighed. "For the moment, I ask you to keep quiet with the others," he said, lowering his voice with a nod toward the curtain. Then, louder, he said, "As God is my witness, I'll do all I can for you. Ruari, let's take the first man."

"Aye, Elisha," Ruari replied, but the two went over and lifted Maclean, carrying him off to the kitchen.

Once there, Elisha made the man comfortable, and explained his role. Maclean caught on quickly, giving screams of agony such as they'd never heard before. He was at times ear-splitting; other times he shrieked like a woman, until they'd counted off, at regular intervals, all the men who should have been cauterized. When Maclean was once again ensconced upon his straw pallet, with a nearby pitcher for his thirst, Elisha gathered up the surgeon's irons and carried them ceremoniously through the curtain. The officers gazed at him in horror, some few crossing themselves as he returned the tools with a bow.

Washing and re-dressing the wounded filled the time until the horn blew to tell them the hold had been called. This time, Elisha hurried to the head of the stairs, with Ruari at his side, and took up a post before the church tower. As the soldiers straggled in from the field, he sorted the dead from the dying, the wounded from the merely dazed. When the trickle became a flood, and while Elisha plied his needles and set the easier fractures, Ruari went among them and continued the sorting process until all the men had been sent off, or waited in their turn for the barber's attention.

As he washed and rethreaded his needle, Elisha called out, "Ruari? What's your trade?"

"A carpenter, same's our lord!" the soldier shouted back.

Looking at the weary men waiting for stitches, and the wailing men waiting for bone setting or the saw, Elisha gave a grim smile. "How'd you like to be a barber?"

"Me? Are ye daft?"

."Most likely," Elisha replied. "All I ask is you can handle a saw."

Ruari gaped across the field of battered soldiers, then slowly made his way to Elisha's side. "You mean for me to cut them?"

"There's a lot more of them than of me. The officers get three bloody surgeons all to themselves, and I've not even an assistant." He looked up from the arm he was stitching to meet Ruari's uncertain gaze. "It's too much for me, and that's a fact."

"But I know nothing about it."

"I'll show you, Ruari."

With a nervous chuckle, Ruari asked, "What if I cut off the wrong leg?" But he knelt beside Elisha as they started the round of cutting—outside this time, rather than spill so much blood down in the hospital for the women to clean up day after day. Elisha showed Ruari how to investigate the extent of the damage and decide which bones to set and bind and which to cut right away.

"Try not to cut at the joint, if you can. It takes longer to heal. For legs, if you give at least a handbreadth below the joint, they'll take better to a wooden leg."

"I've made a couple of those myself," Ruari offered, brightening.

"Likewise, if you draw up the flesh—" Elisha demonstrated, using his left hand to elevate and position the leg the way he wanted, "—it forms a better cushion for the bone afterward."

After tying a tight band above the man's ruined knee, and giving thanks that he was unconscious, Elisha demonstrated how to hold the knives and how much pressure was required at various stages. He'd nearly done when the physician's assistant, Benedict, cried, "Barber!"

Elisha's head jerked up, but he looked back down to his saw and kept cutting, with short, delicate strokes. Just a little longer . . .

"Holy Rood, Barber, you're needed!"

Shooting a glance to Ruari, Elisha gritted his teeth.

"Must be a knight down," the soldier commented.

"I'm not done here!" Elisha shouted back, carrying on the bloody work.

In answer, Benedict suddenly towered over them. "Man's like to die anyhow, come on."

"Just a few more minutes."

Stooping down, careful not to get his robes in the blood, Benedict looked him in the eye. "I thought you understood the system of discipline here. Or do you need a flogging to remind you?"

Taking Ruari's hand, he placed it on the handle of the saw. "Like this, you'll manage." He shifted to allow Ruari to support the damaged limb.

Ruari looked doubtful, but he made a stroke, and Elisha kept his hand on top a moment longer, steady and sure, and Ruari's next stroke was even and strong.

Shaking blood from his fingers, Elisha rose and followed Benedict across to the handful of waiting nobility. On a litter borne by two squires a knight reclined propped on his armor. His leg showed a long, bloody gash, but not too deep.

"This man needs stitching," Benedict said to Elisha.

"Clearly, but where are the surgeons, my lord?"

"Yes," the knight stated shrilly. "I should at least be seen by the surgeons, not some—" He flicked his fingers at Elisha without finishing the sentence.

"They're busy just now," Benedict replied. "Go to."

Darting a glance back at his waiting soldiers, Elisha felt his fingers clench. He brought up his hand, wishing he dared to strike the blank, expectant air from the

young physician's face but was brought up short by a
gasp of horror from the knight.

"He must wash first," the knight insisted. "I'll not
have peasant blood touching my person."

"As you wish, my lord," Elisha snapped, pounding
over to the nearest bucket to splash the blood from his
hands. There was low-born blood enough on the
knight's flesh already, blood from the foot soldiers who
had died to preserve him. Shaking off the drops, Elisha
returned, threading a long needle.

"Wait, won't you give me something for the pain?"

With a little smile, Elisha said, "I ordinarily just
strike the patient unconscious with a hammer. But perhaps the physicians have some superior solution?" He
raised his eyebrows at Benedict, who gave him a look
usually reserved for lunatics.

Evenly, Benedict replied, "You must forgive me, sir,
but we've run a bit low on supplies so far from the city.
I am sure a man of your fortitude is more than capable
of withstanding the pain."

Disgruntled, the knight settled back, gesturing for
Elisha to proceed.

At the first tug of the needle through his skin, the
knight fainted dead away and remained so for the rest
of the procedure. Elisha cut the string when he was
through, inclined his head toward Benedict and asked,
"May I now return to my work, my lord?"

"Please do. You stink of sweat and putrefaction,"
Benedict sniffed.

Elisha forced a brief bow to the physician. By the
time he settled next to Ruari again, two of the un-
treated men had died.

This time, Elisha waited silently as the cullers pulled
the corpses from his hospital. He finished his night's
duties on the verge of collapse and barely made it up

the stairs before his knees gave out. Yanking off his boots, he stretched his weary feet. Lying spread-eagled on the floor, Elisha could smell his own stink, and recalled Benedict's jeer. He knew he'd not sleep easily in any case, not with the faces of the dead waiting to greet him. After a while, he gave it up and pushed himself back to his feet.

Quietly and unchallenged, he limped across the courtyard, stepping over his half-dug ditch. What had seemed a good idea at dawn, now looked like a folly that only made him more exhausted than he should be, and he splashed through the gully without paying attention. He slipped between the off-kilter doors of the main gate and took himself down to the river. On both sides, the king's encampment spread out, the royal pavilion glowing from within. Elisha might pass the entire war without laying eyes on the king. If he did see him, like as not, it would be for no good.

Without taking off his clothes, Elisha stepped into the chilly waters, wrapping his arms around himself. The water here swirled into a wide pool before slipping beneath the bridge and off to the hills. Surrendering to the icy tug, Elisha ducked into the pool, coming up quickly as the cold slammed into him. After a time, he grew used to it and splashed about as long as he could stand it, letting his long hair flow out around him. It felt so good to be wet with something clean, to be covered for a change in purity, not stained by another man's life or death.

Reluctantly, he pulled himself out, shivering, stripped off his wet clothes, and wrung them out. He lay on the grassy verge, his feet tapping ripples in the water. Overhead, dark clouds scudded between the earth and the stars, making an eerie glow around the moon. Elisha shut his eyes while his mind was still full of the moon and stars.

"But can it be?"

Elisha's eyes popped open, and he sat up, searching the night for whoever had spoken. There was no one to be seen.

"I'm no expert in divination, Marigold."

The voice had neither gender nor tone, and Elisha hurriedly pulled on his wet britches, still looking for the unseen speakers. He heard no more and took a step back into the water, peering along the river to see if there might be a boat.

"Then why have you called yourself Sage?"

"Why indeed, Sage?"

"A name, no more."

Confused, Elisha turned a full circle. From the camp came the sound of drums and voices and a flute near the royal pavilion.

"Leave off, it's of no issue what we call ourselves."

"But if I could meet you in person—"

"Unthinkable!"

"Out of the question!"

"Marigold, you know as well as any, and better than most, that secrecy is essential."

Elisha sank back onto a stone. Perhaps his exhaustion had brought on some hallucination. He pressed his hands over his ears.

As loud as ever, a voice said, *"I know, I know. For my mother's sake. But the words seemed so clear—a healing hand that carries death. A healing hand."*

"We've all heard it, Marigold. So your mother caught a glimpse of this man's potential. It happens. It's not a sign."

"It could be, if we let it."

"Not everyone dreams of our people rising up. Most of us are happy as we are."

"And safer that way. Let's not start that argument again."

"I didn't come here for that. Some of you, one of you, at least, is in that hospital."

"Do not speak of it."

"But if I could only—"

"Silence. Safety lies only in silence."

"Why else call ourselves by herbs? So that we cannot betray each other."

"It may be him, it may be the other. Even if one of us knew them, he might not know which."

Dropping his hands from his ears, Elisha hugged himself. These voices were not in the air, that much was clear. They must be either in his head, or—he glanced down at the dark, lapping water. Carefully, while the one called Marigold urged a meeting, he lifted his feet from the water. Silence. Amazed, he placed them back in.

"—did think he questioned me, but for what purpose? If he suspects what I am, would he not reveal me? Yet he has not, so—"

"Suspects," "one or the other," "the hospital"—it sounded as if they were speaking of himself, these spirits in the water. Propping his chin on his knees, Elisha dug his feet into the mud as if he might hear them better.

"—I must assume he doesn't mean to. In truth, I would not even have thought of him, if he hadn't stopped me."

"Gave you a fright when you walked up, though, didn't you say?"

Elisha gasped. "Brigit," he breathed. It had to be. The one called Marigold.

The voices fell silent.

"Who's there?" someone said.

As if this were a command of some kind, other

voices chimed in, *"Marigold," "Sage," "Briarrose," "Willowbark," "Live Oak," "Fennel Seed."*

Again, they fell silent.

"To the air," cried one.

"To the air—" the others echoed, and they were gone.

Elisha jumped up, half expecting to see witches in the sky above him. He splashed in the water, scanning for any sign of them. Then, beyond the bridge, something moved. A man stood on the riverbank, his shadowed face turned toward Elisha and the moon. Stumbling, Elisha lost his footing and fell into the water as his witness ran, vanishing into the night.

Chapter 13

❦oices haunted Elisha's dreams, voices of witches or of demons, he could not be sure. Still and all, he managed to get some sleep before he dragged himself back to work in the morning, strange voices still echoing inside his head. He chewed on his bread as he circulated the room, indicating to Maeve which men should get new bandages. Of the gunshot victims, they had lost only one, a man Matthew had cauterized a little too deeply. The men who had suffered Lucius's boiling oil cure lay feverish, and Maeve set about cooling them down after Lisbet fetched some fresh water. Two of the amputees lay cold upon the floor, and Elisha forced himself to focus, to forget the voices and deal with matters at hand. Both men had been cut by Ruari, who came to peer over Elisha's shoulder.

"Dead, are they? I told you, I'm not the man you need."

"Ruari, no, here—" He pulled the soldier down beside him. "Look, this man has a headwound as well, not bleeding, so we missed it in the night. I checked them all, Ruari, and you did fine work."

Still, the soldier sighed and shook his head, his bandage gone now, leaving a line of stitches and bruising across his temple. "I dunno, Eli, mayhap this is beyond me."

Elisha met his deep brown eyes. "I need you." He thought to say more but instead left the bare words in the air between them.

Ruari ducked his head, raking one hand through his hair in a gesture already familiar. "I dunno." Then he looked up with that mischievous smile and said, "I'll have another go, I will. I've cut the dead heart from an apple tree and had it live, what's pruning a limb or two?"

"That's the spirit." Elisha slapped him on the shoulder. "I'll be about my project then. Once we take care of them." He indicated the two bodies with a tilt of the head.

Crestfallen, Ruari said, "Aye," and lifted the first man onto his shoulders to take to the yard while Elisha managed the other.

Elisha gave thanks that the pick was where he had left it. Inside, Arthur Mason finished up his task with the block, leaving a hole just about the level of the ground, and lining up nicely with the trench Elisha had made. A few hours work would see the ditch done. After a while, when he'd begun to sing again, Lisbet quietly emerged and settled on one of the benches, taking careful stitches in a bit of cloth.

Taking a break, Elisha wandered over to her and admired the entwining pattern of knotwork she had created. "Have you ever thought of barbering?" he asked lightly.

Lisbet snorted. "Course not, I'm a woman."

"I know that," he replied, earning a blush. She fidgeted with the fabric between her hands. "They're asking my help more with the lords, so the foot soldiers have to wait longer every night. If I had someone to handle some of the minor stitching, the men who can go back to their own camps, that'd be a big help to me."

Cocking her head, she shook back her light brown curls and regarded him with a frown. "Not that my mum would approve."

Shrugging, Elisha took up his pick for the final assault. "Consider it, will you? And ask Maeve, or I can ask for you, if you'd like."

"Don't do that!" she cried, looking stricken. "I'll think on it, I promise."

"Thanks," he said, a little ill-at-ease with the glow that came to her face when she went back to her embroidery. Flirting with whores, he found, did not prepare him to handle a girl so smitten. And with himself, of all people. Yet there was no sense letting her attention go to waste, not if she could stitch men's flesh as handily as she stitched that cloth.

At last the ditch snaked across the courtyard from the tiled bank of the stream to the opening in the hospital wall. Underneath, on the inside, sat the repaired barrel. Elisha lined his ditch with some of the loose tiles and paving stones, and considered what he needed to finish the task. He descended into the basement where Lisbet had discovered the barrel and found two broad, broken shovels. One of these was bent, but a good fit for the hole in the wall, making a spout over the barrel. The other he shoved into the ground against the wall of the existing stream.

He swung the pick two-handed, breaking through the tiles, and fished them out of the way in the water. Carefully, he re-traced the route, to find himself face to face with the surgeon Mordecai and his lesser assistant, a chubby lad by the name of Henry.

Beneath the furrowed brow, Mordecai aimed a suspicious look at him. "What are you about, Barber?"

"Plumbing, my lord." With a theatrical gesture, he lifted the shovel head, allowing some of the stream water to be diverted into his new canal. It bubbled and splashed along the channel, losing some to the gaps between tiles. Inside, the soldiers whooped, and someone stuck a pitcher of water out the window.

Glancing back to the surgeon, Elisha nodded to it. "My assistants waste too much time going to the well and back."

"Wasted time yourself in the digging," Mordecai pointed out.

"Aye, sir, a few hours. But think what we'll save over a few days."

"You weren't brought here to dig ditches," the assistant scoffed.

Ignoring him, Elisha watched the surgeon's reaction. "I was brought here to tend the foot soldiers as best I can, sir, I can do that better with a steady supply of water. I've been here when I'm needed."

"Speaking of—" The surgeon gave him a tight smile. "What was that soldier doing with your saw? Last night."

Something in the tone sent a little chill down Elisha's back. "Learning to amputate, sir. He is a carpenter."

"He is a soldier. Should be back at the front, if he's as recovered as to be of use."

"Please, sir, I get fifty soldiers a night at my door, some of whom can't go back to camp, plus assisting with the lords, and the gunshot wounds. I sleep two hours, and I'm back again with a dozen or more of them dying during the night. You three have enough to do with the lords, I know, but if I don't get any help—"

"You're blaming us?" the assistant, Henry, said. "What does it matter if a few more foot soldiers die if the captains and knights can ride out again?"

Mordecai shifted back on his heels, the books dan-

gling from his waist swaying like a flock of disturbed
birds. He held up a firm hand to stop his apprentice.
"King needs soldiers just as he needs captains to lead
them. Keep your man, Barber, if I see he does more
good than harm."

Elisha bowed. "Thank you, sir. I'll see that he does."

From the hospital, someone called out, "Full up, Elisha!"

Elisha pushed the shovel back into place, handily
stopping the flood, and allowed himself a smile.

Noticing the expression, the surgeon stared at him a
moment, then turned away, his assistant following in
his wake, looking chastened. As ever, the books and
papers fluttered, and Elisha's smile became a grin.
Hurrying to the window, he leaned in to see a group
gathered around their new water barrel, filling pitchers
and passing them out.

"Maeve? Get me a pot from the kitchen, can you?"

Rolling her eyes, this time Maeve didn't question
him. She shuffled over and handed a large pot up
through the window. " 'Nother idea, eh, Barber?" She
chuckled. "Should've been a scholar, you!"

"Oh, be off with you. I'm just mixing ointment."
Taking the pot, Elisha sprinted back to his tower. This
time, he didn't stop on the second floor, but climbed all
the way up where the collapsed roof blocked off the upper floor. Carefully, he crept in among the rotting tim-
bers and found what he wanted: rows of sloppy nests.
Disturbing the inhabitants, he gathered as many of the
tiny eggs as he could. They were the size of the end of
his thumb, but he thought they might do for a start.
Frustrated doves pecked at his hands, but he shooed
them away, all the while urging them to get busy laying
more.

Scooting back out, he brushed straw and feathers from

his head. With this precious cargo, he found his way to the
vestry, a small room off the side of the church where
priests would have kept their garments and holy necessi-
ties. As the surgeon had said, the room was stocked with
all manner of dried and powdered herbs as well as rolls of
bandages and suture, a collection of cauterizing irons and
miscellaneous surgical tools all much finer than his own
small assortment. Catching sight of these, he longed to examine them all, to consider their uses and test their fit
against his hand. That, surely, had not been the surgeon's
intent. Indeed, Elisha was not convinced the man wanted
to give him access to any of these supplies.

That in mind, he chose sparingly. When they saw
that his ointment helped, he might just convince the
surgeon to give him a freer hand. Back in the kitchen
behind the hospital, he broke open the eggs, added
only the yolks to a mixture of oil of roses, a bit of vine-
gar and turpentine—a formula similar to one he
learned from his Master Barber; a formula Elisha had
long worked on in the quiet of his own study. As he
mixed, he considered the hospital as the ideal place to
perfect the ointment, and gave himself a grim smile.
The physician, with all of his learning, hoped to do the
same thing regarding his hot oil cure. At least Elisha's
mixture caused no additional pain and might soothe
the burns and infections afflicting so many.

With Ruari's help, he spread the stuff on as many of
the men as he could. Even used sparingly, it did not go
far. All that could be done was to wait and see—and try
to find another source of eggs, larger ones, if possible.
After a supper of cold pottage, since Maclean had been
sent back to camp, they enlisted a new screamer to convince the surgeons that cauterizations were in progress.
Then began another round of dressing the wounds and
trying to abate fever and infection.

Just as the horn sounded for the night's hold, Ruari shook out his weary arms. "How d'ye do this, Eli? Already it's too much for me, and I know we've worse yet to come."

Arching his back to relieve the taut muscles, Elisha pondered the question. He came here to work off the ruin of his brother's family; long hours and hard labor were part of that penance. But, in fact, he had been training for this for years. Since that day of the angel, he had not questioned what he must do, that he must learn the healing arts and be of service at all times. How else could he be sure he would be ready? But how could he explain without being accused of witchcraft? "It's what God expects of me, Ruari. And what I can do."

"I did not take ye for a devout man, Eli, but it's glad I am to hear it."

Together, they went up to stand before the doors as the first of the wounded straggled in. After a little while, Lisbet came to stand by them, her cheeks flushed red and an angry defiance in her stance. Elisha showed her how to anchor stitches and how to draw them firmly, making sure they would not tear. The men she stitched were somewhat dismayed to see her there, but, as Elisha had supposed, she took to the work easily enough. Supervising his two assistants with the easier injuries, handling the difficult ones, and running across to provide whatever service the surgeons felt was beneath them kept Elisha busy until they cleared the court and went below to make room for the wounded among the recovering patients. There, Elisha met the now-expected sight of gravediggers, moving among the bodies. Moans and protests rose up to the sky, and more than one man slapped away a foot about to prod him. As they walked, the cullers glanced back to where Elisha stood, and he could see the bewilderment on

their faces. They cleared away a few, and then their
leader joined him by the barrel.

"You'd best send off some of these who're well
enough, Barber, or you'll run low of space for the new
ones." He spoke sourly, from the side of his mouth, on a
breath reeking of rotted teeth, but the words sent delight into Elisha's spirit so that he wanted to take Lisbet's hands and dance her around the room. What
healer would not like to befuddle the gravediggers,
keeping them from their work by healing too well?

Instead, he slapped Ruari on the shoulder. "I think
he means you. I've a nice room in the steeple, if you'd
care to join me? Second floor, with views."

"I'd be right proud," Ruari answered. "I'll go off to
camp and see if my things are yet there, and not been
taken by my mates."

"Good luck!"

Sending him off, Elisha fairly floated between the
beds of the complaining lords and out into the night,
leaving the surgeons' stares behind him. In the little
yard, he hesitated. He should take himself to bed and
get the few hours he could before it all started over
again, but the quiet rush of the river drew him as if he
could already hear the voices, and he found himself
walking that way.

He chose his spot more carefully for its concealing
bushes and a stone of a height to perch atop. He slipped
off his boots and dangled his toes into the water. This
time, he heard them right away.

"—it is a calling, if such it can be, since I am a
woman."

"And aren't we the stronger sex in any case, Marigold?"

"If you've lived this life of secrecy, Marigold, you
must be wise enough for such a teaching, but don't
overstep your bounds."

"I don't know what you mean."

"Of course you do, much as you wish it otherwise. It may not be given to you to find this one and— Who's there?"

Damn it, Elisha thought, somehow they knew they had a listener, someone who didn't belong. He had hoped to keep quiet and learn the nature of these voices, whatever they might be. Now, his plan must come to naught—unless—he smiled into the darkness. It was worth a try.

"Marigold," "Willowbark," "Briarrose."

After a moment's hesitation, Elisha spoke softly to the water, *"Bittersweet."*

All was silent.

"Bittersweet?"

Cautiously, afraid to ruin it or make some misstep to frighten them off, Elisha whispered, *"That's what I said."*

"What is your nature?"

This caught him up all over again. Was it another code, another question for which they already knew the right answer? He rolled it over and decided to plunge ahead despite the risks. If they were witches or spirits, they might know the secrets of the Bone of Luz, the forbidden knowledge that could right the wrongs he had committed. *"I am a man of flesh and blood."*

Something fluttered in his hearing, like laughter.

"I have not heard your voice, oh man of flesh and blood," someone challenged.

"Nor has any here, unless I miss my mark," said another.

Quickly, Elisha said, *"I have not been here long."*

"Welcome, Bittersweet." The voice had neither body nor tone, but it felt like hers, as if he could see those green eyes gleaming in the glints upon the water. *"It's good to have you among us."*

Us. Who are we? He wanted to know, then caught himself. We? But he was a barber and a serf. An ordinary man. Elisha pulled his feet from the water and leapt to shore, snatching up his boots. Witches, demons, spirits in the water—he had longed for those voices all day and sought out the thrill of this bizarre communion, never thinking of what it meant. Of course they guarded their names, of course they must be secret—if ever they were heard, they would be food for flames. And so would he.

Chapter 14

✦

$\mathcal{H}$e awoke early in the dawn to the sound of horses and wagons creaking below his little windows.

For five days, Elisha had resisted the lure of the river. He lay at night, hearing its call beyond the groans and tears of the injured men, beyond even Ruari's snoring. When he had stolen the child's head, he wished for the witches, to ask for their aid, but he dared not, now that he may have found them. He knew all too well the penalty that could await him or any of those he might contact. Best abandon the project as hopeless, not to mention impossible, which it probably was. In the graveyard, he had promised the child a new life or a decent burial—neither would be served if he died at the stake.

With his guidance, Ruari and Lisbet took on more duties, leaving him free to deal with the most difficult cases, and to do the dirty work for the surgeons and physicians; if he was not earning their respect, at least they no longer felt the need to threaten him. There was a moment after Nathaniel's death he thought he might never take up his tools again—but the work gave him hope and something like peace, as if each man he stitched or bound or set repaid a little of the sorrow he had caused. The chaos which had met him a week before now settled into a routine of late nights and little sleep.

Ruari rolled over, frowning, then his face lit up. "Wagons in from the city; wonder what they'll bring." He sat up quickly, pulling on his shabby boots.

Less enthusiastically, Elisha stretched. "No good for us, I'm sure."

Pausing to glance over at him, Ruari said, "Last time, they brought you."

"That's a recommendation?"

Ruari poked his head out a window, then turned back with a grin. "You'll like this cargo."

Curious now, Elisha sighed and pulled on his own boots. "Very well; I should go down and check on that boy with the broken head in any case."

Ruari made a face. "Do you never think of aught but work?"

"In this place? What else is there?"

That brought a grin to Ruari's face and he urged Elisha ahead of him down the stairs. "This, you'll like."

Outside, carters unloaded parcels from the wagons. The physician, too, had come out and hovered alongside the lead wagon, with Malcolm Carter at his side. Then both reached up to help his passenger dismount. When they stepped aside, Elisha caught sight of Brigit and the breath rushed out of him. Ruari had to nudge him aside with a knowing wink. "Come on, then."

Even as they approached, the physician spotted them and placed a protective arm about Brigit's shoulders. "Good of you to come," he drawled. "This is Mistress Brigit, of the herbalists' guild locally. She plans to remain here, at my request, to assist us with identifying the appropriate medicinals, as well as to view their use in medical applications. I trust"—and with these words, he swept his gaze over the surgeons as well as his own assistants—"that she will be given the utmost respect and assistance."

Elisha managed a bow, though his balance felt shaky. He rose again to find her green eyes upon him, and a little smile playing over her lips.

"Most irregular," Mordecai huffed. "Can't have her leaning over us, can we?"

In an undertone, Ruari said, "I'd not mind a bit!" and Elisha shot him a glower. He worked furiously, trying to find an excuse to greet her, to speak to her, just to have her gaze linger on him a while longer. "I've taken leave of my senses," he muttered.

"Aye, and who wouldn't—cor, she's coming over!"

Indeed she was, picking her way with some care over the scuffed and stained grass. Because they had begun performing urgent amputations here rather than wait to carry the patients indoors, Elisha scanned the area, making sure no stray body parts lingered.

Then Brigit stood before him, a folded bit of parchment in her outstretched hand. "The carter had this for you, Barber," she said, her voice pleasant but with no extra warmth.

Elisha flinched, staring down at it. "For me?"

"Yes, from a woman in the city, he said." She held it out expectantly.

"You're sure?"

At this, Brigit laughed, and the day grew that much brighter. Turning the parchment to face her, she read, "Elisha Barber, that is your name, is it not?"

Wetting his lips, Elisha nodded, and at last put out his hand for the letter. It lay yellow and accusing on his palm, the incomprehensible black markings of his name mocking him.

Brigit gasped, putting a hand over her mouth as she colored the most beautiful pink. Leaning forward, she said, "Do you need me to read it?"

"No," he snapped, crumpling it into his fist. His own cheeks flared to red as he cursed himself for a fool.

At his side, Ruari cleared his throat and announced, "I'll check on that lad, shall I?" then he hurried off without a backward glance.

"I'm sorry I've embarrassed you. I just thought . . ." Brigit drummed her fingers together. "I'm sorry." She took a half-step back as if to go, and Elisha swallowed his pride, though it made a lump in his throat.

"No, my lady, I . . . you were right." He held up the letter. "I would be grateful . . ." He needed to know. He could not think why anyone should write to him, when the few who knew him well enough to send the letter would know equally well he could not read it. With the eyes of the physician and his assistants upon them, not to mention the surgeon with his girdle hung about with books, Elisha wanted to sink into the ground—or perhaps be struck dead on the spot. He did not think they'd heard the exchange but, unless he wanted the letter to remain unread, his public humiliation would soon be complete.

Straightening, Brigit said loudly, "Yes, I believe I know the plant you mean. Why not take me there, and I'll be sure," she said, brows pinched over her green eyes.

Relief welled in him. "This way, my lady." He lowered the hand still bearing the letter into a gesture of invitation.

Turning to the physician, Brigit said, "I won't be a moment." She gave him her most winning smile. "It's good to see you have such an eager staff."

As they set off side by side, Elisha broke the wax

seal of the letter and made a show of examining it, hoping he made no obvious mistake in how he held it or how his eyes traveled the block of black letters.

When they neared the bridge over the river, Brigit turned to him again, her mouth twisting into a rueful smile. "I *am* sorry. I did not even think."

"There's no reason for you to be concerned over my ignorance." Elisha prodded a tuft of grass with the toe of his boot. It would probably have been no more embarrassing for the doctors to know—the worst was that she already did. She was a woman who prized the mind, that was clear enough. Not that he had a chance at her notice, with herself already betrothed, and such men as the physician and his educated comrades to distract her.

Once again, Brigit held out her hand, then gently slipped the letter from his grasp. They strolled slowly at the riverside as the sun rose, painting the sky with pale color. Immediately, Brigit frowned and darted him a worried look. "There's no greeting," she said. "Look, are you sure you want me to read this?"

"Who else is there?"

"Well, the physician, for one," she offered, then drew back at whatever part of his loathing showed plain upon his face. "I assumed . . . never mind, I'll read it."

She cleared her throat and held the letter before her. "'Elisha Butcher'—that should be Barber, perhaps the writer has difficulty with her letters."

Gazing up to the sky, Elisha laughed bitterly. With those two words, he knew who would write to him, who would do so for this very reason, to reveal his humiliation before whomever would read it.

"It doesn't seem funny to me," Brigit remarked.

"Read on," Elisha said, "I'm sure the humor will be made clear."

"'Elisha Butcher,'" she read in her lovely voice, "'I

trust the battlefield is serving your needs—'" Brigit frowned, glancing at him again, but he made no response, so she went on, "'Myself, I am better every day that you are away. The funerals have been held in your absence, and you were not missed. We saw that you planted the cross Nathaniel made. I take it you buried our child and now I am meant to thank you for it.

"'I am writing to demand that you tell me the truth of your brother's death. Sister Lucretia spouts only good of you and will not tell me, nor will that captain who's been about the place. Once I had them together, and both looked pale at my asking. So I put it to you plain, have you killed him? If it were not yourself, then what is the truth of it? How can I recover with this concern weighing down my breast? I may be found at my sister's house if you are not so cowardly as to deny me. All due respect, Helena.'"

When she had done, Brigit examined the letter again, reading it silently and quickly, turning it about to see if there was anything else to know.

Having fallen a bit behind, Elisha shut his eyes on the tears that threatened him. He bit his lip, his hands gripped behind him. Sister Lucretia spoke well of him, the captain held his tongue with all the justice of his office, so Helena reached across the distance to hound him with a question he dared not answer. Nathaniel was at rest, in hallowed ground, but it would not be the first time a man had been disinterred, and that could serve only to punish Helena more than had he told the truth from the moment it happened. Better that she should hate him than turn from his brother's memory. As for himself, he had few friends or relations, but Helena and Nathaniel had many, a legion of admirers who would care for his brother's widow, not to mention the support she should receive from his guild. What would they do on hearing the truth? Let Helena believe what she would, he would not enlighten her. If only he had a way to bring the child back—

Again, Brigit cleared her throat, and Elisha opened his eyes to find her frowning at him. "Are you well, Barber?"

"Aye, I'm well enough," he said, though he did not feel it, and she did not press him.

"Would you like me to write out your response?" She held out the letter, and it trembled slightly.

"That won't be needed. Thanks." He snatched the parchment and re-folded it with jerky movements.

"It's no trouble," she offered.

"Thanks, but no."

"Please yourself." Brigit walked a few steps to the river's edge. After a moment, she slipped off her shoes and dipped in one toe. Glancing over her shoulder, she said, "In this whole valley, I love the river most."

Narrowing his eyes, Elisha watched her step into the water, ripples forming around her bare ankles where she held up her skirt just a bit. Then a chill struck through him as he watched; she was confronting him, challenging him to stand beside her, to reveal his knowledge of the words which flowed in the water. Was she speaking even now to those below?

She lost all trace of smile and said, "Come in, Barber, I swear it will not harm you."

Slowly, Elisha tucked the letter into his pouch. What was the invitation she gave him? Could he accept that communion of the waters she shared with some strange and distant people? And yet, if she could help him, tell him about the Bone of Luz, how could he not? Carefully, he pulled off his boots and set them standing on the river bank. Then, his eyes upon her, he stepped into the rushing stream.

The cold whipped about his ankles, and he shivered,

thinking not of water but of fire, of flames licking at his feet as they had devoured the angel so long ago.

"Bittersweet," the water said, and Elisha twitched, glancing quickly to Brigit.

When she caught his gaze, she grinned, full and triumphant, and the words came again, though her lips did not move. *"I thought it was you, I thought it must be you—twice now, am I right? You've come down here, and heard voices."*

Confused, Elisha looked around, then back to her. "Marigold?" he asked aloud, hearing the strange echo of his own voice somehow trapped in the water all around.

Shaking her head, Brigit gazed at him steadily. *"Do not speak, not aloud. You can hear me, can't you? Let the water be your voice. Imagine you address me, and I will hear you."*

Intently, he focused on what he would say, and asked, *"How is this possible?"* forming the question at the back of his throat, biting his lip to still the words.

Brigit laughed aloud and spun a circle in the water, splashing his knees.

"What is it? I don't understand," he said.

"How is this possible? How indeed," the river laughed. *"You speak as one of us, and yet we know you not. You are a magus, you must be! Why did she not say so?"*

Confused, Elisha put out his hand to stop her dancing, but withdrew. *"I'm not a whatever-you-called-me. I'm just a barber. And who should have said?"*

Stopping, with a hand pressed to her chest to still her eager laughter, Brigit let the water carry her words. *"A magus—a witch."*

At this, Elisha held up his hands. "No," he said into the air. "I am not. I'm a barber, nothing more."

Taking a step nearer, Brigit pleaded with her eyes. *"How else could you speak through the water, or hear my words? You are, just as I am."*

Shaking his head, Elisha felt the brush of his hair warmed in the sun and thought of flames. He backed away, and the stones slipped beneath his feet—treacherous footing indeed.

Brigit pursued him, putting out a delicate hand that hovered, but did not touch him. *"What is it you fear so much?"*

Elisha gained the bank, standing once again on solid ground.

"Is it what you saw?" She asked aloud, her voice in the air seeming smaller, more human. "When you were a child?"

"They burned her," he replied, flinging himself to the ground to jerk on his boots. "She was an angel, I could see it, but they shot her full of arrows and set her afire." He swallowed hard, his eyes seeing not the river now, but the flames. "She had eyes like yours, my lady, and I cannot see you without seeing her, and the blood, and the fire—" He broke off and pulled himself to his feet.

Brigit sprang to the bank and caught his wrist. As he spun to face her, to break her grip, she set her fingers on his cheek, just at the spot where he had once felt the brush of an angel's wing.

Chapter 15

❖

After a long moment, Elisha let out the breath he had been holding, and the warm, soft fingers withdrew. "How did you know?"

"She was my mother," Brigit murmured. "Come back to the water, I cannot speak of this in the air." She beckoned with a turn of her wrist and retreated before his wondering gaze.

Slowly, he did as she asked, slipping off the boots again, afraid to take his eyes off of her. They walked along in the water, carrying their shoes, down to the bend Elisha had come to six nights ago, thick with willows. Here, out of sight, she smiled up at him, but he did not return it, his dismay still too great for him to grasp.

The river tugged at his ankles, saying, *"The woman you saw was my mother. In her final moments, she worked her greatest magic, transforming herself. If she could slip her bonds, she would escape through the air. If not—"* He saw the grief that turned Brigit's lips, *"she would leave the vision of herself as an angel, not devilspawn as the priests would have you think, but a creature of the Lord, as all of us are."*

"She was beautiful," Elisha said in the water.

Again, Brigit smiled. *"I was only four, and a hundred miles away, hidden and safe."*

"Then how could you know about the touch? I have told no one all the years of my life."

"My mother told me. She told us all."

Elisha shook his head.

"You and I are speaking through the water. She spoke through the fire, even as it consumed her. Any of the magi can speak in water—it forms a contact between us, but few can speak in fire. We heard her—everyone. Father thought she meant to talk to me. Instead, she found you. There was a rapture in her voice that I cannot describe." Brigit's eyes focused in the distance. *" 'I have touched a child and seen the man.' "* The green eyes flickered to Elisha's face.

His lips parted, Elisha tried to think of what to say, but there was nothing.

"You came here after the death of your brother. My mother said, 'He will be a man of healing, yet bring death in his hands.' " She watched him closely.

In his hands? Elisha smiled grimly. Not in his hands but in his traveling chest, he had brought death indeed, beyond even the memory of his brother. At least Brigit need not know all. *"How could she say these things of me? I was a boy and still am no witch."*

"Oh, there is power in you, I think all of us can feel it. When I walked across the courtyard that day, I felt it when I neared you, even though I thought my mother had referred to someone else. Some of us believe that when we find this child my mother touched, he will be a leader—and we can finally be as free as other men. Finding him—finding you—is the last sign I need to bring our people together. I think my mother's touch awakened something in you, something even you are not aware of."

"There is nothing in me; I'm just a barber."

"We'll see about that." Her smile grew, along with a light in her eyes very like a flame. *"Let me teach you; let me show you the ways of the magi, and we will see."*

"*Magi?*" His brows drew together, trying to recall what the Bible said of them.

"*Yes. Those kings at the Nativity. The wise men, some say. They were not merely wise, but magi— magic. Can't you hear the very nature of the word? We are the magi. The ignorant term us witches, among many other names, but we are the wise ones, and you are one of us.*"

"*I don't think so.*"

Brigit spread her hands to take in the river around them. "*How do you explain this conversation?*"

"*Perhaps you have enchanted me.*" The words slipped into the water before he could withdraw them, and he gasped, turning away as he knew what he meant to say, and what she must surely hear.

Behind him, Brigit chuckled. "No," she said aloud. "I have only recognized you." Then, in the currents around him, "*Let me teach you, let me finish what my mother began.*"

"*But isn't it dangerous? You say the devil has no part in this—*"

"*And never has. Some of us are born with a skill to sing, others to plan great battles, and others still with this power, to bring up the energy of the world around us and mold it to our will. Gifts from God.*"

Like his gift for healing, Elisha thought, for gift it seemed to be. "*And yet if we are discovered, we're dead.*"

"*I live with that every day of my life.*"

"*Teaching me would be a greater risk to you.*"

"*A worthy risk,*" she answered, and he faced her.

Brigit stood in the river, her feet planted on the slippery stones, her shoulders back and hands raised as if to draw him nearer. Her shortened hair tossed in the breeze that shook the willow saplings, and her eyes shone. Then, flipping her hair to one side, she bent to the stream and lifted a small stone, holding it out to him.

When he took it in his hand, it wriggled and flashed, and a silvery fish leapt from his palm to splash back into its home, disappearing among the rocks it had once been a part of. "*How?*"

"*The principle of affinity: similar things have a sort of relationship. If you can define that relationship, you can cause them to act like, or even to become, one another. A slippery stone, a slippery fish. Let me teach you.*"

Suddenly, scores of tiny fish raced over his toes, and Elisha laughed. "*Yes, teach me.*"

Instantly, Brigit grew serious. "*We cannot meet often. As it is, I'm sure the physician is suspicious that we've been gone so long. But we can speak in the river, even when we are not near.*"

"*How?*" he asked again. He was like a child, discovering the world all over again.

"*Magi can speak through living water—any river, stream, or brook—ponds, too, though that is not so effortless. You've heard us talking twice now. Water is a form of contact, one of the keys to using your power. The closer you are, the stronger the contact, unless the magus is especially sensitive. Of course, touching skin to skin is the closest.*" She shot him a glance that made him long for closer contact. "*All you need do is touch the water, and any others within reach of it can hear you. The more distant, the less likely they are to hear. Please, please, use only the herbal names when we talk. If one of us should be found out, he cannot reveal the others.*"

"*That's why the others won't meet with you.*"

Brigit stamped in the water, sending up a cascade of glittering drops that turned to diamonds and back again. "*They fear too much. This power we have, why should we be so afraid of ordinary men?*"

"*Because they have arrows and torches,*" Elisha said, "*and there are many more of them than there are of you.*"

"*Of us, Bittersweet. Of us. But the magi will listen to me now—now that I have you.*" She stared at him.

Surely her own strength and magic, along with her mother's legacy, were enough to make her a leader among her people. Why should anyone care if she summoned a barber to her side? Elisha could not imagine that his presence would influence even this battle, never mind changing the destiny of a people. Brigit was beautiful, driven, and, where he was concerned, quite mistaken. But her belief would keep her close, and he could not bring himself to discourage her closeness.

From the other side of the monastery, a horn blew into the morning light; the call to arms.

With a backward glance, Elisha stepped from the water and pulled on his boots. "I have to go, my lady. Thank you."

"Come tonight," she said. "There is so much for you to learn."

He grinned and took his leave, making his way quickly to the courtyard. He pulled the gate on his ditch for a little while to replenish the water barrel, then entered through the kitchen. Tending a pot full of the latest hot oil solution, Benedict grunted at him. "I'll apply this lot, Barber. I want to be sure it's done right."

Elated by his talk with Brigit—as much for herself, as for the magic—Elisha ignored the physician's casual slight. "Of course, sir, by all means."

"Probe the wounds and pull the shot—get them ready for me."

"Aye, sir." He popped a bow. Even Helena's hurtful letter he put from his mind: soon enough, the magic might be to hand that he could use to redress the hurt he had done her.

"You are an insolent wretch," Benedict called after him. "We won't suffer it much longer, mark my words."

"Maeve!" Elisha cried, taking her arms and swinging her around. "What've you got for me?"

"Eight with arrows, five shot," she grumbled, slapping away his hands. "Four dead this morning, plus that broken leg."

This deflated Elisha somewhat. "Who are the dead?"

"An amputee and three two gunshots—two cautery, one hot oil."

"God's Wounds," Elisha cursed. "Was the amputee one of Ruari's?"

"Would I know? You've got Lisbet at such a pace, she's checked her men already. As much for the quality of stitches as for their lives."

"She's a good stitcher. I assume she learned as much from you," he tried, donning his leather apron to prepare for the labor ahead.

Maeve snorted. "Don't you butter me up, you. Not right, a girl like her having such congress with common soldiers. She'll be as bloody as a barber." Her cheeks flushed. "Sorry."

"She's saving lives, Maeve. What higher work can there be?"

Irritated, she waved him away. "Go on with you, I've got bandages to wash." She filled up a large pot from the brimming barrel. As she backed away with it, Henry, the lesser surgeon, ducked through the flap and hesitated, shifting on his feet as he eyed the barrel. In his hands, he held a broad basin of various herbs.

Noticing the young man, Elisha walked up. "Rather not carry that thing to the courtyard, I guess?"

Shorter by at least a foot, the assistant surgeon still managed to bristle. "Well, Barber, since you've modified the hospital, it seems just we should all benefit." He brushed past and set about filling his basin. He returned a moment later carefully balancing the full basin.

Elisha muttered, "A word of thanks wouldn't go awry."

The man didn't answer, even as Elisha held aside the curtain for his passage.

At last, Elisha turned to his work. He pulled a long probe from his instruments and chased the round balls of lead—which had battered so many of the men— through blood and sinew. He had a deeper knowledge now about these weapons and the wounds they left behind. As he carefully shifted the probe, plucking free another fragment of lead, he wondered if there wasn't some affinity he could use here, as Brigit had said, to magically remove the metal. Nothing came to mind, but he would think on it as he worked.

Shortly after the late meal, a large party rode through, accompanied by many trumpeters, and the officers got up a feeble cheer from beyond the curtain.

Ruari trotted out to see what was happening and returned with a report. "The king's ridden out to survey the damage from this side of the bombard range. Got some new tactics to work out, I guess."

"What's he look like, the king?" Elisha asked, resuming the binding of one of Benedict's torture victims. He wished he could get his hands on more eggs, but the tower pigeons had run out, and he had found few others in the surrounding buildings.

"Tall fellow, thick beard and all, with these sharp blue eyes. A bit like yours, now I think of it. Very grand, I'd say. You've not seen him?"

"And not likely to, unless he comes to the hospital."

"God forbid!" Ruari cried, crossing himself. "The king's been a bit close lately, I hear. Rumor is there's a plot against him, and he's not trusting even of men he's had for years. Even met one o' the royal messengers stomping about 'cause he's been relieved of duty. King's

had his younger son, Prince Alaric, talking to the nobles hereabouts, making sure this battle don't make for
civil war."

"God forbid," Elisha echoed. All they needed was a
bigger war. King Hugh's dubious succession was meant to
be settled before Elisha was born, yet the echoes lasted
even now. "But how do you know so much about it?"

"Lisbet's brother is a gunner on the king's bombard
crew," Ruari said. "They hear things." He shrugged
and looked away.

Daylight faded outside and the horn would soon be
sounded for the hold. Thankfully, the bombards had
gone silent as the day wore on, and some speculated
that they'd run short of shot. How many rocks of appropriate size could they have piled up in there?

Elisha started to assemble the tools they would need
for treating that evening's patients when suddenly a
blast shook the building, rattling his instruments and
thrumming in the water barrel. Ruari made the sign of
the cross and looked to the ceiling. For a moment, it
seemed they all held their breaths. No stone had felt so
close before.

Elisha let himself relax and gathered the fallen tools.
"I'm off to the vestry for sutures."

"Aye, Elisha."

Dusting off his hands, Elisha crossed through the
infirmary and up the stairs. Even as he reached the
church door, a knight galloped up and flung himself
down from his horse. "Doctors! Surgeons! Come quick,
it's the king!" He braced his hands on his knees, wheezing.

Mordecai and Matthew hurried up the stairs to him.
"What is it, man?"

"That blast struck as the king surveyed the field.
Several in his party down."

Mordecai pushed his assistant in the direction of the physician's cottage. "And be quick! Barber, get your tools!" Elisha doubled back, racing for his leather bundle, and returned to find the physician and his men milling in the yard. With a glance toward the surgeon, he set out for the field. If they waited for horses, they might be too late.

He set a good pace with his long strides, heading for the banners of the king. The blast had shattered a huge tree, sending splinters all around, but apparently missing most of the men. The group was in an uproar, gathered about the king where he sat, his crown askew. From his brief glimpse, Elisha saw the man wasn't bleeding, nor were any of his limbs out of joint, and he allowed himself to relax as the others came up, riding furiously. The physician Lucius pushed everyone back, bellowing for Mordecai and Benedict. Falling aside with the onlookers, Elisha stumbled on a root.

When he tried to free himself, he found a hand wrapped around his boot. A young man lay in a shaded hollow, his face and clothes dirty, his other hand clapped to his throat. "Barber," he hissed.

Dropping to one knee beside him, Elisha said, "I'm with you. It's your neck?"

A slight nod. His eyes flashed wildly one way and another, as if searching for something, or someone. "King," he breathed.

"Looked fine—the physician's with him."

Another slight nod.

Gently, Elisha removed the protective hand, releasing a gush of blood from a tear as long as his finger. "No shot?"

A vague movement in the negative.

"Be still, I'll take care of you," Elisha murmured. He replaced the hand, pressing it firmly to give him the

idea. Carefully, he rolled him onto his side away from
the blast site, then straddled the man's torso.

He drew from his pouch a needle already threaded,
and pinched the edges of the wound together. It should
be probed, cleaned at the least, but the boy had been losing blood. Something struck him oddly about the boy's
hand which yet clenched his leg, but he pushed the
thought aside as he began stitching.

"Barber! Where's the bastard got to?" Lucius
shouted. "Barber! There's a knight with a serious cut
over here."

Praying they wouldn't find him until he was done, Elisha kept at the work. "Don't worry," he told his patient,
"I'll not leave until I've done it. It's a simple wound, just
in the wrong place. Only a few more stitches."

The single worried eye showed white despite these
words, and Elisha began softly crooning another of his
mother's songs.

"Barber, get over here!" Matthew's sharp voice rang
out, and he could hear someone approaching.

"Just a minute—five more stitches." His fingers
worked steadily, the hand on the wound inching along,
the needle pulling and dipping in a regular rhythm.

"Barber." Matthew grabbed his arm.

Roughly, Elisha pulled away. "One stitch."

"Get up, we need you over here."

Growling behind his teeth, Elisha looked back to his
patient, whose ragged breath seemed to have nearly
stopped at Matthew's words. "One stitch," Elisha repeated, placing it with care, keeping the young man's
eye.

Again Matthew grabbed him, but Elisha shook him
off to take the smooth young hand and press it firmly
back over the wound. "Keep it covered, I'll come back
for you." That frightened eye blinked back a tear, and

Elisha smiled even as Matthew pulled him off balance and directed him toward the banners.

"This'll cost you dear, Barber," the physician thundered when he saw them. He straightened from his examination of a knight who groaned and rubbed his head.

"What are their injuries, sir, what would you have me do?"

"Do? Do? Why, we've already done your job!" He gestured toward Mordecai, seated with his back to them as he finished stitching a cut over the brow of one of the lords, who shot Elisha a nasty glance.

"He was stitching a foot soldier, sir," Matthew supplied.

Exhaustion and anger weighed upon Elisha, and he struggled to keep silent, his teeth clamped together.

At this, Mordecai looked over his shoulder, his watery gaze infinitely weary. "None of your concern, Matthew."

"None of my—? But the king himself went down, the physician was calling for aid, and this"—he flapped a hand at Elisha—"wasted time over a peasant."

Wasted time—saving a man's life, the job he had been brought here to do, was born for, in fact, while the physician summoned him to save a knight's vanity. Elisha clenched his fists. With a phrase, Matthew dismissed the foot soldier's worth, Elisha's work, the very heart of what they were all meant to do.

"He is a peasant himself," Lucius pointed out, "Why expect him to rise above his nature? No, rather, with such creatures obedience must be beaten in as with a recalcitrant dog who comes not to its master's hand."

"You are no master of mine," Elisha snarled.

"For our purposes today, I fear you are mistaken. I have the charge of you and the punishment."

"What, will you flog me for disobedience? You, who will not even put a hand out to save a man beneath your station?" Elisha spat at the physician's feet, his still-clean satin shoes peeping out beneath a brocaded robe. "He would have bled to death if not for me."

"Take him to the post," the physician said, not turning his livid features from Elisha as he summoned a few of the milling royal guards. "You're in control here, Mordecai."

The surgeon nodded vaguely, his head downcast as if searching the ground.

Two men caught Elisha's arms, and Matthew turned to follow, but Mordecai drew a long breath and raised his head as if it weighed too much for him. "Stay, Matthew. Get these men to the infirmary."

"Yes, sir," Matthew grumbled, the fervor dying a bit from his cheeks.

"Well, Barber," Lucius said as he mounted his waiting horse, "Now you shall see what righteous fury is capable of."

Chapter 16

❖

As the guards hauled him off, with the physician following on his tall white horse, Elisha tried to calm his anger and keep his footing. Righteous fury, indeed—the few short moments he spent stitching the foot soldier cost their precious nobility nothing. And in any case, they'd rather be tended by their high-born fellows. He should have kept his mouth shut, of course, and practiced groveling. But then, he'd never been good at that. Maybe he'd just grown sick to death of being ill-used. These doctors saw a man's clothes before his humanity, deciding who should be healed and who left to rot based on accidents of birth rather than severity of the wound.

The guards fetched up on the outskirts of the vast encampment, where a post about eight feet high cast its shadow in his direction like a beckoning finger. Once the blond of greenwood, the post had taken on the dull red hue of dried blood, and Elisha had his first moment's pause.

"Take your shirt off," one of the guards ordered, "or it'll be in shreds."

Dully, Elisha complied, removing his apron and shirt to have the garments snatched from his hands and tossed aside as his arms were grabbed again.

A spike held a short chain to the top of the post, with a metal cuff dangling at either end. To these, they fastened his wrists, his face toward the wood. The strain in his arms became quickly uncomfortable; a prelude to what would come.

From the tents and fires, soldiers rose, making their muttering way over to see what was on. Pointing and nodding, they formed little knots, and he noticed money changing hands.

Tucking his head beneath his right arm, Elisha tried to ignore them. Then the physician crossed into view.

"All secure, are we?" he inquired. Benedict trailed after him, looking slightly ill. Carefully, the physician unbuttoned the twenty or more silver buttons of his robe and folded it with the embroidery to the inside to protect it. Laying this over Benedict's waiting arms, he untied the ribbons at his cuffs and pushed back his sleeves, retying them above the elbows. These preparations made, he gave Elisha a cold smile. "This has been a long time coming in your case. I don't expect it will teach you wisdom, but it may encourage you to obey more promptly."

One of the guards stepped up with a coiled length of braided leather. Lucius took it in both hands, and snapped out the curl, inspecting it.

"I recommend a swift strike from the wrist, sir," the guard said.

Eyeing him, Lucius raised his arm and gave the whip an authoritative snap.

Elisha flinched, causing a chortle to ripple through the expectant crowd.

"I have used such on my horses in times past," the physician said.

Bowing, the guard gave ground, and Lucius walked up to stare down at Elisha's face. "This rabble are betting on when you'll start screaming. Oh, you're brazen enough now, but I've got my money on the fifth lash." Draping the whip over his shoulder, the physician sauntered around and out of view.

Tension gripped the muscles of Elisha's back and shoulders, less for the expected pain than for the wait. He clamped his jaw so hard his head began to ache even before the first lash fell.

The whip bit and slashed along his spine, and Elisha jerked, his wrists pulling hard at the manacles.

The crowd roared, calling out, "One!"

The next blow came more swiftly, snaking from one shoulder down across his ribs. "Two!"

Setting his teeth, Elisha shut his eyes, keeping his head down despite the rub of the rough wood.

By the seventh blow, when Elisha still had made no sound, the physician began to fall into a rhythm, and the shouts of the crowd had become a chant of excitement.

Every hit carved agony along his flesh. He could picture the separate muscles, the way they joined to the bones, the way they leapt at every blow. A wail rose in his throat, but he could not give ground, not to this barbarian nor the bastards who egged him on. Instead, he began to hum.

The sound buzzed low in his throat, echoing inside his skull, drowning out the bloodlust and the counting. His Master Barber had taught him to distract himself from other's pain, to use music to flood the thoughts, but never before had he used it in his own defense. Flecks of wetness spattered his arms—the warmth of his own blood. His taut wrists trembled even as his legs threatened to give way beneath him.

Elisha forced back tears as the lash crosshatched his ribs and sliced rivulets of pain into his upper arms.

Weeping could wait for the privacy of night. His eyelids ached with the pressure of holding back.

Suddenly, the whip snagged in his hair, jerking his head around and ripping free. He gasped.

Pressing this unexpected vulnerability, the lash flew again, snapping a line of blood down his exposed throat.

Elisha bit down on his tongue, the hot, metallic blood coating his mouth, and he whimpered, his humming dying away.

The crowd had gone silent—he knew not for how long.

"That's enough now," a stern voice said. "Surely, sir, that's enough."

The physician made a dissatisfied grunt, then said, "Very well. Let him down. However, I am not convinced that I have driven out the arrogance in this one. He'll be for branding before too long, mark my words."

The chain fell loose, and Elisha grabbed for the post, swinging his body around as he stopped his fall.

The physician had his back turned, rolling down his sleeves with short, angry movements, then holding out his arms for Benedict to replace the elaborate robe.

Watching them, Elisha clung to the wood. Every breath tore at his skin. The brush of his hair over his shoulders coaxed shivers of pain.

At last, buttoned up and turned out as perfectly as before, the physician faced him. His lips held in a firm line, he looked Elisha up and down. "I think we know now who is the master."

Silently, Elisha raised his chin.

With a grimace of disgust, Lucius turned away. At his shoulder, Benedict met Elisha's stare, blanched and hurried off behind. The guards hovered a little longer, one of them coiling the whip over his arm, his face downturned. The foot soldiers all around drifted off, solemn, taking their money without saying a word.

At last alone, Elisha slipped to the ground, one arm wrapped around the post, his back sending out spasms of protest. He pressed his cheek to the wood, gasping. His fingers felt chubby and insensitive, his wrists throbbing where the chains ground in. His hands trembled with returning sensation.

Night fell around him before he summoned the strength to rise. His companions had not come for him, whether for fear of showing their support or because they could not leave their duties, Elisha had no way of knowing. He tucked his hands beneath his arms, shoulders hunched against the shaking which assailed him. Slowly, he stumbled his way toward the monastery. His body screamed, but his mind remained numb.

Crossing beneath the main gate, he tripped on the tiled canal and fell heavily to his knees, crumpled into a lump of pain. Water trailed around his toes, finding its way through the holes in his worn-out boots, and he dimly heard voices asking questions, calling for silence, saying too many things he could not comprehend. He inched forward, withdrawing the contact. After a moment, he managed to rise again, taking deep breaths, forcing his hands to hang at his sides.

Could he bear to face them? Could he bear to slink away like the dog they thought him? Resolutely, Elisha turned away from the tower, and took the steps down into the main infirmary. A new demarcation: one side curtained off, and the damaged banner of the king hanging from the ceiling.

Somehow, he stayed on his feet, kept walking toward the curtain. From a bed beside it, Matthew and Mordecai rose. The younger surgeon started to move toward

Elisha's path, but Mordecai put out a hand and drew him back, without shifting his eyes from his book.

Pushing aside the curtain, Elisha entered his own domain, deaf for once to the moans and crying around him. He tried to speak, wet his lips, tried again. "Ruari?"

Looking up from a patient toward the back, Ruari sprang to his feet, vaulting the bodies between them. "Oh, Sweet Lord, Elisha, I wanted to come for you." Worry twisted his features as he held out his hands, still wet with another man's blood.

Elisha shut his eyes and opened them again. Every tiny movement took an age. "Better you were here— someone had to be."

With a half-smile, Ruari said, "I knew you'd say that. Let me look at you. Lisbet, find us some ointment!"

The trembling girl hurried to obey as if she fled the sight of him.

Shaking his head, Elisha said, "Young man, tall, slender, blue eyes." He made a gesture in front of his face, searching for the word. "Sharp nose—the look of a lord. Had a—" He put his fingers to his own aching throat.

Spinning a quick circle to remind himself, Ruari faced him again. "None like that brought in tonight."

"Mary's Tears," Elisha muttered, and began to turn away.

The gentle brush of Ruari's hand sent him rigid with pain. "My God, Elisha, I'm sorry. Ye can't leave—what're you about?"

"I promised I'd see him safe."

Ruari drew close to his face. "Are ye mad? After this? For the love of God, Elisha, leave him lie; ye've done what you could and at such cost."

He had made a promise. He let his brother down, and his nephew; he would not do the same to a stranger

who needed him. Meeting Ruari's dark eyes, Elisha
saw his haggard reflection captured there, but he said
no more, and Ruari nodded.

"I'm with ye, then."

"Don't," Elisha said. "Trouble for me, not for you."

"You are mad," Ruari gasped.

Likely it was true. Elisha mirrored that half-smile of
moments before. "Will they beat me again tonight?"

"They might well, for all that." Bowing his head, Ruari made a little gesture of release. "God be with ye,
Eli, and we'll wait ye here."

As he turned his back, Ruari let out a bleat, and
Maeve cried out behind him, but Elisha had to keep going. If he stopped now, that foot soldier might lie all
night. He had to know, at the very least, if his pain had
bought the man's life after all. Crossing through the
curtain, Elisha was met with silence, which kept at his
back on the long walk to the battlefield. By moonlight,
he found the shattered tree, and stood among the un-
cleared dead, peasants all.

The foot soldier had caught his ankle from below, lying in a sort of dell, which had hidden them both from
immediate view. Elisha re-traced his steps, coming up
as he had earlier that day. There before him, the ground
dipped away, its shadows revealing nothing. He knelt
down, splaying his hands before him, and found a leg
that was still warm. Groping his way along the body, he
came to the exposed throat, to the limp hand which
covered his own line of stitching.

Pressing his fingers to the pale skin, Elisha held his
breath. The pulse beat beneath his hand, slow, but
steady. Kneeling over him once again, Elisha lifted the
young man into his arms, his flesh stinging as the welts
pulled. Wincing, he tried to collect his breath.

"God give me strength for this," Elisha whispered to

the moon. Carefully, he rose, waiting a moment to settle the weight against his chest.

For the third time that night, Elisha crossed the infirmary, drawing a few curses and a few jeers from the
squires and whores. Ruari held aside the curtain and
immediately lifted the man from Elisha's arms to lay
him on fresh straw.

"Blankets, hot water, if you can," Elisha said, just as
his shoulders began to sag, and he felt an ominous
trembling in his knees.

"Aye, we'll see to him. What about you? I tried to go
to the vestry, but they won't let me in, or Lisbet either."

"Fine," Elisha mumbled, putting out a hand to steady
himself on the barrel. "Rest, that's all, water maybe."

Rings rattled as the curtain was once more thrust aside.

Turning, Ruari shouted, "Get out, you!"

"I hardly need obey your orders," Matthew snapped
back. He rounded on Elisha and stuck out his arm. On
his palm rested a copper pot with a fitted lid. "You're to
be back on duty in the morning."

Frowning, Elisha picked up the container, enjoying
the way it fit into his palm.

"Shouldn't be wasted on such as you," Matthew shot
over his shoulder as he swept from the room.

Dumbly, Elisha stood there with the pot in his hand
until Ruari gently unfolded his fingers and pulled it
free. He popped off the lid, filling the room with the
scent of lavender. Raising his brows, he turned it to Elisha, revealing a creamy, cool salve flecked with herbs.
"Sit down, and I'll daub ye as best I can."

"Aye," Elisha agreed, releasing the barrel. With a
soft moan, he tumbled forward into Ruari's strong arms
and felt himself borne to the ground. Blessedly cold,
the stone caressed him, and he shut his eyes against the
rush of pain.

Chapter 17

───────────────◆───────────────

The darkness lifted all too soon, and Elisha squinted one eye open to see Ruari's agitated face. "Elisha? It's sorry I am to wake ye, but there's naught to be done for it. Elisha?" A strong hand gently pushed his shoulder, giving him the slightest shake.

Rolling to his side, Elisha realized the sharp edge of pain had dulled, so he did not cringe too much as he stiffly sat up. Blinking into the candlelight, he said, "What is it?"

Ruari sat back on his heels. "It's this." He held up a folded square of parchment.

At first, Elisha took it for the very same letter he'd had from Helena, but the broken seal upon it was purple, and the squiggles on the front did not look familiar. "A letter?"

"Aye. Found it on that boy you brought. We thought to make him more comfortable, take off that damp coat of his, and this was tucked in the collar."

"It's not our business, Ruari."

Holding it up to Elisha's face, Ruari tapped the seal. "King's seal, that is."

About to shrug, Elisha stopped himself in time. "I'm a bit thick, yet, Ruari; if the king's given this man a letter, how's that our business?"

"But has he given it to him, or has the lad come by it another way?"

"What name is on it?"

Ruari snorted. "And how should I know that any better than you?"

"Sorry. I'm not quite here yet."

"Aye, and who could expect it otherwise." Ruari's shoulders sagged and he tapped the letter against his other palm.

"Don't suppose that woman Brigit is about?"

"Ye sound as if she's naught to you," Ruari teased, trying to coax a smile that Elisha was not ready for, not yet.

"She reads, and she knows more about the lords than either of us."

Ruari brightened. "She did come round, looking for ye, before ye got back, I mean."

"Why don't you trot off and tell her I'm found."

He sprang up, but glanced to the windows. "It's a bit late, don't ye think?"

Clarity dawned faster yet in Elisha's mind, and he answered, "I think that thing in your hand could be worth our lives, Ruari. And if I'm wrong—"

"On your head be it," Ruari completed. "How much can be on your head afore it touches the ground?"

"This head? Not on your life. Get on, will you?"

Tip-toeing between the sleeping or muttering men, Ruari vanished up the stairs toward the room Brigit had taken. Elisha reached a tentative hand toward the welt across his throat. By now, she must have heard what had happened. If he avoided turning his back to her, she might not find out how bad it was. Elisha laughed without sound. And if he could sit still as stone and avoid breathing, and if the mere sight of his face didn't give him away.

Moments later, he heard stealthy treads upon the stair. He gathered the blanket someone had draped over his legs and winced as he wrapped his shoulders. Whatever the ointment had been, the stuff soothed him more than he would have expected, and he determined to find out the recipe. First, though, he must find out who had sent it, for surely it had not been Matthew's idea.

Shielding a candle, Brigit led the way, picking her steps carefully between the men. She settled beside him, drawing her long robe together over her chemise. Her brows pinched together as she studied his face. "I've heard they beat you today, for disobedience."

"Aye, that's true. It's not so bad though." In fact, the sight of her face lifted his spirits through the gloom of his pain.

"Twenty-seven lashes is no small matter."

Elisha goggled and covered his mouth with a hand, but his shock was all too plain, as was Ruari's as he hovered behind her.

Ruari crouched down, aiming a furious look at Elisha. "Ye didn't say it was as much as that! Most get by with ten, maybe twelve or fifteen for hard cases."

Tilting his head to an upraised shoulder, Elisha approximated a shrug.

"Ye're an idiot, Elisha Barber," Ruari huffed. "And t'think I let ye go back for him."

Calmly, Brigit set down her candle and sat back on her heels. "When you did not come, I simply thought something here had kept you back. Or that you had changed your mind about consulting me." Her face softened in the glow. "I'm glad at least you had Ruari here to watch over you."

Ruari snorted. "Much good I did him, letting him go off—"

"How about the letter, then?" Elisha cut in.

"Aye, the letter, the letter." Ruari waved a hand toward Brigit and turned away, still simmering.

"It's to the Lord of Burston Cross—he owns the land adjoining Dunbury—and it has the look of an official message," Brigit replied promptly. "Where's this man you took it from? Perhaps there's an explanation."

Despite Ruari's black look, Elisha rose carefully, holding the blanket over his aching shoulders, and the three went to where the fallen foot soldier lay. Swaddled in blankets, he looked even younger, and Ruari knelt to check his pulse and brush the straggling hair from his face.

Brigit gasped, the candle shuddering in her grip.

"What is it?"

Shutting her eyes, she shook her head. "I thought I knew him, that's all. How is he?"

"Should be fine, just a bit weak with the lost blood." Trying not to sway, Elisha knelt down as well and laid a hand on the young man's cheek. He felt warm enough now and stirred beneath the gentle pressure. He did look familiar, now that Elisha considered him more closely.

Then, like a shot, the young man sat bolt upright, sucking in a breath, his hand clamped to his throat. He stared at Brigit, whose eyes opened wide to meet the stunned blue gaze. Recovering himself somewhat, he swept the room, his eyes settling on Elisha, with a grin as sudden as his awakening. "You came back." Then he stiffened again, touching his arms. Twisting where he sat, he searched the ground around him, his hands ever more frantic.

Again, Elisha touched him, stilling the panic. "Here's your letter." He held up a hand to receive it from Brigit's trembling fingers. "What's this about?"

"Oh, God," he sighed, snatching it back. "But the seal's broken!"

"When ye fell," Ruari supplied. "None's read it, just noted the king's seal, there."

"Yes—king's business, and I'm so late already." He shoved away the blankets and scrambled to his feet.

"You're not strong enough to travel," Elisha protested, though his own body refused to rise.

"Listen, I'm a royal messenger—the only one he trusts. I had this from the king's hand hours ago, and should have had it off by now. I can't think why he's not looked for me." He frowned, taking up his jacket from the place Ruari had set it aside.

"Look around you," Elisha said dryly.

"Were it not for the barber, ye'd still be on the battlefield," Ruari said.

At this, the young man hesitated, then crouched down. "Were it not for him, I'd be dead. Again." He flashed that grin, and the voice suddenly called up the memory, this young man, huddled in the darkness, avoiding a witch hunt.

Elisha reached up and brushed aside the blond hair. Faintly, the mark of his own fist could still be seen, with the traces of the other blows that had come before. "I thought I told you to take more care."

"Wasted advice on such as me," the messenger replied. "I'll tell you all, but another time. Thanks. I am in your debt." Briefly, he gripped Elisha's shoulder, turning away before he could see the spasm of pain that crossed the barber's face.

Pulling her robe close about her throat, Brigit announced, "I've got a horse, messenger. I'll happily loan it to you, if you've got none."

Blinking back at her, he nodded once. "Very well, but be quick about it."

Brigit hurried down the aisle with the young man at

her heels, and the two vanished through the yard into the night.

Sitting where they'd left him, Elisha waited for the renewed throbbing to subside.

Ruari scooted over beside him. "So what's that about, then?"

"I've no idea." But as he considered, a chill crept inside Elisha's heart. She had no horse—she'd come on Malcolm's wagon. He had not yet asked Brigit about the night of the fire, when her own little blaze distracted the men who held an accused witch long enough for the witch to get away. Could it be coincidence, the accused and the lady having both been there that night? "On second thought, I believe we've met Brigit's intended."

"What, him? Is he not beneath her station, then? I'm given to think she's local royalty, if ye get my meaning."

Elisha nodded. "I get it. And her—why not acknowledge him? It's not as if you and me are likely to tell her father."

At this, Ruari gave him an appraising once-over. "Unless she's come to reconsider. Just like a lady to change her mind at the sight of something better."

"God, Ruari, don't even think it," he protested, even as he wished it could be true.

"But ye're a fine sight of a man, as I 'spect ye know. And in a good line of work."

"Barbering is not quite a respected trade, or hadn't you noticed?" Elisha looked down at his hands, flipping the blanket off his shoulders. A few fibers stuck, and he winced.

Watching him, Ruari puffed out a breath. "Twenty-seven lashes, Elisha. Ye're not of this earth, are ye?"

"Sometimes I'm not sure."

"Ye picked the right man to save, and that's a fact. We should've kept him a wee bit longer—imagine the look on that doctor's face to see he's lashed ye for saving the king's own messenger."

Bowing his head, Elisha rubbed his aching temples. "So that's what my blood bought," he mumbled to himself, "a royal messenger, Brigit's betrothed." He should be proud, he should be the first to hold it up to Lucius and crow, but in his exhausted state, it was hard to muster any feeling one way or the other.

"Lie down," Ruari urged him. "Get some rest."

Sighing, Elisha pulled himself to his feet. "Now don't look that way. I'm just going to lie in the courtyard. The cool grass'll do me good."

Gruffly, Ruari said, "Ye're the barber." Then he, too, rose, shaking a finger at Elisha. "Mind, I'll be watching. If I see ye step foot beyond the gate, I'm right after ye like a dog on a hare."

This did win him a smile, slender though it was. Elisha made his careful way up and into the moonlit yard. He let himself down beside the stream, cupping his hands in the water for a long drink, letting the water run down his chest. He lay on his side, his fingers trailing in the water. At first, all was silent, then he heard a lone voice offer the requisite greeting, *"Who's there?"*

"Bittersweet," Elisha answered, his lips murmuring the word, never more true than at this moment.

"Sage," the other replied.

The stream babbled to itself for a long time.

"Why've you come?" Sage asked at last.

"I don't know."

After another pause, *"You are not long a magus, are you?"*

Elisha sighed. *"I am not one at all, to tell the truth."*

"I should go to the air, with that remark."

"*No,*" Elisha said, the thought frightening him some-how. "*No,*" he said more carefully, "*I mean no harm.*"

"*Rather the reverse.*"

"*What?*"

"*It's you who has been harmed. There is such pain in you even the river feels it.*"

"*And you feel it.*"

"*Hard to miss.*"

"*I'm sorry, I should—*"

"*No,*" Sage answered swiftly, "*no, you should not. You sought comfort in the river, only your misfortune to find me here, not some other one.*"

"*No matter,*" Elisha whispered. "*Strangers all.*"

"*If Marigold held sway here, we would be meeting in the church, and wearing badges, so as not to be missed.*" Another pause. "*You're the one she sought, aren't you?*"

"*I suppose I am, not that I know what it means.*"

"*You should know she's not the only one. Most of us sat by fires that day, to listen. Fire-speech is difficult, but we hoped Rowena might manage it. They say—*"

Elisha waited, but Sage remained silent. "*My igno-rance is complete,*" Elisha told him. "*I can't even read.*"

"*No shame in that,*" Sage replied. "*They say a magus has the most power at the moment of his, or her, death. In that moment, great things might be done, such as the transformation Rowena wrought upon herself. Trans-formation is hard to work on a creature of will, even oneself. What she gave us, in that moment, were those words, like a prophecy, and the sense of the touch.*"

Elisha knew immediately what touch he meant. Strange that a moment he had held so private these twenty years turned out to have been shared with how many others, he might never know.

"*To send something so delicate as that touch, I can-not imagine it,*" Sage said.

This time, the hesitation was on Elisha's part. He steeled himself to speak, reminding himself that this was a stranger, a man he might well never know face to face. *"Could any magus feel my pain through the water?"*

"Not any, no. Each has his talents, and his sensitivities. You'll learn, in time, both your own, and other people's."

"I'm scared," Elisha admitted.

"You'd be a fool if you weren't." He let the water ripple between them for a time. *"Myself, I was awakened at the age of twelve, crossing a desert with my family. We bent to drink at a well, and I suddenly felt that my mother was with child. I said as much to her, but she only claimed it was the heat."*

In the encampment, a flute played a lively tune and as suddenly was silenced by frustrated sleepers.

"Were you right?"

"Six months later, she died in childbirth."

"My God, I'm sorry."

"You claim ignorance, Bittersweet. You'll also learn that knowledge is rarely enough. A man can think he knows all, and yet not know what he most needs."

"Aye," said Elisha, *"you are Sage indeed."*

"Not enough," the stream replied, *"and not often. Each of us can only soldier on in his own battle, until he falls beneath the enemy and does not rise again."*

Elisha thought of the angel's touch, and how it had enflamed something within him, burning through to this day and to all that he had done. It was the beacon that led Brigit to find him, as well as the inspiration that made him a healer. He smiled to the darkness and added, *"Or rises in a way that even he cannot foresee."*

Chapter 18

❧ lisha awoke with the dawn, stiff and sore, the welts stinging with dew. Dragging himself up, he walked back to his own room, not surprised that Ruari wasn't there. No doubt the man had spent the night in the hospital, the better to keep an eye on him. He sorted his lightest shirt from the chest, then hesitated. Beneath the layers of instruments and packets of herbs, he could make out the lid of the pot he had carried with him, the relic of that terrible day, patiently waiting his attention. If only he could consult the physician's books or even the surgeon's, he might find the truth about the Bone of Luz without endangering any life but his own. As it stood, though, the magi were his best hope.

He slipped Helena's letter from his pouch and studied it, her bitter words echoing in his head. The worst was, she was right: He was a coward, at least where she was concerned. His apologies had come to naught, along with his efforts to save her. Oh, he had prevented her death, true enough, but now the specters of her husband and child haunted her, the ruin of her family and dreams weighed in every word she had written. Some things could not be forgotten. Or forgiven.

He stuffed the letter down behind the pot and covered both. Next, he pulled off his boots and rearranged the padding inside. They should be re-lined, if he had a chance, though that chance seemed unlikely to come any day soon.

His stomach rumbled, and he realized how long it had been since he'd eaten anything. Pulling his boots back on, he reached for the shirt, dropping it over his head without thought and gasping as it seemed to catch on every one of the twenty-seven blows. When the fire in his skin had died down, Elisha stood and returned to the hospital. Avoiding the lords' infirmary this time, he came in at the back and stood a moment surveying the sleeping men.

A few whimpered or moaned, but most lay quiet, and one or two even had the strength to snore. Many empty spaces gaped between them, and he frowned over that, making a note to ask Ruari what had happened in his absence. For now, though, he remembered the city hospital, with its beds crowded with screamers and corpses, the whole place reeking of sickness. This place was surely none too fresh, but the women kept it swept and mopped as best they could and lay down new straw mingled with woodruff to mask the scents. Having the water barrel made a world of difference, and he wondered how the idea might be applied in a larger hospital.

One of the men gave a sharp cry, and Elisha went swiftly to his side. He had a broken leg not yet set, and he had rolled too far in that direction. Looking into the worried eyes, Elisha smiled. "You're all right. We'll get you taken care of first thing."

"You're back," the man croaked, and Elisha gave a short laugh at the unintended pun.

"Where else should I be?"

The man whimpered again, sweat standing out on his forehead despite the chill. Elisha pulled out his little vial of opium and tilted the man's head back to swallow a pinch. "That should take away the pain while we straighten you out."

He made brief visits to any of the others who lay awake, then went up to the courtyard to pull his gate and refill the barrel. This done, he carried water to the patients, topping off a few pitchers spaced at intervals around the room. Once, those pitchers marked who would live, and the wall had shown who would die.

From a place by the barrel, close beneath the windows, Ruari stirred and stretched. Rubbing his head, he pushed himself up, his eyes widening, then glaring at Elisha. "Ye should be sleeping, yet."

"Not likely," Elisha returned, "Not the way I'm feeling. I'm surprised I got as much as I did." Coming nearer, he dropped his voice. "Look, where've all our patients gone? Please tell me we didn't lose so many."

At this, Ruari grinned. "Indeed, no, Elisha, they've gone home."

"Home? How is that possible?"

"Well, and we were running short of space already, so any who were able climbed on board the wagons back to town and off wherever. A few were judged well enough to return to the lines."

Brushing at his eyes, Elisha tried to blink away sudden tears. He thought again of the king's messenger. The duty of a single man could win the war, and Elisha's hands could hold sway over that man's life. Sage's words, too, echoed in his mind with this conviction. When he chose to become a barber, Elisha knew that many would disdain him, that he condemned himself to a life of ruined shirts and blood beneath his nails. He did not need respect or company or even love to fight this battle of his.

"Are ye well?" Ruari asked gently.

Elisha smiled. "Aye, that I am. That physician has

taught me something I needed to know. I should thank him."

"Tell me yer joking!"

"Am I? Come on, we've got work to do."

Together, they pulled and twisted the broken leg back into place, and Elisha spent a tedious time crouched on the floor, making sure there were no splinters, and tending the torn muscles and skin.

Straightening out the ache in his back, Elisha winced as Benedict came through the door, no doubt on his way to the kitchen for his pot of boiling oil.

With a regal air, Benedict surveyed the remaining men, examining them as he approached. "It appears you've lost a few, Barber," he remarked.

"Aye—lost them to their wives and children." He longed to stand and stretch out his legs, but didn't want to betray any pain before this lordling.

"I don't understand you." Benedict frowned, but his eyes kept roving over the wounded soldiers.

"They went home."

This brought the assistant's attention back to Elisha, and the barber laughed at the consternation on the long face. Shaking himself, Benedict strode on toward the kitchen. "I'll be taking over with the cure. Lucius wants to be sure it's done by a man he can trust. Oh, and I think Matthew will be along for the cauterization."

"Excellent, I'll fetch some wool to plug my ears."

At the door, Benedict turned back, still wearing that frown. "I fail to see how you can laugh after the events of yesterday."

"I'm a peasant, sir, it's not in my nature to brood, or I'd be brooding all my life."

"Ah. I see your point." He gave a tight smile. "In that case, laugh on, Barber, your lot is unlikely to improve any day soon." Benedict disappeared through the door.

Just as he had predicted, Matthew shortly entered, walking quickly, his jaw locked like a vise as he ignored the barber and shut the kitchen door behind him.

Ruari and Elisha shared a look. "It appears I'm on the outs with everyone this morning."

"Only the high born," Ruari pointed out. "Ye're practically a legend among the rest."

They busied themselves with a few more broken bones, interrupted once more when Lisbet appeared, holding up her apron like a little girl, her face aglow. Maeve looked up from the patient she was dressing and said, "It's about time, now."

With only a brief look to her mother, Lisbet crossed over to Elisha. "See what I've brought you!" She knelt down with extreme caution. Held in her gathered apron lay a half-dozen eggs. "I remembered you asking, and I found these out walking this morning."

"She means that *she* was walking, not the eggs," Ruari teased, and Lisbet cast him a mock-angry pout.

"Lisbet, you're a wonder!" Elisha crowed. They were few, but large, and they gave him an idea. He rose unsteadily to his feet, waving away Ruari's offered hand. "I'll get us a pot."

Beaming, Lisbet stepped out of the way.

In the kitchen, a charged silence hung in the air as both assistants jerked up when he entered. It seemed he'd come in on an argument. Immediately, they returned to their separate labors, and Matthew barked, "I'm ready for the first, if you'll bring him in. I'll be doing the amputees as well."

"Aye, sir." The thought turned Elisha's stomach and seemed to throb through every stinging lash. Quickly he snatched a pot from the wall and left the room. As he lifted the eggs from Lisbet's apron, he said over his shoulder, "Ruari, I hate to ask it of you," then broke off and sighed, bowing his head over the pot.

Holding her skirt up a bit longer, affording a view of her strong legs, Lisbet fidgeted, then dropped it.

"What's the question?" Ruari asked lightly, but his face went solemn.

Still, Elisha hesitated, and Lisbet retreated to join her mother, hiding her face.

"It's the cauteries. Matthew says he's ready, but I—" He rubbed a bit of dirt from one of the speckled eggs. "Oh, God, Ruari."

"Ye're not up to it, are ye, then?" Ruari ruffled his hand through his hair. "Sweet Lord, Elisha, course ye're not. Go on, I'll handle it."

Relief cleared the ache in his throat. If that made him a coward, so be it. "What would I do without you?"

Snorting, Ruari replied, "Ye'd have to pray to find me, that's what. Go on. I'll spin a yarn to Matthew that ye've got more important things to do. And won't it be true in any case." He got up and brushed off his britches before finding the first man to undergo the hot irons.

Taking his pot of eggs beneath his arm, Elisha hurried through the infirmary before he could regret his cowardice. The drapes were gone around the corner where the king had rested, and all seemed at peace there. Mordecai raised his eyebrows at Elisha's passage, but kept his head bent over an enormous book spread upon his lap.

In the vestry, Elisha gathered the ingredients for his ointment, then made a packet of flaxseed as well, dropping them all in the pot of eggs and nodding to the attendant as he made his escape. Crossing the courtyard, he saw Lucius and his younger assistant seated on sunny

benches, with Brigit before them. The stylus in her hand
sketched quickly over a waxed board, illustrating some
herb she was describing. For an instant, her eyes flicked
up then back, and there was no break in her voice as he
passed by.

Finding a place by the river, Elisha emptied the pot
onto a flat, table-like stone. He cracked and separated
all but one egg, holding it in reserve. They made little
ointment, but it might ease a few hurts. Again, he wondered about the salve he had been given. There was
nothing like it in the vestry supplies, nor would he expect to find it there, for the ingredients were almost
certainly too rich to hazard in open stores. The mixing
done, he rolled his shoulders, plucking at the cloth of
his shirt to try to prevent it sticking more than it already had. The welts hurt with every movement, but he
did his best to pretend otherwise, and was, on the
whole, successful in his self-deception. The heat of the
springtime sun tingled on the welt across his throat,
and he was about to go back inside, despite the screams
from cauterization that he could hear faintly, behind
him, when Brigit crossed over the bridge.

Taking no notice of him, she tucked a basket handle
over her arm and walked down to the river. Once there,
she slipped off her shoes and waded in from the shore.
Carefully, she dug her fingers into the riverbed, bringing up a plant by its roots, and let the dirt be washed
away.

Elisha took up his egg and the one packet he had not
opened, casually strolling to the shade beneath the
bridge. Here, he sat on a stone and kicked off his own
boots, placing his feet with the water lapping at his toes.

"Hello, Bittersweet. I trust you slept well?"

"Aye, that I did. Better than expected, really. And
you?"

"No, not well. The pain of others is never easy to bear, especially if they themselves will bear it in silence."

"I take that for reproach, Marigold. Was it you who sent me the salve?"

Upstream, she paused, then bent for another root. *"Not I. What do you mean?"*

"Someone sent a salve, rich stuff, better than any I've had care over."

"Why not ask the bearer?"

"It was Matthew."

"Oh." Brigit continued up until a stand of willows blocked her from view. *"Why does Matthew hate you so?"*

"He wants his master's praise and the physician's notice. Lately, I'm a distraction to them both."

"Professional jealousy, most likely."

"Of a barber?"

"A very skilled barber, by all accounts."

Elisha's laughter echoed beneath the bridge. *"By whose account?"*

"Well, the soldiers at any rate. I'm afraid I have no skill at healing magic, or I should do something for you." She paused. *"Did you bring me here simply to pass the time of day?"*

"Bring you?"

"Didn't you want me to follow?"

Elisha had to admit this was true. *"I had a thought, about what you told me yesterday. How like things have affinity. Do you think a seed could be turned to an egg?"*

The river brought him only cold for a long while, then she said, *"Why, Bittersweet, I think you have hit on an idea. I don't know that it's been done, at least, I've not done it, but you're right. It may be difficult though, since one is of earth, and the other is air."*

"But a stone is of earth and a fish is of water."

"Still, that's a difference of only one degree. There's a natural order to the elements: earth, water, air, fire. Think of trying to turn water to fire. Water to air, or air to fire—one degree each—is not so tricky, but to change water directly to fire would be two, a step beyond in the hierarchy."

Elisha nodded to himself, cupping his hand around the egg. Then her comparison reminded him of something. *"That night I threw my cloak over you. How did you come to catch fire?"*

"That chapel burned because of two boys with a candle, afraid to come forward, even when an innocent man was caught and accused. If I spoke in his defense, I couldn't reveal how I knew the truth. At best, I'd be ignored, at worst, I'd stand accused myself. So I made a diversion, and hoped he could handle the rest."

"You lit your own hair on fire." Elisha stared at the bend where she had vanished, and caught sight of her slim figure picking her way among the plants.

"It worked, though there was a moment I thought no one would come put me out, and to douse my own flames would reveal all that I wanted to hide. If you'd not come along . . ."

Elisha squinted, wishing he could make out her face. *"The messenger last night was that same man."*

"He told me, and that you hit him in order to save his life. Truly, you must have been sent to defend us that night." She mused a little longer, then said, *"But you asked about affinity. Find a place where the power is close to the surface—the ancient holy places are best, but the church here is one such. Bring a talisman. Do you have a talisman?"*

"That's a magic charm?"

From the ripples in the water, he could tell that she was laughing. The longer he spoke this way, the more he seemed to understand it, to find the nuances of ordinary conversation, and sometimes an undertone of emotion, not easy to see when you spoke face to face. Especially when the face was as lovely as Brigit's.

"*It isn't magic in itself, but in what it means to you. It's something you hold very dear, a repository of power outside yourself that you can draw on. The longer you've had it, the better. Or if it's associated with strong emotions—a birth or a death, for instance.*"

Or both, Elisha thought grimly. "*I have something like that, yes.*"

Brigit hesitated in her answer, as if some of his emotion had flowed along with the water. "*So, take it with you. Keep the egg and the seed. Begin with the doctrine of Knowledge: For the spell to work, you have to understand both the thing to be transformed, and the thing which you desire. It's difficult to explain. Think of all you know about them, and how they are alike. Imagine the one becoming the other. Try the egg to the seed first, it's easier to descend the hierarchy.*"

Mystified, Elisha studied the egg in his hand. "*Is that all?*"

Laughter and a school of tiny fishes swam the river around him. "*All? When you try, I think you'll see. There is little of technique in this, and much of attunement. It may take you months.*"

"*I haven't got months,*" he protested. "*I need eggs.*"

"*Then you should buy yourself a chicken, Bittersweet!*" Her hair flashed red in the sunlight, and he felt her laughter all around him, a joyous breeze, cooling the sting of his wounds and rippling through his hair.

Elisha shut his eyes and breathed her in, her laughter filling up his soul.

Chapter 19

✦

"**B**rigit!" a voice called suddenly. "Where have you got to, my lady? I thought you needed only a moment."

Peeking out from the shadow of the bridge, Elisha saw Lucius descending the bank, his elaborate robe lifted as delicately as a lady might carry her gown. He ducked back again, but the physician turned, scowling, and Elisha could not be sure if he'd been spotted.

"Here I am, sir—and I've found the roots I wished to show you." Brigit trotted up along the bank, holding out her basket.

Still scowling, he said, "It was not necessary that you should come out just now."

"Sorry, sir." She gave him a glowing smile. "I do tend to get carried away. But look, can you see how the root divides?"

With a glance to the gathered plants, Lucius put an arm about her shoulders. "Come, I have many more questions better discussed over supper. You will, of course, join us."

"Certainly, if you serve again such a feast as we had last night. Since the battle began, we've had little commerce here for spices and the like. Still, I'd best wash first. This root can be deadly if you handle it wrong."

The grin on Lucius's face revolted Elisha as he
watched them go off side by side. He emerged from his
hiding place and walked over to where he'd left his ointment to cool in an eddy of the river. As he retrieved it, he
noticed the assistant Benedict standing not far off, his
face impassive as he watched. With a precise movement,
he turned and followed his master back into the monastery.

What could they have seen? Nothing—Brigit splashing in the stream, himself resting in the shade; they had
even come from opposite directions. And they could
not be overheard, at least not by such men. Brigit tu-
tored him in forbidden arts beneath their very noses,
and they had not the slightest suspicion.

Elisha allowed himself a grin of his own as he
mounted the bank and returned to the hospital. The
screams of cauterization had died away, but it was not
hard to find the men who had suffered it and apply his
ointment. His own pain flared again to life, now that he
did not have Brigit's distracting presence. Perhaps he
could presume upon her charity and claim she must
stay by him, to let him heal. He tried to sharpen all of
his tools, but the welts protested his steady movement,
and instead he taught Ruari how to do it; a skill that
came easily to his woodworker's experience.

When another day was finally done, Elisha bid his
assistants good night and returned quickly to his room,
removing the packets that hid the sealed pot. In an instant, his optimism drained away. What right had he to
feel joy or hope after what he had done? Although he
worked hard in the hospital every day, and men went
home to their families who might have been buried in
the yard if not for him, it was not enough. Still, he had
carried out his plan thus far and owed it to his brother's
memory to try.

Elisha draped the sealed pot with a cloth to bear it away with him. This was the start of his magical learning. If he learned well, he might one day restore what his arrogance had destroyed. Walking into the ruined church, Elisha sat beneath the altar with the pot before him, a single flaxseed in one hand, the egg in the other.

The seed winked brown in the moonlight reflecting from its slick surface. Given time and tending, it could grow to a long grass, to be cut, soaked, beaten, and slowly transformed into linen for spinning—an almost magical transition in itself. He dredged up all he knew of flax, its growth period and its medicinal properties, and the way the stiff grasses felt beneath an outstretched palm. As he studied the tiny seed, a sense of awe filled him, that this little thing had so much potential. He had never before considered the miracle of it, nor its place in a cycle that supported generations of farmers like his father, and the spinners and weavers and vestiers of many a town. Such a simple thing, this little seed, or so he had thought. Was this the Doctrine of Knowledge Brigit spoke of? Still and all, no matter how wondrous the process of seed into clothing, he couldn't see what that had to do with magic.

With a sigh, he turned to the egg and shook his head. Speckled and beige, the egg lay in his palm like a cipher. He had no idea what sort of egg it was and knew not the first thing about where it was found or how the thick liquid inside might become a bird. Brigit had mentioned something called "attunement," but the physician interrupted before she could explain.

He sat on the hard, damp earth with a thing he knew intimately, and one he could not begin to understand. Brigit spoke as if he were something special, an undiscovered talent in this murky realm of the magi, and yet he could not pretend to understand a simple egg. It might take months, she had told him, and he leaned his head back to study the stars. How could he accomplish even the simplest spell if he must research every little ordinary thing, never mind work such magic as it would require to draw the dead again to life?

Popping the flaxseed into his mouth, Elisha crunched it and swallowed. The egg he set aside. For magic, it might serve him little, but for medicine it had some use.

Before him in the grass sat the accusing metal pot, the pale wax of its seal preventing any hint of its contents from escaping into the night air. He lifted it in both hands, feeling the scant weight of its terrible secret. Such a thing should weigh more. It should be borne down beneath the crush of the sorrow it embodied, not simply for its own sake but also for that of the mother recovering from the full trial of childbirth, but without the joy of the child. And still more so for Nathaniel, believing he had betrayed that joy and willing to go to Hell rather than live with his betrayal. Elisha considered Heaven, that reward his brother strove for—would God and his angels be fooled by Elisha's deceit? Would Nathaniel stand before them and freely confess his own guilt, only to be cast below? Or was it all a farce, as Elisha had long believed—a tale told by churchmen eager to lure the faithful to their own service and betterment? For why should God exact such punishment from those most in need of Him? Elisha's own angel was shot at the behest of the churchmen—a sign, or so he had long believed, that the church itself no longer knew the Lord. Now he knew the angel was no angel, but she seemed no less miraculous.

"Have you decided to purchase a chicken?" asked Brigit's voice, startling Elisha so that he fumbled the pot and saved it by clutching it against his chest.

He rounded on her with a glare. "What do you mean by sneaking up like that?"

"Attunement," she replied simply. "It means sensing all that goes on around you. The finest magi can cast their awareness even beyond walls, perhaps beyond the skin of those around them. For now, you ought at least to begin by knowing your place."

"The physician beat me for that very fault."

With a cool smile, Brigit came toward him. She wore again that long robe of the night before, tied at her waist with a dangling cord. "I think you know that's not what I meant."

Elisha shied away from her eyes, which seemed to radiate a light of their own. "Sorry. It's a sore point for me."

"So I see. That's understandable." She maintained that seductive pace until she came up before him. "How is your egg?"

"I've no idea. That's the trouble." He replaced the pot in the grass, close by him, and held the egg between thumb and forefinger. "I know nothing about it. Here I've lived with eggs all my life and never really saw one before now."

Drawing her robe around her, Brigit settled on the ground with the grace of a princess. "And the seed?"

Tossing the egg in the air and catching it lightly again, Elisha said, "I ate it."

Brigit let out a peal of laughter. "Oh, what is the matter with you?"

"Nothing at all," he snapped. "I've got plenty more seeds where that came from. The seed is not a problem."

"Oh." Her lips compressed as she regarded him. "I think I am beginning to see what the problem is." Her gaze never wavered.

Staring back, Elisha asked, "What's that?"

With a quick gesture, she reached out and tapped the center of his chest. Elisha jerked back as if she had struck him. "You," she said bluntly. "There is so much potential in you, and yet you yourself will thwart it. Why?"

"Don't be ridiculous; I'm not getting in my own way. I've been working on the accursed thing for hours now. Maybe it's the talisman." Once the word was out, he could not retrieve it and slipped a protective hand over the pot.

"I was coming to that," Brigit said, her tone more soothing now, and curious. "What's in there?"

Elisha shrugged, sending twinges of pain all down his spine. "Something that met your description, something associated with a powerful moment. Perhaps it's not strong enough."

Brigit's mouth actually dropped open, her breath whooshing out. "Not strong enough?"

Studying her, Elisha felt suddenly wary. "I've said something wrong, haven't I?"

"Not strong enough," she repeated faintly, shaking herself, again she reached out to touch him, but he drew back instinctively, and her hand hovered in the air, a spectral form in the moonlight. "You can't feel it."

Feel what, he wanted to say, but he knew enough to hold his tongue this time.

The silence stretched between them, her eyes tracing the shape of his face, the set of his shoulders, returning over and over to that place on his cheek—the inner mark of the angel's touch.

Finally she said, "That thing you have, that thing you don't wish to show me, Elisha, I can feel it from here. It woke me in my room, and the power of it drew me on. How is it possible you can hold it in your hands and not feel it?"

Tapping a finger on the lid, he watched her stunned face. "I told you I am no witch. I should think this clinches it, if it's as powerful as you say." As he spoke, a secret hope ebbed away within him, but a spreading relief took its place. Perhaps, in spite of his speaking through the water, he could not truly make magic, could never perform the feat he had been planning, and must let go of his brother's memory, but at least he would not live in the shadow world of witches, with fire waiting at every turn.

"But my mother spoke of you, I'm sure she did: a medical man with death in his hands. You were there, she touched you so that we would know you." Brigit shook her head fiercely, her trimmed hair bobbing about her shoulders. Then she looked up at him again, her eyes gleaming. "It's clear you have no wish to share this talisman with me, but let me show you how it feels. Perhaps the trouble is that you do not understand what it is yourself."

Worry marked her face and eagerness as well—she did not want to let go of him, not without a fight, and the idea made him tremble. "Show me," he breathed.

"Take my hand and shut your eyes. It may take a moment to make contact this way."

Contact? He was about to ask, when the warmth of her hand grew hot within his grasp, and he could see her face—or, not her face, but herself, strong, beautiful, daring. At that same moment, the lid of the pot turned cold, so cold his skin fused to the metal. Elisha tried to peel back his fingers, but they would not obey him. His heart beat a little faster.

Cold crept up his hand, suffusing his wrist and arm, until he began to shiver. His breath came in short puffs as the cold insinuated itself throughout his chest, reaching down into his legs and feet, crawling up his spine.

The welts on his back tingled and burned until the pain of them took even the misty breath from his frozen lips.

His head jerked backward, his throat constricting and going rigid. He screamed but there was no sound, or else his ears, too, had shriveled on his head.

His eyes iced over, first with the delicate ferns of frost, then deeper and deeper until the cold stung through into his skull.

Panic welled up in him. His wild heart struggled to keep its pace. His memories froze, his thoughts stilled and crumbled until only fear remained. A black and all-consuming terror howled through him. It scoured the agony from his skin and swept the blood from his heart.

Still hot, his left hand twisted and fought. His fingers tore at the skin which held him. All the strength of his body wrenched at her grasp. The tempest of horror blasted into his fingers, ripping at the other hand in a final attempt to be free.

The grip exploded, throwing Elisha to the ground, his body convulsed with fear, the scream tearing from his throat. The scream echoed through emptiness. He slammed onto his back, and the lashes carved into his flesh all over again as he writhed against the chill.

But pain grounded him. It snatched him back from the awful cold, flinging him into his body with terrible force. His head smacked the stone altar, and he lurched back onto his side, knees curled toward his chest. Sobbing, he fought for breath. He shuddered with the effort. His fingers clenched into talons, ripping at the grass.

Heat hovered near his forehead, slowly seeping in as his breathing finally settled into a rhythm. The heat took the shape of fingers, a light touch at his brow, smoothing back the hair which had sprung free to tan-

gle across his face. The racking sobs died back as well,
his heartbeat slipping back from his ears and throat,
back to his chest to calm itself more slowly.

"What," he croaked, coughing, "what the hell did
you do to me?" The words came out in a gasp, warring
with breath.

"I'm sorry, oh, Elisha, I am so sorry. I thought to
keep it under control. I thought I could guide you
through, to give you a glimpse only."

The door behind slammed open. "Who's there?"

Elisha shook, biting his lip.

"Only me," Brigit called out, her voice undisturbed.
"Sorry about the noise, I stumbled in the darkness."

"I'll fetch you a light," the speaker said gruffly, but
Brigit called out, "Oh, no. I'm searching for night-
glowing mushrooms, any light would spoil it." She
chuckled. "Foolish of me, I suppose."

"Are you all right?"

"Fine," she said. "Just took a fright, that's all." She
stood up and faced the door, waving a hand to prove it
was true. The warmth withdrew from Elisha, and he
feared the return of that cold.

"Very well. Be more careful."

"I will. Sorry to have bothered you."

The door thumped shut again behind the muttering
guard.

When he was able to take a deep breath, Elisha felt
the last of the shivers subside, and he managed to sit
up. Something sticky dampened his knee and he discovered the remains of his egg.

Assured that the guard was gone, Brigit dropped
down again beside him, her face a picture of concern.
"Are you all right?"

"God's Wounds, of course not!"

She flinched, and he almost regretted his harshness

but instead gritted his teeth. She could at least have warned him, given him some idea of what he would feel.

"My God, I'm lucky to be alive after all that." He shot her a furious look. "You seem just fine. What happened to me?"

A smile played about her lips. "That was the force of the talisman you thought might be too weak. What do you think now?"

"Can't you speak plainly for once?" Elisha rubbed his hands together, hoping to gain some warmth by the friction.

Inclining her head, Brigit said, "I can't tell you what you felt, for I did not feel it all. That talisman—whatever it is—is very powerful indeed. It's death in a bottle, Elisha, it's like having demons corked up ready to spring free upon the world. It's what we call a Universal, a talisman with enough innate power to be used by any magus, rather than an object of solely personal significance. I felt it, that's true, but not so strongly as you. For you, it is personal. If you can control that power"—she blew out a breath, the light dancing in her eyes—"there is little you could not do."

"If."

"Yes, Elisha, *if*. If you can overcome your terror and learn to use it."

"How can I use a thing I can't even touch? I cannot master that."

Brigit regarded him with a gentle smile. She reached out and stroked one finger down the back of his arm, bringing it to rest upon his hand. "Oh, no? That talisman is death, Elisha. But every day, you hold the possibility of death in your very hands. This is what my mother was talking about, why she wanted me to find you. You defend the border of life and death, and your choice at any moment might tip the balance. If anyone could call upon that power, it would be you. But it is still death; of course you are afraid."

Keeping still so as not to disturb her touch, he said, "You weren't. You said it called you here."

"For me, it is not personal. I fear death, I think everyone does. But I also accept that, for all of my skill, I have no power over it. Once in a while, I am reminded that I will die, and maybe soon, but it does not enter my life so very often. For you, it's unrelenting. You fight death every minute of every day, with your bare hands, and your open heart."

At this, he found her expression transformed from worry to wonder, her body leaning toward him, her breath held to hear what he would say. Elisha turned his hand and caught her fingers, drawing her into his arms. He tipped back her head, feeling the sweep of her hair as he kissed her.

Contact.

A heat as brilliant as the ice had been swept through him, until his body burned with the want of her. The kiss turned frantic, a search for the source of the fire. His lips pressed against hers, his tongue stroking them open. Her breath scorched his throat, and he drank her in to quench his thirst.

With a cry, she wrapped her arms around him, her hands strangely light and comforting upon his wounded shoulders. Their bodies arched together, desperate to share every inch of skin.

His hand cupped the back of her head, then smoothed down her neck, his fingers slipping beneath the lace at her throat. She felt so pure and the roughness of his battered hand pricked upon the silk.

Elisha rose to his knees, drawing her ever closer, the urgency of his desire threatening to overcome tenderness.

She broke away from the kiss, her face pressing hot along his throat. "Sweet earth and sky," she whispered, her breath a gasp of wonder on his skin.

"Oh, my lady, Brigit," he murmured, bringing his hand back up to her hair, nuzzling into its softness.

"I can't," she sighed, tingling the welt that leapt with his pulse. "I can't, Elisha, not now, not yet."

His eyes squeezed shut on this new torture. "You are spoken for."

"Can't you feel how much I want this?" She let out something like a laugh, or a cry. "Wait for me, Elisha, I swear to you the day will come."

Chapter 20

◆

$\mathcal{P}$ulling away from him, Brigit tightened her sash with a savage tug and stood up, her pale hands trembling in the moonlight. She turned back to him and smiled. "Do you have another talisman? One more innocent, perhaps more pleasant?"

Wetting his lips, Elisha let out his breath, and nodded, thinking of the little cloth pennant, the one he had flown on the day of the angel. "I have something I can try." He sank back upon his heels, brushing escaped hair away from his face.

"Good," she murmured. "That's good. You'll want more than one anyhow." After a moment, she ventured, "Elisha? May I ask you something?"

"Of course—anything." He looked up at her, her silhouette blocking the stars, her face a shadow with glinting eyes.

"That—" she searched for a word, but did not need to find one. "—that. It's related to the letter you got, isn't it?"

He shoved the hair from his face again, cursing softly. She knew that much. If she knew the truth, she'd turn from him. He did not deserve to have her, and he could not bear the thought of losing her so soon. "Yes, but I'd rather not—"

She cut him off, "I know. I won't ask more."

For a long time they stayed that way, Brigit standing over him as he knelt there, the chill of the earth creeping up through Elisha's clothes.

"Well," said Brigit at last, drawing Elisha's gaze back to her shadowed face. "Well, I should go. Come to the river tomorrow? After supper."

"Aye," he whispered, "I will."

Teeth flashed in a brief smile. "I should be able to make an excuse." She tilted her head to study him. "Perhaps it's time to wash clothes, or something."

Elisha frowned, running his fingers over the sturdy cloth of his britches. "Something," he echoed.

She took a few steps backward. "I'll see you then. Or speak to you, at least. We need to show the others what we have in you." Then she turned and left him, the church door shutting softly behind her.

Her absence dimmed the stars and sapped the sense of magic in the air around him, as if the world itself diminished. Elisha longed to run after her, to catch her up again in his arms, kissing the pale neck her shimmering hair concealed and the long fingers which could summon wonder from water and sky. He willed himself to stillness long after she had gone.

Left alone with the talisman, Elisha watched it from the corner of his eye. Silent and solid, it looked no more powerful than the egg he had crushed. He reached a finger toward it, jerking away when he saw the trembling of his hand. By God, he would not fear death, not in the form of that poor child's head. Thrusting out his hand, he snatched it up, letting out a pent-up breath when he felt its smooth surface, neither warm nor cold. He held it before him, his triumph giving way to doubt. The memory of his terror sent shivers through him.

Clutching it in both hands, Elisha felt himself once

more close to tears, not in fear this time, but in failure. What had he thought when he had chosen it? Dazzled by Brigit's beauty, by her willingness to teach him, he had taken the most powerful thing he could imagine. He had taken his brother's child, his last hope of redeeming himself for Nathaniel's sake, and Helena's. And for what? To make eggs. Eggs he could get from any farmer, or any field as Lisbet had done.

Shutting his eyes, Elisha hugged the container close to him. His ambition twisted this child's un-life for his own ends. He wanted to bring it back, to prove himself in Helena's eyes, taking back the honor he had lost two years ago. But what of the child? Gone incomplete to its grave, unable ever to enter Heaven thanks to his selfish desire to win back a brother who could not ever forgive him. And if he did bring it back, its own mother would revile it for the unnatural thing it would be. He had never even thought of the child until now, so obsessed had he been with what he might accomplish, so fascinated by the fabled Bone of Luz and sure that, if anyone could raise the dead, it would be he.

Shaken now by both his terror, and his passion, Elisha couldn't move, the hardness of the child's entrapment pressed against his chest where so recently he had held the woman he loved. Caught indeed between life and death.

Brigit's words hinted at the power he might hold, at the work which could be made from such a talisman as this, and yet what would he be if he used it? The worst of all that witches were supposed to be. Not magus, not wise-man, but necromancer, building an empire for himself on the loss of a child. Shame enflamed the lashes on his back—punishment for a crime none knew he had committed.

At last, he raised his face to the sky, the final tears

running toward his tangled hair. "I am sorry," he said softly. To God, or to the child, or to Nathaniel gone untimely to his rest.

When he could trust his legs to carry him, he got up and walked down the rise to kneel before the altar. Then he dug his fingers into the grass, pushing aside the roots and scooping out handfuls of dark earth. He settled the pot into its tiny grave and bowed his head.

"I don't know the words to say. Prayer has never been my strength," he confided to his nephew. "God keep you safe and hold you close, and tell your father that his brother is a fool. It's not likely we shall ever meet again." He caught his lip between his teeth, the tears now stinging at his eyes. "I wish I'd had the chance to know you." He pressed the back of a dirty hand to his forehead, trying to master himself.

"Amen," he whispered, piling the earth over the lid, replacing the grass roughly with unsteady hands. This time, he had not even a cross.

Elisha rose and fled. Covered with the dirt of the grave and the blood of the soldiers, he ran to the river, plunging in fully clothed.

The cold bit into him at once, but he barely felt it as he ducked beneath the water in the pool hard beside the bridge. He held his breath as long as he could, remembering the way it had been taken from him by icy power.

Cold soothed the welts, dulling the pain as he burst to the surface again. He let his feet settle into the mud, keeping his knees bent so that his shoulders remained submerged, his arms drawn out by the current like a drowned man's.

As he kneeled there, the water swirling around him as if startled by this remarkable fish, he felt a sense of warmth within it, like the touch of a hand.

"Who's there?"

The warmth held a chuckle. *"Sage,"* the other replied. *"Oh, very good."*

"What's good?" Elisha muttered, more to himself than to Sage.

"Bittersweet indeed. Good, I mean, that you knew I was here, when I have just this moment arrived. You shall be magus yet."

"No," Elisha replied, the water carrying the force of his word, so that the touch of Sage's presence faltered.

Louder, into the air, Elisha said, "Leave me be. I will be no witch. I came here to be cleansed not cursed yet again."

"Cursed," Sage mused. *"In truth, it is a curse, a burden to be borne, but not by all. The curse lies not in magic of itself, but in the way it comes. Some it takes as gently as a mother, some it shakes like a rabid dog."*

At first, the man's continued presence irritated Elisha. Had he not said he wanted to be left alone? If Sage wanted to remain, let him at least be silent. Instead, he prattled on with more of his morose philosophy. And yet—and yet—the angel's touch still warmed his face. He thought to turn his back on witches and their ways, to abandon his pretense, yet his impulse was to refute this man. *"Marigold does not speak so."*

"Marigold. Magic has taken hold of her not as mother or as dog but as a princely lover, promising to make her wishes true. She dances ever in that embrace and never knows that others might be clenched too tightly 'til they break. She would use you to rally the magi, even if it means war. She is the most insensitive magus that I have ever felt."

This rankled, and Elisha stood, as if his height might serve him now.

Again the river brought him laughter. *"Teach your-*

self patience, Bittersweet. Teach yourself control, or you will find that others know your heart before you know it yourself."

Startled, Elisha said, "*You feel my anger.*"

"*I am a sensitive,*" Sage replied. "*Like you. We spend our strength to avoid being too attached to others, else their feelings cloud our own. When I first awoke to magic, I thought I had gone mad. At every touch I was assailed by fear, by love, by joy, by fury. Unlike you, I had to learn to ignore them.*"

"*First you say that you are like me, then you say that you are not.*"

"*You send out your emotions as a hurricane around you, but you feel little in return. Tell me, have you yet cast a spell?*"

This touched a nerve, and Elisha hesitated to answer, knowing at the same time that this was answer enough.

"*How long have you screamed your own emotions hoping not to listen to those of others?*"

Elisha considered this. He hummed during surgery for this very reason. He was never unaware, but unaffected, unwilling to accept that Nathaniel and Helena might be in love, not counterfeiting to escape—her position, his loneliness. Trampling the hopes of Martin Draper, pushing aside the warmth of Lucretia's affection, even taking the child's head on this mission of his own when he suddenly realized all the damage he had done. How long?

"*Since that day.*" That day when he had watched them kill an angel.

Sage's presence warmed again. "*Thought as much. Cursed we are, Bittersweet, but it is not a choice. Not a thing you say I will, or I will not. You are, or you are*

*not. Cast off the trappings. Refuse the knowledge. Ig-
nore the voices. You'll not be the first."*

"*Then I'll say farewell,*" Elisha concluded.

"*Cut off your arm,*" Sage continued, as if he had not
heard. "*Carve out one eye. Cripple your leg. Does it
change what you are? Makes it harder, that's all. Each
of us is as God has made us, cursed and blessed in
equal measure.*"

Elisha let himself drift, his hair drawn out by the
current, his feet anchoring him in the river's bed.
Cursed and blessed in equal measure. Even these last
few hours, he had found it so—at last to love, at last to
face what he carried with him. "*Take from me this
cup,*" he murmured.

Sage answered with a laugh so deep and rich that Elisha swore he heard it through his entire body, and so
responded with a smile. Cursed and blessed, blessed
and cursed. There was a talent in his hands which not
all possessed, a talent which brought pain as well as
comfort. Why should this magic be so different? He
hunted it for the basest of reasons—to assuage his own
guilt—but why should he not accept it for the purest?

"*I thank you, Sage. Again, you are here when I most
doubt.*"

Abruptly, the laughter died. "*Do not thank me yet,
not until you understand this cup we all must drink
from. As to my presence, in truth, I am as fickle as the
rest. I am no friend of yours, nor any man's, nor woman's either. Do not depend on me, Bittersweet—I cannot afford to let you near.*" The touch washed away with
the current, taking away the last vestige of warmth in
the night.

Something echoed in those last few words, a sense of
the other man's own worry, a sort of hollow, hurtful

place as if the heart had gone from within, or kept itself
so secret that even its keeper had forgotten it.

Elisha rose up from the river. Water rushed down
one leg, and he realized that his emergency pouch, always at his side, had filled with the water which escaped
it now. "Holy Mary!"

Then he laughed, grateful that Sage had left before
he started cursing. On a post of the stone bridge, he
emptied the contents of his pouch—a card of needles,
small rolls of suture, the vial of opium, a little bottle of
rose oil, a few tightly rolled bandages, the long strip of
cloth Martin Draper had forced upon him, and the
packet of flaxseeds taken from the vestry earlier that
day. Thankfully, most of these things would recover
once dried. Only the seeds might suffer from the wet.
He thought of the egg, crushed and unknowable, and
like Sage, a cipher begging for answer, yet fleeing the
question. The details of the world chimed with sudden
resonance, as if he recognized a pattern he had never
considered before.

He freed a single seed from the soggy parchment
and saw it not as a familiar thing, but as a mystery, a
wonder unto itself, a thing inviolate. He could list all
that he knew about it and yet never understand how
sun and earth could make it grow. Seen by that light,
the seed concealed its truth from him. Earlier, he had
been humbled by all there was to know about it. Now
he realized that he knew nothing, for its essential nature escaped him utterly, its private magic held within,
awaiting some secret signal to arise and unfurl itself
into the sky. Like a bird, hidden in the potential of its
egg.

The seed felt suddenly warm and expectant, ready to
transform itself. As a boy, Elisha had sometimes
checked the eggs of their few hens, noting the heat of

the hen's body, captured by the egg, and the changing weight and balance as some small miracle took place inside. He remembered asking how the thick liquid of white and yolk became the soft, wobbly chick, exhausted from pecking its way to freedom. Nobody knew. Laying, hatching, care and feeding, the thousand uses of the egg, the hundred ways to cook a chicken— every farmer and his family believed they knew all that could be known about an egg. As with the seed, they knew nothing. Ignorant, the physician called him, and arrogant. On both counts, correct. But ignorance was not always a bad thing, if it led a man to learning.

Elisha focused on the seed in his hand, near-invisible in the gloom. He remembered all he knew, or thought he knew, envisioning the tough, shiny hull as the shell of an egg, the tender meat inside as white and yolk, and at their center: What? A secret, a mystery, a miracle he could marvel at but never quite discover. To crack the egg, to crush the seed destroyed their power. Almost, he thought he should apologize, but the seed was gone.

An egg lay cupped in his tingling palm, dully reflecting moonlight from its expectant shell.

Chapter 21

❖

Brigit called his discovery the Doctrine of Mystery.
She clapped her hands and danced in the river
like a little girl when she saw the egg. She even let him
kiss her, swift as the rushing current, under the bridge,
before she danced away again.

"You found another talisman, then?" the river asked.

Shaking his head, Elisha laughed at himself. *"No,"*
he said. *"I thought of one, but I had not gone for it."*

Downstream, Brigit basked in the sunlight. *"You
must have had something. What did you bring with
you?"*

*"Only my clothes, which are nothing to speak of.
Oh—and my pouch. That's just a few medical things, a
sort of emergency kit."*

"Nothing special or sentimental?"

And he remembered the cloth, that long and narrow
strip of mystery given him by Martin Draper, a man
who cared much more for him than he should. By daylight the silk gleamed purple, the color of kings, but the
gold threads worked into it formed birds, not lions. The
piece of cloth had some significance, but he was damned
if he knew what it was. *"Maybe,"* was all he said.

Every day, they found each other in the water, and
Elisha learned to recognize her presence, and that of

the other magi. Sometimes these others chimed in with their own lessons, helping him concentrate, helping attune himself to his surroundings, to the possibilities which seemed now to hover in the air around him. Elisha believed he would recognize Sage if he felt that touch, but it did not come, neither by day when Brigit or Willowbark or even Slippery Elm gave him their advice, nor by night when he came alone, and he gave up waiting.

The encampment grew tense with the long siege. Sorties issued from the duke's castle, taunted the king's army and retreated, causing just enough havoc that the army couldn't merely sit and wait. Meanwhile, many soldiers kept busy building new ladders and siege towers to prepare an assault. So several days passed with fewer casualties, giving Elisha ample time to practice his eggs and seeds. At first, it seemed he must recall his list of similarities over and over, and discover the mystery anew before he felt that tingle of power. Heat transferred from him to the seed, then it grew heavy and full in a breathless moment. Any distraction and the seed stubbornly remained. He never made so many eggs that he could not pass them off as findings, or purchases from some farmer of vague description who happened to be a friend of Brigit's. Applied to those cauterized by Matthew Surgeon or scalded with the physician's hot oil cure, the ointment kept the burn to a minimum and helped them heal that much faster.

Some six days after Elisha's first casting, the siege engines were ready, and the blast of horns called all again to battle.

The bombards, silent for several days, blasted many of the new towers, sending shards of wood through limbs and smashing bones. When a handcart brought the first victims, Elisha and Ruari shared a grim look. Where before they might see a handful of men who had survived such a blast, with the army's steady advance, they now faced dozens, screaming for attention or for death.

Mordecai and his assistants handled the officers and even captains who were not of noble blood, but this did little to ease the barber's burden. He and Ruari got down to work. Many required careful setting of compound fractures, amputation of crushed limbs, or deep cuts to pry out the long daggers of wood impaling them. Rather than divide as they generally did, Elisha worked alongside Ruari, doing the cutting while Ruari held the patient, or steadying a wounded limb for Ruari's careful labor. He couldn't hum for fear of missing anything Ruari or the patient needed to tell him, so the screaming and the sound of the saw through bone burrowed inside his skull. He kept his teeth clenched wishing, for the moment, that his sensitivity had never re-awakened. Whoever he might be, Sage was surely wise enough to avoid such work where raw emotions tore at the soul every moment. Defending the border of life and death, as Brigit had said.

A few of the king's company grudgingly toted the fallen into the hospital and the dead out of it, the pile in the yard growing much too fast for Elisha's comfort. Most of the corpses were men they'd not even seen yet, men who succumbed to their injuries even as they lay within reach of help.

This day, Brigit and the physicians holed up in Lucius's little cottage. A musician joined them, his desperate fiddling a vain attempt to block the noise. Elisha caught snatches of music once in a while, when the tide of the wounded slowed.

Long after he should have eaten, Lisbet tugged Elisha into the courtyard for a quick meal. On his return—

urging her to escort Ruari likewise—he saw clouds gathering over the castle. The counter attack would be that much harder in mud.

As they worked, they moved steadily further from the monastery, leaving their patients where they lay and going on to the next. Elisha's arms ached from wielding the saw and immobilizing men so that arrows could be plucked. Even his callused fingers showed the jab of the needle too quickly used.

Ruari winced every time he moved, exhaustion etching circles under his dark eyes, drawing down his merry cheeks.

Then a horn blew long over the battlefield. Clouds darkened the sunset, and at last the day was done.

Distant cheers rose up from the battlefield, and Elisha looked up, his stiff neck creaking. A few of the siege towers yet stood, somewhat nearer to the castle than they had been. He made a disgusted sound at the back of his throat, and Ruari looked up.

"Here," Elisha said, gesturing over the field. "All these men wasted to gain such little ground."

Following the sweep of Elisha's arm, Ruari sighed. "It's sure that Jesus weeps tonight." Then his head bowed to his chest, and his shoulders quaked.

Elisha dropped down beside him, resting his fingers on Ruari's arm. "What is it?"

The tearful face turned up to his. "This lot," he pointed to the man they'd just finished and those still scattered around them. A few moaned, a few lay with eyes wide open, taking in the sky for the last time. "This lot are my company. I grew up with these lads."

"Why did you not say earlier?"

Ruari's shoulders gave an eloquent roll. "I see you bent over another, and another, every minute fighting for somebody's life. How can I say, leave off that man, this's my mate? Sweet Lord, Elisha, we are all just so many corpses."

"No," Elisha said, tightening his grip. "No, Ruari, you can't give in to that—" He bit off his words. Instead he pulled the soldier's head against his chest and held him, his own face turned to the heavens, his breath scorching in his throat.

Ruari struggled with his sobs, finally pulling away and dragging a hand over his eyes.

"Is that Ruari, the carpenter's lad?" called a rough voice.

Startled, both turned to stare at a stocky, dark soldier gripping his bloody shoulder with his opposite hand.

"Sully!" Ruari cried, leaping over the man in between. "Sully, old mate, you lived!"

"Aye, so far. Don't tell me ye've gone soft on us, boy." He flashed a grin with more spaces than teeth.

"No, sir," Ruari protested. "Not on your life. This here's Elisha Barber. He's come to save your lives." As he spoke, his eyes yet shone with tears and something else: a pride so fierce that Elisha turned away, blinking back tears of his own.

Night was half over before their work was done and the two stumbled back to their room arm in arm lest they give in to the temptation to fall and sleep where they lay.

Swaying up the stairs to the room they shared, Ruari fell in a heap upon his cloak and started to snore in the next instant.

With a fond smile, Elisha followed, ducked to his own place beneath the stairs, and paused. Something felt wrong.

He cocked his head to listen—no, it was not anything

he heard, nor any strange scent in the air. Since his awakening to magic those several nights ago, this happened more and more frequently, as if he had some other, unknown sense. It had not yet amounted to anything. Elisha shrugged it off, flopping onto his blankets, his head pillowed on the small bundle of his spare clothing.

That sense of wrongness tickled him still, and he sat up again, peering into the darkness, trying to place it. It bothered him more when he lay back down, and he rolled onto his stomach, facing the small trunk he had brought with him. With an idle hand, he turned the latch and lifted the lid. Clouds drifted over the moon, providing curious patches of light in which to see.

At a glance, it all looked well enough, and he started to shut the lid, then raised it up again, leaning on an elbow. Ranks of gleaming instruments rested inside, brought out when needed, returned there when he had cleaned and sharpened them. A pair of long-nosed pincers lay with the smaller ones, and Elisha tapped the handles with his finger. These he reserved for difficult shot wounds. He had a long probe with a crooked tip that always went along with them. He had taken to storing the two tools together, rather than poke through them all to get what he needed, but the probe lay at the opposite end, among some similar instruments.

Carefully, Elisha lifted the leather pad that separated the layers, the tools clinking together as he set them aside. Underneath, his packets and vials stood in their usual neat rows, but again that sense of wrongness urged him on, and he lifted out a few. They were all out of order. He couldn't read the labels, of course, but drew a leaf or other symbol on each to tell them apart, then ordered them according to use.

Rifling quickly through the small collection, he

found nothing missing and narrowed his eyes. A common thief would have taken these—a few of the spices and oils fetched a good price. No, whoever had searched his things wanted something special. Suddenly, Brigit's face flashed before his eyes, her fascination with the sealed pot, her way of asking about it while trying to seem merely curious.

Anger flared to life, and was quickly quenched again. Dropping the herbals back in, then replacing the instruments on top, Elisha shut the chest and jerked off his boots, the more softly to move about.

Barefoot, he padded over to the hospital and up the stairs just inside the infirmary doors. Mordecai's second assistant drowsed in a chair, heedless of his passing. One of the whores looked up from where she lay alongside a fat captain and smiled a little into the flickering lamplight.

Elisha kept on down the hall. At this end, part of the roof had fallen in, and the rooms were unusable. He had not been to Brigit's room, but had an idea where it lay. An indefinable sense of her led him onward, and he knocked softly at the door. "Brigit," he whispered against the gap in the frame.

Almost immediately, the floor creaked within, and then the door popped open, Brigit's startled face confronting him. "What are you doing here? You can't come like this, it's not safe."

He shot her a look as he pushed past her. "Then shut the door."

"Elisha," she hissed, "You can't stay."

"I don't want to stay, I want to ask why you've gone through my things."

Shutting the door with a swift movement, Brigit placed her back to it. "I've done nothing of the kind," she said, crossing her arms tight beneath her breasts.

"Who else would want anything I have?"

"Anyone might—surely your instruments are worth something, and herbs or oils are always in demand."

"But nothing was taken."

She scowled. "Then why are you here?"

"Because something was missing—something I took away myself. Something only you knew about."

"I told you, I didn't do it. I thought you trusted me, Elisha." She took a few steps forward, her arms loosening, her voice taking on a tone of hurt, which almost hid the hint of fear that seemed to rise from her like mist.

"If you've done nothing," he demanded, his voice rising a little, then dropping back to a whisper, "then what are you afraid of?"

"Nothing, Elisha, truly. But you need to go. If I am afraid of something, it's that you will be heard. It's not a safe subject, and this is not a safe place."

He spread his hands. "But it's your own bedroom." He turned a slow circle, letting his eyes linger on her trunk, her satchel. Could she have found where it had been buried? Surely he would sense it now.

"Elisha." A note of urgency edged his name. "Please go, Elisha, we can talk in the morning. It's nearly midnight."

Someone tapped on the door, and they both stiffened. "Fire and flood," Brigit breathed.

"Who is it?" Elisha mouthed.

"A magus who won't wish to be known."

He opened his mouth to ask, but she shook her head, pointing toward the window behind him.

"Go, go!" her lips urged.

Catching the sense of her fear, if not all the reasons for it, Elisha turned to the window. He stepped first to the bed, freezing when the tapping came again on the door, a little louder this time.

Holding aside the curtain, Elisha pulled himself up to the window frame. Even as he got his legs through, the old wood cracked and broke.

Ripping down the curtain as he fell, Elisha bit his tongue, trying to turn, to land sideways. Turn he did, taking the blow hard on his left hip and shoulder as he splashed into his own canal.

Somebody shrieked, and Elisha scrambled to his knees. From the deeper darkness by the cistern, a woman suddenly appeared, shaking down her skirts. Then another figure sat up beside her, and a slow smile spread over the face. Matthew, the surgeon's assistant grinned across the distance.

"Scaling the walls on our own, are we?"

"I tripped, that's all, my lord," Elisha answered, standing up, shaking the water from his arm.

"He fell from that window," the prostitute supplied. Elisha tried to look indignant—as if it were she who lied—but his face felt like a mask.

Matthew, too, got to his feet, straightening his tunic and brushing off the grass. He tilted his head to see the window she meant, and the smile grew. "Go and tell the physician he's wanted."

As the prostitute hurried to do his bidding, Elisha contemplated running away, but what would be accomplished except to make himself look more guilty—and perhaps drag Brigit into a dangerous mess. Instead, he crossed his arms beneath Matthew's watchful eyes and leaned against the wall.

In a moment, the physician joined them, with Benedict at his back. "So," Lucius intoned, "I understand you have been visiting."

"No, sir, merely tripping over my own ditch on my way to see a patient."

"How careless," the physician said, with a prim little smile.

"I saw him," the prostitute piped up, wriggling against Matthew's side.

He shrugged away from her. "It's true, sir, he was trying to climb inside when he fell."

At this, Elisha jerked away from the wall. "That's a lie." Matthew had seen a chance to curry favor with the king's physician, even if it cost Elisha a terrible price.

"I believe that's Lady Brigit's room; I wonder what he wants from her that can't be asked in the daylight," Matthew drawled.

By now, the night watchmen had arrived, and heads poked through the windows.

Brigit appeared at her own window. "What's going on?"

By all the saints and martyrs, could this get any worse? Before anyone else could answer, Elisha called out, "I tripped, nothing more. Sorry if I disturbed anyone." He could hear the rising tone of his own voice, the fear that sped his heart, and hoped he sounded annoyed rather than desperate.

"And he accuses me of lying." In a few strides, Matthew snatched up a broken piece of wood, holding his trophy aloft for all to see. "From her window."

"It broke earlier," Brigit said. Her vantage point would not reveal the coldness in the physician's face.

"Matthew, you've been here longer than we have. What is the punishment for the second offense?"

Tapping the wood against his palm, Matthew supplied, "Branding, sir."

"Sir, I swear to you I was not climbing the wall, I simply fell into my own ditch." Which was all true, as far as it went. Elisha's mind raced, but he could find no way out. His own statements made it hard for Brigit to defend him, had she been so inclined after his accusations, and these others had no reason to believe him, not if the jealous glare on the physician's face meant what Elisha thought it must. Any word Brigit spoke sent him nearer to Matthew's irons.

"Branding," the physician mused. "Excellent. Benedict, why don't you assist Matthew here. Oh, and gag him, would you? There's no need waking everyone." He turned on his heel to walk away.

Chapter 22

❖

From her window, Brigit called out, "Wait, wait!" She disappeared and shortly emerged through the side door, knotting the sash of her robe. Elisha clenched his fists, willing her to stay away, as if the talent she claimed he possessed could be used in such a manner.

Lucius stood straight as a whipping post, waiting, but his sharply arched eyebrows twisted downward in displeasure. At the sound of her step, he swung around. "Yes, my lady, what have you to add?"

"I called this man to my room," she said. "I felt unwell, and I hesitated to trouble yourself, my lord physician."

For a moment, Elisha dared hope this ruse would deflect the physician's ire, but Lucius gasped and placed a hand upon her arm. "My dear lady, you should not be consulting with a—a barber! Not for anything! You must know that we are at your disposal."

"I see that now, kind sir," Brigit began, but the physician was already shaking his head, giving Elisha a black look.

"And he should know better than to answer such a summons. Alone, in the night, with you, my lady? My goodness, anything might have happened!"

Elisha leapt to the aid of his defender, swallowing

his annoyance with them both. "I should have come for you, my lord physician, rather than tend her myself."

"But there's no harm done, is there? I feel better now for having spoken with him," Brigit continued.

"You are an innocent, my lady, and not expected to imagine the worst of any man, even such a one as this," the physician said, narrowing his gaze as if he were aiming an arrow at Elisha's heart.

Elisha stepped away from them, his foot striking the chill water of his channel. Brigit caught his movement, and her face went still as she edged a toe into the water.

The moment he felt her presence in the water around him, Elisha said, "*Brigit, your defending me is only making things worse.*"

"*Nonsense. He likes me, he'll listen.*"

"*Likes you? He's as desperate for you as I am, and that won't make him sympathetic to my part.*"

"This barber," the physician said, his smile warming a little as he looked down on Brigit, "is a particularly poor example of the breed. *Mea culpa*—I brought him here myself, saving him from the gallows, in fact, as a comfort to these common soldiers. The more fool I. Now it's my duty to see that he conforms to military discipline."

As Lucius droned on, Brigit stared at the ground and the little stream where she dangled one foot. "*Don't be ridiculous, he's like a father to me.*"

"*Do you know what punishment for the third offense is, Brigit?*" A slight shrug answered him. "*Hanging. Look at his face. If you continue to take my part, he'll find a way to hang me.*"

Her mouth dropped open. "I'd no idea."

"Well, naturally you didn't," the physician said, taking breath for another explanation. "A man like this, coarse and unrefined, a criminal really, well . . ."

"*I appreciate what you're trying to do, but it'll only go the worse for me the longer you stay.*" Elisha forced himself to maintain an attitude of resignation, much as he longed to stare at her, or to ferret out the truth of her other midnight visitor.

"I see, sir." Brigit's voice was soft and calm. "I did not understand all of your considerations." She turned back to the physician with a faint smile.

"I hope now, you can appreciate what is at stake here, my lady. A scoundrel like this cannot be allowed to violate a lady's presence. If you have need of medical knowledge, I am at your disposal."

"Yes, thank you. I'll be returning to my bed then." She tightened her sash and walked toward the door, without a backward glance.

Once she'd gone inside, the physician stalked a little closer. With his hands, he gestured Matthew and Benedict in closer. "Get him to the front, I don't care how. I want him away from here, away from her. Who knows what notions he might take up now that she was unwise enough to invite him?"

"But, sir," Benedict began.

"My lord physician," said Elisha at the same time, but Lucius ignored him.

"Have I made my wishes clear, Benedict?"

With a quick nod, he said, "Yes, sir."

"Get on with it, and make it quick. There's one of the captains in the infirmary headed back before dawn, send the barber along." Lucius grinned at Elisha, a nasty expression of pointed teeth. "Welcome to the battle, Barber. Perhaps we shall meet again, if you find yourself in need of the hot oil cure."

Elisha stared, hardly believing what he heard. He knew the way the battle went, hundreds wounded when the siege towers exploded or went up in smoke, more from the arrows and the bombardelles when they got too near the wall. "Sir, I—"

"Save the apologies for God and bid Him good day for me—if you're heading that way." The physician stalked away to his little house and shut the door with a resounding slam. Elisha twitched at the sound; it was the sound of his coffin-lid falling shut.

Matthew jumped the ditch and grabbed Elisha's arm, jerking him off balance in the direction of the kitchen. "Come on, then, Benedict, we've work to do."

Trailing behind, Benedict did not answer.

Two of the night guards fell in along with them, to be sure that justice was done, Elisha thought, or perhaps to join in the fun.

Once inside, Matthew turned him over to the guards, then went in search of the right iron and stoked up the ashes to heat it. He could fight and run. What was the penalty for desertion? What would be his chances on the battlefield—unprepared, unarmed? He imagined the smoky blast of a bombardelle that hurled him backward, shattered and screaming. He would die, or survive, only to be scalded by the physician's cure. Even Helena at her most furious would not condemn him to such a fate.

Arms crossed, Benedict settled on the edge of one of the damaged chairs, frowning at the table.

"Hard to believe the king brought Lucius all the way here just to torture me, isn't it?" Elisha said lightly, enjoying Benedict's little flinch, his obvious discomfort giving Elisha a moment's distraction.

"It was my master's own idea," Benedict muttered, "coming to the front to better examine this type of wound and develop practical methods for dealing with it."

Elisha cast his mind back to that day in the cell. Lucius had distinctly claimed the invitation of the king. Evidently, Benedict had been told a different story, but why? "I didn't think he had much interest in practical medicine."

Benedict glared. "You would do well in your position to use my title."

"Sorry, doctor, I am a bit rattled."

At the hearth, Matthew pulled out his iron and pressed it to a scrap of leather to test its heat. The leather sizzled, smoke curling up from it.

Elisha's stomach gave a lurch. He drew back from the fireside and the guards' grip tightened.

"A little hotter yet, I think," Matthew murmured, replacing it in the fire. He had chosen an iron with a broad, flat face, suitable for cauterizing the stump of a leg with just a couple of burns.

Turning away, Elisha looked through the door at his hospital. Most patients kept their noise down at night, but he could hear a drone of prayer above the whimpers and moans. "Pray for me, too," he whispered. His dread of cautery arose from the day of the witch, when the smell of burning flesh became anathema to him.

"As the senior man," Matthew said brightly, "perhaps you'd like to take over?"

"No," Benedict cried out. "I mean, you have much more practice than I."

"Very well then, doctor, why don't you hold him?"

"But we've got the guards for that, I—"

"Does your master know what a coward you are, doctor?"

"There is no call for that." The chair scraped as Benedict got up. "I'm only tired is all and concerned that he may struggle."

Rough hands dragged Elisha back, shoving him to his knees before the fire. Then the guards withdrew a few steps. "We'll be at the ready, my lords, if he gives any trouble."

"Off with the shirt, Barber, unless you'd like a hole through it." Matthew smiled down at him.

Slowly, Elisha stripped off his shirt, delaying his fate a few more breaths, a few heartbeats. Matthew's smile turned sharp.

Benedict took the shirt from Elisha's grasp and set it on the table. Then he knelt behind, locking Elisha's elbows with one arm.

Elisha pushed down the rising panic. Fighting could only get him one step closer to the noose. The effort of holding back strained his shoulders, bunching his muscles against the pressure of Benedict's arm. The physician's assistant had an unexpected wiry strength, born, perhaps, of a dread akin to Elisha's own.

With his other hand, Benedict turned Elisha's face toward his shoulder, almost delicately, then he clamped his palm over Elisha's mouth.

Benedict's pulse jumped in his throat, his Adam's apple working furiously.

Elisha caught the intake of breath when Matthew pulled the iron from the fire, and he shut his eyes.

Searing heat slammed through his chest, just over his heart. His skin sizzled, the thick dark hair scorched. His body went rigid against his captor. The muscles shrieked.

Benedict's hand twitched over Elisha's mouth.

His teeth slid open to suck in a breath, then bit hard into Benedict's palm.

A howl of pain rent the air.

Through the stench of his own burnt flesh and the fog of his pain, Elisha tasted blood and fear. Remorse and sorrow twined beneath Benedict's pain, self-loathing tinged the blood along with resignation. Hatred, too, tainted the skin, even as the pressure slackened with the injury.

The burning ripped through Elisha leaving him

breathless and shaky as the iron finally withdrew. Tears steamed down his cheeks, wetting the hand at his mouth until it, too, withdrew, shaking, blood seeping from torn skin.

Benedict let him go, but slowly, separating them and rising to his feet, his breath ragged.

Elisha remained on the floor, his knees bruised by straining against the stone. His right arm ached a little from Benedict's grip, but the left had gone numb. The pain shot out from his chest, tightening his neck and shoulder on that side like a man whose heart has failed him.

At last, he moved, cupping his left elbow with his right hand, drawing his arms close beneath the burned skin. He blinked open his eyes.

For all the pain that they had caused him, the welts had been only a surface ache. To be sure, they protested his every movement, while this new wound confined itself to the left side of his chest. But it felt that much more personal, a patch of himself burned away, the pain reaching deep inside so that his ribs groaned with each quick breath.

He had seen Matthew burn to the bone, when the bullet had gone so deep. It would not have surprised him to open his eyes to the sight of his own ribcage gleaming pale through a rend in the flesh, a rend that could never be healed.

Singed black hairs, curled tighter than before, surrounded a ring of pink skin, growing more livid toward the center where it turned to angry red, then a sunken bull's eye of blackness, the skin so tight that every gasping stretch and release of his lungs pulled against it. He would never be the same.

"Come on, then, we've got beds to get to," Matthew said.

A hand grabbed Elisha's right arm, pulling him to his feet and hanging on until Elisha grew steady enough to stand.

Drawing breath, Elisha raised his head, bending his neck against the quivering of the injured muscles. Matthew stood before him, his lips upturned in the devil's imitation of a smile. Gloved, his right hand still held the iron, steam rising from its head. Elisha's eyes traced the forms, the strong, concealed hand, the flat black iron with its curls of steam from the moisture of his flesh. He wet his lips, tasting again the tang of Benedict's blood, but, without contact, it was only blood.

Shuffling in a half-circle, he faced Benedict who held his wounded right hand, the blood dripping down to his wrist. "Have that seen to," Elisha said thickly. "The bite of a man can kill you."

Ducking his head away, Benedict darted out his hand and plucked Elisha's shirt from the table. With a careless gesture, he flung it over Elisha's left shoulder, draping it to hide the brand. Benedict was cowed by his master, to be sure, but he did have some compassion.

One corner of Elisha's mouth twitched up, and curved itself into a tiny smile. For a moment, he studied Benedict's face. The assistant was a few years younger than himself, with sandy blond hair just brushing his shoulders. He had thin, handsome features—the sort of boy Martin Draper would admire, Elisha thought in some back corner of his mind. His brown eyes were rimmed now with pain that went beyond the body. As Elisha gazed, Benedict looked away again, his lashes quivering.

He was a sensitive, that much was clear from his reaction to the branding, and Elisha wondered idly if he might be a magus, as well, if he might sneak down to the river to trade philosophy with a man he would not acknowledge by day.

Abruptly, Benedict walked through the door into the commoners' end of the hospital, prompting the little group into motion. Elisha followed at a dream pace, unaware of his feet as he drifted in the haze of shock. A few of the men around him called out, their voices demanding or concerned, uncomprehending. Their voices did not penetrate very far.

They greeted Matthew, bringing up the rear, with a chorus of curses and booing, which he ignored.

Benedict held aside the curtain letting them through into the infirmary. Here, the lords snored or drank, trading murmured comments with their companions. Ahead, on the stairs, a figure stood in the darkness, then descended the last few steps. Ruari burst in behind, his face pale. His lips moved, but Elisha couldn't gather his lost concentration. He allowed himself to halt with the others, glad to take someone else's lead.

Stepping down, his head at the level of Elisha's chin, Mordecai reached up and twitched aside the draped shirt. Behind him, Ruari looked faint. The surgeon turned his head just a little, his dark, wet eyes seeking his assistant.

Matthew came around to stand beside his master, the branding iron held now in both hands. "Physician's orders," he said. "The barber tried to get into Mistress Brigit's room."

With the slightest of nods, Mordecai returned his gaze to the wound. His other hand clutched a substantial book bound between covers of wood, though he had left behind the belt of dangling pages; the expression on his face did not change as he dropped the shirt back into place. "So deep?" he asked, his voice a blank. "For so long?"

As if he had been upbraided, Matthew winced, pulling the iron slightly closer to his chest. "A firm lesson," he stammered.

"Need this man to work, don't we?" Mordecai continued in that flat, dull voice, as if he repeated a lesson which bored him.

"Not any more, sir," Benedict supplied. "He's been ordered to arms."

This got some reaction, as the surgeon again took his book in both hands. His graying eyebrows quirked up for an instant. "I see. Who's to do his work, then?"

"Well, he's trained his own butcher and seamstress," Matthew put in, some of the haughtiness returning to his posture.

"We'll see who's a butcher," Ruari shot back, propelled into motion at last. He flung himself down the steps to Elisha's side. "I can't do it without you," he said urgently, searching Elisha's face for some sign of recognition.

Elisha felt himself adrift, as if he had suffered too long a bleeding, detached from anything around him, and most especially, from the throbbing pain at his chest. Ruari's search became ever more desperate, and Elisha found words at last. "You'll do fine," he whispered.

"You'll die," Ruari hissed back.

"It's not in my hands, nor yours." Then he smiled that tiny smile. "Not yet, anyhow."

"Henry," Mordecai said, and his chubby second assistant jumped up from his chair with an eager face. "Fetch some of your burn salve. And bind up the physician's hand. Bite, is it?"

Benedict nodded.

"Barber, your assistant may wish to bring me your tools, for safekeeping," Mordecai went on in his dead voice, his eyes unfocused somewhere beyond Elisha's chest.

This got Elisha's attention at last, and he stiffened.

Safekeeping indeed. Why should he worry about a barber's tools, unless he knew there might be something of greater value? Had he been wrong to accuse Brigit of the search? "Don't do that, Ruari," Elisha said, the power of speech returning with a vengeance. "You watch over my things. Give the tools to Lisbet—she'll keep them well. And you'll need to use them yourself."

"But I don't even know how! By God, Elisha, this is madness."

Coldly, Elisha said, "Ask the surgeon, maybe he'll teach you. I wouldn't take help from his assistants, though. I don't think healing is in their trade."

Ruari drew himself up to martial bearing and nodded sharply. "I hear ye." He put out his hand for the salve as the man returned. "It's honored I am to have worked beside you."

Elisha shook his head ever so slightly. "They're not rid of me yet, my friend."

Chapter 23

✤

efore dawn, the guards roused Elisha from the corner where he'd been allowed to doze. He had finally managed to convince Ruari that he, too, would need his sleep for the morrow. He did not truly sleep himself, but drifted through consciousness and dreams with little to tell one from the other. He thanked the guards when they came for him—at least he need feign sleep no longer.

Ruari had reunited him with his boots so, shod and half-dressed, Elisha went to the encampment when the sky was just lightening from black to sooty gray.

The captain who led his escorts hailed from the western coast where, by God, they'd have a better plan than this frontal assault, especially with the bombards exploding at them all day, not that they'd had much of that yesterday, mostly flaming arrows toward the end, really, which likely meant that they'd get the towers up to the wall today and overrun the traitors . . .

As the man went on, Elisha stared dully at the tents and fires. Cider warmed on a few of those fires, and onions baked on sticks. Soldiers rose from their blankets and groaned, taking bread from the passing wenches. A few of the men furtively shared sausages, apparently unaware that the scent gave away their secret wealth.

The lords in charge emerged from pavilions adorned with awnings and pennants flapping in a rising wind. These were the lesser lords and field commanders. More than one had a woman behind him, strapping on his breastplate, or holding a coat of mail at the ready. To a man, everyone Elisha saw looked defeated, worn down by this ceaseless assault and retreat. He wondered if the barons and knights and squires in the king's retinue across the river had the same hollow expression.

Back on the day of his arrival, he recalled hearing laughter and music, the camaraderie of fighting men, eager for the excitement of battle. Now, a bare two weeks later, they dressed silently, accompanied only by the clink and rattle of their gear and the scrape of a blade receiving its killing edge. As for himself, he dodged execution by coming to battle, only to be given a death sentence in any event. For a chilling moment, he wondered if his efforts at penance had been found unworthy, and this was his reward.

At last they stopped in the furthest group from the monastery, the nearest to the field, and the captain called out, "Madoc!"

A thick-set bearded man rose from his place by the fire. He had a leather tunic, with a copper platter stitched over his breast, token of some woman who cared for him. "Aye, Cap!" he answered, looking them over.

The captain glowered. "You're lucky I haven't flogged you for that, Madoc."

"What, and lose your best man? Never! What's your pleasure?" he boomed, grinning in a way that made Elisha think he always smiled, and that the expression had lost all meaning.

"This here's for your command. He's no fighter, so

put him on a wheel or somewhat. Strong enough, I think."

Madoc came forward, circling Elisha like a curious hound. "What's he, then?"

"The barber. And just in time by the look of that beard!" the captain laughed.

Bristling, Madoc said, "Be off with you! I promised my Alyse no' t' cut it until she could see with her own eyes that the thing was gone." He returned his attention to Elisha. "The barber, though? It's a joke, eh?"

"Demoted." The captain shrugged. "I don't know the story. Just back from the infirmary myself." He displayed a neatly bandaged wrist, the linen so smooth and pale it had to be new, not the re-washed rags Elisha had for his own patients. "Well, I'll leave you to it." He nodded his head, and the escorting guards broke away to return to their own brigades while the captain strode off whistling toward his tent, where a blonde woman opened her arms to him.

"You're the barber?" Madoc inquired.

Elisha raised his head, still holding his left arm. Some sensation had returned, and none of it was good. "I am, yes. Or I was."

"Elisha Barber?"

Startled, Elisha nodded. "Aye, but I don't think I've worked on you."

"No, indeed." Again the scruffy beard split in a wide grin. "But you did Ryan's stabbing and Collum's head-wound." He gestured to a pair of men who rose from the fire to join them. "Not to speak of my brother's leg—he's gone home, he has!" Turning to his men, he placed a hand on Elisha's back and gently pushed him into the circle. "We've got the barber, men."

They brightened at this news, waving their arms in

greeting, but Madoc raised his hand to silence them. "No cause for joy, lads, he's to go to the field."

"But who'll see to the injured?" someone called out.

"I've left an apprentice," Elisha said, "and there's still the surgeons."

"Faugh!" the speaker cried. "As if they'd spare a look for men like us. We can't bring ye to the lines."

"I wish I could leave him here, but I can't think how, without raising the cap's ire agin' the lot of us. As it is, we'll have to watch his back."

Elisha smiled. "My front, too. I've never so much as held a pike." Then the smile slipped a little. "And my left arm's no good. Not yet."

"Branded, are ye?"

"Those filthy bastards!" one of them said. "Was it for stealing? Ye hardly look the type for brawling."

Madoc brought him up, and gave him a stump to sit on.

"For falling in the night, actually," Elisha supplied.

"Falling down? Well, that's a new crime."

The men around him laughed, but Madoc shook his head. "Seems like they get stricter every day."

Elisha watched his new companions prepare. No armor here, just boots to pack with padding, and some had not even that. A few sharpened hunting knives, in case it should come to hand-to-hand. These were the men he'd been brought to serve, the yeomen and tradesmen summoned away from their work and family at the king's conscription order.

"What's this battle for, anyhow?" he asked of no one in particular as Madoc pressed half a sausage into his hand.

"Well," Madoc answered, taking a seat crosswise on a log, "The king's second son was to wed this duke's daughter. And the duke ordered up a lot of fancy new weapons to deliver as dowry. All been arranged months back, see?"

"I've heard that much."

"Set for midsummer's it was, and Prince Alaric come down to stay with his betrothed's family. Then the boy calls it off, can't do it, he says. Why not, says the king?" Madoc made his voice higher, and richer, his bright eyes full of ferocity in imitation of their ruler. "Well, says the prince, but she's no virgin, is she?"

All the men had a good laugh over this. A commoner took what he was offered, as long as she seemed a good woman, but a noble had other priorities. Elisha took a greasy bite of sausage that melted in his mouth and chewed through a bit of gristle. The chill gray of morning and the flavor of meat stirred him back toward life.

A young man in the background called out, " 'Twas a lie! I've got a cousin works in the castle kitchen."

"Just so, say a lot of us," Madoc agreed. "Clear enough, the prince got a look around and turned her down flat. Boy thinks he can get himself a better bride."

Finishing his sausage, Elisha asked, "But why tell a lie that any midwife might disprove, not to mention the lady's own companions, for surely she has them?"

"And wouldn't they all lie for their lady, says the prince? So the duke, he tells the king the whole thing's crooked, and here's his daughter defamed by the prince. Now, mind you, without this duke's support King Hugh would've been thrown over in favor of the French boys back when old Edward and young Edward both died." He paused to cross himself in memory of the long-dead royals. "So it stands to reason the duke's expecting some backing from the king as well. What's he to get for compensation, now the lady's not like to be wed?"

Catching the mood the tale was taking, Elisha guessed: "But they've now insulted the prince, by calling him a liar. And reminded everyone of the mess about the succession, which the king would like everyone to forget."

"Right you are! So the king says, I'll not have my son so accused. And you'd best deliver those guns I was promised."

"But he gave nothing, and the king gave nothing," Elisha guessed. "And here we all are, laying siege to a duke's castle because some snobbish royal couldn't tell his father he didn't like the girl."

"And it's wise you are, Elisha Barber." Madoc nodded agreeably. "You ask me, this is more for the rest of the barons, to show who's master lest they all take up against him. We're a poppet-show and them the children meant to learn by it."

Again, the soldiers showed their mirth at the foibles of the nobility—the kind of gallows humor adopted by those who hadn't the power to change their fate. But Elisha could not bring himself to laugh. For this childish exchange of insults, a thousand men might die. Common but good men, sacrificed to the nobles' pride until one or the other would back down or until the whole bloody castle came down around the duke's ears, and his daughter's disputed virginity fell to some conquering knight in favor with the king. He suddenly wished he hadn't eaten the sausage, for the bile rose in his throat as he considered the day that faced them. Even as he thought it, the trumpet blew a hard blast as distant from music as the battle from a ball.

Madoc jumped to his full, if lacking, height. "Saint's

blood, and I've not even made us a plan. Look, you, Barber. When the bombards start, you drop, you see? Close by one of the towers, if you can, and if it's not afire. Plenty of men get stunned by that, first time out and all."

Elisha, too, rose. "I'm not afraid to fight," he said softly.

"And did I say you would be?" Madoc scowled. "You're worth a damn sight more to us alive, aren't you? So you'll do as I say, and myself'll watch out for you."

"Aye, sir."

"There's a lad!" He moved as if to slap Elisha's shoulder, then checked himself and apologized quickly. "By God, you must think me a clod."

"No more clod than the rest of us!" someone shouted, and all laughed.

"And hope there's no clod over you, the end of to-day," said another, stilling the laughter.

The young man who'd spoken up about the duke's daughter raised a long staff topped by a flag of gold with a hare encircled by battlements. The others formed up behind him, most bringing pikes as tall as two men, a few with axes or spears of their own. Gritting his teeth, Elisha pulled on his shirt, forcing his left arm to work despite the throb of the wounded muscles. Catching sight of the burn, Madoc pulled back his lips in a sort of cringe. "Cor, man, they sent you on with that?"

"They'd like me to die," Elisha said lightly, "To save them the rope."

Eyeing him warily, Madoc nodded. "The duke'll do his best for them, I'm sure. And we'll do our best for you."

"Thanks." Elisha smiled. "Where do I march before my great exit?"

"Keep by me, I'll give you a sign." Madoc guided them to the middle of the bunch, placing Elisha at his right, protecting Elisha's wounded side.

Suddenly Collum—the man whose head Elisha had wrapped—appeared beside him, holding out a large kitchen knife, hilt-first. "Take this, Barber. It beats nothing at all."

Elisha wrapped the wooden hilt in his fist. "Your wife must be missing this."

"Oh, she'll get by. Wouldn't let me leave without!" Collum nodded and hurried back to his own place.

A drum beat somewhere behind, in the ranks of men who followed, and they marched out into the steely dawn.

The golden banner led them to one of the remaining siege towers, and the first few rows of men caught hold of the wooden cross-timbers that supported it. Cart-wheels creaked and groaned as they heaved the siege tower into motion. Now that the darkness had receded enough, they became easy targets for the duke's gunners, and a few men prayed as they pushed.

Close-to, although the siege tower was huge, Elisha had to admit that it didn't look like much. He trudged along in its wake, looking at the hastily bound crosspieces and the pegged rungs which climbed inside. It had a long outthrust arm to reach over the moat formed by the river, if they ever got that close.

Almost immediately, a cry rose and then arrows struck before them, instantly feathering the ground, the siege tower, and a few of the men who were careless in their cover.

Reflexively, Elisha put up his arms, but Madoc had placed them both behind the tower, and the arrows couldn't breach the pine boughs bound to its front.

A scream turned his head to see one of the fallen, the arrow protruding from his belly, blood streaming from the wound.

Starting forward, Elisha jerked short as Madoc caught his arm. "You can't, not now, they'll only shoot you, too."

Cries echoed all around him, and the second volley of arrows brought more.

Everywhere he looked, men lay dying, this one taken through the eye—a lucky shot at such distance. Another pierced through the chest, another already gone, five shafts at least bristling from his body. Still more lay wounded, clutching an arm or leg, struggling to stem the flow of their own blood. "Good Lord, Madoc, I can't leave them."

Madoc tightened his grip, giving Elisha a fierce look. "They're well back, and most'll make their way from the field, those as are likely to live in any case. Wait'll we get beyond. When the fight's well passed, you'll come back." He grinned. "Aye, I believe that you'll come back."

Something cracked, and Elisha flinched, looking up to the tower. When the sound came again, he realized it was thunder. As the rain began, a cheer rose from the men. Elisha couldn't figure why this should make them happy. Presumably, mud could only bog down their progress.

Then the next flight of arrows fell, many of them tipped with balls of flame. A few struck and ignited the branches, but the flames died as the rain fell harder.

Brigit's oath echoed in the back of his head, "Fire and flood," her merry voice cheering him, if only in memory.

A shape of flame fled past them, accompanied by a keening wail.

"Get down!" he bawled to the burning man, who struggled with the arrow which stuck from his side. By the time the soldier fell, it was too late. Rain sizzled on his charred flesh, and Elisha felt a wave of nausea.

He staggered, colliding with Madoc who caught him up in a strong arm. "Soon," Madoc muttered, "Soon, I'll let you fall."

Dizzy, Elisha barely felt the rain that soaked him, weighing down his already heavy hair. Terror and agony surrounded him, thick in the air as a swarm of bees. Again and again he felt the cold touch of death, familiar now and still awful as it played along his flesh with the rain. Madoc's arm alone kept him upright and in the shadow of the siege tower.

Elisha numbly went over his recent training. There must be something he could do, some affinity here that would save these men's lives, some mystery or knowledge. Days of changing seeds into eggs, eggs back into seeds again now haunted him as time he'd lost in idle play.

Arrows fell like rain, he thought, and rain like arrows, sharp and stinging on his burned chest. He hugged his arms closer, Collum's kitchen knife held close to his side.

Feeling the icy bite of death, Elisha raised his head. Rain splashed on his upturned face. Rain flowed like tears down his cheeks, like a river down his back.

Elisha willed his presence into the rain. He shook off Madoc's arm and dragged his pouch around to the front, laying his left hand over it, feeling for the strip of cloth given him by someone who cared.

Arrows to raindrops, wind to water—one degree only, wasn't it? Was it? He bent his will to it, picturing Brigit, almost thinking he could hear the voices of the others around him. Concentrate, hold the image, transform the image, touch the talisman, feel its power to support you. Touch the thing you must change.

Arrows swished through the rain. Elisha felt them falling, a thousand tiny pricks along his skin.

Contact.

Far away, soldiers cried out in astonishment. Some cheered, some cried out for the Lord or for His angels.

From the heavens, thunder answered them.

Thunder and rain.

Chapter 24

❖

Elation flushed Elisha's skin. He stared in wonder as no arrows fell. Men stumbled, searching the sky, the downpour suddenly heavier. Shouts echoed down the line. Off to the left, a spear and pike quickly became a cross, raised up to the sky.

"Sweet Jesus and Mary," Madoc said. "Where'd they go?"

Stifling a giggle, Elisha did not trust himself to answer. The casting left him giddy and weak, as if he'd spread himself too thin and had trouble to get himself together again.

"The king'll think he's blessed now for sure."

The banner bearer piped up, "It's we who're blessed. May God stay with us."

"Aye, you've said it."

"Maybe the rain took them down," someone suggested in a hushed tone.

"Or witchcraft."

A hiss rose at this suggestion. "Heaven forbid!"

"No, lads," Madoc assured them, "the devil has no wish to save such as us."

A boom sounded up ahead, and the ground lurched. "Bombards," Madoc shouted.

Elisha nodded as a second blast rocked them.

"Falling well short though. What've they done with the big 'un?" Madoc was muttering, keeping his head down. Noting a pit they passed, he nodded to himself. "Almost in range. Cross yourself, Barber, we're at it soon."

Another boom, then the air around them cracked open, a man-made wind blowing their clothes as the concussive passage knocked down a few men on the right.

Yanking Elisha half off his feet, Madoc dragged him in that direction. "Down and quick!" he shouted, throwing Elisha into the mud and following himself as the men around them scrambled to do likewise.

Moments later, a second blast shattered the air around them, shaking the earth. The unseen stone smashed through the siege tower, sending up a fountain of debris as it slammed to earth behind. The tower groaned and tilted, shuddering. Men hesitated, then flung themselves away as the bulk that had once protected them came crashing down.

Slivers of wood and a shower of branches rained over them.

The screams of the dying, momentarily silenced by Elisha's own miracle, broke in along with the timber, shattering his reveries. Elisha moaned, touched by so many. He covered his ears, but it wasn't the air alone that brought them.

On the contrary, as he had touched the rain to turn the arrows, now the rain struck back, carrying the horror of the maimed and dying. This was not the directed communication of one magus to another—he could not sense their thoughts or hear their voices, but the contact he forged conveyed their emotions with an awful clarity. Sensitive, Sage had called him, but he did not know what that meant until now.

Darkness whirled around him. From all sides came

the eager cold of death, not so strong as that in his gruesome, now buried talisman, but rather as an army of a hundred deaths. As each death faded, two more swelled to take its place. The rain brought them down upon him, piercing as arrows of ice. Worse yet, the mud which embraced him carried their cries through the very earth, in through the wetness of his clothes, in through the brand upon his chest. A gale of tortured souls surrounded him, such moaning and weeping that he was lost within it. The fingers of Death caressed his skin, leaving a wake of frost.

His teeth chattered so hard he feared they must break. Desperately, he fought the freezing mud, only to find the warmth of a hand pressing him down. Words penetrated his pounding skull.

"Down! Stay down," Madoc urged. "Be dead. The line's well ahead now." Shifting the branches that covered him, Madoc brought his lips close to Elisha's ear. "Keep still a while, let us get on—you'll hear the horsemen pass you, then do what you will."

Shaking his head urgently, Elisha only made himself more dizzy, and his face fell again, the mud smearing his cheek where once an angel had touched him. Now the panic threatened to overwhelm him. He had to get up, somehow, to escape the ooze, even if he could not flee the rain.

Madoc had thrown them into the pit of a previous blast where water gathered that much more quickly. Elisha rolled over, shivering, his hands shaking so much he could barely turn them to his will. With elbows and flailing knees, he flung off the branches and scrambled uphill.

More debris rained down on him, more screams added to the din. He couldn't see, his chilled hands couldn't tell if he climbed on mud or stone or the ruins of the siege tower. Then they struck something warm.

Elisha let out a cry and collapsed again onto his belly, gathering the heat to him, the small warm body of the banner bearer.

Mastering his fear, Elisha held on to the warm, unconscious boy, feeling the life in him. His palms thawed with the sense of the boy's faith, and his onetime eagerness for glory, for the admiration he had toward Madoc, and the fleeting heat of memories Elisha could not quite touch as they raced by.

Grudgingly, Death gave ground, retreating one terrible step at a time, withdrawing the freeze, then the pain, then the horrible sounds of men who could no longer speak.

Some time later, the earth trembled as the cavalry rode by, accompanied by shouts and the clanking of steel, sending a brief shower of mud down upon them, and a few more wails from the wounded, wails that shivered into Elisha's heart.

At last, Elisha lay quiet. Rain washed away most of the mud clinging to him, but it was just rain, and the mud was only earth after all.

He took a deep breath, and let it out. His second breath went deeper yet, drawing in a sense of his own aches, and the burn on his chest soothed by the mud plastered against it. His third breath ruffled the curly locks of the boy who lay beside him. After a moment, Elisha reached out his hand to touch the boy's throat. The pulse beat slow but steady. He inched himself up just a little. His arms still trembled. Elisha ran his hand gently over the boy's arms and legs, finding no arrow strike or obvious wound. Carefully, he turned the face toward his own.

A reddened patch stood out in sharp relief on the lad's temple, remnant of a heavy blow. Still, the skull beneath held no fracture. Even as Elisha smoothed back the hair to check the extent of the blow, the boy's eyes flew open, and he flinched from the touch.

Immediately, the banner bearer started to rise, then slumped back, both hands at his head. "By the cross," he muttered, blinking at Elisha.

"You're all right," Elisha told him, "but you'd better rest a bit to get your senses back."

"I've got to find Madoc," the boy said, trying to shake his head and giving up with a groan. With one hand, he groped across the mud until he found the pole and the banner lying beneath him. "Got to take them on."

"Wait, wait," Elisha murmured. "Like this, you'll only blunder up and be killed."

A pretty blare of horns sounded some way off, and the boy rolled himself over, his head swaying as he tried again to rise. "That's the charge!"

Still shaky himself, Elisha caught his arm.

"Let me go, I'll not go home to Mum and tell her I've spent the battle lying in a pit."

"Lad," Elisha said, "You saved my life; let that content you until your head clears at least."

Turning wide dark eyes on him—the pupils two different sizes—the boy breathed, "Me? I don't remember that."

Elisha smiled faintly. "Take my word for it, if not for you, I'd be a dead man."

Sinking back to the earth, the boy grinned. "That means every life you save here on out is due to me."

Laughing, Elisha tested his left arm, finding it adequate, if still throbbing. "Yes, my boy, it's true."

"Well, I'd better rest up for my next feat." He drew one arm up over his face as his eyes slid shut, the concussion overcoming him once more.

"I'll come check on you," Elisha murmured, then he raised his head.

At the bottom of the pit below, three men lay in the mud. Two had their eyes wide in that unblinking astonishment of death, but the third moaned, hand scraping feebly at the earth.

Shimmying back down the slope, Elisha retrieved Collum's kitchen knife—it might yet come in handy—and tucked it at the back of his belt. He shifted his emergency pouch to the side and crept over to the wounded man. Heaving aside one of the corpses, he quickly saw the twist of the wounded man's arm at his back and the blood seeping through his hair.

"I'm the barber," he whispered to the man's ear, and the eyes fluttered open, a trace of a smile touched the soldier's lips. "Good. You've got a break in your arm, it doesn't look bad, but it'll hurt when I set it, hear me?"

As he spoke, his strong fingers searched out the break, judging where to hold, where to press just so. Relief welled up in him; watching the shaking of his hands, he had thought of his boast to the physician. His hands were the only thing he had faith in, and they had looked to fail him not so long ago. Now, the power returned, if a little slower than he would like.

Carefully, he placed his hands and eased the shifted bone back into place. He tore the sleeve from one of the corpses, the worn fabric washed by the rain until it was nearly as clean as any bandage back at the hospital. With the break bound, he probed the back of the man's head, finding a small scalp wound, bloody, but not serious.

Withdrawing, he inched over to lie face to face with the soldier. "You're fine, but lie still. There's a cut at the back which should give up bleeding soon."

"Thanks," the soldier said.

Nodding his acknowledgement, Elisha crept on past, climbing the opposite bank on his stomach to get a view of the battlefield. Elisha pushed his hair back from his face, spending a minute to bundle it all together again. Ahead, and nearer than he'd ever seen it, stood the duke's castle.

As he watched, he heard the bombards blast, but on the far side. One of the tree-topped hills beyond the castle trembled, then slipped from view in a cloud of dust, quickly dissipated by the rain. The ground shook as from an earthquake and finally lay still again. Elisha brushed raindrops from his face, staring at the place where the vanished hill once was. On the tall castle towers, storm winds shook bold pennants like taunting tongues.

Between there and the bulk of the last siege tower, the battle raged. Men on foot and horseback crossed swords with a ringing of steel. Banners waved and fell and were taken up again by other hands. Shouts and cheers warred with the cries of the fallen, but Elisha had taken back his touch and heard only as a man should, and no more. Behind him, a patch of ruined earth showed the reach of the bombards' blast, but there were few bodies, and Elisha let the glow return, that euphoria tingling inside him. Few bodies because the arrows never struck another man. The archers must have stopped shooting, whether from superstitious awe or by order of some worried superior. Beyond that, arrows sprouted from the ground and from the distant soldiers like unholy saplings, and Elisha's glow faded. If he had only done it sooner. But it was the living that must concern him, and he turned his attention again toward the battle. Those behind had lain long enough that either they were dead, or they had bound up their own injuries with whatever came to hand. The ones ahead still had need of him.

Keeping his head low in case of stray arrows or bombards, and to keep from the sight of the captains who watched for shirkers, Elisha wriggled along until he came to the nearest man who showed any life. This one had a nasty gash down one side from the splintering of the siege tower, and Elisha freed a few shards of wood before binding his ribs tight with a dead man's tunic.

As he went on, checking pulses, setting breaks, and stitching the wounds he deemed most in need, Elisha took up whatever came to hand to bind them. Some soldiers sported bandages torn from their captains' banners, while others made do with the tunics of the dead. Many would have to wait for more serious care at the hospital; these he wrapped with tourniquets and bandages of their companions' belts and baldrics. Here on the field, he treated lords and soldiers alike, any who might be too hurt to last until the hold was called. He wielded the kitchen knife against his private foes, cutting out arrows, spearpoints and shafts of wood. He hoped, even here, he could make Ruari's task a little easier. Once in a while, he looked up to check his progress. He tried to work his way across the field, back toward the river, without getting close to the battle.

After a few hours of this, his throat began to itch, and he realized he had been humming. The wounded groaned or wailed or cursed him as he worked, and the humming started up as it always did. As he broke off, taking a drink from the rainwater collecting in a fallen shield, Elisha heard a voice call out not far off, a shout of pain and helplessness.

Taking another quick swallow, Elisha set out again, crawling around the corpses when he could avoid them, or treading gently when he could not.

"God help me, it hurts!" the victim screamed to the leaden sky.

Elisha risked raising his head, spotting the writhing figure just to the left. Angling that way, he quickly reached him, lifting his head again to survey the man's wounds.

The wounded man wore a breastplate of steel, embossed with a pattern of animals most likely related to his coat of arms. If Elisha paid more attention to such nonsense, he might even be able to put a name to the man. It was enough to see that one of the buckles of his armor had ripped loose, leaving a gap by his left arm. From the gap thrust a crossbow bolt at a wicked angle, little of the short shaft emerging.

Blood soaked the man's cotton padding and ran down his pale throat, which worked to swallow his pain. The strap of a skewed helmet cut across his cheek.

Wetting his lips, Elisha reached out and touched the man's face.

His head whipped around to stare at Elisha, the white showing at his eyes. "Who are you? What do you want?"

"I'm the barber—I want to help you," Elisha said. He brought his other hand around and freed the buckle to draw off the man's helmet.

Settling his head back with a little moan, the noble maintained his frightened gaze. "What'll you do? I'm for the Lord now," he gasped. His body quaked with the shock and pain as he crept a hand up his chest.

Darting a glance toward the moving hand, Elisha saw the flash of the dagger in its grasp.

Biting back a curse, he shot out his arm as the blow came. Elisha grabbed the man's wrist, his fingers slipping on the metal bracers. Still, he managed to shake free the blade and sent it tumbling away among the dead.

Frustration knotting his brow, the noble struggled, trying to reach Elisha's face.

"Stop it," Elisha said through gritted teeth. "Just

stop it and let me help." His own strength hadn't fully returned, what with the force of his casting and the damage of Matthew's iron.

Side by side they lay, locked in this one-armed battle until the nobleman's desperation was spent, and he let his arm fall back, panting with the effort it had cost him.

"That's better. I'd advise you to keep as still as you can, if this arrow burrows any farther, you're a dead man, hear me?"

With a whimper and a flash of those agonized eyes, the man nodded.

"I'm taking off your armor," Elisha warned, as he fumbled with the clasps he could reach. He guided the breastplate around the shaft and flung it to the other side, leaving the man's padded chest heaving and exposed.

Reaching for the handle of the kitchen knife, Elisha paused. "I'm bringing out a knife, but it's not for you."

The lord flinched as the blade came between them. He shut his eyes, screwing up his courage for a killing blow, his lips twitching in the Lord's Prayer.

Elisha pulled up a bit of cloth around the wound and cut through, swiftly shearing away the padding, as well as the linen shirt beneath. This done, he replaced the knife. Gently, he snuck his fingers under the layers, against the warm flesh.

With a sharp breath, the lord popped his eyes open, swiveling his head to frown at Elisha.

"Didn't I tell you I'm not going to kill you? Good God," Elisha muttered. His palm lay flat over the man's heartbeat. He flicked his eyes to the man's face, gratified that the eyes which met his looked more brown than white by now, as the fear left him. Elisha smiled.

Placing his right hand around the shaft to steady it, he instructed, "Take a breath, deep as you can."

The man whimpered as he did, but the arrow didn't move any more than expected. Good. Shifting to lean over the nobleman, Elisha wrapped his left arm underneath, lifting him up just enough to creep his right hand along the man's back. No exit wound; judging by the angle, the arrow was likely lodged against the shoulder blade, and too much movement could well force it back to the vital organs.

Now to stabilize it until a small knife could be found to get it out. The awkward kitchen knife couldn't handle such delicate work, and the little knife in his emergency kit would never do. Horses whinnied nearby, probably roaming the field riderless, the sound at odds with the moans of the men who still needed his attention. Elisha brought his head up to search the noble's person and those around him. He needed a long strip, or something which might be knotted together to anchor the shaft.

Nothing struck him as readily useful, and he was out of bandages in his own little stock. Then he remembered Martin Draper's queer gift, the long bit of cloth he carried coiled up in his kit.

Elisha hesitated, then fished it out. It was not his only talisman, and it might well save this man's life, depending on how gently he was brought from the field. He could send to Ruari for his chest. If he made it off this field himself.

The man's head lolled as he lapsed into unconsciousness. Carefully, Elisha began his wrappings, tying off the shaft and binding the man's arm so he wasn't tempted to flap it around. He'd just brought the end around again when he was jerked back by the hair.

Letting go the cloth, Elisha grabbed at the hand that held him. Then two and a half feet of steel flashed before his gaze, and the sword swung up beneath his chin.

Chapter 25

❖

$\mathcal{P}$ulled backward as he staggered to his feet, Elisha held his breath, trying to lift his throat away from the edge.

"Teach you to loot from the Earl of Blackmere," muttered the voice against his ear. "Like to slash your guts and leave you to the crows, so help me, if I'd not get your cursed blood upon him."

Before him, three men dismounted their horses, tossing the reins to a few already on foot. The smaller of the three led them, a paunchy man in battleworn mail, who dropped to his knees at the side of Elisha's patient. "Praise the Lord—he's alive!"

A fourth man stood a little back, steadying a blackened bronze tube on the end of a wooden shaft. With a sickening jolt, Elisha realized this was a bombardelle, its deadly shot aimed at his heart.

"Get back inside, your Grace—it's not safe out here," Elisha's captor urged the paunchy man.

"I saw Phillip go down," the man replied. "The least I could do for him is to attend his body."

"This bloody murderer would've hacked him with a kitchen knife!"

His head jerked back again, his hair yanked tight to stretch his neck over the man's shoulder. Time for that haircut, Elisha thought distantly. He wrapped his right hand around the mailed fist which held the sword, but he was no match for its iron will. Between gasps of breath, he swallowed, his feet finding a bit of ground at last.

"His armor's off," a different voice remarked, "and his dagger taken."

"Let's execute the bastard and have done," someone advised. "At this range I could blast a hole in him the size of his head. Once my lord Robert steps aside, of course."

"Still more certain with the sword," replied the man at his back—presumably Lord Robert. The blade snicked the skin along Elisha's jaw, and he grappled with the implacable hand, even as the grip made the subtle shift to kill him.

"Hold," another voice commanded, stern and striking.

"Blast it," muttered Elisha's assailant. "Your Grace, this is no time for mercy."

"Bring him here, Robert, and gently, if you please."

Stumbling, Elisha was dragged on and thrust to his knees before the horsemen. "Hands on your head." His captor briefly removed the sword to enable this action.

"Don't move him," Elisha called in his momentary reprieve.

The sword drew a stinging line of blood across his stomach, and Elisha cried out, stifling the sound as the sword leapt back to his throat. The barrel of the bombardelle thrust nearer as well, searing his nose and throat with the scent of death.

"Now, really, Robert," chided the shorter man, looking up at Elisha's cry. He knelt at the wounded man's head, examining the protruding shaft. His round face creased with concern, and he stripped off his gauntlet.

"Don't move him," he muttered, echoing Elisha's admonition. With careful fingers, he lifted the trailing end of the strip binding the wound. "What's this?"

Elisha's throat moved against the blade, but he couldn't draw breath to speak. His arms trembled, his hands clamped to his head as ordered.

Cocking his head with a weary sigh, the man said, "Robert, it's all well and good your wish to defend me, but let the man speak, would you?"

The sword wavered and withdrew to hover just a few inches away, easy striking range.

"The shaft struck against his shoulder blade in back." Elisha spoke quickly, his words tumbling in a desperate rush. Whoever he was, this man held power over his life. "If he moves much, it might harm the lungs or heart. I tied off the shaft to steady it. You'll need a narrow blade to slide along it and back it out." His chest heaved, the taut skin of his brand aching as he drew a few breaths, watching his questioner.

Surprisingly, the man gave a tired smile. "We've had a medical lesson, gentlemen. I hope you've taken notes." A few offered tight laughter. Fingering the cloth, the man repeated his question, "What's this? The cloth, I mean. Where did you get it?" His words took on a soothing tone, not dissimilar to the one Elisha used on his more frightened patients.

Given a little space to breathe and overcome his initial fright, Elisha considered. The other's manner, and his question, gave notice that he probably knew more about the cloth than Elisha himself, but was he Martin's friend or foe? "I had it with me," Elisha admitted. "Just a scrap."

Nodding, the lord stripped off the other gauntlet, and carefully tied the end of the binding before stepping over his comrade and coming to gaze down at Elisha. "And who are you? A medical man, evidently, but not one of ours—they're still at the far end of the field."

"Elisha Barber," he said promptly, "I've been serving . . ." He let go the words he would have said.

The only men on the field were the king's men weren't they? He took a furtive glance around and saw how close the siege towers had come to the duke's own walls. Inside, they would be running short on shot and arrows. When Elisha ruined their barrage, they probably sent out a sortie of armed knights to repel the besiegers rather than waste what little ammunition remained. *Your Grace*, the man was addressed, *"not one of ours,"* he had observed. Elisha blanched. It was none other than the renegade Duke Randall of Dunbury, and the man he had saved was the enemy. "Oh, God," he murmured.

The duke removed his helmet, handed it back to one of his men, and ran a hand through his thinning brown hair. He puffed out a sigh and bent his knee, bringing himself down to Elisha's level. "I see you've worked it out, Barber."

In his voice, the name of Elisha's profession did not come out as an insult the way lords generally applied it. Warily, he nodded.

"Do you know the man you doctored?"

Elisha slowly shook his head.

"Phillip, Earl of Blackmere. He only led the sortie because he was furious the king refused to parley. He thought he might shame him into it." Duke Randall settled his elbow on his upraised knee and dropped his chin into his hand. "Does that fool Hugh even know what he has in you?"

At this, Elisha frowned. He thought to speak, then thought better of it. Let the duke tell him what he would. Maybe by the time they returned to the subject at hand, he would know the right answers.

"Yes, Barber, I have been on a first-name basis with kings, and now I am a marked man. But before I die, I would know from you how you came by that piece of cloth."

That mournful air, the way he brought himself down to look Elisha in the eye inspired a sort of trust Elisha was not familiar with. He risked his voice. "My lord— Your Grace—I don't know that I should tell you."

"Now you speak him fair, Barber," the lord said, bringing up the edge of his sword.

"I cannot speak you fair, Your Grace, but I can speak you plain. Someone's given me this bit of cloth. I don't know where it's from, and I don't know what it means, and I don't know what he meant in giving it to me." Elisha gave a giddy laugh. "Perhaps he meant someone to kill me, Your Grace. You've already got my life in your hands. But regardless of what he meant, I'm damned if I'll reveal him and give you his life as well."

Duke Randall considered this, his round face wrinkling with thought. "The trouble is, Barber, that in order to take it, I'd have to be a free man. The only time of day I can even leave my house is during the hold, and only then as long as I trust Hugh to keep his word. But you have a commendable loyalty to this unnamed friend." His face cleared as he glanced up to Robert at Elisha's back and then to his other lieutenants. "The cloth is from my daughter's wedding gown. I had it made up to her design and hired a man of the city to get it done. He swore to me to let no scrap escape him, lest her special gift be worn by whores or even the queen's ladies in imitation. And here I find a piece of that selfsame gown employed to bind my best friend's wound. And by an honest barber."

With the groan of a tired man, the duke rose to his feet and smiled down at Elisha. "Martin Draper is your friend's name," he said, "and he meant, if ever you came my way, that you should go free, and with my blessing. Clever man, our Martin. Let him go, Robert. For the life of the earl, if not for Martin's sake, he deserves better than he's had from us."

Grumbling, Robert sheathed his sword and even gave Elisha a hand up to regain his unsteady feet.

Slightly dazed, Elisha glanced from one to the other of them. A few faces still looked suspicious, including the tall, fierce Robert and the gunner who scowled as he put up his weapon. But Duke Randall smiled. "Give Martin my best, would you, when you meet again? I doubt I'll have that pleasure."

"Don't talk that way, Your Grace," replied Lord Robert immediately.

"Once I believed this could all turn out well in the end. I thought Hugh's rascal boy would recant, or Hugh himself would see reason, but I think now it is not to be. Go on," he told Elisha, indicating the king's encampment with a tilt of his head. Quietly, he replaced his helmet. "Don't move him, you say?"

Elisha, already leaving, turned back. "Yes, Your Grace, unless you make him a litter. Better to have your surgeon do it here and avoid the danger."

"Thank you, Barber. God be with you."

Bowing his head, Elisha returned, "And with you, Your Grace," and thought he had never wished something so true in his life, even as he turned his back. Across the field of the wounded, he saw parties of the king's men approaching, some gathering the soldiers into carts while others in twos and threes took up the lords. Several of these stood still, staring in their direction. Quickly, Elisha called out, "Your Grace!"

"What is it?" Robert's voice answered.

"I think I must ask you to kill me."

"Sorry?" said Duke Randall's soft, puzzled voice. "I've just set you free."

"Aye, Your Grace, but the king's men have seen us talking. If they think you've tried to kill me, I may yet live through this."

"Ah, I see your point. Go on gunner—but leave out the lead."

"Aye, Your Grace." The gunner tipped his weapon and shook out the lead ball, then refilled it with black powder and stuffed in a bit of wadding, poking it down with a rod. For a moment, their eyes met over the open mouth of the bombardelle, and Elisha wondered how many of this man's victims had died in his hospital. His stomach roiled. He knew too well the damage that thing could cause. He took a step back, shaky.

"Go on, then," said the gunner, "might's well run and make it look good." He leveled the weapon in Elisha's direction, bracing the wooden shaft at his foot, then lit a twist of cloth from a hooded lantern at his belt.

Elisha stumbled back another step, then he ran. He leapt a few bodies before the gun went off with a terrible boom and a puff of smoke. A blast of hot air slapped his back, stinging through his shirt, and he fell with an unfeigned scream, his ears throbbing with the sound of the blast. For a moment he lay gulping for breath, and he could see why even the bravest of men feared the shot. The black smoke swirled over him and dissipated, leaving its acrid stench.

Boots tramped nearby. Looking down as if to be sure the captive was dead, Robert winked and walked away.

Elisha soon discovered how hard it is to lie still for any length of time. He heard the duke's men speaking softly amongst themselves, and the occasional ripping of grass as one of the restless horses chomped a meal while he waited. After a time, a surgeon came, muttered over the wounded Earl, and apparently followed Elisha's repeated instructions. At last, the duke's party moved on, ignoring Elisha just as they had since his "death."

Moments later, booted feet tramped up around him. "That the man?" one asked.

"Aye, I think so. Long hair, covered in blood—seems about right."

"Here," said the first, "Bring over that lad."

"The barber! Thank God you've found him," fluted the youthful tone of the banner bearer. "Is he hurt? They've shot him!"

Even as he lay there, holding his breath, Elisha knew he was lost. Warm hands rolled him over and touched his throat. "Thank God," the lad repeated fervently. "Just stunned, I guess. Won't Madoc be glad to hear."

"Go back to your company, boy, we'll take him," the man said gruffly.

"I should get him back to Madoc, if he's all right," the lad replied. "Sure and he's been worried enough."

"We'll take him," the man snapped, and one set of footfalls hurried away.

A boot prodded Elisha's chest, sending a spasm of pain through the burn that radiated along his rib cage. Elisha gave an involuntary gasp, and the men around him laughed. He braced himself to play the role he had claimed, but his heart sank.

"Get up, you traitor. The king'll have a word with you."

Opening his eyes at last, Elisha asked, "Have they gone? Thank God."

"Don't give me that," the soldier snapped. "We saw you talking to the duke."

He should have asked Duke Randall to kill him for

good rather than face whatever was to come. Firm
hands dragged him to his feet, taking the knife and his
belt with its pouch. For good measure, they stripped off
his boots, searched and discarded them. Slipping away
his pouch—no doubt to be used as evidence or sold for
private gain—the guard pulled Elisha's wrists together
at his back and bound them tight with Elisha's own
leather belt. The skin of his chest strained at the brand,
a pain that gripped him with every breath.

With a guard on each arm, Elisha trudged back toward camp. As they walked, heads looked up among
the search parties to watch him pass. A man gathering
fallen weapons into a cart called out to him. The rain
still fell, softer now, but the world seemed empty of
magic, and he had given up his talisman to save the
earl. That bit of cloth had given him a slight reprieve as
well as the chance to be executed for betraying his king,
rather than for tending the wrong man. The banner
bearer might believe the gunner had missed him, but
the soldiers clearly were having none of it. At least, he
might see Brigit one more time before he died.

Shaking back his hair, he raised his head and tried
to keep his feet. What had been farmers' fields were
transformed by furrows of the dead, freshly turned.
The acrid smell of powder hung in the damp air, along
with the reek of perforated bowels. Here and there, soldiers staggered up and leaned together, making their
way toward camp. The ruins of the siege towers hulked
over all, deepening the darkness. A few men with a
pike struggled to raise part of a trebuchet to free a man
trapped underneath. Even as he passed, Elisha could
see the rend in the man's chest, pumping blood. His
battle was over, but his friends still fought for him.

Ahead, a soldier crept toward them, dragging a
crushed leg. "Please," he groaned, reaching out.

Elisha's hands strained against the binding, twisting and unable to get free. "A tourniquet," he said. "Sir, if I can just—"

The guard jerked him off balance, towing him forward. "The cart's coming, you be still," he told the injured man.

With a sob, the man slumped to the mud, his fingers digging in.

"It won't take a moment, sir," Elisha said. The guard cuffed him hard, and he staggered a few steps, hauled along by the grip on his arm.

The coppery taste of blood stained Elisha's tongue, the blow spinning him so that he could still see the wounded man left behind them. "I'm sorry," he whispered. For a moment, in the shimmer of the rain, the man had his brother's blond hair.

They reached the strip of earth where the farthest arrows of the duke's archers had reached, and the battlefield was marred by blackened towers and scorched corpses. So many died that he might have saved, by magic or by the skill of his hand. So many lived who still needed him, clutching bloody wounds and arrow shafts, and he could do nothing but stumble on, his hands growing numb, arms aching with his thwarted need to help. "I'm sorry," he told them, but there was none who could forgive him. The injured watched him pass with tears and pleading, the dead with vacant, staring eyes. One of the corpses wore a little tin cross.

Chapter 26

❖

Elisha's journey ended at a gaily striped pavilion complete with an awning to hold back the absent sun. Once inside, they thrust him to his knees. The three guards seated themselves on campstools. One drummed his fingers on a small table with a heap of blankets tucked behind it. The only other furnishing was a rug.

For hours, Elisha waited as the tent grew darker and darker. When they first arrived, he would periodically try to stretch his legs, but his guards drew their swords, and so he stilled himself. He sat on the ground at the center, alternately wondering how his patients on the field were faring and studying the richly patterned rug. His family had had dirt floors, but the king could afford to throw down such a rug in a war camp.

On the way, Ruari had hailed him as they walked past the monastery to the bridge, but Elisha dared not acknowledge him, and he knew his silence would give his friends little comfort. Who knew where Brigit might be.

At last, the flap swept open, and a tall, fair man ducked underneath.

Instantly, the guards leapt to their feet and bowed.

Elisha, sore from his long wait, rose more slowly, but bowed the more deeply to make up for it. From the growl of the guard behind him, he realized his actions could as easily be taken for insolence.

The physician and the surgeon's assistant, Matthew, stepped through a short time after, staying at the tent wall as the man who must be the king strode forward. Clad in a tabard of royal purple with a hound's head emblazoned on a field of white, he had the thick beard and sharp blue eyes Ruari had described, with a sharp nose as well, giving him rather the look of a falcon, ready to rip Elisha to shreds. The duke had called him "Hugh," a name that sounded much too small and plain for such a man. Glaring at him, the king parted his lips and intoned one word. "Kneel."

Elisha sank to the ground, his heart racing. In all his nearly thirty years, he had never been called before the lord who owned his village, nor even the burghers of the city. He had no idea how to speak to a king, and evidently had already gone wrong without saying a word. The throbbing from his chest spread into his muscles. Keeping his head down, Elisha watched the king's highly polished boots, the left toe moving slowly up and down as if he kept time with distant, unheard music.

"You were seen speaking to the renegade duke, can you deny it?" the king demanded at last.

"No, Your Majesty, I cannot," Elisha mumbled.

"Speak up," the king snapped.

"I cannot deny it," Elisha repeated, finding his voice.

A sword suddenly jabbed at his chin, and Elisha flinched away, forced to look up to the king's impassive face. "You are a mere barber, and little expected to understand the ways of your betters, but my title, at the least, you should understand."

Elisha wet his lips. "Yes, Your Majesty, please forgive me."

Slowly, the sword withdrew.

The blue eyes narrowed. "Forgive you? Against your other crimes, that one pales to insignificance. What did you discuss with the duke?"

"I was bandaging a lord on the field," Elisha began, adding "Your Majesty," quickly, "when the duke's party arrived. We spoke of the man's wound." The blood seemed to be draining to his cold feet as he knelt there, knowing that nothing he said, neither truth, nor lie, would be of any use.

"What lord?"

"The Earl of Blackmere, they said, Your Majesty."

"Ah." The single syllable carried both illumination and disgust. "The Earl of Blackmere, the duke's loyal man—the enemy, Barber, if you failed to notice. Though how you could fail to notice such a peacock in a field of hawks is beyond me."

Elisha wasted a moment trying to conjure up a picture of a peacock. "Your Majesty, until this battle, I have never left the city. I did not have even the heraldic descriptions your soldiers must know."

The king let out an exaggerated sigh. "So you claim ignorance."

Noticing the stillness of the king's left foot, Elisha held his tongue.

"To continue," the king said as he began to pace a short track in front of his prisoner, "you doctored the duke's best man, and the duke's party found you there—leaving aside the question of how you came to be so far afield at the time of the hold—and he talked to you about the earl's wound, he seemed about to let you go, then they took a shot at you with one of my guns."

"Yes, Your Majesty."

"Why didn't he cut your throat right away?"

Elisha hesitated and chose the truth. "He was grateful about the earl, Your Majesty."

"I imagine that he was. What did you say about the earl's wound?"

"That he should not be moved for fear the bolt would . . ." Elisha's mouth went dry, and he trailed off. The king's heels stood before him now, with silver spurs shimmering by the light of braziers, twitching as the king listened. "That the bolt would puncture the heart or lungs, Your Majesty."

"Did you save his life, do you think?"

Miserably, Elisha wet his lips, tasting the blood that lingered still. The truth became another weapon to use against him, another blackened mouth ready to blast him with fire, and he could do nothing to stop it.

"Answer me, Barber. Did you save his life?"

"Yes," Elisha whispered. "Yes, Your Majesty, I think I did."

"Ah." The king suddenly took two long steps forward. "Who are you?" he demanded of one of the bystanders.

Elisha risked a glance to see the king standing toe to toe with Matthew, who shrank before him.

"Matthew Drake of Gilbertston, Your Majesty. I am Mordecai Surgeon's first assistant."

"What are you doing here when I called for your master?"

"It's the Sabbath, Your Majesty, I'm not sure where he is—where he is at worship, that is. Your man brought me in his stead."

"The surgeon's a Jew?" the king asked, turning away without an answer. "I thought my father had expelled the lot of them. Should've known they'd be creeping back in." He rounded again on Elisha.

"Some of the best surgeons are Jews, Your Majesty," Matthew supplied, in a voice more timid than Elisha had ever heard from him.

"And the best barbers, what are they?" the king asked, his voice with an edge of humor.

"I am not sure I take your meaning, Your Majesty," the physician ventured, sharing raised eyebrows with Matthew.

"Men who know when to put their tools away." He grinned, a sharp expression to match the sharp eyes. "Fetch my throne and my crown. And Surgeon—"

"Yes, Your Majesty?" Matthew said, springing a half-step forward.

"Have you ever assisted an interrogation before?" He kept his icy gaze on Elisha as he spoke, his gaze like the slightest touch of Death.

"On occasion, Your Majesty. My master has little taste for such work himself." Matthew stood straighter, his voice and bright eyes betraying his excitement at winning the king's attention.

"Fetch what you need." He twiddled his fingers over his shoulder, and Matthew hurried out. Matthew, who did not hesitate to scald their own men, would hold back nothing if granted the king's justice upon a traitor. More so, given the antipathy between them.

"But Your Majesty, I don't know anything!" Elisha protested. "I have met the duke only once, and we spoke of exactly what I told you."

The king settled himself in the throne two of his men carried inside. A servant stepped up to place a gleaming crown upon his head. "A week ago, you saved the life of my messenger," he said abruptly.

Startled, Elisha frowned, glancing to the physician—who stood strangely detached, not even betraying the glee he must feel at Elisha's downfall. Shouldn't this act

count in his favor? If so, why was the king looking ever
more fierce? "Yes, Your Majesty."

At this, the king smiled again, tilting his head as if
sizing Elisha for a noose. "And how did you know he
was my messenger?"

"The message was found, Your Majesty," Elisha replied slowly, "when I brought him to the hospital for
treatment." His knees and bare feet leached the heat
from his body into the cold earth below.

"It was found." The king waved a hand, and someone brought him a goblet from which he took a long
swallow. "By you?"

Wetting his lips, Elisha hesitated. Ruari and Brigit
had both seen the message, and knew the mark upon it.
The messenger knew all this, but apparently he hadn't
spoken of it. Neither could Elisha bring himself to lift
the burden of guilt by casting doubt on either of them.
His stomach clenched, Robert's cut to his stomach
stinging like an accusation.

At that moment, Matthew popped back through the
door. He approached one of the braziers to Elisha's
right and placed a few long, slender irons into it, unrolling on the floor a leather bundle full of tools not unlike
Elisha's own. Elisha's muscles felt rigid as he recalled
how each tool was held—how it felt in the hand and
how it moved against the flesh. He knew intimately the
incisive thrust of the lancet, the bite of the saw into
bone, the smell of burning flesh.

"Did the ground shake while you were on the field
today, Barber?" the king said, distracted by the sight of
Matthew laying out his tools.

"Yes, Your Majesty," Elisha said as Matthew rearranged the irons, adding to them a long blade. "It
looked as if part of a hill collapsed." The brand upon
his chest ached as if in warning of what was to come.

"Why did that happen?" the king mused, stroking his beard.

"I don't know, Your Majesty."

"Could it be that my men tunneled underneath it? That they were nearly to the castle foundation, nearly ready to spring the trap, when the duke's largest bombard, notably absent from the fighting, blew a hole in just the wrong place?"

Elisha bit off a breath, the questions suddenly coming together in his mind. "Is that what happened?" he said, his voice shaky, "Your Majesty?"

Matthew pulled an iron from the fire and tested it by singeing a few of his own arm hairs, then thrust it back in with a satisfied smirk.

Goosebumps tingled on Elisha's skin, his fingers trembling a little. "I don't know about it, Your Majesty. I only saw the outside of the message, and that it bore the royal seal. I swear to God I know nothing about it." The king's left toe went still; with a nod, Matthew rose from his place by the brazier. Elisha's heart pounded. Death he expected. Summary execution, most likely— but the king was not done with him. "Please, Your Majesty, today was the first time I've laid eyes on the duke or any of his men."

"How shall we start, Surgeon?" the king inquired graciously.

"Well, Your Majesty, he has a particular revulsion for burning."

With a graceful turn of his hand, he said, "Proceed."

As Matthew drew out one of his irons, two of the guards stepped forward.

"His hands, if you please," Matthew said.

The belt finally tugged free of his wrists. One guard pulled Elisha's right arm out in front of him, twisting it palm up to expose the more sensitive skin, while the other wrenched his left elbow behind his back. Pain shot through him, his back stinging with the thousand pinprick burns of gunpowder overlaid upon the welts. His flesh was a palimpsest of pain about to be overwritten with hot irons.

"I don't know anything!" Elisha cried, in a last bid for the king's ear. Then heat tingled his wrist, and a fingertip of fire jabbed into his flesh. He screamed.

"Who do you know who works for the duke?" the king asked, his voice pleasant.

"No one, Your Majesty, I swear—" A few inches up from the first, another spot of agony flared into him.

"How did the duke intercept my message?"

Panting, Elisha managed to get out, "I don't know." A third crimson burst of pain. He bucked against his captors, succeeded only in getting his left arm pressed between his shoulder blades, a subtle twist introduced in his wrist. "By God I wish I knew," he sobbed.

"Your ignorance appalls me, Barber." The king took a long swallow of his wine. "Did you mark me for the bombard shot that day?"

The change of tack bewildered Elisha, and he wondered if he'd gone pain-mad so soon. "What?"

At the king's nod, iron bit his arm yet again, searing into the skin and muscle close to his elbow. His arm jerked against his will but the guard pulled it taut again.

"How about the roots that found their way into my supper? Roots you watched that herbalist woman examine."

Had Brigit tried to poison the king? He couldn't imagine it. Shaking his head, Elisha stifled a yelp at the fresh wound.

"Then you claim to know nothing of these various attempts on my person?"

"Nothing, Your Majesty," he gasped. "Please." Burnt

skin sizzled. Elisha slumped, his shoulders shaking from the strain.

"What did you and the duke speak of today?"

"I've told you," Elisha whimpered, clamping shut his jaw as the iron descended to the smooth flesh of his inner arm.

"Can he really be so in the dark?" the king pondered.

"Indubitably, Your Majesty," the physician remarked. "He is only here fleeing criminal charges."

"Indeed? Well, that may explain it. I find it hard to believe any honest man—even a peasant—would refuse loyalty to his rightful monarch."

Elisha's chin rested on his chest, jogged by quick breaths. Tears stung his eyes, but he refused to let them fall. Ruari couldn't read, no more than himself, and Brigit—well, she could be a traitor, though he didn't think she'd had the message long enough, and Ruari would have little reason to protect her if he knew she read it. But the seal had been broken when Ruari found it. Elisha tried to piece these clues together into a story that might save him. Slowly, he raised his head. "The seal was already broken, Your Majesty."

"Oh? Have you decided to cooperate, then?"

Shaking his head vaguely, Elisha said, "When we— when I found it, the seal was already broken. In his fall, I thought, Your Majesty."

"So you are saying someone else may already have read it, is that what you think?"

"Perhaps the messenger—" Elisha broke off.

Even the burns along his arm chilled with the change in the air as the king rose again to his full height and glared down at Elisha. "The messenger."

Staring sidelong up at him, Elisha swayed a little with his pain and exhaustion, but he did not say a word. His outstretched arm trembled with foreboding.

With a tight smile, the king said, "The messenger is my son, Barber. Prince Alaric himself carried my message that day. The only man about me I can trust these days—I received word that he has delivered his message in spite of his injury. I thought you might have recognized him, and that perhaps you deserved my thanks for tending him. It seems you were merely acting in defiance of orders once again." He stared hard at Elisha's face. "Or that you marked him for my messenger, and took your best chance to spy out my commands. You learned the location of the sappers' mine and slipped the information to your master. If you had known him for my son, he would be dead, just as you've been trying to kill me."

He flicked his fingers, starting his men in a flurry of motion. Two carried off the portable throne while another held back the curtain. The spurs glittered like twin stars. "Give him another, Surgeon. And string him up at dawn. Don't bother to wake me."

Chapter 27

◆

When the king had gone, Matthew caught Elisha's hand in his own, gripping his fingers as he delivered his parting shot to the center of Elisha's palm, a curl of steam rising from the burn. Elisha's fingers jerked, and his hand went ominously numb—the hand that made his livelihood, that made his life, lay twitching, as if it were no longer his.

Elisha screamed for the last time, not just for the pain, but for the knowledge that death would come for him. He had done all he could to forestall it, but he had lost that battle for his own life, and with it, any hope of his salvation: his penance was through.

Dropping Elisha's hand like a thing repulsive, Matthew stooped over his instruments and gathered them up, setting the irons upon his shoulder at a jaunty angle. With a last shake of his head, the physician accompanied him out.

Wordlessly, the two guards pinioned his arms behind him, tying his crossed wrists with no regard to the recent burns. Elisha barely noticed through the fog of confusion and pain. He had looked for answers that would satisfy the king, but the truth only brought more torture. The prince had carried his father's message. Not the elder one, Prince Thomas, who was off defending the northern borders, or extending them, depending on who told the tale. This was the second son, Prince Alaric, who was to have married the duke's daughter, the one who had started it all. Twice now, Elisha had saved his neck, only to find himself undone by the messenger's identity. The thought that followed after stopped him cold, jolted away as the guards hauled him to his feet.

Elisha stumbled between them in the rain, sinking down again to his knees as they tied him, his elbows to either side of the whipping post, his bound hands a hard knot at his back. The muddy ground at the base of the post clung to him, and Elisha rested his head against the harsh, familiar wood. His breath shuddered as he tried to master the pain and the sudden sorrow of his knowledge.

Brigit knew. She knew who the messenger was, and they two had some other dealings, that much was clear. From the look upon her face when she had seen the man, Elisha strongly suspected he knew what those dealings were. Trysting in the chapel, Prince Alaric had told him. With her.

She would come to see him unless she had a heart of stone and even the threat of his death would not move her.

Two of the guards wrapped themselves in long cloaks, dragging up a bench to keep their watch over him. They sat each on an end, facing each other and a pair of dice, shaken and tossed, shaken and tossed.

Unlike the king, Brigit did not keep him waiting long.

He raised his head even as she came, picking her way across the mud, a cloak drawn close about her. She passed within a yard of the guards, but they did not look up. When she drew off her hood, she hesitated, and he could feel her eyes upon him.

After a moment of wary watching, Brigit dropped down before him, hugging her knees, close enough that the rim of her cloak fell over his knee. At least some small part of him would be warm.

"Hanging, is it?" she asked, her fair face streaked with rain, her forehead creased.

"Aye, and what else would it be?" he snapped, then turned from the pained look in her eyes.

"Elisha, don't be angry with me, I'm here to help you—"

His chest throbbed. "You began it all, didn't you? The battle, the siege, it's all because of you."

"What are you talking about?" she asked, her eyes glazing over with a strange detachment.

"Oh, I think you know. Prince Alaric, the messenger, the man who was supposed to marry this duke's daughter. The man you love."

"Elisha," she whispered, reaching a hand toward him.

He could not withdraw from her touch, but he tilted his head away, his face to the rain, and as she let her hand fall back, he went on. "He couldn't tell his father the real reason he wouldn't marry her, so he made something up: the lie for which a thousand men have died. Oh, God, Brigit, I can forgive you loving him, even forgive you not telling me, but that these men should die so that you can love a prince—" He broke off while he could still master his emotions. Memories flashed before him: the tin cross, the shattered leg, the soldiers' struggling to save a man already dead.

"Please," she whispered, "please hear me, Elisha. I never intended any of this. It's true, all that you've said. I met him months ago, in the duke's own court. He didn't like the lady in any case, and when we got to talking, I, well, he . . ."

Rolling his head to the side, Elisha watched her. She bit her lip, brushing away what might have been tears, or merely raindrops. "You can't think he'll marry you, Brigit. He's a prince. He is as far beyond a country lady as—" Elisha laughed, "—as you are beyond me, and further."

"He will," she shot back, her head jerking up. "He will marry me, he has sworn it, but we must go slowly, we mustn't make it seem as if . . ." she trailed off, indicating the battlefield with a backward look.

"As if he started a war for you?" As he studied the line of her cheek and the glimmer of her eye, he thought he himself might have done it. He would start a war for her, if he thought he could win some day. If the countless men who died meant no more to him than so many cattle. Then, he knew he was wrong: he could never have done this. He had been too close to death for any man's life to mean so little.

She held a palm over her mouth, nodding slightly. "I never intended any of this. I didn't understand, when we began, and now it's too late to take back the things that have been said. It's not about him and Duke Randall's daughter, not any more. And neither of us knows how to stop it."

"I know how! 'Excuse me, Your Majesty, I lied! I claimed that girl was a whore just so I could marry someone who really is.'" Elisha stared at Brigit, wanting to hurt her, wanting to matter more to her than he ever possibly could.

Trembling, she kept her face lowered, one palm still at her mouth, her other hand gripped in her skirts.

Looking away, Elisha studied the guards, who still took no notice. Some magic defended them, muting their words and hiding her from watchful eyes. "Does he know what you are?" Elisha asked dully.

"Of course he does. Don't you see?" A pleading note edged her voice. "Suppose I marry him, we take up his estates, we live as respected nobility, and then I can reveal that I am a witch. Don't you see what that could mean for all our people? Not just for me, but for any of us. What if they never burn another witch, Elisha? You say that all these men have died for us, for me—what if their deaths enable our people to be freed? Imagine greeting another magus on the street, speaking openly about yourselves, offering your services to those in need without fear of the fire. Earth and sky, Elisha, the vision is so sweet sometimes it tastes like honey on my lips."

Drawn by the sound of her voice, Elisha saw her green-eyed gaze searching some far distant place, an image only she could see of the world she longed to bring about. "I have no such dreams, Brigit. I'm just a barber sick to death of saving men only to see them dead for such a war."

"Just a barber? You most certainly are not." Her gaze snapped back to him with a piercing intensity. "What happened to those arrows, Elisha? Did you see them fall? Oh, I've heard that Jesus took the field today, turning back the killing for his faithful flock in this righteous war."

"There's nothing righteous about it!" He pulled forward, felt the strain in his arms and slumped back again.

"So what happened to the arrows? If Jesus wasn't there, who was?" Her lovely lips curled into a smile. "I wish you could go to the river tonight, Elisha. The water is abuzz—how was it done? How can so many objects be transported at the same time, or were they destroyed? And could any magus alive have done such a thing? Who has done it? 'Is it you?' 'Is it you?'" She turned one way and another, miming the astonishment, then stared directly at him. "Is it you?"

He dropped his gaze, the breath catching in his throat. She must be exaggerating; there was nothing so complicated in what he had done. Just the first law, the only one he understood. Anyone could have done it, in fact.

"It *was* you," she breathed. Brigit inched forward, her knee pressing against his as she spoke. "How did you do it?"

"The rain," he said simply. "I reached into the rain, just the way you'd reach into the river."

"But the arrows?"

"I touched them as they passed, the raindrops were my contact." He frowned. "I thought they were alike, the fall of arrows, the fall of the rain."

"Affinity," she laughed, catching her hands together like a girl. "You applied the first law to raindrops and arrows? My goodness, Elisha, how did you think of it?"

"I didn't think," he snapped, her glee denying all he had just lived through. "I had to stop the arrows killing one more man. I didn't think, I just did it."

In wonder, she clasped his face in her hands. "Oh, Elisha, you have no idea how special you are."

He cackled, the sound coming harshly even to his own ears. "Does it matter? Tomorrow, I'll be specially dead."

"No," said Brigit sharply. "I won't let you die. I'll come up with a plan, you'll see. I will not let them have you."

Twisting his head from her grasp, Elisha muttered, "Why bother?"

Gently, firmly, she guided him back. "Because I should have met you first." Her green eyes flickered over his face and back to his gaze. "I should have met you first."

Tears stung his eyes, and he longed to shut them, to blink away the pain, but he couldn't bring himself to seal away the sight of her. Elisha bit his lip to stop it trembling.

She stroked her fingers down his eyebrow, across his cheek where the angel's feather still warmed him, down to his jaw line, tilting his chin up gently toward her. Leaning forward, she kissed him, light and sweet, her eyes on his.

With a bitter smile, Elisha murmured, "Not yet, you said, that night. Not yet, and now it's too late."

"Trust me," she hissed, both her hands again upon his face. "Trust me, Elisha, I will not let you die."

Again, she inched forward, her legs widening to straddle his, her breasts nudging against his chest, her breath steaming in the chill rain.

"Don't do this to me, Brigit," he moaned.

"Don't you want me to?" she whispered, her lips brushing his face. "I can help you feel nothing but joy."

He swallowed hard. "Here, like this? How—"

"It's a deflection," she whispered. "They see nothing; they hear nothing."

Her hands moved down his chest, avoiding the brand, slipping for a moment into the slit the duke's man had made across his shirt, her touch tingling in a delicious wave through his stomach. There should have been pain, but her touch carried a desperate desire that urged his surrender, her eyes meeting his as the pain receded, her hands infusing him with wanting her. If it was a spell, he welcomed it, searching for anything that made the pain go away—for anything that brought her closer.

Then her hands continued down. The guards had taken his belt and pouch, so she slid up the hem of his shirt unhindered. Her breathing grew ever warmer. She found the tied cord at his waist, and the knot parted at her merest touch.

Brigit gathered her skirt high up to her hips. Somehow, she edged even closer to him, her thighs pressing hot over his. Her arms wrapped around him, then moved upward. Her hands took hold of the post above his head, high over his own bound hands. She pressed herself ever closer.

Elisha caught his breath. One cheek rubbing the rough wood, the other caressed by her exhalation. The heat of her burned through him, bound to the post, half expecting to feel the sweep of her wings.

Then Brigit opened herself to him, drawing him in.

She sighed against his face, her body warm and soft against his until there was no distance between them.

Contact.

Chapter 28

❖

After she had left him, repeating again her exhortation to trust her, Elisha knelt still in a kind of ecstasy. She would save him. The knowledge seemed as true as if it had already happened. Brigit had such power in her; she could come and go unseen, and yet her presence still enveloped him, as if she, too, touched the rain.

It fell now in soft sheets, soaking his long hair already damp with sweat. He parted his lips to the sky, drinking in the remembrance of her. That giddy weakness spread through his body, as if he had worked magic so great it would never let go of him. He lost feeling in his hands, and it didn't matter. She would save him. Not now, she had said, they were too watchful by night, and her spell could divert attention for only so long. Only long enough to love him.

Elisha opened his eyes to the night, watching the clouds drift over the moon, patches of silver concealed and revealed like the gleam of her eye. He reveled in the sway of her hair against his face, overlaying the angel's touch with a benediction of her own. Somewhere far distant inside himself, the iron yet burned his skin, and the weeping ache of the brand on his chest throbbed with every beat of his heart even as it slowed back to its proper pace.

To the east, by Duke Randall's castle on its hill, pale blue seeped into the blackness of the sky. The stealthy hue crept onward, conquering the dark with a gray and growing steel. Steady rain doused the new pair of guards who huddled in their cloaks, arms crossed and feet stamping against the chill.

Shivering, Elisha summoned up the treasure of her warmth. With dawn, his hope blossomed. There had been enough time, now, for Brigit to make her plan. He couldn't guess what it might be, or when.

Footfalls brought his head down with a start, expecting to see her there.

Instead, a bulky man with a blank expression consulted briefly with the guards, then came forward. He wore dark leather, stained with darker patches. He walked up to Elisha, reached down a meaty hand and plucked up the bundle of his hair.

His head jerked forward, Elisha watched from the corner of one eye as the man drew a long knife from his side. A spasm of terror swept through him. Not now! They couldn't kill him like this, before Brigit had her chance.

But the knife reached over his neck and started to hack through the thickness of his hair. Elisha's head swayed with the sawing of the blade, and some of his euphoria ebbed away.

Stepping back as if to view his handiwork, the man tossed down Elisha's hair and left him.

Elisha raised his head. It had not seemed so light in years, a weight taken from his scalp. Now, the shorn waves barely touched his jaw at the front, and the back of his head cooled quickly in the rain, skin revealed to the air for the first time in at least a decade. The new short hairs quivered on end in the growing dawn.

Already, he missed the regular and comforting movement of his hair upon his back. He turned his head side to side, listening for the soft rustle. It would take years for all that hair to grow back. Of course, he had thought himself impractical, letting it get so long to begin with.

A priest seemed to materialize before him, and Elisha realized that he, too, was barefoot.

"My son, I have come for the cleansing of your soul and to perform the Lord's last rites upon you. Do you wish to make confession?" A small, weary figure, he slumped within the robes of his office as if he had heard too many secrets not his own.

Elisha considered the offer. What would he confess freely before a god he did not quite believe in? That he had faith in Brigit? That he was a witch, who had performed magic against the laws of God and country? Elisha smiled faintly. "No, Father, I don't think I do."

The lines of the priest's face deepened into canyons of disapproval. With a dispirited gesture in the sign of the cross, he blessed Elisha anyhow, then retreated a little way to wait.

More footsteps squelched through the mud as a party of guards approached, the man in leather among them. Behind, he could see shadowy figures passing from the monastery toward the trees along the river. What did the river speak of this morning?

Someone stooped behind him, cutting through the rope at the back of the post.

When two men caught his elbows, Elisha swayed between them, stumbling as he got his feet underneath him again. Mud oozed between his toes.

Surrounded by the king's guards, Elisha walked where they led him. He darted his glance here or there, looking for Brigit. Most of those gathering wore hoods against the rain, and he could not tell which might be hers.

He caught sight of the physician with Benedict trailing after, the second assistant at his side. With a gesture to his own throat, Lucius seemed to be explaining the effects of hanging to his companions. Benedict looked up for an instant, his face drawn, dark patches beneath his eyes. Then as quickly he looked away.

A huge oak stood alongside the river, its roots gnarling into the water, its thick branches dark against the clouded sky. The crowd backed away when the guards drew near, and he caught sight of Matthew and Henry, the surgeon's assistants, though still no sign of Mordecai himself. Elisha frowned briefly, dredging up what he knew of the Jews' Sabbath, which was precious little.

From beneath the corner of a blanket, Ruari gave him a bleak stare. His eyes looked hunted, as if he worried over the truth of Elisha's crimes.

Unsure if a smile would reassure him or merely frighten him more, Elisha hesitated, and the chance was gone.

Toward the back of the small crowd stood a clump of soldiers. Madoc raised his arm, and the others followed suit, their faces sad and solemn as they saluted Elisha's passing.

The guards brought him up alongside the tree, most of them dropping back to form a sort of perimeter. When they shifted into position, Elisha caught sight of Brigit's face beneath a hood. She gave a swift smile, holding up something he couldn't see, and his heart lifted.

Then the rope dropped over his head. In a civil trial, they might have hidden his face, but here, the full weight of the penalty should be revealed for all to see.

Hands behind him snugged the knot up beside his left ear. As he swallowed, hemp pricked his skin and rubbed against the place where his pulse jumped quicker. His gaze darted again to where Brigit stood.

She was gone.

A hint of ice cooled his anticipation as he searched the crowd for her. He craned his neck, the rope shifting like a snake at his throat.

He heard the men behind him. Something thunked against the tree and rustled along its bark. The rope drew up a little tighter.

A bead of sweat trickled down his forehead. Impatiently, he shook it away, shaking back the too-short hair that hung in the edges of his vision. Was that her near the back? By Madoc's men? The banner bearer who had saved him—then discovered him for the king's guard—kept close beside his commander, his lip trembling as he struggled to be a man. Elisha wet his lips and kept looking.

With a smug expression, Matthew watched from the left-hand side. The smaller Henry looked away, scanning the crowd on a quest of his own.

One of the guards who had been present at the interrogation stepped forward. "This man, Elisha Barber, stands convicted of treason against king and country. May God have mercy on his soul."

The voice rang in his ears, echoing in the hollows of his skull.

At the physician's side, Benedict gulped, his fingers entwined down low.

Elisha's hands began to shake, chafing against their bindings. One end of the cord itched against the burn on his palm. His fingers groped toward it and could not reach. He swallowed again, the motion catching at the rope, then sliding past. He bit his lip.

Tugging his blanket tight around his shoulders, Ruari wept. His eyes flicked up to Elisha's face and away, then up again, blinking fiercely.

Elisha's eyelashes trembled, he scanned the faces

more rapidly, ruddy cheeks, vacant stares, gleeful gazes blurring together. He tasted blood on his lips and realized he had bitten too deep. Let go. Trust. Let go.

He dug his toes into the grass, the green blades only adding to his growing cold. The burn on his chest remained warm and angry, a fire held tight beneath his skin. A green fly buzzed past, winking in the rain like her eye.

At some signal Elisha did not notice, the guard intoned, "King's justice be done," and the ground fell away beneath his feet.

Elisha's scream never had a chance.

The waiting rope snapped to its work, ripping into his throat, yanking him up into the rain.

His feet kicked, the grass still caught between his toes falling away with cakes of mud. Cold blasted the exposed skin. His fingers writhed in the air, wrists flexing and twisting against the bond, a cold trickle of blood glazing his hands. His arms shook with the effort of trying to tear free.

Somehow, his eyes still searched. What he wanted was lost in the rising tide of panic. Figures became darkness, faces flashed in and out of his wild eyes. His tongue cleaved to the roof of his mouth, dry and cold. The inescapable grip of the rope bore down all around, burning against his frozen flesh.

His mouth gaped. His eyes seemed to swell and darken, throbbing.

People cheered or screamed or prayed, the voices drowned out by a rushing in his ears—a rushing like the eager crackling of frigid flames. The rushing became a roar, pounding through his brain, blasting away both sight and sound.

Blackness gushed through him. He remembered this terror, the headlong flood of death. A wail started deep in his bowels, tearing up through his chest only to be choked off by the clawing at his throat. It burst instead from his skin, searing into the raindrops, searching for escape, for contact, for anything that might keep death at bay a moment longer.

Through the rain, Elisha screamed and pleaded and everything he touched came to nothing but cold.

Chapter 29

❖

Cold fingers of wind and rain tore at him from all sides as he swung. His eyes and ears went numb, his throat still screaming what none could hear. Slowly, terror gave way to oblivion.

As abruptly as it had been ripped from him, the ground rose up and snatched Elisha from the air.

He landed hard, tumbling on his face, then fetching up against the tree in a blow that would have knocked the breath from him, if he'd had any. It jarred him back to life, and he fought the stranglehold to no avail, his back arched and body thrashing.

"Henry!" someone panted—the voice somehow clear. "Take this!" Hurrying footsteps accompanied a wheezing breath of exertion.

Agile fingers took hold of the knot. "Give," the voice muttered. "You bastard, give!" Those fingers pulled the rope back a precious inch, slipping it from the trough it had carved.

His body convulsing with the effort, Elisha gasped for breath.

"Get me a knife."

Then a different touch slid steel beneath the noose and cut it free.

"Did I not tell you you would live?" Brigit said, her voice shaky from behind him.

"Here, what are you doing?" snapped a stentorian voice as another shouted, "I thought you checked the rope!"

Strong hands stripped off the rope and cast it away, replacing its terrible grip with their own warmth. One at the front, one at the back, they wrapped his cold throat with a heat unlike any he had ever felt—not the sharp burn of iron, nor the delicious fire of passion; this was a steady, urgent heat.

As Elisha dragged air into his lungs, the constriction at his throat eased. Warmth radiated from those hands, forcing back the frost that had hold of him. Until that moment, he had not understood what it was to touch. The simple pressure of those hands cradled the grievous harm done to him. Somehow, they knew the searing pain at his throat, the desperate burning of his lungs, the leap of his heart; they knew how to stroke his skin to calm him into believing that he could breathe, that he could live. These hands existed for such a touch. Gratefully, he surrendered to their knowledge and let himself be comforted. As he rested under their touch, Brigit's fingers and knife worked on his own hands, cutting through the bonds and unwinding the remnants.

"Does he live?" Ruari cried.

"Your blanket, quickly," the man's voice commanded. Shifting Elisha's head to rest upon his knee, he did not take his hands away. Coarse wool draped Elisha's heaving body as he struggled to draw enough air. "Easy, easy," the man murmured. Then louder, "Rub his hands—be firm, the feet too."

Someone else took up his hands, gently at first, then more strongly, rubbing the life back into them.

Overhead, guards argued and the priest prayed

aloud in amazement at God's miracle, receiving the broken rope as a sign of innocence.

"What shall I do, sir? Where do you want me?" Matthew said from on high.

"Get your irons and go home," the voice ordered.

"What? Sir, I don't—"

"I do not repeat myself," the voice thundered, and Matthew made a quiet sound of protest, but spoke no more.

"But this man is a traitor," the physician began, sounding strangely intimidated.

"Don't make me laugh."

Affronted, Lucius went on, "He perused and purveyed the king's own message. We have come to see justice done upon him."

"You idiot," the voice answered, "he can't even read. Did you never think to ask him that?"

"Here, Ruari, let me," Brigit was saying.

His rescuer's voice dropped low. "You should not be here."

"But I—"

"She saved my life," Elisha croaked, then coughed and forced himself to breathe again. His eyes flickered open, peered up through the tangle of his hair.

Mordecai the surgeon stared back at him, damp eyes blinking quickly, then darting aside, in the direction of Brigit. His downturned mouth pinched a little tighter.

"'Twas a blessed miracle, Elisha," Ruari babbled. "I've prayed so hard for ye, and the others, too, we all did. The way the rope just parted, oh, Sweet Jesus! We thought it too late, but ye're with us still."

"Amen," someone said, but Mordecai only stared, his hands enfolding Elisha's throat in radiating warmth.

"Leave him to us for now," the surgeon said, the careful calm returning to his voice, though sweat showed upon his forehead, his cap set askew on the gray hair.

"Yes, you're right," Brigit replied softly. She patted Elisha's shoulder, then she was gone.

In her wake, Elisha whimpered.

Ruari started rubbing his feet, then worked up his trembling legs. A cloak draped over him, joined by another.

The shivering broke out suddenly twice as violently, and Mordecai shifted his grip to support Elisha's head, smoothing away the hair. "Get him up—wrap that around." A few men lifted him, quick hands bundling the cloaks and blankets all around him. Gently, they laid him down again.

"Ah—he's still our prisoner," someone said.

"Bugger off!" Ruari snapped.

"We'll investigate what's happened here, Sir, but he is—"

"My patient now," the surgeon finished. He glanced up darkly. "In the infirmary, until you have orders from the king himself."

"Sir, I don't think you should—"

Mordecai turned over his shoulder. "Let's get him up. Henry, go ahead of us and put some water on the fire. You, take his feet. Barber, here with me."

Elisha frowned within his fog. He couldn't stop shaking, and he had no idea what the surgeon wanted.

After a moment, Mordecai clarified, "Yes, I mean you."

Then Ruari's strong arms bore up his shoulders. Elisha's head rested still in the surgeon's masterful hands, gently upheld. More hands worked beneath his body and legs, then they raised him and he was borne off. He let his eyes slide shut.

After some grunting and shuffling, they got him down the steps of the infirmary, and the rain finally ceased to fall.

"You," Mordecai ordered. "You're well, get out."

"I say! But I've not been called back to duty."

"You are well, my lord. Get out. Take her with you."

Cracking open his eyes again, Elisha saw the rear view of the lovely prostitute and her latest bedmate as they hurried out of the surgeon's way. His bearers lowered Elisha onto a bed, the down of a mattress enveloping him, still warm from its recent occupants.

Mordecai shoved back the curtain that separated the two sides of the hospital, revealing Elisha's barrel. He drew out a bucket.

"I should be doing that, sir," Ruari began, but Mordecai gave a quick shake of his head.

"Work on those hands." He brought out a thick, fresh cloth and knelt at the bedside to soak it. Wringing it out again, he murmured, "Not hot yet, sorry," as he washed Elisha's face and neck.

Frowning at him again, Elisha wondered where he had come from and why he was doing all this, he who rarely put down his books long enough to operate on even a lord.

"I've done it, sir," Henry said, returning from the kitchen. "Three pots, to heat up quicker."

Without looking, Mordecai almost smiled, the nearest Elisha had ever seen to an expression on his face. "Good work. Bring me some of that ointment, the one in the copper."

"Yes, sir." Henry turned, then turned back as quickly. "What shall I do with this, sir?"

Mordecai glanced up.

Henry held out to him the long belt slung about with a dozen books and tablets. He held a broken end in each hand, careful to keep the books from touching the ground. Still, they dripped, and a few had clots of mud clinging to their bindings.

The surgeon turned away, wringing out the bloody cloth. "Lay them by me," Mordecai murmured. Then, "That's fine," when the young man complied and hurried off to fetch the ointment.

In the aisle, Madoc and a small cluster of men hovered. They watched anxiously, but their faces began to relax. Outside, in the distance, a horn blew, and Madoc drew himself up.

"Any further service?" he offered, but Mordecai shook his head.

"You've done what was needed." He mopped his cloth over Elisha's hands and arms, methodically dampening it and then wringing it out in a separate bucket.

Watching the followers turn, Elisha rasped, "Thanks."

Madoc caught his eye and nodded his head, giving the fearsome grin which was his shield. He herded his soldiers on before him, and they clumped away.

Elisha shifted his eyes back to Mordecai, trying to penetrate that brusque efficiency.

Glancing up, Mordecai met his gaze for a moment and looked back down.

Henry reappeared, proffering a round, familiar copper container which Mordecai accepted, unscrewing the lid to release a scent of lavender. "You may go, Henry. Thank you. Lucius will be coming. Fend him off."

"Yes, sir." Henry bobbed a little bow and hurried away again.

"Best get to your rounds, Barber," the surgeon said to Ruari, tucking Elisha's hands back under the covers.

"I'd like to assist, sir, if I might," Ruari said, sounding protective.

Elisha brought Ruari into focus. His friend flashed a worried grin, looking to the surgeon, no doubt recalling Elisha's distrust the day he had left, rejecting the surgeon's offer to watch over his tools. Twitching one corner of his mouth, Elisha gave a tiny nod toward the hospital.

"Tell me when the water's hot," Mordecai said, bending to something on the floor. He came up with a pair of slender silver pincers, then shifted to sit on a stool by Elisha's head. With his left hand on the patient's jaw, he tilted Elisha's head. "Hold still." Deftly he plucked a strand of hemp from the wound, discarded it, and reached for another.

Grumbling, Ruari left them.

With a few more plucks, and a gentle turn of Elisha's head, Mordecai finished. Then he took Elisha's left hand from beneath the covers and performed the same careful operation, removing bits of grass and leaf that were ground into the wounds.

Elisha studied Mordecai's downturned head, the cap off to one side, revealing a patch nearly as bald as a monk's. "It was you," he whispered. His voice had no sound, but it didn't matter, not as long as Mordecai was touching him.

The gray head bowed a little further, then looked up, dark eyes upon him, thin mouth set.

"The rope," Elisha persisted on a breath. "Your belt is broken. You used it to split the rope."

Mordecai let out a little puff of breath and turned back to his task, the heat still radiating from his hands.

Elisha spoke again: "How did she know you were . . . ?"

With a soundless, bitter laugh, Mordecai replaced Elisha's hand beneath the blanket, but let his fingers linger on the back. *Let it go, Barber. You will not like the truth.*

Silent, he rose and rounded to the other side, carrying his little stool with him.

A brief and awful suspicion sparked in Elisha's breast, but died again as quickly—this man was not her lover, that much seemed clear. "I don't understand," Elisha sighed.

Aloud, Mordecai answered, "I know."

Reaching beneath the cover, he drew out Elisha's right hand, turning it palm up.

Although his expression remained bland, he sat that way a long time, with Elisha's pale, cold hand resting on his own hot fingers and staring into it as if he could read the fates scarred forever by his assistant's brand. Mordecai's shoulders hunched, his head dragged downward by some terrible weight. A single hot tear dropped into Elisha's palm. *"I should have acted sooner. I should have spared you all of this."*

"I don't—"

"You don't understand, I know. Don't I know." A familiar, bitter laugh sent recognition and warmth to Elisha's cold flesh.

"Sage," he whispered.

"I told you not to depend on me." A slender edge of pain crept through the contact and was quickly withdrawn, the tear being the only one. In profile, his expression did not change, his control was complete.

"And yet here you are, when I most had need of someone. How, if Brigit did not bring you?"

In answer, Mordecai shut his other hand over Elisha's, gently cupping his palm so as not to touch the burn at its center.

His vision darkened and blurred, then Elisha saw a small grouping of items, a tiny lantern guttering in the light rain, a little cup full of something, a book laid open, with strange letters spelling out words of prayer and devotion. Through Mordecai's eyes, he could read them, and he felt the smile that answered his delight.

The surgeon could read six languages, he suddenly knew, while Elisha could not read even his own. Mordecai's hand turned a page from left to right, then hesitated. Rain fell upon him, seeping against the back of his neck beneath a prayer shawl draped over his shoulders. Rain, and yet not rain. The touch was light at first, then grabbed hold and shook him with terror.

In the vision, Mordecai leapt to his feet, whirling, the book clutched in his hands, the others at his waist spinning and slapping against him. His devotion to knowledge endowed the books with power to ward off the swirling emotions of his work. His concentration should have defended him from any but the most direct contact, for the books guarded his sensitivity. Even as his anger rose that someone dared touch him so, when he did all he could to avoid it, the anger washed away in that tide of fear and pain and betrayal.

Through the surgeon's eyes, Elisha saw the distant scene, and knew Mordecai held his Sabbath on the dormitory roof, safe from prejudiced witnesses. Down below, in the far bend of the river, a crowd backed away. A man hung from the largest tree, struggling for his life. Himself.

Elisha's throat constricted all over again, and a sudden renewed warmth rushed through his hand.

Somehow, the scene blurred even though Mordecai still looked on. The warmth of his compassion withheld what he saw.

Mordecai ran. He searched for salvation and seized upon the simplest way. Taking his belt in his hands, stumbling down the stairs, Mordecai tore at the strands of his belt, urging them to part. All of his will was bent on this, and he kept his eyes turned to the hanged man, imagining the rope, feeling its awful grip through the rain.

Splashing down, he fell into the mud, and scrambled up again.

He reached out into the rain, grasped the fading cry that still quaked inside him. He felt for the rope, to know it, to understand the horror that swamped Elisha's mind.

His belt broke, tumbling the precious books into the mud and himself along with them, shaking. Still, he pressed on, snatching up his treasures as he ran.

Winded, Mordecai shoved through the crowd, throwing himself down as he flung his belt into his assistant's hands. He worked at the knot, his fingers slipping, and finally gained purchase, tugging it loose a few precious inches.

Still, Elisha could not see himself clearly, though he felt the echoes of his anguish through the rain on Mordecai's skin. This, too, the surgeon somehow blurred, leaving only the suggestion of the fevered work, of Elisha's breathing and Mordecai's returning almost together, then a sense of utter astonishment: Mordecai had not expected his casting to be recognized for what it was, but that Elisha should give Brigit the credit left him in dismay.

As they worked over Elisha's shaky form, Brigit's fingers brushed against Mordecai's strong, warm hands. He tried to blur this, but the contact broke too late.

Mordecai withdrew his shared vision, but not before Elisha felt Brigit's own surprise. The truth slapped his breath away once more.

Chapter 30

❖

$\mathcal{S}$traightening, Mordecai took up his tweezers again and pinched away a bit of grass, a strand of rope. His touch faded to the gentle contact of any human hand, his awareness withdrawn even as Elisha recoiled from him.

Brigit had told no one of her intentions. Brigit had watched him hang—again the distant image of himself jerked in the air, the echo of Death—and had not raised a finger to save him. Instead, Mordecai, who had no reason but compassion to be his deliverance, had risked exposure to cast the spell which saved him. Mordecai had run from his worship, broken the codes of his God, and sat there now, holding in his pain, tearing himself apart because he had not acted sooner. He who bore Elisha no special love, while Brigit—

Elisha stifled a cry, burying his head in the soft pillow. Brigit was insensitive, Sage had told him long ago, she did not feel what he felt, neither the sensations nor the emotions. He remembered the feel of her hand, gripping his, showing him the power of the talisman he thought to use, and letting him suffer its full impact. In showing him the power of his own call through the rain, Mordecai had known to soften the fear, whereas Brigit said only that she thought she could control it.

What did she want from him? Why had she come to him last night, and done all that she did? Did she even care for him, or had he let his own emotions overwhelm him—had he seen only what he wanted to see?

Tears seeped from his eyes, and crept into his hair.

"Sir?"

Mordecai twitched at the sound of Ruari's voice, and Elisha clenched his eyes, pushing back the tears.

"Yes? Ah, the water. Good." Mordecai lay Elisha's still-numb hand upon the bed and rose.

"Is he all right?" Ruari whispered, apparently thinking Elisha slept. Just as well he should.

"What do you think?" Mordecai asked. Then, as if regretting his harshness, said, "This ordeal has been harder on him than you can imagine. Ruari, is it? He'll need healing beyond the flesh. It remains to be seen whether the king will believe this was a miracle. We may not have much time."

"Aye, sir, I hear ye. What can I do?"

"Let's get him warmed up, and cleaned up, and see how he fares." He rounded the bed once more and started stripping away the layers of wool that wrapped Elisha.

The chill air brought out gooseflesh on his damp skin, and he started to shiver again, his teeth chattering.

Mordecai made a harsh sound in the back of his throat. "We'll take him near the fire, I think." He lay a hand on Elisha's brow as if summoning his return.

Elisha blinked his eyes open.

"Can you rise? You'll get help, of course."

Swallowing, Elisha tested his voice. "I think so."

They helped him to the edge of the bed, then each took a side, draping his limp arms over their shoulders. As he rose shakily to his full height, he found that Ru-

ari was taller than he by a few inches. He hadn't noticed before. On the other hand, Mordecai, despite his
formidable presence, stood a full head shorter. Letting
his head droop to his chest, Elisha shuffled between
them into the kitchen. The fire's warmth greeted him
immediately as they sat him on one of the chairs.

"Sorry," the surgeon muttered, a preface to his tearing Elisha's ruined shirt down the middle and drawing
it off by each sleeve.

While Ruari gently washed him with soft rags and
warm water, Mordecai sprinkled herbs in one of the remaining pots. He disappeared for a moment and returned with his pot of ointment, folding back his
sleeves.

"Should I . . . ?" Ruari asked, indicating the pot.

With a shake of his head, Mordecai studied Elisha's
face. "I should do this." He drew up a chair. "Find him
a dry blanket, will you?"

Ruari nodded and left.

Holding out his hand, Mordecai offered a sad smile.
"I did warn you about the truth."

"Aye," said Elisha faintly. He lay his right hand,
palm up atop the offered hand.

Taking a bit of the ointment, Mordecai smoothed it
gently over the round burn. One by one, he dabbed the
cooling stuff over each of Matthew's burn marks. It
seemed to penetrate with a lingering sense of Mordecai's healing warmth. "You have good hands," Mordecai murmured.

Elisha managed an inquisitive sound. His throat still
ached too much to speak at any length, though whether
from the noose or from his knowledge of Brigit's betrayal, he couldn't be sure.

"I wondered why your patients didn't die. Forgive
me, Barber, for I have met too many of your peers to be

impressed by any." Again, he smiled, a fleeting movement of the lips before he moved on to the larger brand
over Elisha's heart. His lightest touch still brought a
whimper of pain, and he flinched then hesitantly tried
again.

Ruari ducked through the door clutching in his
hands a thick blanket of several layers stitched together.
He draped it over Elisha's shoulders, smoothing it
down with a clucking sound as if he tended an ill child,
but his hand lingered with a gentle squeeze.

Looking over Elisha's shoulder at Ruari, Mordecai's
eyes narrowed, and he nodded. "As I say," he continued, "I wondered why your patients lived. When you
took on Ruari and that girl, I felt sure the charm would
be gone, that it was your skill." Glancing back to Elisha, he took another smear of ointment. "Your skill extended even to choosing your assistants." He paused a
moment, then continued. "There are three things that
make a good doctor." His touch on Elisha's skin said
Four, but he did not elaborate, and Elisha knew he referred to the sensitivity they shared. "Skill—what you
two share, even with Matthew." His lips turned down at
that thought, but he went on. "Empathy, which that
other one has not. And knowledge, which can come
with time. Should you pursue this labor, Ruari, I would
encourage it."

"Oh, aye," Ruari said with a laugh. He released Elisha's shoulder and found a mug, drawing a draught of
the brewed herbs. As he held the mug for his friend to
drink, he spoke to Mordecai: "And ye be all high and
mighty wi' the rest of us, sir, as if yer encouragement
should make me eager t' be like ye."

Elisha bit his lip and let it go. He tried to speak, to
defend the surgeon, but his voice had gone again.

Slowly, Mordecai shook his head. "You shame me, Barber. You both have. So long have I kept myself apart. I work among the lords because they know my skill, and more because I know theirs. What good can one man do, a common man? He has no power, nothing to contribute but his life for the cause." His voice turned self-mocking, and he drew his hand away, bringing the blanket around to cover Elisha's chest. "So I believed, so we all believe who are born above that station, for how else could we go on as we do? I serve the lords, they make the wars, they make the peace, they move this brutal little country that much closer to civilization."

Standing abruptly, he jammed the lid on his pot, screwing it down tight. "Why risk your back for a peasant, what difference can he make? Then the peasant somehow becomes the messenger, becomes the king's own son, and instead of embracing you, he hangs you from a tree." Mordecai bit off the words, his hands shaking with his anger. "And, yes, I am ashamed that I chose such service." He took Ruari's arm in a quick motion and slapped the pot of salve into his hand. "Reapply in a few hours." The surgeon strode from the room, casting eddies of frustration and guilt in his wake.

Carried only by the air, and by those words, the emotions still stung, and Elisha caught his breath. Two men as sensitive as himself and Mordecai should not meet so often—it threw them both off balance to feel too much.

"What's that about then?" Ruari asked, assuming the surgeon's chair, tossing the little copper pot from hand to hand.

"Thinks he should have defended me sooner," Elisha whispered.

"As well he should, if he's thought so much of you."

Mordecai had too much to lose if his secrets became known, but Elisha could hardly tell Ruari that. "He had good reason for caution," Elisha said, then a rustle drew their eyes to the door.

Lisbet hesitated on the threshold, then stepped inside and dropped a slight curtsey, flicking her lowered gaze from one to the other. "Mother says I'm not to see you," she mumbled. "We're going. I'm sorry." She darted another glance at Ruari, and rushed off in a flurry of long skirts.

Rising from his place, Ruari stared after her, his hands half-raised to hold her back.

Something in the line of his friend's back told Elisha all he needed. "Go on," he whispered. "I'll wait."

Turning his head, but not his eyes, Ruari said, "Ye're sure?"

"Go, get on." He made little shooing motions with his concealed hands.

At last alone, Elisha slumped in his seat. There was not a patch of skin which did not burn or ache or throb or shiver. He shut his eyes and let out a long, shaky sigh. His bruised throat protested, and he winced.

"Is it very bad?" Brigit said.

Jolted from his chair, Elisha turned his head to look at her, his eyes flaring. He stood, staggered, grabbed for the back of the chair, but a thrust of pain from his hand struck through him and buckled his knees.

Holding up her hands, Brigit rushed toward him. "Sit, please, sit before you fall down." She caught his arms with a concerned smile.

He let her ease him back onto the chair, disgusted by the rush of heat her touch sent through him.

Still smiling, Brigit set a hand upon his knee, her fingers finding his flesh through a tear in the worn-out fabric. "Attunement," she said, teasing.

"You would have let me die," he rasped.

Brigit's face fell, her smile turned in an instant to trembling lips. "*What did he tell you?*"

"I'm not a fool," he said, the lie twisting his mouth.

She held up a twig of oak, twirling it in her fingers. "*I was about to break the branch, to let you down a little easier.*"

His throat hurt too much, so he resorted to the witches' way, the words not quite reaching his lips. "*You let me down enough as it is.*"

"*Don't talk that way, Elisha. You know I had to make it plausible, you of all people know what I would risk by any magic, I had to save us both.*" Her fingers stroked a small, hot circle.

"*Did he risk any less?*" Elisha turned his face from her, struggling for his lost control.

"*Either way,*" she snapped, the energy crackling in his skin, "*You are alive, with magic to thank for it, and to all of them, it looks like divine providence has proved your innocence.*"

"*Even a moment longer, Brigit, and I would have been dead. I could feel it, like that night you showed me the talisman, only this time for me. Death already had one hand on me, and it wasn't you who fought it back.*"

"*I did what I could, Elisha, I never left you.*" She smoothed the hair back behind his ear with a delicate touch. "*Earth and sky, you act as if I wanted you to die.*" She held her face still, an expression of compassion fixed upon her beautiful features. What if she did? A chill tingled deep in his bones, as if death had not fully relinquished its hold.

Brigit flinched. "*Is that what you think? That I*

*wanted you to die? My God, Elisha, what for? What
purpose could your death possibly serve? That's just
your fear talking."*

Before he could answer, he felt Mordecai's approach.
He allowed himself a slender smile, pulling away from
Brigit's touch and looking toward the door.

Her eyes narrowed, then she, too, turned as the surgeon paused at the doorway. "I only wanted to ask,"
Mordecai began, "but I do not wish to interrupt." He
inclined his head, and turned to go.

Wait, Elisha wanted to say, and Mordecai stopped, as
if the word were spoken. A man as sensitive as Mordecai
did not interrupt by accident; ignorant though Elisha
was, he was beginning to grasp the meaning of the magi.

Slowly, the surgeon turned. A knot held his belt together, the damaged books hanging limp. "I merely
wished to ask what became of the rope."

"The rope?" Brigit asked, slipping her fingers away.
"I don't take your meaning, sir."

But she did, Elisha had caught that much in her
quick suppression.

"Only that there are some," Mordecai explained in
his best over-educated tone, "who believe a hanging
rope is a thing of power. No one seems to know what
has become of it."

Shrugging with a roll of her shoulders, Brigit said, "I
cast it aside. It may have gone in the brush, or even in
the river."

For a long moment, Mordecai simply stared, his lim-
pid eyes looking too weak to even see so far, never
mind to carry the warning Elisha felt in waves around
him. "As you say, my lady." He inclined his head.
"Sorry to bother you." Turning back, he stepped lightly
away into the hospital.

A thing of power. A talisman marked by Elisha's own death, and all of the fear, the pain, the betrayal that went along with it.

Brigit's smile returned as she reached toward him.

Suddenly stronger, Elisha snatched her hand from the air. "What purpose would my death serve? What indeed?" Cold certainty pooled in his heart. *"Is that why you made love to me? To make the rope that much stronger?"*

"I made love to you for your own sake, Elisha. That old man knows nothing about me, or you. Can't you see how much I care about you?"

Dropping her hand, Elisha felt the first waves of grief rise up to overwhelm him. "No," he said aloud. "I can't see you at all, Brigit, because I love you too much. You say that your prince knows what you are."

Again, she reached toward him, shaking her head, warning him not to speak such things to the open air.

He blocked her touch with an upraised arm, the thick blanket coming between.

Her green eyes flared to life. "My prince, as you call him, knows all about me."

"He knows that you would sacrifice my life to further your own ambition."

"That's not so, Elisha, it never was." She sank to her knees before him, her posture and tone beseeching even as hints of magic thrilled through her, trying to woo him. "With you, I could be so much more," she whispered. "No wonder my mother marked you for me to find. Two such powers as you and I—you speak through raindrops, Elisha, I speak through fire— together, there is nothing we could not do. You want an end to war? You want to save lives? Think of it, Elisha, so much strength between your hand and mine."

Resting his head on the back of the chair, Elisha followed the cracks in the ceiling and laughed to stave off weeping. "Yes, Brigit, oh yes, offer me your hand. Haven't you figured out by now it's not your strength I'm after?" He squeezed his lips shut and stared at the cracks until he felt her go.

Chapter 31

❖

When weariness overcame him, Elisha got up from his chair before the kitchen fire and lay down in the pile of fresh straw in the corner. He slept immediately, the herbs from the pot filling his nostrils. He awoke to the dull throb of his injuries, but felt strangely clear-headed and calm. Some combination of the surgeon's potions and the potency of his touch worked to make Elisha feel much better than he should, even if he remained miserable.

At the hearth before him, he could see a pair of feet beneath a long gown, feet clad in expensive boots with pointed toes. Elisha moved the arm under his head and blinked up at the figure of Benedict, his back toward him, stirring something over the fire. He recalled the brief moment when he'd thought Benedict might be the magus who called himself Sage, and smiled a little. When he felt up to rising again, he would go to the river and listen to what they said. Then he thought of Marigold-Brigit and the smile slipped away. Who knew what she wanted, or what she might do? If he hadn't noticed Mordecai's broken belt, he might never have known the truth. Brigit would have been willing to take credit, and Mordecai willing to let her have it if it meant none would know the truth about him. As a Jew, the slightest whiff of witchcraft would get him killed out of hand, and without the trumped up charges brought to bear against other witches.

Benedict muttered over his pot and checked a scrap of parchment he carried tucked in his belt, then added a pinch of something else. Lying there a few feet away, Elisha thought he could sense the tension in Benedict's actions. Elisha, drifting in the haze of his recovery, began the process of attunement, reaching out with his new inner sense to every corner of the room and everything in it.

He sent his awareness further with a sense of creeping along the floor like a beetle, as if some hitherto unknown antennae could feel the vibration of Benedict's presence in the air. Mordecai's touch, and his conversation, had shown Elisha what it meant to be attuned, not in the physical, grounded way that Brigit seemed to imply, but on a different level. It began with the physical, with an uncanny knowledge of how Benedict stood and moved, almost as if they might inhabit one body. Knowledge—the sort that Mordecai carried in his books, that Elisha had learned from setting a thousand bones and treating ten thousand wounds.

From this new perspective, Benedict radiated tension. His fingers clutched the wooden spoon so hard that tiny slivers pricked beneath his nails, though he was unaware of them. Tension gathered in the muscles of his neck and shoulders, his posture rigid with the strain. His jaw tightened until it ached.

Of Benedict's mind, Elisha could sense little. Vague washes of emotion drifted there, understood not through direct knowledge, but through how they influenced the pulse and breathing: a hint of fear, a twinge of pain from the bite Elisha had inflicted, and a pang of regret. The knowledge was intimate, fascinating, and exciting—and more than any man would want revealed about himself.

Elisha pulled back from that intimacy, tamping down his awareness, despite his curiosity. Somewhere upstairs, he heard footsteps, and felt a sudden draft of shock and fear, which blew away as quickly as it had come, leaving him chilled. He would have risen, but footsteps approached the door as well. Voices murmured, then the physician stepped into the kitchen, his presence catlike in anticipation.

Lucius glanced toward where Elisha lay, but Elisha was perfectly motionless, allowing the skill of attunement to reveal his surroundings. "Still sleeping," the physician muttered, then joined his assistant, staring down at the concoction on the fire. "Ah, very good," he said, then set his hand on the younger man's shoulder. "I need to speak with you, Benedict."

"Of course, Sir, I'm nearly done here." The voice shook a little, and the physician's hand patted him in a manner intended to be soothing.

"Come along with me now. That will keep."

Clunking the spoon against the pot, Benedict turned. "I thought you wanted me to—"

"Yes, yes, but the king's guard, you know, they've been prowling about, so it seems wise we should speak now."

Looking back as if he could see the guards, Benedict slowly withdrew the spoon and laid it on the table with curious precision. "As you wish, sir."

Lucius used his comforting hand to gently propel Benedict toward the door by Elisha's head.

"Must we go through the yard, sir, it makes me—"

"I have not made you my assistant in order to hear your complaints."

It sounded as if Benedict were to have his ears laid

back for some offense. Elisha almost smiled. In their wake, he remembered the fear he had sensed earlier. Pushing himself into a sitting position, Elisha waited. He felt stiff and weary, but not on the verge of death, as he had a few hours ago. Rising slowly, he shifted the blanket closer and hobbled over to the stairs. He shuffled up them, and down the hall, which he found empty. At each door, he paused and knocked, but had no answer. Two doors in a row stood open, opposite the one which was Brigit's. His small chest stood on one of the beds, abandoned when Lisbet and her mother did their packing.

Frowning over it, Elisha considered what to do. He hadn't the strength to move it, not far anyway, and it contained little worth protecting. Still. He dropped onto the rope webbing of the bed and flipped open the catches, pulling back the lid.

His one remaining shirt lay neatly folded on top, and Elisha slipped it over his head. He found a length of rope to use as a belt and emptied out a tied-leather bundle of herbs, replacing them with an abbreviated version of the emergency kit the guards had taken from him. At the bottom of the chest lay the little cloth pennant, but his tools had shifted in all the moving about, and a knife had torn through the painted hawk, leaving one wing nearly severed. Elisha plucked it free and held it on his palm, a miniature of the angel's wing. He wondered for a moment if his own pennant-waving that day had inspired her, even as she waited for her death, to try this one last miracle. Her daughter's betrayal tainted the memory, but he pushed it aside. Whatever Brigit had done to him—or not done, as the case may be—her mother's touch meant something still.

Folding it gently, he placed the cloth wing into his packet and re-tied the leather thong, tucking it into his waist. Elisha replaced the lid of the chest and let it lie. Rising again, he continued down the hall. Above the infirmary, he found another door standing open, a scatter of pages blowing in a breeze from the window. This must be Mordecai's room, but he wasn't there.

Abandoning his blanket, Elisha gathered up the pages and placed them on the neatly made bed. He turned to go but frowned. The place felt hollow in a way that worried him. Perhaps it was only that sense of loss he found in the man himself, the echo of the secrets he still held. Downstairs, he stopped at the entrance to the infirmary, but found no sign of Mordecai there either.

Perhaps he, too, had sought the river. As he walked, Elisha realized he had not heard the bombards' blast all day long, for surely that would have awakened him sooner. Indeed, a large number of knights gathered across the river by the king's pavilion, talking and laughing, apparently at their ease.

Elisha glanced back, but could see nothing of the battlefield from here. Shrugging it off, he walked the few paces down and plunged his feet into the rushing water.

Silence.

But not silence, not really. A low moan shivered around his ankles, more a feeling than a voice, and Elisha looked upstream. At a bend beyond the monastery walls, he saw a figure emerge from the reeds and stride up, fastidiously lifting long robes, though they dripped with water. Lucius. But where was Benedict?

Elisha sprang up the bank and pushed himself into a run, his hands curled into fists.

He slithered down the rise where the physician had emerged and stumbled into the brush, fetching up against the massive roots of an upturned tree.

"Benedict?" he called out, trying to push his way past the reaching roots. "Benedict!" The sense of fear, the pressure of the physician's hand—he should have put it together.

Bursting free from the entangling brush, Elisha found himself standing ankle-deep beside the downed tree, looking into the swirl of a pool sheltered by the looming of its branches. Something splashed like a dark, pointed fish. Benedict's expensive boot.

"Don't do it, Barber," Lucius's voice suddenly cracked behind him.

Spinning, already up to his waist in the water, Elisha stared.

The physician stood on the bank, his gaunt face twisted as he drew a small crossbow from the folds of his ridiculous sleeves and held it casually at his side. "It's too late for him."

But the river said differently. Even though it carried the chill of death, it carried too the submerged struggle for breath, a struggle Elisha knew all too well. He backed another pace into the river's flood.

"Don't, I tell you. It's for your own good as well as mine. He's the traitor, don't you know. He wants to kill the king."

"Then bring him before the guards," Elisha shouted back.

"I'm just going to fetch them," Lucius said, but he did not move.

Taking another step, Elisha drew a deep breath, even as the physician slid a bolt into place. As he shot, Elisha fell back into the water.

The bolt slid in after, as subtle as death, as swift as the river, and Elisha reached out with his mind. Contact. He caught it and forced it into the water, dissolving it into the flying current.

Another followed in a moment, Lucius turning to keep his prey within range, as Elisha swept toward the tree.

Elisha rolled and kicked, grabbing a branch near the entrapped figure of Benedict.

Fighting with the tree that held him, Benedict flailed. Blood streamed in the water around him.

Diving beside him, Elisha forced him down and dragged him back against the flow, one arm wrapped about his chest. Both popped to the surface, drawing a curse from the physician.

Lucius aimed another bolt, but Elisha splashed his hand through the air, bringing up a stream of water that consumed the weapon as it flew.

His mouth flapping, the physician drew back. He pointed a finger in Elisha's direction, a finger that struck Elisha with more fear than had his bow. A gesture of knowledge and accusation.

Their eyes met across the distance, and the physician crossed himself quickly, pulling the bow close to his chest like a crucifix. Then he backed away, stumbling over his robes and falling.

Elisha hesitated, the water lapping around his knees, Benedict clutched in his arms. If Elisha dropped Benedict, he might catch Lucius. What had Benedict done for him, that Elisha should risk the fire?

Caught up in the extra yards of fabric, Lucius floundered and pulled himself up.

"*Who's there?*" came a sudden voice in the water.

"Oh, God, Benedict," Elisha murmured, shifting his grip and hauling Benedict toward shore against the current. By the time they arrived, Lucius had already sped off to sound the alarm.

Flopping Benedict onto the shore, Elisha climbed up after him, his chest heaving, his feet cold. Too cold.

He turned Benedict's face toward him, and the eyelids fluttered open. "Barber," came the raspy voice.

His master's bolt had taken him in the back, just to the left of his spine and Elisha felt a sick dread.

"You've got to live," Elisha said urgently, even as his hand probed around the wound.

"Take . . . letter. To him, not me," Benedict said, his hand fluttering at his waist. "Not me."

Elisha found a slender waxed packet tucked in Benedict's belt. "Lucius received it?"

A slight, stiff nod.

"Who's it from? Benedict? I can't read, Benedict."

The fair head lolled to one side, but the eyes flickered open again, and the blue lips trembled. "Prince . . . Thomas. Build him a medical school." Almost, he smiled. Lucius had talked about that school in the same breath that he'd lied to Elisha about coming to the hospital at the king's invitation. On the contrary, apparently Prince Thomas, impatient for his crown, had lured the physician to assassinate his father the king, while he remained hundreds of miles away, above suspicion.

Cold seeped from Benedict, but Elisha pressed his hand to the wound. He willed it warm, but he did not know how to work that magic the surgeon practiced. "Please, Benedict, stay with me," he muttered. Elisha's own interrogation had revealed his innocence regarding the assassination attempts—so Lucius had got himself a new scapegoat.

Benedict expelled a gout of blood and the single word, "Sorry."

The sound of tramping boots echoed from the monastery wall, and Elisha pulled Benedict up onto his shoulder, struggling through the brush back toward the bridge. His aches returned and redoubled, but he dared not stop. They emerged onto the grass, a troop of armored men hurrying up with the physician babbling after them.

"Get the surgeon!" Elisha shouted. "This man's wounded."

"So let him die."

At the drawl of those evil words, Elisha turned. On the opposite bank stood the king, with a few of his company, and some distance off, two men in the colors of Duke Randall.

"Your Majesty," he gasped, his raw throat closing over the words.

"I little expected to see you up and about so soon. Is this more of your magic?" the king inquired coolly. "Oh, yes, the esteemed physician has been telling us. I was told a miracle had saved you. Now it seems there is another explanation."

"This man is nothing to do with it, Your Majesty. Let me bring him to the surgeon," Elisha begged.

At this, the king let out a boom of laughter. "The witch wants to consult the Jew. But he's here already." He waved a lofty gesture toward the bridge.

There, among the tall, armed men, stood the slight figure of Mordecai, stripped of his cap and gown, thin shoulders stooped. Someone had wrapped his prayer shawl around his waist, and its tassels fluttered in the wicked breeze.

Chapter 32

"Come here, Barber, come to me," the king beckoned.

Tearing his eyes from the bridge, Elisha lowered his burden to the ground. A glance confirmed what the chill in his back already knew: it was too late for Benedict. Elisha shot a glare at the physician. Slowly, he rose again, trying not to reveal his sudden weakness. If he was to become a trembling child after every casting, how could he ever put the magic to any use?

He walked a few strides into the river.

"Who's there?"

"Bittersweet." Elisha crossed to the shallows below the bank where the king stood waiting.

Around him in the water echoed other voices, betraying their confusion. *"Briarrose," "Slippery Elm," "Arrowroot," "Willowbark."*

"But you were not alone," someone said, a brief touch of dismay.

"I am now." Bowing his head, Elisha watched the rush of tiny silver fish around his feet, the muck of the bottom oozing between his toes.

"Where is Marigold?" asked Briarrose. *"She was to meet me."*

"I have a guess." Looking up to the king, Elisha

sighed, the sound catching a little at the band of pain around his neck. He thought of the other empty rooms: Brigit's, Lisbet and Maeve's. The men might believe their prayers had saved Elisha, but the king would not—he would be looking for traitors. "What is your will, Your Majesty?"

Indicating the duke's men, the king said, "Those good gentlemen have come under a flag of truce. Why so? As well you may wonder. They wish to bargain for your life."

Elisha frowned up at them. It made no sense.

The king shrugged his broad shoulders and smiled. "Even before the physician started spouting his nonsense," —this brought a cry of outrage from Lucius— "I have intended your death, for one crime and another. But how has the duke heard of it, and, more importantly, why does he care?"

Wetting his lips, Elisha bent his thoughts to that question. *"One of you is in the castle of the duke,"* he whispered in the water.

"We do not speak of politics," someone answered.

"I don't give a damn about politics." Elisha's frustration cracked through his attempts at control.

"Then why turn the arrows to rain?" asked a gentle touch upon his feet: the voice of Willowbark. *"You have already taken sides."*

"Men were dying." He glanced back to the bridge, to the silent scarecrow figure of Mordecai, surrounded by the king's men. *"They still are."* When he searched in that direction, despite the distance, despite the fact that Mordecai stood on stone, and Elisha in the water, he felt the tremor of the older man's bones. Fear and worry gathered at the back of his throat, and a strange serenity centered around the prayer shawl.

"I am waiting for your answer, Barber. Why should

the duke be interested in you, when you have so vehemently claimed not to know him?"

Turning back, Elisha noted the king's too-casual stance, the slight drumming of his fingers. He had no sense of attunement to the man. But while he did not know the king as he knew the surgeon, his eyes could serve him well enough. Elisha did not need to feel the emotions in the air to know that they were dangerous. "I've already told you the truth of the one time I met the duke. But he is besieged, Your Majesty, what does he have to bargain with?"

Narrowing his eyes over his hawk-like nose, the king appraised him. "I discovered my traitor, have you heard? That very lord who received my message." He gave a grim smile. "He was meant to assemble the force that would take advantage of my tunnel. Instead, he waited a few days to allay my suspicions, then turned over both message and messenger to the duke." The sharp blue eyes leveled at Elisha as he realized what this meant: The duke had known to aim his bombard at the sapper's tunnel because this unnamed ally of the king—now proven false—had told him, and given him Prince Alaric as a hostage.

He wondered if Brigit knew where her lover was now.

"Your Majesty, I—"

"Apparently my son has offered to recant his claims against the duke's daughter in exchange for his freedom, but why does my enemy want you? Why is he ready to offer such a prize—my own son—for the life of a miserable barber?"

Miserable indeed, Elisha thought. "Your Majesty, I wish I knew."

Still staring, the king flicked his fingers.

Elisha whirled in time to see the guards shove Mor-

decai against the bridge rail. One of them caught his
arm, jerking the hand flat against the stone.

"No!" Elisha ran with the current, but the guard had
drawn a hatchet.

The blade arched through the air, descending with a
cold whistle, splitting skin, hacking bone, chinking into
the stone below.

Elisha screamed, grabbing his own wrist. His knees
buckled, dropping him into the river.

The severed hand tumbled like a shot dove and
splashed beneath the bridge. Blood streamed after it.

Mordecai remained silent, his wrist lifted by the
guard, his eyes shut, but a wave of anguish shot through
Elisha's body from his right arm, and his right hand felt
cold, quivering as if water washed over it. Fear, pain,
loss all eddied in the river.

Up on the bridge, Mordecai's head pitched forward,
and the guard let his arm slip free as the surgeon crumpled to the stone.

Elisha gripped his own wrist. If he felt the pain, then
it must be possible for Mordecai to feel the cure. Doubled over in the water, Elisha pulled free the cord
which should have tied his shirt. Using his teeth and
left hand, he jerked it into a tight circle at his wrist, the
cord sliding easily into the grooves already worn by the
leather belt the guards had used to bind him. As he had
once felt through the surgeon's vision, he now joined
the two of them together, reaching out to know the angle of the cut, which bones snapped, and where the tendons shriveled. He pulled the ligature as tight as he
could stand, then a little tighter, his hand going numb
and stiff. He couldn't see Mordecai behind the stone
rail. He could only pray it would work, but he would
have to get to him soon.

"Usually," the king observed, "I have to threaten

wives and children, or other lords, at the very least.
Killing Jews and peasants hardly seems sporting." He
laughed as Elisha raised his head. "Oh, yes, there's
more. A girl, a soldier, a few men fighting under a banner of a hare." He flipped his hand negligently. "Anyone who visited you. Anyone who helped you up this
morning, or dared to speak your name."

"What do you want from me?" Elisha howled. Icy
fingers seemed to take his hand. He was running out of
time. Waves of shock shivered through him. "To get
your son back, you need only let me go."

At this, the king laughed again, and fury began to
supplant the cold in Elisha's blood.

"*Sage?*" someone asked. "*What's happening?*"

"*Sage can't answer,*" Elisha cried in that secret way.

The king strolled along the bank until he drew
abreast of Elisha again.

"*I thought I felt him.*"

"*You did. He's dying—shut up!*" His teeth clenched
to hold in the start of the giddy laughter.

Dropping to one knee, the king leaned out over the
water to get close to Elisha, who shot him a glare.
"Now, Barber, it's just a Jew, after all. Think of the others yet to come."

"What do you want?" Elisha repeated.

He dropped his voice to a murmur. "I'll make the
bargain; you'll kill the duke."

"I'm not a murderer."

Sharp teeth flashed through the king's bearded
smile. "But I am." He rose swiftly. "Bring out the girl."

Elisha jerked to his feet, fear flooding his brain, but it
was not Brigit the guards held between them. Not Brigit—
Lisbet, and Ruari bound behind her. The girl's frightened
gaze flitted here and there, searching for an ally.

"You were expecting someone different," the king

murmured, "No, *that* girl deserves something special. She seems so very like her mother."

Elisha met the king's eyes. "I'll do it."

Losing his smile, the king said, "His body in the river at dawn, or I'll pitch them from the tower. One by one. You can watch." Turning, he summoned the two men in the duke's livery to approach. "Well, he knows no more than you reveal about your master's purpose, but I will accept your bargain. Send out the messenger in one hour, and I will do the same."

Bowing briefly, the two men hurried away, glancing all around them, giving the king all the trust he was due. Perhaps they guessed at his whispered command, or perhaps the brutal amputation had shaken them, not understanding its cause. They hurried over the bridge, past the king's guards, scuffing Mordecai's blood into the dirt on the other side.

Giving them a cheery wave, the king turned again to Elisha. "Are you truly a witch?"

"What do you think?" Elisha muttered. The river voices, which had grown silent at his rebuke, began to reach out again, tentative and frightened.

With a hearty laugh, the king shook his head.

"I have seen it!" the physician said, stomping along his side of the bank, pointing back at Benedict's body. "When I was defending myself from the treachery of my assistant, this man sought to defend him with the dark arts, turning my bolts into serpents of the water." His outthrust finger shook.

Again, the king laughed. "Is it true, Barber?"

Elisha merely stared up at him, ignoring the mottled colors of his hand as he tucked it beneath the opposite arm.

"I thought not. He's too dull-witted for magic. If he could do it, he would defend himself now."

They might argue all day over his head, while Mordecai lay dying on the bridge—so near, and yet unreachable while the king's guards surrounded him. Shutting his eyes, Elisha reached out into the water. The touch faded quickly, but he found what he sought, and called it back, by the bond between them.

From their opposite bank of the river, the king called out insults, and the physician sought to counter them, to convince the king of Elisha's complicity. How much more dangerous could a witch be on the side of the enemy, surely there was—

Focusing his will upon his own ends, Elisha drowned out their words. He opened his eyes, searching the shadows on the far side of the bridge.

There! A small, pale thing bobbed in the water, slowly but inexorably moving upstream.

One of the men on the bridge saw it first. He gasped and blanched—crossing himself as Mordecai's hand passed from sun into shadow and emerged again.

"Your Majesty!" someone shouted, leaning over the rail. Beside him, two men were sick, one fainted, the rest started to back away.

Lisbet's keepers hurried back the way they'd come with the girl flung over a shoulder.

A young man broke and fled the waterside, crying aloud for divine salvation. In moments, half the guards were with him. Some of the rest drew weapons and sprang after the deserters, relieved to have a reason to run that would not look like cowardice.

In his trance, Elisha reached down to the water, lifting the sad and severed thing in his palms. Hours before, this hand had saved his life.

Taking a deep breath and letting it out slowly, Elisha turned to the king. He raised his head, feeling his shorn locks along his cheeks, and started to smile. "The hand of a healer is a powerful thing, Your Majesty," he said, his voice even and deep. He took a step toward the king, water tugging at him with a thousand questions.

Scrambling to his feet, the king stumbled back a pace. "What can you do?" he sneered. "Abuse me with a Jew's remains?"

"I will tear your face off," Elisha replied, taking another step. "I will rip the intestines from your belly and bind you to the tail of a horse from Hell." He reached the bank. "I will cause your eyes to boil in your head and collect your screams to summon a thousand demons. I will snap a hole into that skull of yours and laugh while your brains ooze out into your beard."

Retreating inch by inch, the king darted a glance around. His few defenders trembled as they shifted toward him. "If you can do all this, why haven't you done it?" he shouted boldly enough, but his voice quavered.

Elisha's gaze never faltered.

As he mounted the bank, Elisha stripped the seeds from a frond of grass. Bearing Mordecai's hand upon his bound right palm, he flicked a seed at the king.

"Now is your doom upon you!" Elisha howled.

An egg struck the royal forehead, spattering the king's face.

Reeling at the blow, the king screamed and ran. He flailed at his hair, flinging off the sticky stuff. His guards sprang to his aid, some glancing backward, staring at Elisha wild-eyed.

Elisha sprang onto the bank and sprinted for the bridge.

Mordecai lay sprawled against the rail, footprints tracking through his blood in both directions. Dropping to his knees, Elisha gently touched his neck—still warm—and found his heart still beating.

Bending over Mordecai, Elisha carefully raised the

stump of his arm. No blood flowed from the severed veins. Maintaining a firm grip, he untied the bond around his own wrist with his teeth and quickly bound off Mordecai's wounded arm.

Lying the hand upon its owner's bare stomach, Elisha gathered Mordecai into his arms, awkward as his own hand tingled with returning life. His sense of connection with the surgeon wavered, despite their contact.

Moaning, Elisha pulled Mordecai closer. *"Live!"* he urged without voice. *"I have already lost a man today, I will not lose another."*

There was no answer.

Struggling to his feet as a chill swept through him, Elisha took a moment to steady himself. Mordecai felt light in his arms, a fallen bird. An angel.

Again, the brief wind of death ruffled his heart.

Wetting his lips, Elisha remembered the warmth of the surgeon's hands, reaching him in the dark and cold. Mordecai in his arms, he stumbled toward the church, toward the altar where he had lain to rest his unholy burden. The talisman of strength enough for such powerful magic.

Slipping on a bloody step, Elisha twisted in his fall to strike his own back rather than cause Mordecai more harm.

At the jolt, the surgeon's dark eyelids fluttered, and the lips parted to let out a sigh of breath.

"Sage?" Elisha cried.

"It's you." A touch as fragile as frost.

"Of course. Of course I'm here." Staggering, he regained himself and started to run.

"I am not dead."

"You will not die." Elisha countered fiercely.

Again, that sigh. *"Pity."*

The delicate warmth of contact slipped away again, and Elisha cursed. He splashed through the brook and fetched up at the door of the church, only to find a barricade built across it. As he panted for breath, he heard the rise and fall of Latin liturgy—a desperate Mass to ward off the evil of himself.

The blood fled from his face, and he felt again the hangman's rope burning at his throat, the hand that could heal him lying cold forever.

Chapter 33

◈

His back to the mossy stone, Elisha sobbed. He pulled the fading warmth of Mordecai to his chest in his strong, helpless arms.

Too much had already been lost—too much blood, too much time, and now his last resort was closed to him. Not that he had even been sure what to do with the talisman if he had it. Without it, he was nothing, and even Brigit was out of his reach. He had only that torn scrap of a pennant to call upon. It had been enough for eggs and arrows, but it could not stand against this enemy. Alone, he had not the power nor the skill to save a man. The loss of hope left him shaking.

Tears streaming down his face, Elisha stared at the barren blue of the sky. Not even a raindrop to give vent to his anguish. Each man must fight his own battle, Mordecai had told him, until he falls beneath the enemy and cannot rise again. If it was death he fought, then death had overcome him at last, and he had agreed to become its messenger.

His back scraping on stone, Elisha slumped to his knees.

His chin dropped to his chest, ragged with sobs. Mordecai lay in his arms, pale beneath his olive skin, his ribs barely rising. His left hand draped at his hip, his right lay upon his chest, separate and terrible. Through his shirt, Elisha could feel the prayer shawl, still warm; that worn and faded width of fabric, symbol of a god who had let this happen. An edge of darker threads resisted the blood that soaked the rest.

Freeing one hand to wipe away the tears and his own dark curls, Elisha brought up one end of the shawl. Not dark threads, but hairs—some of them long and thick, others shorter and softer—human hairs, woven in alongside the white wool.

They had sought to humiliate Mordecai, stripping him of his robes and using the shawl of his faith as a loincloth. Instead, they had left him the one thing that mattered: his talisman.

Elisha suddenly knew that he was not alone, that even if his bit of painted cloth was not enough, the Jew's prayer shawl rippled with power of its own.

He pushed himself up again. Not the church, then, but to find another place for magic. A place where power was close to the surface. Unbidden, the image of the hanging tree flashed before his eyes, a great, sturdy oak of uncounted years, where he had nearly died and been called back from the house of death.

Striding purposefully, Elisha ignored the growing ache at his wrists and neck as they throbbed with every step. He winced at the sight of the tree and shied away, following closer to the reeds at the river's edge. He came around to where the tree's roots thrust into the water and sank down there, settling Mordecai in grass which showed the marks of heavy treads—three men leaning into a rope to swing him . . .

Elisha jerked his attention back to the moment. He inched his toes into the water and called out, *"I need you."*

"*What?*"

"*We are magi, not dogs, we do not come when called.*"

"*What do you need?*"

Unrolling his leather emergency kit, Elisha said quickly, "*Sage has fallen. He's not dead yet. He's lost a hand. I think I can save him, but I have no skill.*"

"*With the wounded? You have skill enough, I'm told.*" A gentle touch, but strong. Willowbark, he thought.

"*I am still weak,*" he said to the dissonant voices. "*And this is beyond me—too much shock, and pain—I felt it like my own hand.*" Even as he told them, the trembling returned, dizzy bubbles of weakness drifting up into his mind.

"*You use too much of yourself,*" Willowbark replied. "*Let the talisman be your strength.*"

"*But how have you felt his injury?*" asked another voice, querulous and detached.

From the packet, he lifted the tattered strip of parchment with its single painted wing. The irony struck him in an instant, and he giggled. "*We are too sensitive, we both are. Something he shared with me bound us together.*"

"*That may be enough.*" A strong, soothing touch in the cool water. "*I will send what I can.*"

Elisha took the truncated arm gently in both hands, studying the wound. The ends of the bones showed clean, cut above the joint. That should make things easier. The tendons, already curling back, would be more of a challenge.

"*We cannot help him,*" the other voice scoffed. "*Too much focus is required for such sharing. What if we are discovered?*"

"*Then you have not hidden yourself well enough,*" Willowbark advised.

"*But after he's declared himself before all and sun-*"

*dry? And he's been a magus less than a month—how
can we trust him? I won't do it. No—not for any Jew or
stranger."*

At this, a spark leapt in Elisha's spirit, igniting the
anger still simmering there. *"He's not only a Jew, he is a
healer and one of the magi. If you can't lay aside your
prejudice even for this, I would rather see you burn!"*

*"Don't cast your curses on me, Bittersweet—save
them for the king when he comes for you."* The forceful
touch slapped against his ankles, and was gone as the
magus withdrew.

Another woman's voice joined them, lighter, and
more distant. *"Marigold is right. If we do not stand together, who will ever stand for us? I will do what I may."*

"But what may we, at that?" Willowbark asked.

*"Perhaps a binding spell, to fix the spirit into the
body,"* someone suggested.

*"With what components to establish the affinity?
There is little time."*

"A summoning," said the other woman, *"calling him
back."*

"A simple healing?" suggested another.

"He may be too weak for healing alone."

As the magi discussed in the ripple of the river, Elisha heard them with only half his mind. The rest of his
concentration turned to the task of understanding the
wound, recognizing the damage done, and the amount
of blood spilled. But their words at the back of his mind
began to form a pattern and a prayer. Binding, summoning, healing. If he could call forth blood from the
marrow, if he could beseech the return of the departing
spirit, if he could bind it all together. His fingers remembered the heat of those hands together, cupping
his own.

Spilling out the contents of his kit, Elisha hunted

and found a strong needle. His hand throbbed with the pain of the brand, his fingers feeling thick and unresponsive, so it took him a few tries to thread the needle with a length of suture. Affinity: the joining of the stitch, the joining of the flesh, and of the spirit to the flesh. The likeness of this man to his angel, wounded and in need.

In preparation for stitching, he brought together the severed hand with its lonely wrist. Knowledge: how the wound was made, how the bones were cut, how the veins and tendons should work. The way Mordecai had touched his throat, as if the surety of his knowledge were enough.

Elisha shifted his grip, sending his awareness into the cold flesh of the hand, feeling out the pathways to be joined. When he settled the hand just so, something tingled in his own wrist, a rightness of place, and he took the first careful stitch.

As he worked, forcing his numb fingers to obey, Elisha reached out for the witches in the water, their focus buoying him up. He remembered the year his father bought their only horse, teaching his boys to guide the reins. Now he drew in the reins of the power all around him. Warm wishes flowed to him from the river, dark strength gripped him from the tree roots running deep, the painted hawk's wing fluttered in a breeze of its own making.

At Mordecai's waist, the hairs woven in his prayer shawl resonated with an inner current.

Mystery, Elisha thought, the mystery of this man's soul, of his faith, and his pain. Elisha had felt but the keenest edge, masking a wound that cut into the surgeon's heart, long healed over, bearing a scar that reminded him every time he spoke, and especially when he came close to smiling. "*Pity*," Mordecai had said, when Elisha refused to concede his death.

Elisha began to hum, drawing energy from the others in the water. They might be around the bend, or in another county—one, at least, sheltered in the castle of the renegade duke, while another might be in the camp of the king, terrified lest Elisha spark a witch hunt. As he sank deeper in his work, the howling cold of death rose up around him, spreading darkness through every contact Elisha made: through the earth, through the water, through the chill flesh he fought to save. Elisha shivered at the touch. His heart pounded, and he struggled to maintain the easy rhythm of his breath.

The earth beneath him writhed with angry tendrils of oak. The tree that stood so long sentry by the river, the tree that had lifted his weight so easily to kick at the air, now groped toward him, branches creaking overhead, leaves cackling. It would drag him up again, his hands useless, his legs trying in vain to run away.

Elisha's throat constricted, choking off the humming in a gasp for breath. He had chosen the wrong place, a place of evil. He had to run. His fingers shook, his hands going numb in remembered horror.

Reaching out to gather Mordecai and take him from this terrible place, Elisha brushed the torn cloth of the pennant, and the touch blew away his panic like so much mist. He drew breath again and forced his dull fingers into motion, joining the skin as he urged the bones and tendons to join.

Suddenly, the water seemed to echo with strangers, with harsh laughter and jeers. It sucked at his feet, offering deliverance in drowning, carrying the mournful touch of Benedict, lost at the moment he might have been rescued. The presence of the other magi felt treacherous, their offered contacts stung him, distracting him just as he must gather his strength. The magic he sought to control turned against him, perverted by the depth of power all around him. His mind reeled, the echoes of the hanging tree, the talisman, the memory of dying reverberating within his skull.

Elisha's toes edged him forward, his feet working to free themselves of the dangerous water. Voices called him, but shrieking laughter battered out all sound.

His knee brushed an edge of bloody cloth, and warmth rushed through him, causing a swirl of cold that ripped at his ankles.

"No!" Elisha dug in his feet, sending out clouds of silt.

He called forth the memory of Mordecai's touch, the strength of his hands, the tenderness of the vision that had bound them together. He had to go on, to concentrate on binding and summoning.

"*Yes, yes, Bittersweet, we are with you,*" the water sang.

The third assault crept from the still flesh under his feverish fingers. It stole down from the blue of Mordecai's fingertips and seeped through Elisha's skin like poison. Death could not be fought. It could not be defied.

What he wanted could not be done. The body was too complex to be known, too familiar to be mysterious, and this man he worked over with all his hope did not even wish to live. Did not Mordecai himself call out for death? Did he not long to escape the horrors of earthly life, to hide forever from his persecutors? Had he not spent his life in hiding already, keeping his faith in private, defending himself with books from the touch of other magi? It had taken Elisha's own death to draw any compassion from him. He was a Jew, a witch; he was alone in the world and did not seek for company. He should not live.

And Elisha, who dared to defy this fitting death, what right had he? By what authority did he try to summon this man from death's door? They were not friends, not even colleagues—Mordecai's knowledge was so far beyond his own. This struggle was absurd, a losing battle, and one that would only leave Elisha weak and pathetic, lost as he ever was. How stupid of him to try, to fight so hard for something which was not his to win. He was not a magus, only a barber, despised by all as a butcher, responsible for his brother's death, for the loss of the child, for the loss of affection they could have shared, and betrayed the widow with his wicked theft.

Tears coursed down Elisha's face. Even if it could be done, he was not worthy to work such magic. His arrogance had caught him once again. Pride goeth before a fall indeed—and daring even to quote the holy book of a god he had forsaken. He was cursed as surely as his sins deserved.

Elisha's shoulder's hunched, his hands drawing in close as he shook with weakness and despair. His hair, once a source of pride, swung forward in its butchered state.

One dark wave brushed along his cheek where once an angel's feather had found him. The touch flared to life beneath his skin.

Elisha gasped as wonder flooded through him. The last moment of her life, this woman, witch, angel, had reached out to him. It had been Elisha she struggled for, Elisha whose presence had been a comfort to her, even as arrows bit her flesh and flames snapped at her feet. From the very heart of death, the angel sent out her vivid gaze to him. Even as she died, she marked him as her own, blessing him with the transcendence of her flight.

Blindly, Elisha set the final stitch, his eyes drawn away to a distant day as bright and fair as this one, and as full of warmth. The warmth of sun on his shoulders dispelled the darkness. The warmth of his companions in the river dispelled the cold.

And despair left him at the merest touch of the warm fingers which, impossibly, gripped his own.

Chapter 34

❖

Elisha drew a full, deep breath for the first time in nearly an hour. He held Mordecai's hand gently in both of his, the row of small stitches showing like a pale bracelet against the olive skin.

"How?" the surgeon sighed, his dark eyes searching their joined hands in wonder.

The tension fell away from Elisha's arms, and a helpless wave of laughter welled through him. He had done it! He laughed, bowing his head as his shoulders quaked.

"But I . . ." Mordecai began, his thin voice trailing away again.

Shaking his head, trying to quell the laughter, Elisha watched him through the screen of his hair.

Turning his wrist first one way, then the other, Mordecai puzzled. "Sutures? But the bones," he murmured.

Elisha couldn't answer. There was too much to explain, and too much he wasn't sure he could.

Gently, Mordecai slipped free his hand and brought it close to his face. He raised the other hand as well, tracing the line of stitches. "Are they real? I cannot feel them, nor find their beginning."

"I don't know," Elisha said at last, his voice hoarse. He let himself turn away a moment, bending to scoop water from the river and drink deeply. He poured a handful over his sweaty forehead and sighed.

He felt the slightest touch, bearing with it a heat familiar and humbling.

"*Elisha Magus.*"

His chin rose, and tears shimmered at his lashes. He blinked them away. "I'm just a barber," he whispered.

"*A man of flesh and blood,*" called one of the magi.

Laughter rippled like gold in the water around him. "*Welcome,*" "*Welcome,*" "*Welcome!*"

But their acceptance reminded him of the duke's trust, and the memory of the king's command returned to him with full force. He squinted at the sky. The hour must be up by now, and they would be coming for him.

Elisha shook off the last of his giddiness. Despite the magnitude of the casting, he felt stronger than he had after the arrows in the rain. The magi's advice about the talisman and the place, not to mention their own support, had carried him through. With an extra lift from the angel's wing.

Turning from the river, Elisha glanced down at Mordecai. Although conscious, he had not lost his pallor, and would need a long time to regain his strength. Still, Elisha could not afford to leave the king another captive, especially not one he thought already dead.

"The king has given me a charge I must complete."

The surgeon nodded slightly. "Trading you for the messenger. He asked what I knew about you." At this, a slender smile trembled on his lips.

Stifling a chuckle, Elisha replied, "Everything."

"Nothing," murmured Mordecai, "Not if you are capable of what you have just done."

"I can't risk leaving you here. Can you walk?"

"*I asked you that myself not so long ago.*" Mordecai

pulled himself to a sitting position, steadying himself on Elisha's arm. "*A lifetime ago.*"

"Two lifetimes," Elisha said in return. He slipped an arm around the thin shoulders, and they rose together, both shaky, leaving the shadow of the hanging tree.

As they made their way toward the hospital, a strange wind stirred the reeds on the opposite bank, as if they startled the air itself. In the lords' encampment, nothing moved but a few pennants and the billowing of the tents, their flaps all lowered. The breeze carried a stamping of hooves from unseen horses. For the moment, Elisha was simply relieved to have few onlookers as he helped Mordecai up to his room.

Wind scattered the pages Elisha had stacked so neatly, and the surgeon made a soft sound at the back of his throat. "All of my books," he sighed. "I had so many books." Disconsolate, he gazed about the room as if they would appear.

Letting him down onto the bed, Elisha retrieved a scrap of parchment and offered it up.

With a glance, Mordecai's eyes brimmed with sudden tears, as quickly blinked away. "The prayer book. That alone could have no value, not to such as these."

Elisha bowed his head and sank to the floor. All the weariness of the past few days stole over him. "I was here," he said, "looking for you. I should have guessed—" He interrupted his regret upon hearing a gentle chuckle, and looked up.

Sitting nearly naked on his bed, his most loved possessions carried off, still Mordecai managed to sit tall, his chin raised. Without a word, he raised his right hand before him, his dark eyes on Elisha's face, and smiled gravely. That air of knowledge Elisha had once found so intimidating seemed to grow again around him, the crinkles around his eyes and lips holding wisdom Elisha might never know. But then again, he might.

A grin broke over Elisha's face. Whatever happened next, whatever dark deeds he might be responsible for, this moment would shine. Impulsively, he asked, "Teach me, Sage. There is so much I still need to know."

The gray eyebrows dipped downward, and Mordecai dropped his hand, his head already shaking. "Too long in secret, Barber, I wouldn't know how to undertake that. Only went to the river for a little company."

"But you've had surgical assistants," Elisha protested, then wished he hadn't reminded him as pain flashed across the other man's face. "You know what I mean. I know I'm not worthy of such a teacher, I'm just—"

"A barber? Can you still believe that? Dear boy, you are a miracle worker. I am grateful, of course I am." He glanced away.

A brief cloud of sadness passed over Elisha's heart, causing the brand to ache. "No," Elisha murmured, "I'm not sure you are."

As if unaware, Mordecai's hand held one corner of the bloodied prayer shawl, his fingers running over the darker band where the hair was woven in. "Sarah," he whispered, "My wife. Jacob, the eldest, Joshua, my little Rachel." He blinked fiercely, and Elisha felt the tightening in his own throat as he knelt before the surgeon. "Baron brought me in to heal his son—a Jew, a last resort. Too late, of course. I had no choice but go." His voice sank so low that Elisha felt the rumble of grief long held as if a storm approached across an empty sky. "We never have a choice, my people. I called even upon my skill, and could not save him. Such anger rose. I have never felt such anger. How could a Jew know what it was like to lose a child? We murdered Christ. We slay good Christian children for evil rites— the force of his anger almost overcame me. I went to the library at the college of surgeons. I sank myself in words until the weakness left me. I came home." His voice died away completely.

By instinct, Elisha reached out, setting his hand on Mordecai's arm.

"*Too late.*" A bitter echo through Elisha's heart. "*He made sure I understood.*"

After a moment, Elisha swallowed his own pain and weakness. He wondered if Mordecai had ever considered the desperate notion that captured him in his grief. "*Do you believe in the Bone of Luz?*"

Mordecai stirred slightly. "*I have been a surgeon longer than you have been alive, and I have never found evidence of that. However they are to be raised up, it is not for man to know.*"

Elisha longed to offer some comfort, even some condemnation of the terrible injustice, but he was spent, and this grief was too old, too deep for any words to reach it. The knowledge fell heavily upon him that his own quest for resurrection had been a fool's errand. Slowly, Elisha withdrew his hand and laced his fingers together.

A thoughtful movement of Mordecai's right hand brushed his wiry gray hair across the thinning patch atop his head. "If you'll excuse me a moment?"

Elisha scrambled up, swaying a little. "Of course. I'll wait outside. I don't want—" He shrugged. "I can't leave you alone."

"Understood." He hunched on the bed, waiting.

Drawing the door shut behind him, Elisha propped

himself against the wall. The memory of death chilled him even across such a distance. He tucked his hands into his armpits to stop them shaking.

"Elisha Barber!" a voice shouted from outside, and Elisha jerked upright.

Footsteps echoed on the stairs. "Elisha Barber!"

"I'm here," he called. No good in hiding from them now.

Cautiously, the guard peered around the corner, then stepped into view with two of his fellows behind him. "Get a move on, then," he snapped, but a cross of newly whittled branches hung around his neck along with a sprig of something fragrant.

"I'll be down," Elisha said, softly but firmly.

Glancing at his companions, the guard adjusted his helmet strap, then nodded once. "Hurry it up." They turned and descended in a clatter.

After they'd gone, the door opened at Elisha's side, and Mordecai stepped out, clad in a long, hooded robe, his prayer shawl out of view. He was stuffing the remaining pages of his brutalized prayer book into an inner sleeve. "Shame I have no knowledge of deflection. Always meant to learn." Looking up to Elisha's face, he gave a brief smile, as if to show he'd recovered, but Elisha saw a few more lines around those eyes, and Mordecai gave up the pretense. "Shouldn't be around you so much—I'll have no secrets."

Elisha offered a rueful smile of his own. "At the very least, you shouldn't try to cheat if we gamble together."

"If we partnered, though, could be a new line of work." Mordecai flipped up the hood to hide his face, and slipped his arms deep into the sleeves.

They descended carefully, both still weak, and stopped for a breath at the landing. How they were ever to cross as far as the castle, Elisha had no idea. Perhaps the duke was eager enough for his company that he would send out a carriage. Lord only knew what the man wanted to begin with.

Together, they took the last few steps and emerged into the sunlight. Two dozen men awaited them, and the leader stepped up quickly, though he halted a few paces short, scowling. "Who's that then?"

"Ah, my assistant. I can't leave him."

"We don't have orders for that," the man replied.

Elisha gave a savage grin. "Then maybe I should go before the king to explain." He took a step forward, projecting menace.

"Still don't know why we're not gathering wood for the stake." The leader narrowed his eyes. "Take him, then, just let's be off."

The man radiated tension, poised for violence, and Elisha felt impressed with himself all over again. Apparently, his ruse at the bridge had gained him more than the chance to retrieve Mordecai: he had earned the fear of the king's men. Good.

As they began the long walk, Mordecai swayed, and Elisha shot out a hand to steady him.

One of the guards falling in behind let out a derisive snort. "Assistant? He's got a woman under there!"

Elisha nearly succumbed to another fit of giggles, and the hooded head rose with a note of indignation. Smothering the laughter, Elisha turned his gaze ahead, to the rough ground of the battlefield and the distant ramparts of the castle. As he gazed, the drawbridge inched downward, and finally lay open. A small group crossed over and started on their way.

As they walked, sun beat down on Elisha's dark hair, and he could only imagine how Mordecai must be sweating in his heavy robe. Since that moment in the chamber, Mordecai guarded his every emotion and sensation. Exhaustion crept through, however, and a nagging ache at the sight of his injury. Amputees often complained of feeling the need to scratch their missing limb, and Elisha wondered if Mordecai might now and again feel as if his hand were still lost.

After all the events of this day, Elisha found it amusing that he retained any scientific interest at all.

Still, as the walk wore on, entering the realm of pitted earth and ruined engines of war, sweat trickled down Elisha's neck, stinging the rope's path like a thousand insects. He flicked his hair, but it wasn't long enough any more to relieve that tingle. He gritted his teeth and walked on, turning his mind to the question of the assassination he had agreed to perform.

This duke seemed a man of honor, from Elisha's brief meeting, but who could tell with a nobleman? And did not the lives of all Elisha's friends outweigh this one? Assuming the king could be trusted to let them go, especially after Elisha's little show on the riverbank. He tried to think of a way around their bargain, a way to counterfeit death, but the body in the river was an obstacle he could not surmount, not without much more knowledge than he possessed. If he got a chance on their arrival, he would consult with Mordecai, to see if he might have any suggestions. Of course, once they got there, he had no guarantee of how they would be treated. Not knowing what the duke wanted left him at a severe disadvantage. Perhaps the messenger-prince had spun some tale about Elisha's value, or perhaps the wounded earl—the very reason Elisha had come face to face with Duke Randall—had begged his life, if he'd been aware enough to know who tended him.

In front of him, the lead guards suddenly halted, calling out.

The party of the duke's men had met them, exchanging salutes. As they separated, Elisha saw the figure of Prince Alaric, grubby and still clad in his messenger's garb. One of the men leaned down and worked the lock on his manacles. Rubbing his wrists, the young man started forward, entering the company of the king's guards.

From behind, someone screamed.

Piercing Elisha to the heart, the shriek rang on the wind, then was silenced by a crunch that sickened him even at this distance. Elisha whirled in time to see a second figure brought out atop the tower. He reeled. "No!" he shouted to the treacherous king. "No! You promised me time!"

Elisha started to run, but his guards had already drawn their swords, as if they'd been waiting for the signal of that scream. A breath of steel wind slashed at his back, and Elisha threw himself to the ground.

Someone grunted and rolled.

The startled guards hesitated, giving Elisha enough time to scramble back to his feet.

The lead man lay gaping, a dagger stuck in his side.

Standing over him, the prince flashed a familiar smile. "That's one I owe you, Barber."

"What the devil is going on here?" Elisha cried.

Knocked down in the scuffle, Mordecai stayed on the ground, one hand holding his hood in place.

Feet approached behind, and Elisha stiffened, but Prince Alaric called out, "You men, stop there!" He leaned to the guard he had killed and took the dead man's sword. "My father made a bargain. Surely you're meant to carry it out."

Arrayed behind him, the duke's men likewise froze, exchanging worried looks, hands gripping their sword hilts.

"We got orders, Highness," one of the king's men said, advancing.

Elisha darted a glance back, then returned his eyes to the prince.

"What orders?"

"To fetch 'im back to justice, alive or dead, once we had you. 'e's a witch, Yer Highness! Take care."

Throwing up his hands, the prince replied, "He's a barber, you fools. He saved my life not long past."

"We've got orders: Get ye back, and get rid of 'im!"

The prince eyed Elisha sidelong, his hesitation just enough for his father's men. The king's guards sprang forward, several of them rushing to encircle Duke Randall's soldiers as well. Even if the prince did choose Elisha's side, the duke's men were sorely outnumbered.

Rolling out of range for the nearest man, Elisha crawled toward Mordecai, reaching for attunement at the same time, despite his thundering heart. Neither of them was armed, but they might at least watch each other's backs using every sense at their disposal. As he approached, the hooded figure rose in a swift movement, throwing off the hood.

"Behold! I rise again!" Mordecai cried in a voice like thunder. Elisha froze in astonishment.

"It's the Jew!" called a panicky guard.

"Kill the witch!" the leader roared in turn.

A few men backed away, but a booted foot struck the small of Elisha's back, shoving him down to the dirt, knocking the breath out of him. The brand flared into terrible life on his chest, igniting the series of burns down his arm, and Elisha cried out.

He grabbed at the ankle, struggling to dislodge it as a sword flashed in the corner of his eye. He had not even a seed of grass to defend himself and a sudden cold shivered through him like Death's own laughter.

Chapter 35

❦

Then, through the disturbed earth, Elisha heard hoofbeats. Many horses, riding hard from the direction of the duke's castle. The king's treachery had not gone unnoticed.

"Lord preserve us!" cried Elisha's attacker.

"To the prince!" shouted another.

As they regrouped, the leader ordered, "Bring him!"

A mailed hand grabbed hold of Elisha's shirt hauling him up and dragging him in the opposite direction.

As he fought to get himself loose, Elisha caught sight of Mordecai, sprinting for one of the fallen siege towers. As if feeling the glance, the surgeon flashed him a look and dove for cover. Beyond, Duke Randall's cavalry came on, fifty horses, followed by men on foot. Elisha lost his tenuous footing, and was pulled headlong back toward the king's encampment.

He finally got one leg under him and launched himself ahead, tangling into the legs of his captor.

Both went down hard. As Elisha clambered up again, he heard another shriek on the wind, another resounding crack. Had it been Ruari, or one of Madoc's men? Christ!

With a glance to be sure Mordecai was safe, Elisha started to run. One way and another, the king would have him back: best return of his own free will and see what he could make of it. Unarmored and urgent, he quickly outstripped most of the king's guards.

He caught sight of the prince in the midst of a ring of soldiers, all moving toward the king's encampment. "Go, Barber!" the prince shouted, his mouth dropping into a mask of surprise as Elisha ran up, dodging a guard's hasty swing.

"You're going the wrong way!" Prince Alaric pushed through for a moment, and Elisha hesitated, meeting those familiar blue eyes.

"He's got Brigit," Elisha snarled.

The eyes flared wide as the prince caught his lip between his teeth and let it free. "But why?"

Even as Elisha turned away, panting, he saw the darkening of recognition in the other man's face.

His heart in his cramped throat, Elisha ran toward the royal encampment. What would he do—what could he possibly do?

Suddenly, the hoofbeats caught up to him. "Holy Cross, man, what are you thinking?" someone snapped down over the battle-ready snorting of his steed.

At that moment, Elisha didn't know. But he must try to reach the hostages, try to figure out a way. His head swam with the urgency of his need, and the futility of his action. The king would shatter them all by the time he could get back.

"Get to the castle, you fool! Don't put me through this for nothing!"

His hands balled into fists, he risked a sidelong look at the horseman who kept pace with him.

Duke Randall's round face watched him from the frame of his helmet, his visor thrown back. "I dunno what's going on, but Hugh's got no more patience for you, that's for sure."

"He's taken my friends!" Elisha shouted, turning back to his path to leap over a fallen soldier.

"My God, man, what for?"

Gritting his teeth, Elisha said, "If I don't kill you, he'll kill them, but he's already started."

"He's got no honor," the duke fumed. The horse lunged ahead, then made a tight circle to come up beside him, slowing.

A hand snatched at Elisha's arm.

"Come on!"

Stunned, Elisha tripped, then righted himself.

"Hurry."

He locked his hand around the duke's upper arm. Swinging himself up to the horse's rump, he clung to the saddle.

"Let's meet the snake in his lair," the duke muttered into the wind.

Tightening his grip on the saddle, Elisha struggled to maintain his balance, the natural impulse to embrace the rider thwarted by breast and back plates. Sword and twin daggers hung at the duke's sides, and he ducked low against the horse's neck, letting him run. In a moment, it could be over, Elisha saw with instant clarity. A slash from a stolen dagger, even a well-placed shove could send the duke tumbling back to be trampled by his own horsemen. The king on his tower had planned all of this, the hostages merely a way to keep hold of Elisha. He would be watching now, his two enemies coming on one horse. If Elisha carried out the deed, the king might be surprised into lenience. He would fulfill the bargain just to learn why Elisha had done it.

"Will you?" the duke called over his shoulder.

"What?" Wind whipped tears from Elisha's eyes.

"Will you kill me! It's your best chance right now!"

Elisha wet his lips and swallowed. The life of this one nobleman could hardly outweigh those of Madoc's regiment, or his friend Ruari—assuming they had not already died. Or Brigit. Her face flashed before him, green eyes glittering.

His wrists throbbed with the effort of hanging on, and Elisha shut his eyes against the wind, his head lowered into the shield of the duke's broad shoulders. He had conquered Death today, would he now become its ally?

"God damn me for a fool," he muttered, his face twisted into a bitter smile.

"I thought not," the duke replied. "You love life too much." He spurred the horse a little harder. "Then let's take the bastard down."

As he listened to the snorting of the horse, he remembered the stillness as they'd left camp, the lowered flaps on the lords' tents, the strange rustle by the river. The king's camp seemed deserted, his men vanished. Or hidden. Why start killing Elisha's friends? Because Elisha had no choice but to respond. Why order his men to disrupt the prisoner exchange? For the very same reason: the duke's honor would never stand for it. "Your Grace! It's a trap!"

But they had already entered the river's bend, the monastery looming up before them. Too late! In the cottage and hospital, the doors flew wide and soldiers poured forth. Mounted knights dashed around the corner, singing out their warcries.

The duke pulled hard at the reins, wheeling about as he cursed.

Elisha lost his grip and tumbled from the horse's rump to roll hard along the ground. Curling into a ball, Elisha hid his head as a horse sprang over him. Metal clashed, and someone stumbled on top of him, falling in an arc of blood. His body seared Elisha with the freezing cold of death.

He could feel it mounting all around him now. Horses whinnying their terror, men screaming and cursing and praying while that frigid wind passed through them. Yet they remained unaware.

Elisha moaned, pushing the corpse away. The cold stung his fingers and burned his injured wrists, as if seeking its revenge.

On the battlefield there was room to run. Here, the duke's men were trapped, ambushed by a treacherous king who had baited his snare with Elisha himself. The duke had brought only fifty men—a show of strength to intimidate the king's guards—and many of these were outside of the ring of battle, separated from the man they had sworn to serve.

Death cackled in the horse's dying screams. It frosted the eyes and lips of the men falling all around him, the common soldiers cut down by weapons wielded from horseback. Agony struck through Elisha as if he felt every blow. He whimpered.

Not far off, Duke Randall's voice rang out over the battle: "Come out and fight me, Hugh, you cowardly bastard!" But any answer was lost in the driving wail of death that beat at Elisha's ears.

Another man tripped over Elisha's huddled form, giving his opponent the advantage, giving Elisha another spatter of blood that turned cold too soon.

Elisha forced himself to move, shaking off the soldiers. He lurched toward the door by the vestry, and fell through into a silence that stunned him more than any sound.

Blinking, wiping blood from his face, he pushed himself up. He lay on the grassy slope behind the altar of the ruined church. Flowers trodden by the feet of

waiting soldiers already sprang back into the sunshine
of spring. The grass trembled in a warm breeze, and a
butterfly landed on a broken bench, its wings closing
once, twice, resting before daring again to touch the
sky. In here, the world lay at peace, becalmed beneath
the glorious day. Life surrounded and enfolded him,
taking over the fallen stone of this god's house. A place
of power indeed.

Breathing heavily, his muscles shaking, Elisha crept
to the altar. Soft moss and new grass cushioned his aching palms as he went. Fragrant earth touched his knees
with moisture. The sun warmed his bruised back, invit-
ing him to lie down and rest. But he found he could
hear the battle. He could hear the men and horses
tramping one way and another in their one-sided fight.
What was missing was the terrible sound of death that
sapped his strength and cleaved from him all awareness
of life. Yes, men were falling, wounded or dying, some
already dead, but all was not lost, not yet. And he had
come to what he needed.

Even before he began, the dissonance of what lay
there chimed a false note in the quiet hum of life. Digging in his fingers, Elisha pulled back the roots he had
packed in place. He scraped away the dirt, and drew
forth the grubby metal pot, its lid firmly sealed with
wax. As he set his fingers on it, they stuck, frozen, and
he lifted the thing awkwardly into his lap, breathing
moisture onto it to free himself.

Gleaming dully in the sun, the thing looked darker
than ever, as if the dirt had covered it for centuries,
concealing its malevolent power. Oh, yes, he could feel
it now. Not just the brush of death's cold hands, but the
aching injustice of the child who had never known life,
and the tearing anguish of its parents, bewildered in
their grief and Elisha's own pain, knowing it might

have been prevented if he had not betrayed his brother's trust. Layers and veils of emotion wrapped around him.

The death he held tried to break free, a wild lashing of panic sprang through his skin. He bit his tongue to stifle a scream as the ice took hold. But he must control it. He must overpower Death once more and bring it to heel. Only then could he send it hurtling forth against his enemies.

Elisha knew Death now, as he had not when first they met through this talisman. For so long, he had struggled against it, without ever understanding what he fought. Now, he recognized its terrible laughter, the sharp bite of its wind when it flung away another man. Now he knew the evil edge of cold that cut a wounded man and the ripping sensation as it tried to tear him from the world. And he knew the grip of its talons at his own throat, squeezing out his breath, and its howl of rage when he was snatched away by other hands.

Fighting down his fear, Elisha invited Death to join him.

He raised his hands and summoned it, calling out the madness and the pain. Death stole in through his flesh. It wrapped fell mists around him. It creaked along his spine and shivered his lungs so that he could not breathe. Death insinuated itself in every taut muscle and drop of blood. It crept through his bowels, and set its stealthy hands upon his heart. It sang within him, a humming so intense he vibrated to its rhythm, his body shaking as he took it in.

Elisha invited Death, and it accepted, curling up inside him like the serpent in the apple tree, lurking, waiting for its chance to strike. It sang to him with subtle voices, a song of strength and power, of an end to time and tyranny.

No longer weak, Elisha rose.

No longer giddy with spell-struck lunacy, Elisha laughed.

He held the talisman close to his heart, the metal sliding easily in his cold, cold grasp.

Chapter 36

━━━━━━━◆━━━━━━━

Bearing his pot of Death, Elisha turned to the door. He heard nothing now, though a wounded man stumbled inside and fell at his feet. The mouth gaped with words, but they could not penetrate the soothing hum of Death inside him.

Stepping over him, Elisha walked to the churchyard. He surveyed the fight, seeing the little knot of horsemen, hemmed all about by the king's knights and soldiers. They looked so weak and fragile, their bones struggling against their flesh. He imagined it putrid, falling from the crumpling bones in strips, these men who thought themselves bold dissolving into rot and dust and foulness. He searched for someone, but did not see him.

A figure loomed up before him, calling out, the face contorted with anger.

Elisha gazed around the soldier, cool mist enveloping him.

Raising his axe, the man charged, his teeth showing in an open roar that issued no sound.

Lifting his hand, Elisha caught the axe haft.

Brittle, dry and ancient, it splintered in his grasp, the axehead dropping to bury itself.

Waving his arms before him, the man stumbled back, then turned and fled.

As well he should run, for Death stalked this field.

Ignoring the fighting knot of men, Elisha walked into the courtyard, still seeking. He sniffed the air and found that Death had gone before him. In his steps, the grass browned and withered. Flower petals fell from the dandelions. Their naked stalks rotted where they stood. A small darting bird swooped through his shadow, and its wings trembled, then it fell from the sky.

Elisha strolled forward. He remembered hurrying, as if there were some race on, and he must win it. It didn't matter now. Whatever he had been after, he would find it in time, or it would come to him.

Another man sprang up to challenge him, waving a sword.

With a casual sweep of his hand, Elisha knocked the man aside. At his touch, the flesh shivered and grew cold, darkening to leather. Something trembled through his fingers, a disturbing something that wanted to distract him, to make him falter. Withdrawing his hand, Elisha frowned, but the sensation was gone, and he relaxed.

Two broken bodies lay at the base of the tower, soldiers still bound needlessly. Again that distraction arose, but he pushed it away.

Across the yard, beyond the stone cistern, he saw the man he had been looking for, the man with the crown on his helmet. Framed in the empty arch near the bridge, he stood in a ring of his own men. Holding a long sword before him, the man circled with a shorter, stocky figure. The crowned man laughed and sneered, twisting his bearded face.

The stocky man stood between Elisha and his goal, the sword in his grip shaking a little as he stood.

Beyond the wall, someone died. A rush of power flowed through the earth, up through Elisha's feet and legs, taking root in his breast. The heady scent of it filled him, tingling through his senses. Elisha grinned, then laughed.

Heads turned among those who watched the duel. Three ran forward, more fell back, tripping over their own feet.

Elisha's walk took on a suggestion of purpose. He stepped in a narrow channel, frost racing out from his ankle as he crossed over. The water froze and cracked and thawed again under the distant glitter of the sun.

Another familiar figure slunk along the wall, using the distraction of Elisha to make for the tower. Elisha laughed again. In time, all in time.

Another death rippled through the earth to him. He reached out and caught it, taking it over his hand like a ferret in a lady's sleeve, sleek and sharp. He played it over his fingers in a dark coil. More like a snake than a ferret—nothing so soft, something slick and darting, tasting the air, hungry for more.

As the crowned one attacked, the stocky man fell aside and his sword flew from his grasp. Elisha stepped over him. Intent on his quarry, Elisha felt only the hint of the cold wound as he passed by.

Drawing back, the crowned man shouted.

Elisha stepped on, shriveling a clump of weeds.

The ring of guards, shattered by Elisha's approach, tried to rally to their king. Elisha glared upon them and watched them sink to their knees, tears tracking their faces, hands begging for the gift he could not offer.

The king retreated, his sword thrust out before him, his lips gibbering with useless sound.

Inevitable and unmovable, Elisha walked toward him.

With a cry, the king slipped. He slithered down the bank on his belly, his feet splashing into the water.

Elisha did not fall. He knelt down at the riverbank and held out his hand. Performing this final baptism, he placed his palm on the king's crown.

Blue eyes widened. The head shook, the lips turned pleading.

Elisha's icy grip shattered the metal, tumbling the helmet in pieces into the water. His fingers combed the tousled hair.

The king's mouth broke into a horrible wail as death poured over him. His eyes sank and shriveled, his tongue twitched and lashed as he spoke ice crystals into the sunlight of April.

His hands flew up from the freezing water, grappling with Elisha's arm. For a moment they stuck, his skin frosting over. He tugged and twisted and could not break free until he tore his skin. The fingertips ripped away like dried-up mushrooms, his flesh powdering the surface of the ice. His cheeks withered. His powerful shoulders arched and wrenched, then sagged into his chest. His heart gave a final desperate pound and froze like a lump of stone within him.

Death raced up Elisha's fingers, kneading itself into his arm, crowing the victory.

He lifted his hand, and the king fell, his desiccated corpse breaking on the already-melting ice.

A familiar word echoed suddenly through the mist, and Elisha rose, frowning. Again, it came, like a breath of history, long dead. Elisha smiled and turned. The word meant nothing now, just another fleeting thing to fall and be consumed. All the words of the world meant nothing.

People ran at him, people without weapons, save one. They stumbled to a halt beside the crumpled form of the stocky man.

Elisha tilted his head, seeing them through a sort of prism, their faces magnified in horror. A tall one caught up a smaller one in his arms and backed away. A short, hairy one held up his hands before him, gesturing wildly. The one with the sword grabbed the red-haired one.

You are all mine, Elisha thought. You all belong to me, however much you struggle to avoid me. He laughed, and even his own sounds were unable to reach him.

The one with the sword advanced, pushing aside the red-haired one. Its mouth flapped, its hand waved in a gentle rhythm.

Recognition dawned in Elisha's cold mind. Oh, he remembered this one. He remembered those keen, blue eyes, and the moment of hesitation when he might have been Elisha's savior. This one had held the power to set him free, and had not done it. This one possessed something he longed for. What was it? What could he ever have wanted that he could not now take of his own will?

Gathering the mist around him, Elisha strode out to meet it. He rolled death into his fingers, squeezing it like a child's toy, a plaything only he could enjoy.

Before he could get there, the man fell under a sudden deluge, tumbling away to one side, floundering. The red-haired one let the water she had summoned fall back.

Elisha felt a twinge, and he shook it away.

Running, the red-haired one stood suddenly before him.

He raised an arm, but her hand snuck past him, her fingers brushing his face.

Shocked, Elisha froze. A fistful of death held close and ready, but she did not darken or fall, and the touch of her hand crashed through him like a wave of sudden sound. Around him, people screamed and prayed. The tall man—Ruari—called down his god of vengeance on a witch. Beside him, Lisbet cowered beneath his arm. Madoc intoned the words of an antique language, one they spoke here long ago, the rhythm of his hands trying to ward off evil. The prince dragged himself free of whatever entangled him and broke into a run.

The woman before him held out her hand. Her fingers indeed had darkened.

His cheek twitched with warmth, and Elisha shook his head to clear it, to maintain his focus. But the touch went too deep. It twined inside him, hot and growing hotter by the second, flaming through the veils of mist. Her touch dashed away the darkness in his eyes. It spread through his skin and radiated into every finger.

Elisha trembled and gasped. He struggled to keep his contact.

Then her eyes gleamed into his, and she spoke again that single, familiar word. "Elisha," she said on a breath of fire.

The heat seared a pathway into his heart, casting off the icy grip that lodged there, and he screamed.

The pot tumbled from his spasming fingers.

Something snapped inside him. Elisha collapsed, and darkness took hold.

Chapter 37

❖

Elisha's eyes flew open. A woman shrieked and something clattered. He jerked upright, flung off the bedcovers, and leapt to his feet, looking around wildly. He remembered cold. A cold so deep it coursed through his veins and shot from his fingers.

On the tiled floor, a strange woman scrambled to her feet, her hair in disarray, a basket of stitchery over-turned around her. "Don't hurt me!" she wailed. Getting her feet beneath her, she crossed herself.

Elisha swallowed hard. His mouth felt dry as sand. His throat convulsed with pain, and he brought his hands up, feeling a bandage wrapped over a remembered injury. He did remember that, didn't he? But it, too, had been cold.

As his hands fell, he stared. Something was wrong there. Elisha wriggled his fingers, turning his palms up and down. No, not his hand. Mordecai—the name sprang to his memory, and a rush of others followed: Ruari and Lisbet, falling in love in his absence; Madoc and Collum and all of his men; Benedict sinking cold from his arms. The prince, whose name he should re-member, and Brigit, whom they both loved. Brigit who had melted the ice from his heart.

Elisha clapped his hand over his mouth, reeling with

memory. Taking a few paces, he dropped to his knees
before the terrified woman. "Did I kill the duke? Tell
me! Did I kill him?"

Shrinking away, the woman swayed.

As she fainted, Elisha caught her and lay her on the
ground. He leaned back on his heels.

"Elisha."

He jerked as if someone had struck him, pulling
himself half up as he turned.

Even as he did so, the air in the room grew warmer,
somehow comforting, as if he drew a breath of lavender. The fallen maid stirred and sprang up to make her
escape.

With a twisted smile, Mordecai bent down to him,
holding out his hand. "Shouldn't've left you. Sorry."

Touching the bracelet of pale markings, Elisha
grasped the offered hand. Comfort flowed through
the contact, and he drank it in, letting out a shuddering breath as he shut his eyes. "Thank God," he
breathed. "Thank God."

For a moment, Mordecai waited, and Elisha raised
his head at last, letting himself be drawn up from the
floor. Nausea swept through him, threatening to topple
him once again, but Elisha clung to Mordecai's hand,
and the feeling receded.

Wearing a new cap, and a robe of practical brown,
Mordecai studied him. "It's been three days, Elisha,
you are entitled to some weakness, yet."

"Three days? But it seems—" he broke off. How
could it be so, when the memory of cold still chilled his
mind?

"It requires terrible strength to stop a war, and terrible weakness is bound to follow."

Nodding, Elisha released his hand. "Terrible indeed.
What have I done?" he murmured. As he stared at his

hand, he remembered more than cold. He felt again the leaping joy of death flooding through him. So much power in this hand.

Mordecai closed the distance in a step, and set his hands on Elisha's shoulders, gazing steadily up at him. *"You have taken one life to save many others. Yes, you might have done much worse, you have held what no man should, and you have borne what no man should. Elisha Magus, you struggled with death on my behalf, and won. Death fought with you and might have taken you, but still you have won. In spite of all, you are a man of flesh and blood."* He smiled then, and the warmth of it banished the last of Elisha's shivers. *"Blessed and cursed, as we all must be."*

"Only one life? Can it be?" Relief set him to trembling inside, and he sat back onto the bed.

Mordecai stood before him, his touch more gentle now. *"It was the king's life, Elisha, and there will be a reckoning for that."*

A reckoning indeed. The king had been wicked, of this Elisha had no doubt, but a king nonetheless. Elisha hardly knew how vast a thing his death might be.

"You touched a guard," Mordecai went on, *"and might have killed him, but instead merely delivered an injury even the learned physician cannot account for."*

"What about the duke? He fell before me—I can't see it clearly."

As Mordecai parted his lips to answer, Elisha felt the ripple of someone approaching. *"You will."* He stepped away, breaking the contact.

Tapping on the door left open in the nursemaid's wake, Duke Randall strolled in. His arm was in a sling, and his eyes were still rimmed with darkness, but he walked confidently enough. "I heard a scream, and assumed you must have woken." He nodded to Mordecai, who bowed slightly. "Are you still demonic?" he asked lightly, his lips curving a little.

"No, Your Grace, I think not." He considered rising to bow, but decided against it as his vision wavered yet again.

"Glad to hear it. Welcome to my home." It was the duke who bowed, his neck once again exposed to Elisha's potential.

"How . . . ?" Elisha asked, ruffling the hair out of his face, then, "Wait. I need water."

"Still no manners," the duke observed.

"A poor nurse I make," Mordecai sighed, rising and slipping back out the door.

Wincing, Elisha said, "Sorry, Your Grace. Manners have never been my strength."

Duke Randall let out a hearty bark of laughter. "Don't take me seriously, Barber, I beg of you. Do you mind?" he inquired, pulling up a chair and sinking into it. "I'll take a bit of recovery yet."

Elisha started to rise with a frown. "What's the damage?"

Flapping his free hand, the duke said, "Tush, sit. I've been well cared for, by your own man."

"The surgeon?"

"The barber," he corrected. "Your assistant, as I understand."

"Then Ruari's all right."

At this, the duke lost his smile. "Yes, yes, he's fine, and his lady-friend as well. A captain called Madoc, I believe, and all but two of his men survived."

The softening of expression did not escape him. "Then what is the matter, if I may know?"

"They will not come to you. I'm sorry. They saw," he broke off, shaking his head. "They know what you are."

Nodding slowly, Elisha said, "Then so do you, Your Grace."

"So why have I come? Why have I taken you into my home? Aside from the fact that you won this battle for me. Alaric, the king's pig of a son, promised to recant if I released him, and he's kept his word about that, so at least my daughter's honor is no longer in question, even if her marriage prospects are shaky. Now I'm hearing his brother Thomas is discredited for plotting against their father, we'll have to hope that Prince Alaric proves worthy in other ways."

With a little shrug, Elisha invited him to continue.

"But that's nothing to do with you, really. I might have released him for the apology alone, but I thought I could get a little more than that." The duke resettled his injured arm. "My wife is a wonderful, compassionate woman—you must meet her—the Duchess Allyson." Then a grin split his face. "But you have already met her, under the name of Willowbark."

Relaxing, Elisha flopped back onto the comfortable bed and sighed. "I knew someone had to be here; how else would you know what went on?"

"She told me you were too good to lose—as if I'd not seen it myself; that you deserved a better chance, and I gambled she was right. I won, quite handily, too."

"I was the lure in a trap to catch you."

"Not your fault. I should have expected as much from that back-stabbing bastard. No matter, here we all are, safe and mostly sound. I think I might have come after you even without my wife's bidding."

"Did she know I was sent to kill you?" Elisha glanced toward him, and the duke narrowed his eyes over a slender smile.

"Something was on, we knew that much. Some of my men argued to let you die instead or bring you back in chains. I took another gamble."

"With your life."

Again, Duke Randall shook his head. "I thought self-knowledge was one of the laws, but never mind that. That day we first met, on the field, my man dropped his sword for just a moment. You did not plead for mercy. You did not pray or rant against me. What did you say? 'Don't move him.' You were on the verge of being executed, and you thought first of your patient—a stranger, and an enemy."

"I didn't know that," Elisha replied.

"That's exactly the point. It did not matter a whit to you who he was, if he was lord or servant, enemy or friend—he was wounded, and you had the skill to save him. Of course, I have my own interests at heart in bringing you here. If concerns over the king's death can be assuaged"—he tipped his head to acknowledge the size of this *if*—"I want you to work for me. Even when you were just a barber, I thought to earn your loyalty." He spread his hands. "And now, all the better for me. I suspect I may prefer to have you on my side."

With a grim smile, Elisha said, "I am rather glad I did not see myself, at that moment. But if you will have me, then I will stay."

Mordecai entered, the room warming with his familiar presence, bearing a tray of food with a tall mug of cold water. "From the river," he said, offering it with a flourish. "Drew it myself." He met Elisha's gaze.

Rising heavily from his chair, the duke said, "I'll leave you to it. When you're up and about, I can send you to the city, with an advance on your wages to purchase whatever you need. I expect the things you brought with you this far have been well dispersed by now." He sighed, wincing at the pull on his wound. Again he gave a slight bow and withdrew.

As he laid out the food on a little table, Mordecai said, "She's come, you know, if you've not felt her."

Easing himself into a chair, Elisha took a long draught of water. "I wasn't sure if I should hope for that or fear it."

Mordecai nodded. "I'll send her, then you'll be sure." He disappeared through the door again.

Tipping her head around the door, Brigit watched him for a moment before she stepped through.

His heart rose just to see her. Her pale face looked as radiant as ever, as if an inner glow suffused her skin. She ducked away from his scrutiny, hiding her eyes as she entered. Bundled in her arms she carried a heap of dark wool. Turning from him, she laid it out on the bed and smoothed the cloth with a careful hand, her red hair swinging forward to hide her face. His lost cloak.

"I cast a spell and found it for you," she said. "The coins you sewed in are gone, of course."

"Thank you," he replied, stiff and self-conscious. He must look a mess, with his bandages and his unruly hair.

She spun on her heel and laughed, a beam brightening her face as she dropped onto the bed. She kicked her heels just as she had done on the altar, so long ago, when his hands had held the silken weight of her hair. "Oh, Elisha, it has been such an amazing time. It's May, now, did you know? To think so much could happen in the space of a single month!"

He wet his lips and remained silent as he took another swallow.

"What you did," she breathed, sighing as her eyes searched the ceiling, "I have never heard its like. I was right about you—my mother saw the power in you."

"Not in me," he said, shaking his head. Then he froze and glanced up again. "What happened to the talisman?"

With a toss of her head, Brigit replied, "I don't know."

The lie cut through him with a delicate blade, and his hopes faded away as quickly as they had flared. "Brigit, you must give it back. It's not just a tool, not even just a talisman—"

At least she did not maintain the pretense of ignorance. "I can't do that. I need it. We need that power."

"No, Brigit! You don't know what it is, what it feels like." He tried to push himself up, but a wave of dizziness swelled through him. "I swore an oath to lay it to rest."

"An oath you broke when it suited you."

He winced at the truth of this, but his expression hardened at the thought of anyone using it as he had done. He had been desperate to save lives—in the hands of another . . .

"Elisha, a thing that strong cannot merely be set aside. It must be handled carefully—I know that. I've been a magus all my life and the daughter of one. Of course I know what to do. What if our enemies got hold of it?" Her hands clenched.

"Your enemies are not magi, Brigit, they wouldn't know what to do with it."

"They have bombards, Elisha, and knights and armies, and a legacy of slaughter. You have only just become one of us. When you've lived under this fear for years, you'll know, you'll understand, why we need every advantage we can take."

Passion lit her face and he almost believed in her.

"When the time is right, Elisha, you can fulfill your oath. When the crisis is past."

He stared up at her. Would the crisis ever be past, or would she have a thousand reasons to keep what she had stolen? Weakness prevented him from fighting for it as he must, and the failure soured his stomach. "Oh, Brigit. Why did I ever love you?"

She gave a little moan of pain and dropped to the floor beside him, taking his hand. "Elisha, please. This is not easy for me, none of it! We may be at war, don't you see? Alaric found the letter, the one his brother sent to hire Benedict to kill the king."

"No," Elisha broke in. "Benedict died because he would have revealed his master—it was the physician's letter."

Brigit frowned, her head tilted to the side. "But Lucius is gone already. Not that it matters. Even now, Alaric's brother Thomas will be mounting an army against us. Alaric has claimed the crown, of course, since he was faithful, but it shall not be given up without a fight. That night you fell from my room, I was expecting an ally, a magus who might help us win victory. I've been preparing all my life for this moment. The time is at hand to claim our freedom. Oh, earth and sky, Elisha, the things that lie ahead for me will not be easy."

His voice broke, but he managed, "Easy? You will be queen." Tears stung the corners of his eyes, and he brushed them harshly away.

"*If I had only met you first,*" she whispered in his mind.

Elisha flung her hand away, shaking off the contact as if it burned him. Indeed, the brand over his heart gave a sudden spasm of pain, and he cried out.

"Elisha!" she sobbed, stroking his face, daring to touch again the angel's mark.

Again, he thrust her away, but not before he felt her words, a touch of surpassing tenderness, whispering, "*I love you.*"

"But not enough to give it back," he said bitterly.

Brigit's head fell, her red-gold hair rippling along his thigh. Then she shook herself and rose, drawing her arms about her. "I can't," she said, "Not yet. Someday, I promise you, I will do that, when this is all over with.

There are such terrible things coming, Elisha, you can't know it yet—" she broke off, then said, "Trust me."

Tears spilled down his cheek. "By God, Brigit, what in heaven or earth could ever make me do that?"

With a soft cry, she fled.

Elisha leapt up and stumbled for the door, already dizzy with the motion. "Brigit!" he shouted as if one last try would make her understand.

"No!" she snapped, then spun about, still backing away, step by step. "Elisha Barber. You watched my mother die!" She flicked away a tear from her face. "If you had your accursed talisman then, you would have saved her!" She stabbed her finger in his direction. "And you would deny me that power? No, Elisha. Let no more witches burn."

Her bright eyes reflected the flame of that day, his cheek warm with the memory as he let her walk away. This parting would not last forever: They two were bound, both past and future, by her mother's death, by the talisman, by all that they shared.

Elisha gazed after her and wondered if she knew, if she had set herself upon that road as well, when she first refused his passion, then demanded it. In the stroke of her love, he had felt a deeper stirring, that of new life waiting and growing. Did she know yet that she would bear his son?

Chapter 38

❖

A fortnight later found Elisha in Duke Randall's carriage, returning to London with two of the duke's clerks. There, they would find or order the things they needed to rebuild. During the battle, they had torn down several buildings for the stones launched in their bombards and run through all their medical supplies. There was also a shortage of brooms, for Duchess Allyson had turned every bit of straw into arrows for her husband's archers. When Elisha's spell turned them to rain, she gave up the arrows rather than spend more of her strength against his. Not everyone knew that she was a witch, but those who did kept their peace with her and gave thanks in the chapel for the gifts she could provide.

When they left him in the high street, specifying a day to meet again, Elisha knew he must find Helena's sister and try again to atone. He had so hoped to bring her child's remains back with him, but that must wait; Brigit wouldn't give up such power without a struggle. So he'd avoided her, and, for the moment, avoided Helena as well.

Instead, and on the duke's advice, he walked the few blocks from the gate to the leaded glass panes of the draper's row, and opened the door to Martin's shop.

Samples of elegant fabrics decked the wall behind a counter, and an assistant glanced up while helping a finely dressed lady pick out just the thing to drape her walls. Looking him up and down, the assistant glowered, and Elisha laughed. The young man was fair and tall with a long fall of hair swept back by a ribbon a touch too bright for the average man. He was new since last Elisha had been there, and it was clear what he thought of Elisha's entrance. Even clad in the Earl of Blackmere's cast-offs, Elisha was clearly not a customer. Martin's assistant had already leapt to a different conclusion.

"Sorry to interrupt, sir," Elisha said, still amused by the assistant's jealousy. "I'll just wait, shall I?" He stepped to the counter and started to finger a delicate sample of silk which was probably worth more than the duke would pay him in his lifetime.

Stiffening his spine, the assistant snatched up a silver bell and shook it, then slammed it back onto the counter. The customer jumped a little and frowned. The pretty young man murmured something soothing, and they bent together over the samples.

A paneled door popped open. "What is it, Brian?" Martin called out, then stopped, his hand on the knob. A brief grin flared across his face, and he gripped the latch a little tighter. "Ah, yes, about the duke's orders? I've been expecting you," he babbled, adding to his assistant's discomfort.

Stepping lightly forward, Martin swung up a section of the counter and invited Elisha through. "Come to my office," he said, then followed, shutting the door swiftly.

Once inside, Elisha turned.

Martin slumped with his back to the door. That ridiculous grin threatened to swallow his eyes, which welled with tears. "Mother Mary, I thought I'd never see you again."

Returning the smile, Elisha plucked something from his belt and shook it out—a long strip of purple silk. "But you have, thanks, in part, to this."

Shaky, Martin dropped into his chair, pressing a beringed hand to his cheek. "What's happened to you? Tell me all! And your hair," he moaned. "Oh, your glorious hair."

"I cut it all off to save you from temptation," Elisha teased, dropping into a chair opposite. He had found someone to trim it short, so that the dark curls clung to his head. Perhaps one day, he would let it grow again, but maybe not. He smoothed the fabric against the leather desktop with his palm.

"You've been badly hurt, haven't you?" Martin asked, leaning forward. "I can see it all over you, and not just in the body, either."

For a moment, Elisha wondered if the draper might have more secrets than one. "I fell in love with a lady," he sighed, still aching at the memory.

"Oh, it would be a woman," said Martin crossly. "But go on."

Elisha told him most of the story, glossing over his injuries, finding ways around the witchcraft, as he had rehearsed it all those nights in the duke's castle. He foisted off the king's death on a stranger, but suspected his voice revealed too much in any case.

When he had done, he gazed at Martin's smooth, handsome face.

Martin sat back in his chair, one arm across his chest, the other propped against his face. "You loved the lady who will be queen." He whistled softly, shaking his head. "Only you, Eli." He frowned, toying with an end of the cloth. "'Tis a curious tale, and somewhat different from the one I heard."

"Where there's a battle, the rumors will fly as thick

as the arrows," Elisha replied. "When that man Robert had hold of me, and the duke asked where I got this—" He tapped the fabric. "I thought for a moment you might have set me up for death, instead of life."

"Perish the thought!" Martin clapped a hand to his chest, setting his rings glittering in the afternoon sun.

"Forgive me for doubting you," he said, and pushed himself up. "I should go. I think your assistant has already gotten the wrong idea."

Rising with a sigh, Martin said, "I'll reassure him, though I wish there were some foundation for his jealousy." His smile turned rueful. "You'll stop and see me before you go back?"

"As you wish." Elisha held out his hand, and Martin grasped it in both of his.

Through their joined hands, an energy flowed which was not familiar, yet instantly recognizable. Both men looked up, catching each other's eyes.

If it were possible, Martin's grin grew even wider. "*I knew it! I just knew it*!"

Impulsively, Martin flung his arms around Elisha in a quick embrace, not long enough to make him uncomfortable, and broke away again, letting his hand linger. "*How long?*"

"*Just after I got there, I met*—"

Martin drew back with a stern expression. "*Don't tell me, please! You must know the rules.*"

"*A few of them anyhow. I've only just started.*" He spread his hands and smiled, that trace of regret running through him as he watched Martin's expressive features. Martin remained his very dear friend, never to be more to him than that.

As if he sensed Elisha's regret—and well he might—Martin glowered. "*Get out before I fall in love with you all over again!*"

Bowing slightly, Elisha took his leave, with a cheery wave to the disgruntled assistant as he left the shop.

Feeling lighter, and, perhaps for the first time in his life, connected with something greater than himself—a people of whom he could truly be a part—Elisha leapt the drainage ditch and dodged around a party of bickering beggars. With Martin's good will, he felt strong enough now for what he must face. He shied away from the hospital, its miasma of misery touching him briefly as he passed by. Shuddering, he hurried his pace, and soon stood before the little house in the mews with its sagging roof and crooked steps. His brother's workshop stood to one side, smoke rising from the chimney.

Elisha's heart gave a lurch, then settled down again. She must have sold it, or found another smith to take it up. As he stood, unsure what to do next, a man emerged, rubbing his hands on a cloth.

"Help you?" he called out.

Approaching a few more steps, Elisha said, "Yes, I'm looking for Nathaniel Tinsmith's widow, do you know where she's living?"

The man nodded his head to the house. "Still here, ain't she? Go on through."

"But who are you?"

"Roger Ironman, new to the parts. She's rented me the shop 'til I get meself settled."

As Elisha walked up, the door sprang open, and a child darted out, giggling like mad and bounding down the steps into the yard.

"I'll get you!" a woman in a nun's habit cried, springing after, then stopping short, her mouth dropping open. "Elisha!" Sister Lucretia wrapped him in an embrace, pressing her cheek against his chest.

It still ached, but he didn't mind. Somehow, he freed his arms from the tangle of hers and returned the ges-

ture. "Sister, I can't tell you how glad I am to see you,"
he murmured. He felt the return of his sentiment and
trembled. So long he had been surrounded by emotions
he denied himself, from Martin's love to Lucretia's admiration. Since his awakening, he hurt more deeply, it
was true, but he also laughed from that depth—cursed
and blessed, and glad of it.

At last, they broke apart to gaze at each other.
"You've changed," she observed.

"Aye, that I have, Sister, and you don't know the half
of it." He shivered in the suggestion of a breeze.

"Come inside—we've just got supper on, if I can
catch that Annie!" her voice rose at the end, and a trail
of giggles emerged from around the back.

Elisha looked toward the darkened door. He had
last gone through it alone, bereft, and dripping with
blood that should never have been spilt. "Am I welcome?"

Hesitating, Sister Lucretia kept his hand in hers,
gazing with him. "Much has changed here, too."

"Like Annie?" he asked, his surprise returning.

Lucretia brightened. "Aye, like that! She's been
God's gift, and not his only. I convinced Helena to bury
her grief in charity, and so she has. She takes in the
country children, the ones recovering from the hospital, you know, who mightn't be welcome back to their
families as more mouths to feed." She crossed herself
quickly. "There are some as would rather their sick
ones went home to the Lord."

"I know, I've met them." He took a deep breath. "I
worried she might return to her old life. Nate would
never . . ." But his brother's name stopped his throat.

"Between what she's given for the children and the
rents from the workshop and your old rooms—sorry,
Eli—she gets by." Lucretia nudged him toward the house.

With some trepidation, but with the strength of her hand, Elisha walked toward his brother's door.

At the steps, Lucretia detached herself and climbed inside, speaking in a low voice. From within, a baby wailed, and Elisha looked to the cloudless sky, mastering himself for what was to come.

After a moment, Sister Lucretia peered around the doorframe. "Come in," she said, "It's all right."

The cry of the child had not prepared him for what met his eyes, and Elisha sucked in a breath. His throat seized up a little, and he forced himself to relax. What could be more natural, after all, than a woman nursing a baby?

Except if the woman were Helena, so recently bereft of her own child, and her husband as well. All that she loved had been torn from her, and Elisha had been the surgeon who made the first cut. He never thought he would see her again, so he sank himself in his work as if healing others could repair the wounds he had caused.

She glanced up from the child's face, one of its tiny hands wrapped around her finger. The smile she wore faded away, leaving her solemn and yet radiant. No woman had glowed like that save the Virgin Mother. Or Brigit, when she looked on him.

Elisha's head bowed to his chest, and he folded his arms together. His lips trembled, and he fought to keep them still. "Helena," he said, "I am so sorry. For you, for the baby, for Nathaniel—" His voice broke.

"Come here," she said, "Kneel down where I can look at you." Her tone brooked no refusal, and he obeyed, only too glad to sink to his wobbly knees. "This surprises you, does it? To see me with a child at my breast? Look closer, Barber, look."

Her words drew up his gaze, and he saw as she lifted the infant away, turning it to face the other breast.

Although the other side of its face had glowed with that bliss particular to babies, this side seemed stiff, the eye sloping and twitching, the arm a stub with fingers too small even for a child. "The mother took one look and turned it away," Helena murmured, caressing the child's cheek with her finger. "Sister Lucretia came to me." Her voice faltered, then grew stronger. "She came to me because my milk had just come in. I hurt in so many ways, then, and that one seemed the most terrible. God had taken my baby to be with Him, she said, but it did not mean I should be alone, and here was this child . . ." She looked toward where Lucretia hovered at the hearth. The smile that touched her lips echoed the joy he heard in her voice: She had found the blessing beyond the curse, in this giving of herself.

"Everything is changed," she said. "Even our king is new, and his betrothed. They say the battle you fought has been only the rumor of a greater war."

"It was not my battle," he murmured, thinking of all of those who had died, the men under his care, the men felled by arrows, by fire and stone. "Not mine alone."

"Forgive me."

Helena's voice rang in his ears, widening his eyes as he looked up to her face. "But what have you done to need forgiveness?"

She glowed with that smile and with something like sorrow, or pity. "The letter I sent you," she said. "It was cruel in its words and its intent. I had not yet healed. I still have not, but at least I've come far enough not to inflict my pain on others. I'm sorry. I still hope you will one day trust me with all of your story." At his expression, she shook her head. "Not today. It's still too soon."

Elisha's hands gripped each other, almost like a prayer. He rubbed one thumb over the nail of the other. "That night I left, do you recall your curse to me?"

After an instant, she drew a quick breath. "I do," she said, "I cursed you to love, and to lose your love."

He nodded, missing again the weight of his hair, the way he could hide behind its darkness. "It came true." He swallowed hard, trying to hold back the pain of this strange wound.

She sat silently, only her breath betraying her presence.

He had drawn into himself again, not daring to feel whatever emotions rocked her—not even to punish himself.

Then her soft words fell through the still house. "Oh, Elisha, I am sorry."

With a strangled laugh, he whispered, "I forgive you."

Then her hand brushed against his hair, and she did not need to speak to answer him, for his defenses fell away, and she drew him close against her knee. His brother's widow stroked his hair, and Elisha felt the chill slivers of Death rise away from him toward Heaven.

Available July 2014 from DAW,
the second novel of *The Dark Apostle*
by E. C. Ambrose:

Elisha Magus

Read on for a sneak preview.

The gray of the evening sky deepened as Elisha walked to the churchyard. The church itself leaned a bit to the left, its ruined steeple pointing up toward the duke's castle, accusing or beseeching, it was hard to say. Riders jangled by, talking and laughing, on their way for the grand masked ball, their chatter drifting over the walls into what should be a peaceful place. His business here would likely be brief, and he would be back to the castle in plenty of time to dodge the visitors and return to the comfort of his infirmary. He wanted to check on the scullion's new baby, not to mention that man-at-arms with the wounded leg. So far, no sign of putrefaction, but the fellow was terrified he'd have to lose his leg, and his livelihood. Elisha hoped the noise of the ball wouldn't disturb them, and that the flow of wine and ale wouldn't mean a flow of drunken nobles tumbling into his own domain.

The ribs of burned-out houses and barns still loomed over the streets, but a few had been dismantled, fresh stone laid for new foundations, and piles of cut saplings waited to be woven into walls. Two houses, at least, had already been built to the roofs, tiles gleaming dully with the rays of the distant sun, and smoke curled from their chimneys. Elisha took careful stock of all that he

saw, looking for movement, looking for new places
someone might hide. Tension crept into his shoulders,
much as he tried to keep it back, to focus on the duty he
maintained here. Nothing else caught his eye, but Elisha still stretched his awareness, allowing tendrils of
his strength to move over the ground, aware of the families in each house, the sheep in each fold, the cat that
slunk through a blackened barn in search of mice returning.

Even the graves lay unquiet after the battle, crosses
askew, the handful of stone monuments broken or flat-
tened by the bombards' blast and the rumble of siege
engines. Elisha picked his way toward the far side,
where the low wall had been dismantled to expand the
yard, and a series of mounds still high over the new
graves showed where the soldiers lay. A hunched figure
bent over, shovel across its shoulder, examining the
shrouded remains of the latest corpse.

The figure gave a twitch and turned, straightening as
much as possible, the lumpish face curling into recognition. The fellow had been here through the battle,
burying the dead of the king's army, and of the hospital
where Elisha did his best. Now he worked for Duke
Randall's village. Gravediggers didn't choose sides. Elisha gave a nod, but noticed the flutter of the shroud as
if the gravedigger had been searching beneath it, not
merely measuring the corpse for a grave. His eyes narrowed. "Which side did he fight for?"

"Who can say, now? Anything worth money's been
stripped, eh? And his clothes don't tell much—been a
month in the woods, ain't he?" The gravedigger grinned
and shrugged, then set his shovel to the earth. "Didn't
expect nobody but the priest."

Elisha moved past, facing the grave between them,

and the pale cloth of the shroud. The cracked bell in the crooked tower gave a thunk, then another, and a third, each with a groan of rope over pulley that suggested how hard the priest must work to get even that pitiful sound.

A week had passed since the last funeral, and they had thought it might be truly the last, until a few children found this sorry fellow half-buried in a blast pit by the trees. The first funerals he attended here included relatives of the deceased, the camp followers or near-by townsmen who still recognized their own. But time degraded the dead until their families would not have known them and most had been already laid to rest. The gatherings dwindled to a few sympathetic townsfolk, and even then they wanted to know if the fallen were of the king's army—which had set the torch to their homes—or of the duke's, as if the duke's bombards had spared them any grief. Elisha had effectively fought for both sides, impressed to the king's army before delivering the ultimate victory for the duke himself. He came as much for his brother's sake as for the soldiers, for the funeral he had missed.

Father Michael crossed the yard, wringing his hands and shaking out his fingers, the lines of his face deepened by the sinking sun. He, too, nodded at Elisha. The three men stood around the grave as the priest crossed them and the corpse and spoke in Latin. Elisha's outspread awareness as much as the monotone of the priest's voice suggested that this task had moved from reverence to rote.

Father Michael led another prayer, followed by Elisha's quiet, "Amen," and the grunt of the gravedigger, then sprinkled holy water and turned away for the church.

"Give us a hand, mate," the gravedigger muttered, waving Elisha closer with a flap of his wrist.

Pushing back his sleeves, Elisha came forward, squatting to lift the corpse's shoulders. The body gave in his hands, a softness foreign to healthy flesh, and Elisha swallowed the bile in his throat.

"Give 'im the toss." The gravedigger chuckled, but he moved carefully enough to lay his end of the body into the grave.

Still, Elisha stumbled and nearly slipped in afterward, the head and shoulders flopping heavily from his hands into the hole. A ripe odor drifted from the shroud, along with a few flies, and Elisha drew back, looking away for a breath of fresher air. Just to breathe in the stench of corpses opened one to disease. He straightened and tipped his head back, the clatter of hooves and merry voices rising from the road. The slightest thrill of interest touched him from afar and Elisha turned.

A bolt whizzed past, snagging the cloth of his shoulder with a sharp tug.

With a curse, Elisha leapt aside, tumbling into the half-filled grave as a second bolt whipped through where he'd been standing and cracked against the dirt wall. His shoulder stung and the corpse beneath him gave an exhalation of foul air. Recoiling from the stink, hand pressed over his mouth, Elisha froze. If he stuck his head up now, the archer might have a third shot. Damn it! His heart hammered loud in the narrow space. His eyes watered as the stench invaded his nostrils, but he held his stomach in check. Even without his extra senses, he heard the horses galloping off.

"Christ on the Cross, two in one grave!" The gravedigger peered down at him, a shovelful of dirt poised in his hands.

"Barber! What's happened?" Father Michael ran up. "I was checking the garden when I heard you cry out."

Elisha blinked up at the two faces silhouetted against the evening sky. "Someone shot at me," he managed. "Probably gone."

The priest paused a moment to look around, then reached down and Elisha took his arm to climb out of the grave, brushing off the dirt and shaking his head. He frowned down at his shoulder where a thin line of blood marked the rip in his tunic. The evening breeze swept over him, wiping away the reek of death.

"In a churchyard, no less!" Father Michael frowned as well, or rather his lined face fell into the expression it seemed made for, then he bent to lift the fallen bolt, short and new, with a sharp head for piercing flesh. Holding it close to his nose to examine it, he said, "No fletcher's mark."

Hefting his shovel, the gravedigger started to scatter dirt over the corpse. "Woulda been convenient, eh, dying in a graveyard?"

"Not tonight," Elisha replied. He wiped his face and took the bolt. The tip gave a chill tingle, marked with the intention of his death. A small crossbow could be carried loaded, easily hidden beneath a cloak or simply dangling at a horse's pommel, ready for use. Half the barons called for his blood, but they wanted a public execution. This wasn't an attempt at justice, but an assassination.

"Come wait in the church—Morag here will send a boy for the duke's men to see you home."

The gravedigger huffed as he tossed in another shovelful.

"Go on," Father Michael prodded.

Morag gave a long look to the corpse, then put up his shovel and stumped off into the streets. A moment later, he could be heard banging on a door. Elisha kept glancing around as he followed the priest. His magical senses warned him, true enough, but they told him little else. A boy ran off in the direction of the castle, the gravedigger stumped back to his task, a pair of dogs snarled and tussled over something they'd found in a cellar hole. With a grand gesture, the priest ushered Elisha into the chilly church with its high, rectangular windows cutting bits of sky through the heavy stone. Father Michael paused to cross himself with a little bow, more like a lady's courtesy, then raised a brow until Elisha followed suit, then he shut the door at their backs with a solid thud.

The priest busied himself lighting a few tapers from the massive spiraled candle kept burning at the Lady altar—a donation from the duke, its curled length representing the number of dead.

"So . . ." Father Michael found a cloth and began to wipe down the altar. "Have you repented yet?"

"Sorry?" Elisha turned from the windows.

"Have you repented of your regicide?" The priest met his gaze, dark eyes reflecting the thin light of candles.

Elisha gripped the bolt a little tighter. Repented of killing a tyrant? At the time, he wanted the killing to end: the deaths of the common soldiers and of his own friends, held hostage to the tyrant's own ends—not to mention saving Duke Randall, whom the king wished Elisha to kill. He had not meant to take magic into his own hands to slay the king, but it had brought the end of the battle that caused so much pain. The idea of killing, and the manner of it, still disturbed him, but to regret that the man was dead? "It's not a simple matter, Father."

"It is to God."

"Then I'll take it up with Him."

"Not if you are in Hell," the priest said, bracing his hands on the altar and leaning forward so the flame turned his wrinkles into crevasses of darkness. "Not if you are bound there sooner than you think. Myself, I have doubted the rumor of sorcery, believing that any man so devoted to attend to funerals cannot be so. . . diabolical. But if I am mistaken, Barber, then only true repentance can save you."

"I will repent of my actions when God repents of killing babies—or the mothers who would bear them." Elisha turned away, blowing out a breath, but his shoulders ached, the bolt wearing a line into his palm. He had not meant to speak so harshly, and he could sense the stillness of the priest at his back.

"It is not up to you to judge the Lord."

He could leave now—likely the archer was already in the castle, masked and dancing, camouflaged by a hundred others. If Elisha found a mask of his own, he might hide likewise, and seek among the company for the one who sought his harm. He jerked at the knock on the door, then relaxed as Lord Robert, one of the duke's staunch retainers, stuck his head in.

"Father? Elisha! What's happened? The boy said somebody'd been shot."

"Nearly." Elisha held up the bolt. "One of the duke's guests, or somebody riding with them, tried to kill me."

"The prince's guests—surely his Grace wouldn't abide anyone who'd shoot his surgeons." Robert crossed himself and ducked his head, then gestured Elisha toward the door. "No matter, we're with you now. I've got seven men."

"Think on what I've said, Barber," the priest called

after them. "An eternity of torment awaits the sinner down below."

Elisha said nothing as he moved into the night. Ambushed twice on holy ground—the first time for his body, and the second for his soul.

E. C. Ambrose

The Dark Apostle

"Ambrose's fantasy debut depicts a 14th-century England in which magic and fledgling science exist side by side. Elisha's struggle to bring relief to those in need is complicated by his own need for redemption and his innate fear of what he cannot understand. This beautifully told, painfully elegant story should appeal to fans of L.E. Modesitt's realistic fantasies as well as of the period fantasy of Guy Gavriel Kay."

—*Library Journal* (starred review)

"In a grim world of medieval warfare, witch-hunts and primitive surgery, E. C. Ambrose has crafted a shining tale of one man's humanity and courage. A gritty read for those who like realism as well as hope in their fantasy."

—Glenda Larke, author of *The Last Stormlord*

ELISHA BARBER   978-0-7564-0836-7
ELISHA MAGUS   978-0-7564-0926-5

To Order Call: 1-800-788-6262
www.dawbooks.com

DAW 190

John Marco
The Bronze Knight

"A sprawling tale of military battles, personal and political intrigue, magic, and star-crossed love set against a richly detailed land of warring kingdoms and hidden magic."
—*Library Journal*

THE EYES OF GOD
978-0-7564-0096-5

THE DEVIL'S ARMOR
978-0-7564-0203-7

THE SWORD OF ANGELS
978-0-7564-0360-7

"Finely crafted, fluid writing and fully realized characters."
—*Publishers Weekly*

And don't miss
THE FOREVER KNIGHT
978-0-7564-0751-3

To Order Call: 1-800-788-6262
www.dawbooks.com

DAW 150

Kari Sperring

Living with Ghosts

978-0-7564-0675-2

Finalist for the Crawford Award for First Novel

A Tiptree Award Honor Book

Locus Recommended First Novel

"This is an enthralling fantasy that contains horror elements interwoven into the story line. This reviewer predicts Kari Sperring will have quite a future as a renowned fantasist."
—*Midwest Book Review*

"A satisfying blend of well-developed characters and intriguing worldbuilding. The richly realized Renaissance style city is a perfect backdrop for the blend of ghostly magic and intrigue. The characters are wonderfully flawed, complex and multi-dimensional. Highly recommended!"
—*Patricia Bray, author of The Sword of Change Trilogy*

And now available:

The Grass King's Concubine

978-0-7564-0755-1

To Order Call: 1-800-788-6262
www.dawbooks.com

C.S. Friedman
The *Magister* Trilogy

"Powerful, intricate plotting and gripping characters
distinguish a book in which ethical dilemmas
are essential and engrossing."
—*Booklist*

"Imaginative, deftly plotted fantasy...
Readers will eagerly await the next installment."
—*Publishers Weekly*

FEAST OF SOULS
978-0-7564-0463-5

WINGS OF WRATH
978-0-7564-0594-6

LEGACY OF KINGS
978-0-7564-0748-3

To Order Call: 1-800-788-6262
www.dawbooks.com

DAW 121

Kristen Britain

The GREEN RIDER series

"Wonderfully captivating...a truly enjoyable read."
—Terry Goodkind

"The author's skill at world building and her feel for
dramatic storytelling make this first-rate fantasy
a good choice." —*Library Journal*

"Britain keeps the excitement high from beginning
to end." —*Publishers Weekly*

GREEN RIDER
978-0-88677-858-3 (mass)   978-0-7564-0548-9 (trade)

FIRST RIDER'S CALL
978-0-7564-0193-1 (mass)   978-0-7564-0572-4 (trade)

THE HIGH KING'S TOMB
978-0-7564-0588-5 (mass)   978-0-7564-0489-5 (trade)

BLACKVEIL
978-0-7564-0779-7 (mass)   978-0-7564-0708-7 (trade)

MIRROR SIGHT
978-0-7564-0879-4 (hardcover)

Saladin Ahmed

Throne of the Crescent Moon

978-0-7564-0711-7

"An arresting, sumptuous and thoroughly satisfying debut."
— *Kirkus* (starred)

"Set in a quasi–Middle Eastern city and populated with the supernatural creatures of Arab folklore, this long-awaited debut by a finalist for the Nebula and Campbell awards brings *The Arabian Nights* to sensuous life. The maturity and wisdom of Ahmed's older protagonists are a delightful contrast to the brave impulsiveness of their younger companions. This trilogy launch will delight fantasy lovers who enjoy flawed but honorable protagonists and a touch of the exotic."
— *Library Journal* (starred)

"Ahmed's debut masterfully paints a world both bright and terrible. Unobtrusive hints of backstory contribute to the sense that this novel is part of a larger ongoing tale, and the Arab-influenced setting is full of vibrant description, characters, and religious expressions that will delight readers weary of pseudo-European epics."
— *Publishers Weekly* (starred)

To Order Call: 1-800-788-6262
www.dawbooks.com

DAW 205